Summer of the Mariposas

Summer of the Mariposas

GUADALUPE GARCIA McCALL

Tu Books
AN IMPRINT OF
LEE & LOW BOOKS
New York

This is a work of fiction. Names, characters, places, and incidents are either the product of the author's imagination or are used fictitiously, and any resemblance to actual persons, living or dead, business establishments, events, or locales is entirely coincidental.

Mariposa definition on opposite page loosely based on online information referencing the following sources: Sheena Morgan, *The Real Halloween;* Dr. Carlos Beutelspacvher, "Las Mariposas entre los Antiguos Mexicanos" (*Butterflies of Ancient Mexico*), 1988.

TU BOOKS, an imprint of LEE & LOW BOOKS Inc.
95 Madison Avenue, New York, NY 10016
leeandlow.com

Manufactured in the United States of America
by Worzalla Publishing Company, July 2014

Book design by Isaac Stewart
Book production by The Kids at Our House
The text is set in Minion Pro

HC 10 9 8 7 6 5 4
PB 10 9 8 7 6 5 4 3 2 1
First Edition

Library of Congress Cataloging-in-Publication Data
McCall, Guadalupe Garcia.
Summer of the mariposas / Guadalupe Garcia McCall. — 1st ed.
p. cm.
Summary: In an adventure reminiscent of Homer's Odyssey, fifteen-year-old Odilia and her four younger sisters embark on a journey to return a dead man to his family in Mexico, aided by La Llorona, but impeded by a witch, a warlock, chupacabras, and more.
ISBN 978-1-60060-900-8 (hardcover : alk. paper) —
ISBN 978-1-62014-010-9 (paperback) — ISBN 978-1-60060-901-5 (e-book)
[1. Adventure and adventurers--Fiction. 2. Sisters--Fiction. 3. Llorona (Legendary character)--Fiction. 4. Supernatural--Fiction. 5. Dead--Fiction. 6. Mexican Americans--Texas--Fiction. 7. Family life--Texas--Fiction. 8. Texas--Fiction.] I. Title.
PZ7.M47833752Sum 2012
[Fic]—dc23

2012014845

mariposa (mah-ree-PO-sah)

from the Spanish, *mariposa*, the apocopate *Mari-* (Mary in English) and *posa* (to rest or repose)

Butterfly. Mariposas are slender, delicate insects with four wide, colorful wings. In almost every culture, butterflies are associated with transformation. The Aztecs held the butterfly, *papalotl*, in high regard and had a special celebration to welcome the migrating monarchs in early August every year. They believed that mariposas were the cheerful souls of their loved ones, the angels of women and children, their fallen warriors, their ancestors, returning home transformed to assure them that they were well and that life, however brief, was beautiful.

Table of Contents

Part I: The Departure

Prologue:	*El Cazo*/The Pot	1
Chapter 1	*La Calavera*/The Skull	5
Chapter 2	*El Pájaro*/The Bird	23
Chapter 3	*La Estrella*/The Star	44
Chapter 4	*El Venado*/The Deer	59
Chapter 5	*El Mundo*/The World	70
Chapter 6	*La Mano*/The Hand	83

PART II: THE INITIATION

Chapter 7	*El Árbol*/The Tree	105
Chapter 8	*La Sirena*/The Mermaid	118
Chapter 9	*La Araña*/The Spider	143
Chapter 10	*La Garza*/The Heron	160
Chapter 11	*El Alacrán*/The Scorpion	171
Chapter 12	*La Muerte*/The Death	184
Chapter 13	*Las Jaras*/The Arrows	194
Chapter 14	*El Diablito*/The Little Devil	212
Chapter 15	*La Dama*/The Lady	238

PART III: THE RETURN

Chapter 16	*El Nopal*/The Cactus	261
Chapter 17	*La Chalupa*/The Canoe	277
Chapter 18	*El Corazón*/The Heart	286
Chapter 19	*El Músico*/The Musician	299
Chapter 20	*La Rosa*/The Rose	312
Chapter 21	*La Corona*/The Crown	321
Chapter 22	*La Luna*/The Moon	328
	Author's Note	335
	Glossary	338
	Acknowledgments	353
	About the Author	355

To my *cinco hermanitas*
whom I love *con todo mi corazón*:
Alicia, Virginia, Diamantina, Angelica, *y* Roxana
the Garcia girls, together forever—
no matter what!

PART I

THE DEPARTURE

In which my younger sisters and I find a drowned man in the Rio Grande and how, with La Llorona as our mystical guide, we take a trip across the Eagle Pass border to return him to his family in El Sacrificio, Coahuila, Mexico.

Prologue

El Cazo: *"Hazme caso o te caso con un sapo."*

The Pot: "Listen to me or I will make you marry a toad."

—a play on the multiple meanings of the word *caso*

(pay attention and wed/marry)

Almost a year after our father left the house, never to be heard from again, the long, miserable drought ended in Texas. The heavy summer rains had more than enchanted everyone; the days that followed had brought forth a most unexpected, spectacular surprise. To our delight, an unusually large brood of American Snout butterflies swarmed Eagle Pass by the billions.

Indiscriminate in taste, the *mariposas* flittered over cultivated gardens as happily as they danced over thorn-ridden lots and neglected fields. To them, nothing was safe, nothing was sacred.

Because they were everywhere, clinging to freshly scrubbed laundry on clothes lines, or stuck to the bottom of well-heeled shoes, the butterflies were on everyone's most wanted list, including Mamá's. She hated sweeping their brown, dusty corpses out of her kitchen and off her porch, but she especially hated how they followed her everywhere like a dark little cloud.

That same summer, Mamá stopped being a housewife. After admitting to herself that Papá wasn't going to send any more money, she'd done the responsible thing and gone out and found her very first job.

As for us, we *tried* staying indoors and playing *Lotería* like Mamá instructed. It was difficult, however, because to play *Lotería* we needed a caller, *un cantor*, and Papá had always been ours. A good *cantor* can recite the traditional riddles for all fifty-four cards in the *Lotería* by heart as he reveals each card to the players. Riddles like "*El caso que te hago es poco*" were all right, but to keep things interesting Papá had always altered the riddles and personalized them to fit our family. We'd squirm and giggle with joy and excitement every time a new riddle featured one of us. One day, however, right before he left, Papá made up a particularly ominous riddle.

"*La Sirena*," he called, holding up the card for The Mermaid. "*La mujer* who wants to take your Papá away! No! We won't let her!"

My parents were like any other parents; they bickered and made up all the time. But that day the riddle upset Mamá so much that the fight it stirred up between them soured the game for Papá. From then on, we played *Lotería* as a family with less and less frequency. So it was no surprise that after he left, we lost interest in playing the game altogether.

The summer of the *mariposas*, we abandoned our beloved *Lotería* for good, neglected our chores, and went completely wild. We cared for no one but each other, not even Mamá. Because we were always unsupervised, we finally had the freedom to do whatever we wanted, wherever we wanted, whenever we wanted.

On rainy days, I'd read a book and watch the girls as they played in the crowded shed behind our house. But on scorching summer days, when the pavement was so hot you couldn't sit on it, they made aluminum bracelets and arm cuffs out of the bottoms of soda cans they rubbed against hot cement sidewalks. Sometimes, they even costumed themselves with dusty curtains and old tablecloths, scissoring through the faded fabric with Mamá's gardening shears or tearing them apart with their bare hands. And when Mamá would get upset because we weren't helping, we'd whine and then scrub out a pan or two before we'd take off again. Honestly, there was just too much fun to be had to pay her any mind.

Some days, we'd hike the hills beyond El Indio Highway, following the swarm of *mariposas*. They'd become our dusky shadows, our companions, as much a part of us as we were to each other. Most days, however, we rode our bikes as far away from home as we could get, a flighty brood of the tiny butterflies straggling behind us. With our chubby little sister, Pita, sitting precariously on the handlebars of my bike, we pedaled down to the river, rode through one of the large gaps in the eleven-foot border fence, and swam for hours at a time without drinking or eating anything more than the watermelons we chilled in the bank of our river.

The waters of the Rio Grande were unruly and loud, but we had found an alcove far off El Indio Highway, a pebbled niche where the current swirled in peacefully and stayed for a while, as if to rest from its long, draining journey over boulders and through canyons all the way from California down to our miniature bay in Eagle Pass. There it pooled, relaxed, cleansed itself, and bubbled into laughter at the sheer joy of having us in its midst. We splashed around in that cold, clear water like river nymphs, born to swim and bathe till the end of days. It was a magical time, full of dreaminess and charm, a time to watch the *mariposas* emerge out of their cocoons, gather their courage, and take flight while we floated faceup in the water. And that's exactly what we were doing the morning the body of a dead man drifted into our swimming haven.

1

La Calavera: *"La calavera del muerto está en su huerto."*

The Skull: "The skull of the dead man is in his grove."

Juanita reacted first. Being fourteen and only second oldest, she didn't usually take charge. But when she felt the corpse floating beside her, she started pulling Pita out of the water as if she were a sopping Raggedy Ann doll.

"Holy shiitake mushrooms!" the twins, Velia and Delia, shouted in unison, frozen in place by the sight of the body bobbing up and down and side to side only a few feet away from us.

I shrieked the way Mamá would have if she'd been there with us. "Get out! Get out! Get out!" Grasping only the sleeve of Velia's shirt, I yanked her toward me with all my might.

"Odilia!" she complained. "Let go of me!"

"Get out of the water! Now!"

"Okay! Fine. But I thought you were yelling at him," she defended herself.

I pushed her and Delia ahead of me. "Why would I be yelling at him? He's dead!" We stood, all five of us, drenched with fear on the bank of the river, staring wildly at the first cadaver we'd ever seen in our lives.

It was spooky, like seeing a ghost floating facedown in the water. His dark hair was long for a man. His thick tresses floated loosely around his head like the black tentacles of a sea monster.

"We should call someone." Pita shivered, pushing her wet hair out of her face and scooting over to stand behind me as if she were afraid the man was going to suddenly get up and come after her.

"The authorities," I said, my mind still reeling from the shock. The only thing I could think of was how Mamá was going to give me one historical *paliza* when she found out—and she'd find out if we called the authorities. But I had it coming to me. After all, I got my sisters into this by bringing them here. The waters of the Rio Grande were dangerous, and Mamá wouldn't care that our swimming hole seemed safe to me. How many times had we heard of drowning victims turning up on its banks?

The twins, Velia and Delia, chimed in. "The cops for sure."

"No. We should call the border patrol. I bet they know what to do," Pita said, sounding older than her ten years.

"Guys," Juanita whispered, her face suddenly pale. "Do you realize what this means?"

"What?" Velia asked, still staring at the body floating in the river. I didn't respond. Juanita's brain always worked differently from my own, so I couldn't begin to guess what she was about to suggest.

Juanita's face broke into a grin. "We're going to be on TV!" She sobered a little when she glanced down at the body again.

"Mamá is not going to like this. You know how she feels about talking to strangers," Velia reminded Juanita. She was right. Mamá was more than paranoid about giving out personal information. In her mind, everyone was a potential predator, and we were under strict orders never to speak to anyone about anything if she wasn't around to protect us. We weren't allowed to use the Internet anywhere other than school, where we were semiprotected. No e-mails, no instant messaging—not only couldn't we afford a computer at home, but Mamá worried that we didn't understand how to distinguish our real-life friends from dirty old men. "Besides, we're in no condition to be put in front of a camera. Look at us. We look like bums."

I looked at each of my sisters in turn. We were wearing cut-off shorts and ripped tank tops. Pita tugged at her wet shirt, squeezing out the water and pressing it down over her round belly to smooth it out, while Velia and Delia tried in vain to straighten out each other's clothes. And to say nothing of our hair, which was not only wet but thick and clumpy with dirt residue from the river water. Pita had leaf particles clinging to her bangs. I reached over and picked the bigger pieces of debris out of them as I mulled over our predicament.

"Well, it's not like we'll have a choice. This is big," Juanita tucked her shirt into her shorts, as if that was going to make a difference.

The twins nodded at each other. "This is more than big—this

is *huge*," they said in unison. They had a habit of finishing each other's sentences. They were even closer to each other than all five of us were as a group. It was a game they played—presenting themselves as the "twin front," fooling people who didn't know them all that well by making them think they really were exactly alike.

I tried to think of a way out of it as I chastised myself for bringing the girls to swim in the river all summer long. Calling the authorities brought with it consequences, but we couldn't just leave the dead man where he was in the water. He'd pollute our swimming hole—not to mention that he should be put to rest somewhere.

"Ginormous," Juanita whispered beside me.

Delia pulled her ratty tennis shoes off her feet and beat them against each other, trying to loosen the clumps of dirt from their soles. "You think they'll get here that quickly? Like right away? Can't we go home and change before we call them? I don't know about you, but I want to look my best for my first-ever television appearance."

"No, we can't," I said, looking at the twins. They were the pretty ones. With their long honey-brown hair, hazel eyes, and perfect smiles, they had nothing to worry about. They didn't look as pretty right now, after a day swimming in the river, but it didn't matter. The camera would love them, no matter what they were wearing or how disheveled their hair had become. Not me—like Juanita I was big boned, darkly bronzed from being out in the sun every day, and homely as a gingersnap.

Juanita undid her droopy ponytail and tried to comb her wet hair with her fingers. "This isn't a movie set, and you're not starlets yet," she reminded the twins, who had aspirations of someday making it in Hollywood. "This is about him, not us."

"That's right. This is real life, and that's a real dead man in there." I pointed to the river. What if bringing an investigation here meant no more swimming? "Whoever we call is going to want to interrogate us. The cops, the border patrol, everyone's going to want to know how and when and where we found him. And that's when the news people get involved."

Velia looked at her twin sister for validation, not grasping the full meaning of what I was getting at. "But we're filthy. My shorts are ripped. See? We can't be seen on TV looking like this. What will people think?"

Delia put her hand on her twin's shoulder. "They'll think we're poor, and that our father has abandoned us," she stated sarcastically. The painful truth set off my sisters. Suddenly everyone was talking at once.

Pita's voice cut through us all, saying aloud the one thing that worried us more than Mamá finding out about this. "Do you think Papá will see us? On television?" Pita asked, biting the inside of her lip. "I hope we don't embarrass him." I couldn't help but wonder, myself, what Papá would do if he saw us. Would he feel sorry for us? Would it make him come back?

"It'll be fine," Juanita assured her. "Here, let me fix your hair."

As Juanita used her fingers to scrape back Pita's hair and re-secure its braid, I thought about where our father might be now. "We don't know if he even watches the news," I reminded them. "The truth is, we don't know much about him nowadays. Not where he's living, where his band is performing, or why he hasn't called or come home in almost a year."

"Well if he does watch the news, he should be embarrassed," Juanita retorted through the ponytail holder clenched between her teeth. "Leaving without saying good-bye—I don't know why I'm even surprised." She spat out the rubber band and bound up the bottom of Pita's braid. "Did you know that seventy percent of men aren't as attached to their female children as they are to their sons? It's true. I read that somewhere."

Delia let out an exaggerated sigh and rolled her eyes. "Can't you ever talk like a real person? I'm tired of listening to you quote stupid stuff!"

"If you two *taradas* are done arguing, we need to go home and change before going up to customs," Velia said, taking the focus away from Papá and back to the situation at hand. The body was still floating gently in the same place. The way the current worked here, once something floated into an eddy it had to be pushed out again.

Juanita smacked Velia in the back of the head, then pushed her away. "If you call me *tarada* ever again I'm gonna show you just how *ignorant* I am by kicking your behind all the way across the river."

"Knock it off," I said, stepping between them. If we kept bickering, we'd never make a decision about the dead man and what it meant for the future of our swimming hole. After a quick glance at Juanita, I turned my attention to Velia and Delia. "What's wrong with you all? A man is dead in the river and all you can do is fight? We should be pulling him out and going to get help."

Delia didn't look at Juanita. Instead, she turned to look at the drowned man. His blue shirt clung to his back in a crumpled mess. It was still semitucked into his belted jeans. He was wearing brown cowboy boots that were probably made from rattlesnake skin, like the ones Papá had on his feet the morning he walked out of our lives. "We could push him out again and move him downstream, then cut him loose in the water down there." She pointed downriver.

"Or we could just lug him back out to the deep end, have the river carry him further away, then call someone," Delia said.

"I think pushing him out there is a good idea," I said. "So who's going to help me here and who's going up to customs to report this? Remember the rule of the five little sisters—*cinco hermanitas*, together forever, no matter what! No one's allowed to go off on their own, so we'll travel in packs. Delia? Velia? What are you two doing and who are you taking with you?"

"Now hold on," Juanita interrupted. The twins waited in the water a few feet from the dead man, caught between their older sisters' argument. "We're not calling anyone. We can't turn him in to the *migra*. They'll throw him in a hole somewhere and forget all about him." The concerned look in Juanita's eyes told me she truly believed the rumors. Like Juanita, I'd heard the horrible *rumores* from the *comadres* in our neighborhood too. They whispered about unclaimed bodies in sacks and shallow unmarked graves. I was sure the rumors were grossly exaggerated, but we had no way to know one way or the other.

"They throw them in a hole?" Pita stood behind us, away from the riverbank as if afraid of getting too close to the corpse. "Why?" she wailed. Her plump face twisted with anguish and her eyes brimmed with tears.

At the sight of our baby sister in distress, I put an arm around Pita's shoulders, hugging her to my side. "They don't treat them like animals. They bury them," I corrected, trying not to scare her any more than she already was.

"Maybe we should just let them do that," Velia said, inching back toward the shore. "I'd rather not touch a dead body if I don't have to." She didn't come out of the water, though.

I tried to signal to Juanita with widened eyes that it was enough, but she either didn't get the hint or decided to ignore it. "Hello?" she burst out, arms flailing. "Those customs agents are ruthless! To them, illegals are no better than stray dogs. They'd shoot them before they'd help them."

"You're so full of it," I said, shaking my head. "Customs agents are government workers. They have to take care of the bodies they find."

"Shows how much you know," Juanita mumbled, looking at the dead man floating in front of her.

"And what makes you such an expert?" I demanded, still hugging Pita. I pulled her closer, turning her away from the sight of the dead man. "One of those stupid books you read all night. No, wait. You were just born knowing it all. Sorry. I forgot."

Pita scrunched up her face, on the verge of sobbing aloud. "I'm scared."

"Shut up. We don't have time for crybabies." Juanita scowled at Pita. The dead man continued to float in front of us like a giant water-logged voodoo doll—a bad omen to be sure.

Juanita paced along the bank, agitated. I let go of Pita to sit down on a rock, the weight of the decision we needed to make unsettling my stomach with a queasy feeling that no matter what we decided, our lives would change.

"I'm telling Mamá!" Pita wailed, but when she started toward the bikes, Juanita pulled her arm and forced her to face us.

"No you're not, you little snitch," she said. "We're not telling anyone anything. We're going to do the right thing."

I didn't like where this was heading. Knowing Juanita and her quixotic ways, this could turn into one of her many hare-brained schemes. Next she'd be starting some kind of crusade to prevent the drowning of illegal aliens in the waters of the Rio Grande. "And what's that? What is the *right thing*, Juanita?" I asked, exasperated. Arguing with her always had a draining effect on me.

"Help me pull him out," Juanita said as she waded into the river. "Water quickens the rate of decom—decomp—decay. So we need to hurry up."

"I'm not touching *that*," Pita announced, stepping behind me.

"*Him*. You're not touching *him*," Juanita hissed at Pita, who pressed her face against my back. "He's a human being, even if he is dead. Now help me pull him out. Pita, you go sit over there if you can't handle it." She directed our little sister to a chinaberry tree with giant overhanging branches a few yards away. Obediently, Pita went to sit under the designated tree. Delia and Velia looked at each other, shrugged, and followed Juanita deeper into the river where the body was still floating in the gentle water.

"We should call the authorities, Juanita," I said, trying to control the situation like Mamá would've wanted. "I don't think we should pull him in. No telling how long he's been dead."

As usual, Juanita ignored me. Although she was only a year older than the twins, who were thirteen and full of cuss words and spite, Juanita was much taller and more muscular. Next to them, she looked Amazonian. Like the female warriors in Greek mythology, she could've pulled in the man's body without help from any of us.

I stood my ground.

Delia and Velia stood waist deep in the river and stared at me with the exact same expression on their faces, an expression that said I should do something.

"What?" I asked them. "I'm not helping her. She's crazy. Always has been."

"I'm not crazy. I'm compassionate. No, I'm more than compassionate; I'm . . . considerate," Juanita said, using the word correctly. Unlike the twins, who were having fun exploring the criminal side of language, Juanita had recently discovered the pocket-sized dictionary, and big words flew out of her mouth every day. Most of the time, I complimented her on her vocabulary, but at that moment her consideration was making me sick to my stomach.

"He's heavy," Juanita huffed as she pulled the dead man toward her by his right arm. Delia and Velia screamed when the body made contact with their midriffs. They sprang out of the water like sleek *mojarras*—two slim, delicate fish flying out of the river. So Juanita ended up bringing in the dead man by herself. I only helped her when she was having trouble dragging him over to sit him up against the trunk of a mesquite tree.

Juanita moved his arms up and down and side to side. "He hasn't been dead very long," she hypothesized. "See, no rigamorphus."

"Rigor mortis," I corrected. "You still have some work to do on those dictionary skills."

"Whatever," she said, sounding embarrassed. "I think he just drowned, like a few hours ago. He doesn't smell and he's not swollen." But I could tell he was definitely dead, to the point where I was sure pumping on his chest wouldn't have done him any good.

"Drowned? What do you know about drowning?" I asked her. While I wasn't sure she knew what she was talking about, I was relieved to hear the news. Even if she wouldn't listen to me, at least Juanita wasn't exposing the other girls to some super-decayed dead man's germs.

"Hello. I watch *Crime Dawgs*. It's like my favorite show." The sight of her turning the body over and pressing and prodding at the head and torso with her bare hands turned my stomach. Juanita had nerves of steel. I had to give her credit for that. "Besides, it's obvious he drowned. There are no other signs of trauma, no bullets, nothing. See?" She flipped the body onto its back again.

"We should really go up to customs and get some help," I began.

Juanita's brown eyes were warm and dark with the genuine concern she was so proud of. "I wonder where he came from. If he has a family . . . do they know where he went? Did he tell them?"

Because I knew exactly where this was coming from, I put my arms around her shoulder and pulled her close. "He must have," I assured her.

"Papá didn't," Delia whispered to Velia as they stared at the drowned man. His brown hair was slicked back from his face now, as if he had just gone for a swim, and his face was expressionless, serene, as if he were now sleeping in the hot sun to dry off. Except, of course, that he was still fully clothed.

Juanita ignored the twins and crouched back down to inspecting the body. "He's soaked."

"Duh," Velia said, rolling her eyes toward Delia.

"We should take off his clothes," Juanita suggested. "Let him dry out before he starts to grow fungus or something."

"Gross! I'm not doing that!" Velia and Delia exclaimed in unison.

I pushed Juanita gently away from the corpse. "We should leave him just the way we found him."

"We should have left him in the water, *babas*," Delia said, thumping Juanita on the shoulder with the back of her hand.

"Watch your mouth!" I warned. I was tired of the twins calling everyone stupid. Delia mumbled an apology under her breath.

Ignoring my command to leave the drowned man alone, Juanita tugged at the dead man's left boot and yanked it off his foot, almost falling back in the process. To everyone's surprise, a tightly wound plastic bag fell halfway out of his sock. Juanita pulled it all the way out and looked at us before she opened it.

"Money," she whispered as she pulled out a huge wad of rolled up American bills and laid it down beside the drowned man. Velia snatched it up and started sorting it, divvying it up between herself and Delia.

"Look at this. Hundreds, fifties, twenties," Velia announced. She and her twin unrolled the bills, laying them in neat stacks over a flat rock a few feet away.

Their announcement piqued Pita's interest. Like a curious kitten, she crawled out from under the chinaberry tree and came over to join us. She picked up a hundred dollar bill and turned the foreign object over in her hands. "He was rich."

"There's a wallet, with an address," Juanita whispered, pulling the man's Mexican driver's license out of the wallet and staring at it. "His name is Gabriel Pérdido. He's from El Sacrificio, across the border."

I stood up and stepped away, wiping my hands on my wet shorts. My palms suddenly felt sticky and dirty, and I couldn't breathe right. "We have to turn it all in—the wallet, the money, everything," I said resolutely.

"We can't do that to him," Juanita said, looking up at me with those big brown eyes.

I felt like a jerk for not caring as much, but I had to be reasonable. "We don't even know this guy, so stop acting like we owe him anything." There had to be something we could do that would be right, but also not get us in trouble with Mamá. If she realized we'd been swimming so close to the deep end of the river all summer, she'd never let us come back here. On the other hand, we had no other choice but to report the poor man. Mamá would be even more upset if she found out that we didn't. And knowing Pita's loose tongue, Mamá was bound to find out sooner or later. We were doomed either way.

"He's probably got a wife and kids, and they're worried about him," Juanita insisted. "And right now they're wondering what he's doing, if he made it across all right."

"We don't know that." I snatched the driver's license from her. "Look. His driver's license expired *six years ago*. He probably doesn't even live there anymore. Truth is, we don't know who he is or what he does, or even if he has a family."

"He has a family!" Juanita yelled. She threw his worn-out

wallet at me. Pita picked it up and looked at the picture flap inside, which started her tears again. Velia and Delia took it away from her and stared at it too, but they didn't say anything.

"He has a family and a home and a life," Juanita said as she took the wallet back from the twins and passed it to me. Behind the plastic, on the right side of the beat up wallet, was a picture of the man with his family. "We can't just leave him here. We've got to find a way to take him back to his family."

"El Sacrificio?" I asked, the name getting caught in the back of my throat.

"Hey, isn't that close to . . . ," Velia started.

"Where Papá is from?" Delia finished Velia's thought, looking at her twin first and then turning to me with an expectant look.

"We can't go to El Sacrificio," I said. The idea of possibly encountering Papá terrified me. What if he didn't want to see us? What if he walked away from us again?

"Why not?" Velia asked.

"Abuelita Remedios still lives near El Sacrificio, in Hacienda Dorada," Juanita said, a plan to visit Papá's mother forming vividly within the shine of her dark brown eyes.

"We can't go to El Sacrificio," I repeated firmly.

Velia and Delia clearly questioned my sanity, from the looks on their faces. "Why not?"

"I'd like to see Abuelita Remedios again," Pita whimpered, taking my hand in a silent plea. I felt sorry for her. She had only met our grandmother once before, when she was around three.

"We can't," I insisted. I shook my head and let go of Pita's hand. I stepped away and turned my back to them. I stared off into the woods, down the worn path that led back into town, wishing we'd stayed home today.

"Look. It's been years since we last went to Hacienda Dorada. I'd like to see Abuelita again too," Juanita said, plopping down between the rock with the money and the dead man. "Experts agree children need to be close to their grandparents. It makes them feel secure, and when they grow up feeling loved they make better parents themselves."

"That's a bunch of horseradish! I'm *never* becoming a parent," Delia interjected.

I held up my hands in a vain attempt to stop this runaway train of thought. "We can't go *because* . . . ," I began. Then, dropping the wallet on Juanita's lap, I closed my eyes and fought past the raw, agonizing emotions that threatened to overwhelm me. It was painful to know that our paternal grandmother lived less than a day's drive away and we had not seen her more than twice in our lifetimes. If only Papá had been more willing to do his job and make us a family, maybe El Sacrificio would be more than just an exotic name printed on a dead man's driver's license.

"Because why?" Juanita demanded doggedly. "Give me one good reason."

"Because it's all the way in friggin' Mexico, that's why!" I growled.

Juanita waved the wallet up at me again. "Don't you see?

There's a reason we found him instead of the border patrol. He came looking for us because he knew we could help him. It's not a coincidence that he's from the same place as Papá."

"What are you talking about?" I asked. "You're not making any sense."

Juanita continued passionately. "Don't you get it? We were meant to find him, so we could go see our *abuelita* in Mexico again. It was fate that brought him to us."

"Do you even know what you're considering?" I asked. The man was *dead.* There had to be a law against what she was proposing.

"I know it's going to be hard," Juanita concluded. "But if this man's family is ever going to see him again, we're going to have to be the ones to take him back. And maybe while we're in El Sacrificio, we can find out . . ."

"If Abuelita Remedios knows what's happened to Papá?" I whispered, more to myself than to them.

My comment was met with silence. I hadn't meant to make the connection, but it was too late. The thought was out there. Their eyes said it all. The same question had been on everybody's mind, not just mine. I was about to take it back when something caught my eye. On the other side of the Rio Grande, on a hill, something moved . . . a woman?

She stood still—watching us from afar. I tried to focus in on her face, but the sun's reflection bounced off the surface of the water and her form wavered in the afternoon light. One minute her long, white dress was billowing against her legs, and the next she was gone. Disappeared. Like a ghostly apparition, she vanished into the surreal light of the fading sunset.

"What is it?" Juanita asked, looking across the river.

I thought of La Llorona, the legendary Weeping Woman said to have drowned her own children. Mamá says she roams the rivers of the world in search of them. Goosebumps rose on my skin and my body shook slightly. "Nothing," I said, rubbing my arms briskly and turning my attention back to the girls. "Let's get out of here. It's getting dark."

2

El Pájaro: *"Pájaro, pajarito, encántanos con tu canto bonito."*

The Bird: "Bird, little birdie, enchant us with your pretty song."

"We can cross the border at dawn, pretend we're going on vacation with our father," Juanita suggested. We walked our bikes out of the woods and mounted them, ready to ride the rest of the way. "Once we're through the checkpoints, we can drive straight to El Sacrificio."

"Excuse me, and how are we going to do that? Are you going to call your fairy godmother and ask her to turn a watermelon into a chariot?" I asked. "Because I don't know about you, but I left my magic beans in my other shorts."

Juanita gave me the evil eye. "*¡Calláte!* I'm not stupid, so you can stop acting that way."

Velia patted her shirt pocket with a flattened hand. "It's not like we're broke; we have money now."

"You took his money?" Juanita asked, shocked. "I can't believe you stole from a dead man."

"It doesn't belong to us. We can't just take it," Pita said, looking scared.

"We can if it's for a good cause," Delia said. "We're not using it to buy ourselves stuff. It's not like we're really taking a vacation. We're using it to take him home."

I thought of the drowned man again. We'd left him sitting by the riverbank, drying under a mulberry tree, the tiny *mariposas* clinging to his mouth and nostrils as if trying to resuscitate him.

"Well, technically, we will be using it on ourselves, because he's dead," Juanita pointed out.

"Okay," I said, looking up at the darkening sky in frustration. "So how are we gonna get there? Do you even know where you're going?"

"We can take Papá's old car. There's an old map of Coahuila in the glove box," Juanita said. She hit my arm with the back of her hand and then grabbed the handlebars of her bike as she pedaled off.

"That car's a lemon," Velia yelled after her. She smacked her lips in disgust and then pedaled after Juanita.

"It's worse than a lemon," her twin elaborated. Shaking our heads, Delia and I pushed off and rode our bikes at full speed trying to catch up with Juanita and Velia. I had to work extra hard because Pita was riding behind me, her arms wrapped tightly around my shoulders and waist, like a heavy backpack. "That car's a pile of junk, Juanita," Delia continued. "Not even a dung beetle would want to push that old ball of *caca* around, much less hold on to it. Mamá should have sold it a long time ago."

"Bought us some new school clothes or something," Velia added, slowing down to talk to us.

The girls were right, of course. About everything. The car was still running, so it was sellable. Since Mamá didn't know how to drive, preferring to take the bus everywhere she went in Eagle Pass, she made me start it once a week and drive it around the block to keep the tires from going flat. But my *hermanitas* were mistaken if they thought I was going to drive them around in that death trap. It needed an oil change and the brakes squealed—and those were just the things I knew to watch out for. God only knew what else might be wrong with it.

"See? You can't even agree on how to get there," I said, looking at Juanita for acknowledgment.

"Well, we're going. You can join us, like a good big sister, *cinco hermanitas*, together forever—or you can break our motto and stay behind like a coward."

I turned around, gritting my teeth. "That's insane," I growled as I pedaled on, wondering how to fix things without any real solutions coming to mind. Velia and Delia rode around Juanita and flanked me.

"Listen, if you don't take us Juanita is willing to drive," Velia said without looking at me as she slowed down to match my unhurried pace.

"Don't be ridiculous," I said. "Juanita wouldn't know how to find a gas pedal if it had a rattle on its tail. At least I have a driving permit. Let's just get home for now. The right thing to do will come to us."

We let the conversation die off and pedaled our bikes back to the house in silence. When we got there, the sun was a luminous orange globe touching the horizon. Mamá had already left for work. She was a waitress at Mr. Gee's, an all-night café off Main Street on the edge of town, so she was always gone by eight o'clock and didn't come back until the next morning.

Soon after we got home from the river, the girls had another one of their yakking sessions in the twins' room, and as a result, they were running around the house packing for their trip to Mexico. I didn't intervene or stop them from packing. They were exhilarated by the idea of taking a long, adventurous journey, but I knew very well how this was going to turn out. They weren't going anywhere. They just didn't know it yet.

I ignored them and went to the kitchen to fix them welfare burgers for dinner. We called them welfare burgers because we used regular sliced bread instead of buns. Mamá said buns were more expensive and they were the same exact thing, so she just didn't see the point in wasting money on them.

As for me, I wanted a sandwich. The long, hot summer day had made me hungry for something cold; so I took out the bologna and cheese. Because there was no mayo, I ate my sandwich dry as cardboard as I stood over the kitchen sink and looked out the window at the darkening sky. When I looked up at the kitchen clock on the wall by the back door I realized it was much later than I thought, so I went to talk to the girls.

I poked my head into the twins' room, humoring my sisters as they sorted through a pile of unfolded laundry in the middle of the full-size bed. "Dinner's on the table. You need to eat to keep your strength up for that *long* drive."

"Do you think we'll need sweaters?" Velia asked her twin, pulling an old tattered sweater out of the cluttered closet. She tucked it under her chin and displayed it over her flat chest.

"It's the middle of the *canícula*," I said, stepping all the way into the room. "Why would you need a sweater during the hottest part of the summer?"

"It gets cold in the desert," Delia said. She sat cross-legged on their dilapidated dresser, smug as a cat.

"We're going to a desert?" Pita asked. "But I wanted to wear this dress." She had put on her best church dress, a baby blue, short-sleeved silk dress she'd had for a long time. She twirled around and watched the full skirt swirl around her like an open umbrella. Then she stopped, looked at herself in the mirror, and tugged at the snug waistband. Clearly Pita wanted to impress Abuelita. She always had to try so much harder than the twins to feel pretty.

"That dress doesn't even fit you anymore." Delia uncrossed her legs and jumped off the dresser. She poked Pita's baby fat and pulled on the dress collar's silk ribbon bow. "Too many *tamales*. You've got to stop eating so much, *Fajita Pita*. Wear something else. You look like a *chile relleno* in that."

"I don't care. It's my favorite dress, and I'm wearing it," Pita whined as she slapped Delia's hands away. "And don't call me that!"

I took Pita's round face in my hands and squeezed her cheeks. "You don't have to worry. We're not going to any deserts."

"Coahuila is a desert, isn't it? It's next to Chihuahua, and Chihuahua is a desert," Velia asked no one in particular.

"Think so?" Delia furrowed her eyebrows. I rolled my eyes.

"Of course not, *calabazas*. You're such knuckleheads sometimes," I said, looking around and talking to all of them at once. "Okay, let's get this straight. First of all, only the western part of Coahuila is a desert. El Sacrificio isn't, even though it's just as hot as Eagle Pass in the summer. But we're not going there anyway. So just get in there and eat your dinner. Then go to bed. It's almost eight, too late to worry about the body tonight. We'll talk about it tomorrow."

"Tomorrow!" Juanita complained as I turned around and started out of the room. "What do you mean tomorrow?"

"But we have to go back tonight," Delia whined. "To prep him."

"We'll talk about it tomorrow," I insisted. Then I turned around and left them there, whining and fighting again.

I went to my room and entertained myself by reading a few pages of *The Great Gatsby*. It was on my summer reading list, and so far, I had not been able to get past the third chapter. My mind was on other matters, like how to settle the girls into bed without causing a riot.

I played again with the idea of calling customs, to tell them about the body, but there was something else none of us had considered. Not even Juanita with her presumed giftedness had realized that once our swimming hole was discovered, we'd never be able to go back there. At the very least, the border patrol would keep an eye on that particular area of the river in case anyone else tried sneaking through that gap in the fence. We were lucky they hadn't noticed us swimming there already. They might even close it off, making us leave our swimming days behind.

By the time the girls burst into my room, frayed backpacks and old bucket purses busting at the seams, I was all ready to go. I stood up, picked up my own backpack, hiked it high up on my shoulder, and faced them.

"I'm going to Marisol's house. I think she's having a sleepover tonight."

"What? When did this come up? You didn't mention it before!" Juanita's continuous demanding tone was the most frustrating part of her. "What about the body? We said we'd take him back."

"I told you. We're not going to Mexico," I said decisively. "Mamá would kill us. Besides, she's already mad. I called to tell her I won't be here tonight to take care of you. She was so upset, she threatened to cut her hours short and come home. I think she's already working on it."

It was a total lie—but they needed a reality check, and they wouldn't call Mamá to confirm my story. Besides, while I made dinner, I'd developed a plan to have Mamá "be home" that night, if not in body, then in spirit.

"So you all better be in bed by the time she gets here," I continued. "You know how she gets when she's in a bad mood."

"This isn't fair!" Juanita screamed, her arms rigid and her face reddened with rage. She was actually crying. Juanita never cried. Her stubbornness usually led to yelling or bullying. It was unnerving. I don't think I'd seen her cry since she found out Santa Claus wasn't real. Suddenly I felt like the wicked stepmother in Snow White.

Juanita, probably embarrassed at her tears, stormed out of the room. She didn't go very far though—I could hear her mumbling under her breath in the hallway.

Delia threw her backpack on the floor and kicked it to the corner of the room. "You're an ignorant, goody-goody, wanna-be saint! *¡Una santurrona!*" she declared.

"And a sissy-face!" Velia added spitefully. Their remarks didn't bother me. I was used to the twins' stylized brand of cursing by now. They'd been doing it all summer, pretending they were old enough or even brave enough to curse like sailors, but never quite getting the words out. I was more worried that Juanita, who was glaring at me from the door, would do something drastic like storm out of the house and go back to the river.

"I bet Marisol kicks her big fat behind out and she has to sneak back in here like a sewer rat," Delia told Velia, flopping down next to her twin on the bed. They both looked at me like they were about to spit in my face, eyes glistening with wrath and frustration.

Juanita came back into the room, looking more like herself again. "You're a lousy sister!" she yelled.

"Enough!" I finally raised my voice the way Mamá does when she's done putting up with them. "Now go to bed before I call Mamá back and tell her what's really going on. And you, stop cursing, or I'll wash your mouths out with Clorox."

To my surprise, the twins flounced off the bed. All four of my sisters marched out and down the hall to the kitchen without another word. I went out the front door, locked it, and put the spare key to the deadbolt in my pocket. There was no other set of keys in the house to that door, so if they wanted to open it again, they'd have to wait until Mamá came home or jump out a window.

The thought had barely entered my mind when I heard the unmistakable sound of a window being slid open. I turned around to look at the darkened house. The only light was in Pita's room, which faced the front.

"You can't back out of this! We out-vote you four to one!" Juanita screamed, her body halfway out the window.

I lifted my hand in the air, my index finger extended. "Rule Number One of the code of the *cinco hermanitas:* The eldest sister has the final word. Always. Good night."

I left the yard, closing the gate behind me noisily, so they could hear me leaving even in the moonless night. Then I walked resolutely up the sidewalk toward Brazos Street. The thought of them escaping through a window made me cringe. I froze momentarily before I reached the corner, but then I realized they wouldn't do that. They might be wild, but they depended on me for everything. If I wasn't in on it, it usually didn't fly. That was the beauty of following the code of the five little sisters. We really did do everything together.

I walked around the corner, past the Aguileras' house, and cut across two empty lots, where I got the left leg of my jeans tangled up on some bramble weeds. I had to stop to pull the brambles off, and then I turned up Zamora Street toward Mr. Gee's. Peering in through the glass door, I saw that Mamá was standing at the counter, slicing pie with a heavy knife. Her black hair was twisted up in a haphazard knot and the dark circles under her eyes were more pronounced tonight. She'd been working so hard lately. Guilt stabbed at me, but I pushed it away. Even though I knew it would make Mamá mad, I needed to talk to her.

As if she had ESP, Mamá froze in midslice and looked up, making immediate eye contact with me. The sight of me standing there with my nose pressed against the glass made Mamá clench her mouth, and she cut through the crust of that pie like she wanted to kill it. She finished plating the slice of pie before she left the counter. I opened the door and started to go inside, but she hurried to meet me. Taking my arm in a vicelike grip, she turned me around and marched me back outside.

"What are you doing here?" She massaged her forehead with her fingertips, rubbing at the worry line between her eyebrows as if she wanted to erase it.

"It's important," I started, noticing the deep-set lines on her ring finger where her wedding band used to sit. It had been months since she'd stopped wearing it, but apparently wearing it over the years even after gaining a lot of weight had left her finger scarred.

Mamá used to be skinny before she got married, then she got really fat. I mean really fat, like almost three hundred pounds fat. But she lost it all in the eleven months since Papá left, so she was back to being thin again. Not *skinny* thin like she used to be when she was a girl, the way the twins are now, but definitely thinner. So thin, in fact, she didn't look like our Mamá anymore. But I wasn't worried about her anymore, because she wasn't as sad as she used to be and she was eating again. She looked more like me and Juanita now, strong and voluptuous, but tired from working so hard.

"We talked about this, Odilia," Mamá warned in Spanish. "Unless it's an emergency, you can't come here. One more incident like the last one, and I'm out of here. Is that what you want? To get me fired?"

Last time I was here, I was trying to get Pita to come back home. She'd made such a scene, bursting into the café to whine to Mamá that the girls were picking on her again. "No, but . . . the girls—" I started again.

"I don't want to hear it, Odilia," Mamá warned, her upper lip getting thinner and tighter as she spoke. "I've told you before, if nobody's dying and the house isn't on fire, it's not an emergency."

How could I convince her without giving anything away? "But they're being ridiculous," I continued, blinking nervously now, because we had caught the attention of Mr. Moore, the restaurant manager.

Mamá tried to control her temper by closing her eyes and taking a deep breath. "I mean it, Odilia. Take care of your sisters. I can't be in two places at once." This wasn't working. I was only bothering Mamá, and she couldn't help me anyway. I wanted to scream at Mamá and tell her that everything wasn't going to be okay, that I couldn't take care of it, but then Mr. Moore burst through the door, almost knocking us both down.

"Is there a problem?" Mr. Moore asked, standing halfway out of the restaurant and holding the door open. His bald pink head was covered in sweat. It glistened like a Christmas ornament under the fluorescent lighting spilling out from the café. I felt like taking the cleaning rag from his apron pocket and wiping it down for him, but that wouldn't have been nice, no matter how good it would have made me feel to do it.

"Oh, no. Odilia just came over to pick up some money for eggs," Mamá assured her boss, quickly switching to English. Reaching into the front pocket of her apron, she made a show of pulling out a couple of dollar bills and handing them to me.

Mr. Moore shook his head. "And this is more important than keeping your job?"

"No. It's not. And Odilia knows better. It won't happen again," Mamá whispered. Normally, Mamá doesn't let people mistreat her. She knows how to defend herself, but she had to act all meek and mild because Mr. Moore was a big fat slop-eating hog and she needed this job. After all, it wasn't like she had many career options without a high school diploma. She spoke English well enough despite the fact that she only went as far as the third grade in Mexico—which was all her parents had money for—and she hadn't come to the States until she met and married Papá when she was just seventeen years old. Up to now he'd always taken care of her.

When she first started working, the only jobs she qualified for were janitor, maid, and waitress. After a few trial runs, she decided she hated the other two, so she was doing her best to keep this job. She couldn't stand Mr. Moore, but she got along with the customers and they tipped her well.

"Then let's get back to work, shall we?" Mr. Moore raised his eyebrows. When we didn't move, he cleared his throat. With his lips clamped shut and his eyes bulging out of their sockets, he looked like a toad on steroids, but Mamá knew he was about to explode, so she nudged me aside.

"I'll be in in a minute," Mamá said, taking me by the shoulders and turning me around so that I was facing the parking lot.

"I'm sorry," I whispered as soon as Mr. Moore was inside the restaurant again. "I didn't mean to . . ."

"Whatever it is, deal with it, Odilia," Mamá insisted. "You are the eldest. It's your responsibility to take care of your *hermanitas*. I can't do it all. Now, go home before I lose my job."

Because I'd known how going to see Mamá would turn out, I left Mr. Gee's without feeling one bit of remorse over not telling her what was going on. At least I'd tried. There was nothing more I could do when she wouldn't give me the time of day. I couldn't help but think she wouldn't get in so much trouble at work if she and I had cell phones. Money was just too tight, and calling the restaurant would only get her in more trouble. Mr. Moore didn't approve of personal phone calls. But then, a cell phone would probably be yet another reason for Mr. Moore to accuse Mamá of neglecting her work. Last week I saw him chew out Mamá's younger coworker for texting instead of finding something "useful" to do on her break, like tidying up the break room.

Feeling less than thrilled at having to once again "take care of it," I walked back down Zamora Street the same way I'd walked up. The truth is, I needed to stall for a while if my plan was going to work tonight. So, instead of turning right on Brazos, I just kept going until I hit our old elementary school.

The campus fence wasn't locked, so I was able to walk right up to the classrooms. I dusted the powdery corpses of half a dozen dead butterflies off a cement bench and lay down on the quad under the moonlight for a while, contemplating my sisters and our rebelliousness. We were taking it too far, this rowdiness. Maybe I needed to tone down my part in it, become more responsible, listen to Mamá—wash some dishes or do some laundry for a change.

At that exact moment, a star shot across the sky. Its sparkling life faded into the horizon as it died away, unsung, unwept. Immediately following behind it, another star fell from the sky. It went down in the same direction. Then another one; and another, and another. On and on they all went, one right after the other, all five descending in the same direction.

Something told me I should hurry up and make a wish before the magical moment passed me by, so I closed my eyes and thought about the one thing I truly wanted—Papá.

Yes. If I could have anything, I'd have Papá come back into our lives and take care of us. I wanted him to stop touring, get a real job, and be home every day like he used to be when we were young. I wanted Mamá to stop working and worrying all the time. It's not like I wanted her to tuck us in at night and sing us a lullaby in Spanish like she used to. We were too old for that now. No. I just wanted to be a family again. With that longing in my heart, I closed my eyes and actually fell asleep right there on the school bench.

When I woke up, I lit up the face of my thrift store watch and couldn't believe how long I had napped. It was ten past midnight. Two hours had just flown by! I jumped up and trotted past the empty lots, but instead of going straight down the street toward home, I took a detour. I turned into the alley behind our house. Hiding behind the Olivarez family's dumpster, I opened my backpack.

Hastily, I took one of Mamá's blue dress uniforms out and slid it over my own clothes. I unzipped my jean shorts and slipped out of them, shedding them like a snakeskin and stuffing them into my backpack. Then I changed into an old pair of Mamá's work shoes and twisted my hair around and pinned it up into a half French twist, an easy, well-rehearsed styling technique I'd learned from Mamá, who always wore her hair that way. I completed the outfit by tying a white apron around my waist.

By the time I got to the house, the lights were all out. I could see that in Juanita's bedroom a nightlight was shining, but, when I jiggled the latch on the chain link fence, it went out. I kept my head down as I walked into the yard. Just as Mamá would, I struggled with the doorknob, pretended to look in Mamá's apron pockets for her keys, and finally opened the door. I didn't turn on any lights or make any noise. Like Mamá, I chose to walk in darkness. Quickly and quietly, I slipped into her bedroom.

I didn't undress, but instead lay on Mamá's bed fully clothed with my back to the door. Soon, I covered up with her blanket and pretended to snore, congratulating myself the whole time. I was *bien águila*, the queen of ruse.

Not even ten minutes went by before the bedroom door clicked open, and I heard someone enter Mamá's bedroom. But I didn't stir. Instead, I continued to fake snore.

"Mami?" Pita said quietly, sweetly, reaching the bed and touching my shoulder. She tried to shake me a bit, whining softly under her breath, but I snored again, loudly this time, like Mamá does when she's really tired.

I heard another noise, more like a rap, then another—a knock, then two, three, four more. I shifted in bed and halfway turned. In the mirror, I saw the dark silhouettes of at least three of my sisters locked in a muted struggle. In the darkness, I could hear their muffled grunts, and then the intake of a sharp, deep breath before they knocked each other to the floor, taking Mamá's ironing board with them.

I clicked the table lamp on and saw Velia, Delia, and Pita all tangled up on the floor. "What's going on?" I yelled.

Pita wailed, "They're trying to kill me!" She took a sharp breath, struggling to free herself.

"We are not!" Delia and Velia exclaimed even as they held her down.

"They had their hands over my nose and mouth. I couldn't breathe!" Pita whined, wiping at her eyes with the heel of her hand when they finally freed her.

Juanita entered the room and looked from the girls on the floor to me on the bed. "What are you doing in Mamá's clothes?"

"Stop biting me, you little traitor!" Velia spat out. She was so mad, she kicked at Pita's leg.

"Aw!" Pita scooted away from them and stood up. "I wasn't gonna tell, I just wanted to give Mamá a good-bye hug."

"Sure you were! *¡Chismosa!*" Delia scolded. "You're the biggest gossip there ever was." She turned around to give me a dirty look.

"Don't kick her." I let Pita sit on the bed with me. "You should be ashamed of yourselves, treating her like that. She's a little girl, not a spy on *Mission Impossible*."

"And you're not Cinderella, so why the stupid get-up?" Juanita threw back at me.

I undid the knot on Mamá's apron, slipped it off, and laid it on the bed beside me. Then I pulled the pins out of my hair and let my hair loose. It felt good to let my scalp breathe again. "Never mind me," I said. "Didn't I tell you all to go to bed?"

"You were bluffing, weren't you?" Juanita's dark brown eyes narrowed in disgust. "There was no sleepover, and you never called Mamá. It was all a trick—to stall us."

Delia got up and dusted her rump. "Well, it didn't work; we're going anyway," she announced.

"That's what this little snitch was doing in here. She was going to tell Mamá we're leaving," Velia said, kicking at Pita again before she stood up too.

"I said, don't kick her," I warned Velia. Then, looking at Juanita, I asked, "Oh yeah, well, how're you going to get there?"

I started to unzip Mama's uniform down the back. I felt ridiculous sitting there dressed up like a waitress even as I tried to sound like the voice of reason. Delia went to the door and blocked it, her feet apart and arms crossed like some kind of mobster. "If you won't drive us there, Juanita will. She's been watching you. She knows how to do it."

"She has the keys," Velia said, as she went to stand next to her twin.

"You don't know what you're doing," I said, pulling my clothes out of my backpack. I peeled the waitress's uniform off, put on my T-shirt, and pulled my jean shorts back on quickly.

"Well, we're going anyway," Velia concluded.

They walked out of the room, leaving me and Pita to stare at each other.

I heard a commotion in the living room, the girls arguing again, but the front was locked and I had the only key. "They're not going anywhere," I assured Pita. No sooner had I said that than I heard the front door slam shut.

"What the heck!" I walked out into the hall just in time to hear my father's old Chevy Nova sputter loudly to life. I pulled off Mamá's frumpy shoes and pushed on my own sneakers. Dang it! There was obviously another set of keys, to the *house and the vehicle*! I had no idea where they'd found them, but they had, and now my sisters were trying to drive away in a compromised vehicle without a clue as to how to handle it.

"Ah, you cussed!" Pita followed me down the hall. From the living room window, I saw Juanita, Velia, and Delia jumping into the car. I ran out onto the porch.

"Hey! Get out of the car! What do you think you're doing?" I hollered. Juanita put her arm out the window and waved my old canvas bag at me, taunting me from inside the car, daring me to stay behind. Then she revved the engine like a professional race driver and stared me down.

"Wait for me," Pita called, leaving my side and running out after them. She jumped into the backseat. Seeing that I wasn't leaving the porch, Juanita shrugged, put the car in reverse, and backed out of the driveway. The left corner of the Nova's rear bumper clipped the chain-link post, taking the gate with it and knocking down a good part of the fence. Juanita didn't even look back at the fence damage as she put the car in drive.

I ran into the darkened street as Juanita peeled out. "Come back here!" I yelled, but they were driving off so fast, I had to cut across the neighbors' lawns and through their backyards to keep up with them. Pumping my arms and legs as fast as I could, I followed the car all the way down to the corner. My breath was coming in ragged gasps, and I could barely hear the knocking engine of Papá's old car for the pulse pounding against my eardrums.

"Okay!" I screamed. "Okay! I'm coming with you! Stop! Stop!"

They paused long enough to let me jump into the front seat while Velia made room for me by quickly crawling into the back with Delia and Pita.

"Can you at least let me drive?" I asked.

"You can drive us into Mexico, but not before that," Juanita said, gripping the wheel resolutely.

"Then turn on the lights!" I demanded as we made our way down Main Street in the dark. If they didn't want to get stopped by the police, we should at least look like we knew *that* much about driving. The idea made me think that perhaps I shouldn't have pointed that out to her—getting a cop's attention *would* definitely bring their harebrained trip into Mexico to a standstill. But police involvement was more of a last resort. There had to be a better way. "Use the wipers," I continued. "Get these dead butterflies off the windshield so we can see where we're going."

It wasn't at all how I had planned our night to end, but I figured all hope wasn't lost. It was just easier to let my sisters think they'd won. However, the instant I buckled up I promised myself I'd surrender the body when we got to the international bridge—no matter what.

3

La Estrella: *"La más alta y brillante de todas mis hijas."*

The Star: "The tallest and brightest of all my daughters."

When we got back to the river's edge, the girls exhausted themselves prepping the body for the trip. Velia held a flashlight, while Juanita, who had brought a pair of Papá's old jeans, one of his dress shirts, and his cowboy boots, dressed the body with the reverence of a dedicated mortician. Afterward, we slept with the *mariposas* in the car. At five o'clock in the morning, the girls got up and splashed cold river water on their faces.

"I don't like it," Pita scrunched her chubby face in disgust when they propped the dressed body up against the mesquite's trunk. He was as rigid as the mannequins at JCPenney, with a baseball cap on his head, dim sunglasses over his lifeless eyes, and his arms crossed awkwardly in front of him.

"He looks too much like Papá," Delia admitted, stepping away from him.

Velia scrubbed away the thick layer of rouge Juanita had applied to his cheekbones in the dark. "He looks like a prostitute."

"He does not," Juanita said. "Don't take it all off. He needs to look alive."

Delia helped her twin sister scrub off the excess makeup from the dead man's neck. "He doesn't look alive; he looks ridiculous. Men don't wear makeup, Juanita."

"Fine, have it your way. But we're gonna get caught if he doesn't look half alive," Juanita answered.

I left them there arguing with each other and took a short walk while they figured things out. Once they got the body in the car, I'd drive us up to the international bridge and turn it in. We'd be home in time to fix breakfast for Mamá. Then we'd go to bed and only dream about what could've happened after this night.

I walked alone along the riverbank. In the dawning light, it shimmered with the hues of day fighting away the shadows of night, while the multitude of trees and shrubbery that grew for miles and miles along the riverbank still shrouded the land in shadow. Suddenly, to the left of me, about ten yards southeast along the river beyond the twisted path my sisters and I had worn into the thicket, two small figures ran past me in and out of the dusty brush right up to the river's edge. They ran along the bank, skirting it so closely that pebbles flew off their footsteps and bounced down into the water. Their faces were indistinguishable in the dark and their white outfits were muted by the lack of sunlight, but I could see that they were little boys running away from something—or someone.

It didn't take very long to see who they were running from. Behind them, a woman in a pale dress came running, screaming at the boys, begging them to stop. Her long black hair whipped behind her as she fought through the brush. It was clear to me she was worried—frantic, even—that they might fall into the river.

"*¡Ay, mis hijos!*" she screamed as she side-stepped ruts and rocks with her small bare feet. The short trees tore at her immaculate white dress, but she didn't care. She pulled herself free of any tree limbs that clawed at her and kept chasing after her children, never losing sight of them.

"Hey," I screamed after the children. They didn't turn to look at me or acknowledge me in any way. They were getting dangerously close to a cliff at the edge of the river. I left the security of our path and darted after them. They still ran parallel to the waters of the Rio Grande, much too close to the current that roared furiously below. The waters here were dark and angry, almost violent—nothing like our friendly swimming hole. I sped up, afraid they might lose their footing.

Too late, I screamed for them to get away from the edge. In a second, they were falling, both of them, one behind the other. Into the water they went, making loud splashes as they fought to stay afloat. Without thinking, I scrambled up to the edge and jumped in after them.

The roar and chilliness of the dark water awakened my senses, and my heart constricted in my chest as I came up for air. I had to fight the undercurrent to keep from being swept away. As I struggled to stay afloat, I looked around wildly for the children who I clearly saw fall into the water seconds before me.

They were about fifteen feet away from me, being dragged down, into the body of a heavy current. Their mother, running along the river, cried and screamed for me to help them.

"*¡Ay, mis hijos!*" she wailed miserably.

I swam with long even strokes, trying to remain in control of my body, not letting the undertow pull me down. But my efforts were in vain. The water rose over my head and swirled around me like a whirlpool, dragging me deeper and deeper, until the thin light of dawn turned into darkness, and I couldn't see anything anymore.

All was obscurity and cold, and I thought I would drown. *What would Mamá think? Did I fail my sisters?* My lungs ached with the pressure of unreleased air. Just when I was about to give in, the roaring stopped and I felt myself break through the surface. The fresh morning air hit my lungs like a blow to the chest, and I pressed a fist against my heart as if to stop the pain from killing me.

As I coughed and sputtered in agony in the now-calm water, I saw one of the boys floating before me. I grabbed his arm and pulled him in. Dragging him over my shoulder, I began to swim toward the riverbank, where his mother was crying out for me to bring him to her. When I got close enough, she stepped back.

"You're too late. He's drowned," she wailed as she stood watching me struggle with her son's body. At her words, inexplicably, the boy's body slipped from me. It bobbed in the water and wavered in the pre-dawn light, then disappeared before my very eyes. I turned around to look for his brother and saw him drifting a few feet away from me. Before I could dive for him, he vanished like a strange mirage.

"Here, let me help you," their mother said, extending her hand to me from above. The hand was cold as a corpse, but I took it anyway. At first I attributed the coldness to her state of despair or my own soakedness, but when she pulled me out she spoke again, and what she said made me want to jump right back in the water.

"It is always the same way," she said, her expression helpless in a worn, weary face. The woman's hair was long and disheveled, and her long tunic dress was torn and frayed. I could tell it used to be a white robe of some kind when it was new, but it was so old it was gray now. On the whole, she looked unkempt and malnourished, close to death. "They drown before I can reach them. It is my nightmare, my destiny, my fate to search endlessly for them by night only to find them drowned with the sigh of morning."

Recognition entered my mind, and I froze, unable to speak.

The woman's eyes softened and she looked sad. "You know who I am, don't you?"

"Llorona?" I whispered the dreadful name before I could censor myself. Most women would be offended to be mistaken for the ghostly apparition, but she did not flinch at the horrific namesake. Instead, her smile was apologetic and teary—it evoked compassion rather than fear.

"Some call me that," she admitted, as she tried to take my hand. "Do not be afraid. I cannot harm you."

Was she saying she was La Llorona? As much as the idea of talking to a ghost fascinated me, it also frightened me. I had heard so many awful things about La Llorona that I couldn't help it, I pulled away from her and took a few steps back. "But you . . . killed your children." It was common knowledge, more than a legend. Every mother on both sides of the border warns her children that La Llorona will get them if they wander too close to the river. I couldn't help but wonder if by playing in it all summer, we hadn't cursed ourselves.

"I know what they say," she admitted. "I've heard the stories many times through the centuries. But they are mistaken. I did not drown my *chiquitos*."

"You didn't? Then why do they run away from you?" I looked back at the dark river, wondering if I had really seen her children drowning. Had I imagined trying to save them? Was it possible I was dreaming all this?

La Llorona stepped away from me and turned to the river. She wrapped her arms around herself as if the memory gave her a chill. "We were arguing that night—their father, Hernán, and

I—about his decision to leave. We fought over the children, dragged them into our pain. *Mis hijos* were so scared, so confused, that they fled toward the river in darkness and drowned. It is a nightmare I experience every night, a memory I am forever reliving."

I went to stand beside her. Her loss was unimaginable, and suddenly she was very human to me. "Why do you look for them, if you know they are dead?"

"It is a punishment I impose on myself," La Llorona began. "A penance for my part in it. I should have been more careful, made sure they were always safe. I want them to come back to me, but they won't—or can't. I do not know the reason behind it, but they are being kept from me. I would never take the children that play at the river, the way people say I do. I do not want other children. They could never replace my *chiquitos*. Believe me—you and your sisters have nothing to worry about. I am not here to harm you."

I considered her words and wondered why someone would willingly punish herself for all eternity. It seemed implausible to me. But then again, I was standing on the edge of the river talking to a ghost. Nothing was normal. Nothing made sense. "Then what do you want from us?"

"You were chosen for the goodness in your heart," she explained. "Like Juan Diego, the most humble of the Virgen's children, you are noble and kindhearted. You displayed great courage when you jumped into the water to save my sons. Your sister was right when she said finding the body of the drowned man was not an accident."

She took my hand once again, her touch still deathly cold. Standing beside the hackberry shrubs with hundreds of empty desiccated cocoons still clinging to their branches and a carpet of butterfly corpses under her feet, La Llorona did not look anything like a malevolent specter. She looked more like a tired, heavily burdened woman.

"My sisters are waiting," I said, trying to take my hand from hers so that I might escape if I had to.

La Llorona let go of my hand. "Please, try to have faith. I am here in your service, to guide and protect you," she said.

I put my hands under my arms to warm them. "Protect me? From what?"

"Yes," she said, a wry smile curling around her lips. She had a look of age about her, despite appearing no older than Mamá. It was something in her eyes, the sorrow of long ages lived in them. "It is an eternal atonement, to watch over the children of the sun, the children of my people, the *Azteca* bloodline."

"Aztec?" I asked, surprised. Mamá never said we were Aztec. Papá was fair-haired and light-complected, implying a Spanish bloodline rather than native Mexican, but Mamá did have olive skin, black hair, and dark eyes.

"Yes. You are descendant of a great people," she continued, pulling my attention away from my wild, erratic thoughts and making me focus on the situation at hand.

At that very moment, the sun burst out from beneath the horizon, and La Llorona's features changed. She went from being a tired woman to looking downright frightening. Her disheveled hair suddenly turned completely white. The loose silvery strands writhed around her head like serpentine ghosts, more fearsome than Medusa's. La Llorona's gaunt face shriveled up like a pale raisin, becoming sallow and ashen, creased by centuries of wrinkles and dark blotches. But it was her eyes that scared me the most. They turned a deep, evil black. They glittered like cursed gemstones. I was so terrified I couldn't move, but I trembled where I stood. I couldn't speak for a moment—my throat tightened and I was having trouble breathing.

"Don't be afraid," she pleaded. "I don't have much time. Once the sun rises completely I must go back."

The gentleness of her voice calmed me a little, and I was able to reply, though I wanted to run away, back to my *hermanitas*. "G-go back where? Why are you here?"

"I have been sent here to help you find your way," La Llorona said. "There is a path designed for everyone and everyone must walk in his or her path. This is your path. You must walk it. To refuse would be . . . unfortunate."

Unfortunate. The word felt ominous, coming from La Llorona herself, and my body stiffened in response. I fought to speak, to get out the words to the question that was suddenly weighing heavily on my mind. "Am I going to be cursed, like . . . like . . . you, if I don't—walk my path?"

"Change must take place. It is important. To remain as you are would lead to isolation. You would be doomed to a lonely existence, ripped apart from those you love."

I threw up my arms and let out a frustrated sigh. "You're speaking in riddles." I didn't understand what La Llorona wanted me to do. How was I supposed to change, to find my way? What did that even mean?

"Then let me speak plainly," La Llorona began. "You must go to El Sacrificio and take the drowned man back to his family." The sun had finished rising and its full radiance was dissolving La Llorona's form. She stooped to hide under the shade of a cluster of huisache trees, looking almost translucent.

"But . . . we don't even know who he is. Sure, we have his wallet, but we're just kids," I began.

"It's not all about him," La Llorona assured me. "This is about you and your loved ones too. Your family is lost in turmoil. You must find each other, become whole again." Though La Llorona's body was translucent, her eyes remained untouched—dark and luminous in the shadows of the huisache trees.

"Are you saying that this is about the trouble between Mamá and Papá?"

"This is about all of you: your sisters, your parents, even your *abuela*," La Llorona continued. "You must travel to the other side, into the land of your ancestors, to find each other again."

Before I could ask her to clarify her puzzle—after all, my sisters were all right here with me—I heard Juanita's voice, then

Delia and Velia calling out for me. I turned toward the clearing.

"Here, take this," La Llorona said, reaching for me again. This time I did not pull away as she placed something bulky and cold into the palm of my hand and closed it tightly for me, her bony fingers pressing against my own. Though she appeared to age before my eyes, her skin felt youthful and firm as it made contact with mine. "You will need it, for your journey will be filled with many hardships. Your courage and conviction will be tested throughout your travels. You must accept it and use it."

I opened my hand to look at it, wondering. Before I could ask, she said, "An ear pendant." I held it up to the light, where the gold glittered in the morning sun as I twirled it between my fingertips. At the base of the ear pendant, a serpent's fangs held a small loop. Within the loop five wide rings were suspended, each one larger than the last, nesting snugly inside each other, like the rings of Saturn.

"It is a likeness of Cihuacóatl, *La Serpiente*," La Llorona explained, watching it glint in the morning sun. Along the bank we were almost fully exposed to the sun, though the thick woods continued to stretch for miles around us. "A most powerful amulet. It was given to me by my mother on my fifteenth birthday at the altar of Tenochtitlan, when I became a woman. It has magical properties, gifts from the gods. But you can only use it five times, once for every ring on its axis." I examined the beautiful pendant. It had to be centuries old, if she was telling me the truth. "Take it," she said when I tried handing it back. How could I take

something so valuable? Even half a pair must be worth a fortune.
"It belongs to you now. Wear it on your left ear. When you need help, take hold of it, spin it, and invoke the goddess, the Aztec queen, Tonantzin, the Holy Mother of all mankind, and ask for her magical assistance. Whatever you ask, she will provide."

"I—I can't do this," I told La Llorona. How could I take responsibility for something so powerful? It frightened me more than La Llorona herself to do such a thing.

"This ear pendant can do many things," La Llorona insisted. "It can change your aura and provide you with safe passage as you travel from your world into ours, but be careful to use it wisely; never call upon its power in anger or arrogance. You and your sisters must remain pure of heart on this journey, Odilia. Be courageous, but remember also to be noble and kind. If you do that, everything will be all right."

"Odilia? Is that you?" Juanita's voice startled La Llorona, who stepped back into the brush.

"They're just little girls, dreaming up an adventure. I can't drag them down to Mexico. I can't sacrifice them to follow my path," I whispered fiercely, still holding the ear pendant in front of me. But La Llorona wasn't taking it back. I heard twigs breaking and footsteps getting closer from the direction of the swimming hole. The girls couldn't see us from the path. We were hidden behind a heavy cluster of huisache trees. But if they veered off the path, they'd find me talking to a phantom.

"This is not for you to do alone," La Llorona said. "You must come together, you and your *hermanitas*. You must rejoice in the strength of sisterhood and return the man to his family."

"Because we're *lost*?" I asked. Even as I said it, a pang of recognition that La Llorona was exactly right about us, that we *were* lost, fluttered to life within me much like the mariposas who were beginning to stir in the morning light. At the same time, La Llorona confirming Juanita's crazy plan made me question my own sanity. But what if she was right? If doing something as simple as returning a dead man to his family would save our family, shouldn't I try? Yet the thought of going into Mexico without telling Mamá where we were going or why made me feel awful. We hadn't even left her a note. What would she think? Would she feel abandoned again?

Delia and Velia were arguing with each other in the brush behind us. They weren't more than ten feet away, but the cluster of huisaches sheltered us from their view. "She left!" Delia declared.

"No. She wouldn't do that. She wouldn't leave us out here all alone," Velia said, their voices getting closer and closer, until I knew they were only a few yards away.

I focused back on the spectral woman whose voice was becoming more strained. "It is the only way," La Llorona whispered. "Your mother and sisters need you! They are lost in despair."

They needed me right here, taking care of them. Mamá was depending on me to keep them safe. "I'm tired of your riddles. I'm taking them home," I said, turning to go.

"Please," La Llorona pleaded, standing up and stepping in front of me. "You must take him back. Don't do it for him. He's just a man, one who committed a selfish act. Don't do it for his wife either. She cries for him for her own selfish reasons. Don't even do it for his little ones, who, like many children, have already turned to their play without thinking much of him anymore. Do it for your *hermanitas*. Deliver the man home to his family and then drive your sisters to El Sacrificio to see their *abuela*. Reunite your family, Odilia. It is all part of the journey you must take, the path to true happiness."

"Odilia? Who are you talking to?" Juanita burst through the brush from another direction. I thought she was with the twins behind the huisaches. She stopped abruptly and stared at me. "And why are your clothes all wet?" she asked.

I looked around for La Llorona, but the apparition was gone. "Nobody," I said, suddenly feeling stupid. *I'm losing it*, I thought, as I pushed branches aside, fighting my way back to the clearing.

"But I heard voices," Juanita insisted.

I tucked the ear pendant into my pocket for safekeeping. "Me too. I think it's Delia and Velia arguing again."

"No," Juanita said. "I heard them, but I heard you too. You were talking to someone out here."

"I wasn't." That was one thing I hated about Juanita, the way she clung to things and wouldn't let them go, like a dim-witted gnat stuck on a piece of rotting fruit. I couldn't explain to her who I'd been talking to, but she wouldn't let it go.

"Yes, you were. I heard you," she insisted. "Why are you lying to me?"

"Okay. Fine," I finally admitted. "I was talking to La Llorona. She wants us to take the drowned man home. I tried telling her we couldn't, but she said we have to do it because it's our destiny or something. I couldn't understand her. She talks in riddles. There. I admit it. I was talking to a ghost. Are you happy now?"

"Fine. Don't tell me. I don't care! I don't *have* to know!" Juanita clamped her mouth shut and stalked off. I followed close behind without saying another word. If I'd known the truth was the one thing that could shut Juanita up for good, I would have stopped lying to her years ago.

4

El Venado: *"No es venado, es venada,*

y hay cinco en mi ramada."

The Deer: "It's not a deer, it's a doe, and

there are five of them in my arbor."

Instead of helping Juanita carry the body, I went to sit in the driver's seat of Papá's car to be sure Juanita didn't try her driving stunt again. Looking at myself in the rearview mirror, I took the cubic zirconia stud out of my left ear and replaced it with La Llorona's elaborate ear pendant. The zirconia studs weren't expensive, but they were a birthday gift from Mamá, so I didn't want to lose them. I attached both studs to an old envelope I found in the car and tucked them safely into the glove box. Still looking at myself, I shook my head, trying to get used to the weight of La Llorona's ear pendant. I watched it glint in the daylight and wondered if it really was magical. It looked ancient and mysteriously beautiful, and for a moment, I thought it glittered magically.

Juanita rested her forearms on the driver's window and looked at the ear pendant. "Where did you get that?"

"I found it," I said, twisting at the back of it to make it stay in place. It would take time to get used to the great weight of it pulling down on my small earlobe.

"Nice," she said, touching it gingerly. "Can I try it on?"

"No," I said. "It's not mi—"

"It's not what?" Juanita's eyes narrowed as if she was trying to put together a word puzzle.

"It's not . . . not. Nothing," I said, stammering on my words like a stalling engine. "Don't you have something better to do than stand around looking at me? I'm not that interesting."

Her face dropped sheepishly. "Well, I think I'm going to need some help. He weighs a ton. Dead weight, you know."

"Oh, no," I said, getting out of the car and slamming the door shut. "This is your show, not mine."

"Fine! Whatever!" Juanita walked away in a huff. I leaned back against the car, crossed my arms, and watched as she enlisted the help of Velia and Delia.

Even though I had put on the earring, I refused to admit that I was seriously considering taking the body back home to his wife and kids. It was unfathomable. *This is stupid,* I kept telling myself. *Ghosts aren't real, and they don't give you expensive presents. I should go home and have my head examined.*

"Okay," Juanita said. After positioning the body in the backseat with the side of his face resting against a pillow, looking like he was trying to sleep, Juanita took a list out of her back pocket and started rattling off its contents. "Blankets?" she asked.

"Check," Velia verified.

"Flashlight? " Juanita continued.

"Check." Delia patted her hip, and for the first time, I saw that she had a sort of tool belt full of odds and ends wrapped around her waist. It was one of Mamá's worn waitress aprons with loops and odd-shaped pockets sewn awkwardly all over it.

I pointed at the absurd contraption. "What's in there?" I asked.

"In this?" Delia asked, grinning with ingenious pride, her perfect smile brilliant. "Medical kit, makeup, perfume, scissors, batteries, candles . . ."

"Perfume?" I asked. "Why would we need perfume?"

Velia rolled her eyes at me. "Hello? He's gonna start stinking."

"Oh, great," I retorted. "So now he's not just going to look like a prostitute, he's going to smell like one too?"

Velia gave Delia an elbow shove in the ribcage. "I told you we should've brought Papá's Old Spice."

"It was almost gone," Delia said, rubbing at her side.

"So why not bring both?" Velia looked mad now.

"I did," Delia said, pulling out Papá's old bottle of cologne with nothing more than a few drops left in the bottom of it. "See?"

"People, please," Juanita interjected. "Can we just move this along? We don't have time to nitpick each other."

"That's right," Velia said, watching me intently with fierce hazel eyes. "Today we're on a mission, and we shouldn't let anything stop us from doing what's right. Today, we need to work together. Otherwise, this whole thing could blow up on us."

"You mean, like we could get caught and end up in juvie?" Pita asked.

Delia took off the apron and folded it carefully so nothing would spill out of its pockets. She put it in the trunk, where I saw more supplies. When had they gotten those out of the house? "They wouldn't do that to us, would they?" she said, looking at Velia for reassurance.

"Of course not," Velia answered, sounding like an expert. "It's not like we've broken any laws."

"Actually," Juanita began, "improper disposal of a dead body, even failing to report it, is a crime. That's why we're doing things right, and taking it to his family, who can give him a proper burial. But no matter what happens, we are Five Little Sisters, *cinco hermanitas!* The Garza Girls! Together forever! No matter what!" Juanita exclaimed, and like every time one of us said those words, they all huddled together and hugged.

That's when I started to turn. Being left out of the circle of the *cinco hermanitas* was like becoming an orphan, or suddenly being homeless. I didn't like the way that felt, didn't want to be apart from them, ever, even if Juanita was changing the subject to avoid focusing on what could go wrong. So I did what any true sister would have done at a time like that. I stepped forth and let them pull me in.

I wasn't pretending either. At that very moment I changed my mind, believed in us as a team, believed that together we could get through anything. And for an instant, I wondered if maybe La Llorona was right and this journey was our destiny, our path to true happiness.

So we all loaded our gear in the trunk and got in the car. Juanita rode in the front with me. Delia and Velia sat side by side in the backseat next to the "sleeping" drowned man while Pita wedged herself against the opposite car door trying to stay away from him. At the edge of the woods, before we turned onto El Indio Highway, I paused at the stop sign long enough to turn around to look at the twins.

"What do you think?" I asked, shaking my head to make the *argollas*, the nesting rings on La Llorona's ear pendant, rattle against each other. "Do I look stupid wearing only one earring?"

"What are you talking about?" Juanita asked. "You're wearing two of them. They're a matching set. But really, where did you get them?"

"Them?" To my surprise, I felt the weight of an ear pendant on my right ear even before I reached up and touched it. Feeling the coldness of the yellow gold within my fingertips, I looked at myself in the rearview mirror again. There it was, the other ear pendant, framing my face and winking at me. Its magical power was indisputable in the sunlight.

"I found them," I said, trying to satisfy her curiosity without giving away too much. She hadn't believed me when I tried telling her about La Llorona anyway. "Well? Do I look dumb wearing these giant hoops?"

"No," Velia said, excitedly joining the conversation. "You look powerful, like a woman who knows what she wants out of life."

Delia reached over and flicked the golden rings with her forefinger, making them tinkle against each other. "Yeah, especially with your hair all wild like that. You look like a gypsy, a rebel with an eye for fashion." I reached up and touched my hair. It was more than "wild." It was downright ratted with knots because I hadn't even brushed it once since we got out of the water yesterday, when we found the dead man. I wondered if there was a comb I could use later in Delia's apron contraption.

"I think it makes you look older," Juanita observed. "More sophisticated."

"Good. Good. I like that," I said, putting the car into gear and turning onto El Indio Highway, toward the border. I'd need all the sophistication I could muster to make us believable when we attempted to cross the bridge.

Crossing customs on the American side is always fast and easy. There's a toll to pay, so Velia put the three dollars in the dead man's right hand and rested it on the right shoulder pad of the driver's seat. She pressed her own shoulder under the dead man's arm to make it look like she wanted to be close to her daddy, when in reality she was keeping his arm from slipping and falling into her lap.

When we pulled up to the tollbooth, the duty officer didn't even look at us. Peripherally, he must have seen Velia take the money from the drowned man's hand and reach over me to pay, because he took it from her without once glancing at us, unaware of who or what was inside the car.

That's how much he cares, I thought.

At that moment, I had a choice. I could make him care by informing him that the man sitting rigidly behind me was actually a corpse, or I could just keep driving. As I watched the duty officer straighten up and look at the next car, a brazen breeze picked up around us. It passed through the car, dragging a small bevy of tiny brown *mariposas* into the car. The butterflies flittered around us, beating their wings gently against the windshield then sitting prettily on the dashboard. At least a dozen of them had flown into the backseat and settled on Pita. Four of them clung to her hair, opening and closing their wings in long, luxurious strokes, while the rest of them crawled delicately along her arms.

"I think they like us," Pita said, smiling and sitting as motionless as humanly possible, trying her best not to disturb the delicate butterflies. With one of the *mariposas* climbing up her nose, staring at her eye to eye, Pita looked like Bambi, right before the hunters shot his mother.

The image of Pita looking so innocent and young made me think of the dead man's children, sitting at home, wondering what happened to their *papá.* At that moment, I realized what would happen if we were caught with a dead man's body in our car. These people would call Child Protective Services and that would lead to a full-on investigation of Mamá. They would label her neglectful and make her look like an unfit mother.

It felt like I deliberated our journey for hours, when in reality, we were there for only a few more seconds. The people in the cars behind me started honking, and the toll booth attendant looked into the vehicle for the first time since we drove up. He glanced suspiciously at the sleeping man behind me. Terrified that he might catch us with a corpse in the car, I snapped into action. I reached up and gave my left ear pendant a vigorous spin and asked it for help, low enough for the girls not to hear me, "Aztec queen, Tonantzin, Holy Mother of all mankind, give me your magical assistance. Distract this man, make him forget what he has seen."

"That's a nice pair of earrings," the attendant said, mesmerized by the sight of the whirling *argollas* humming against my cheeks. "Where'd you get them? I'd like to find something like that for my wife."

"They were a gift," I said, watching as the man squinted to avoid the glare of golden light emanating from La Llorona's ear pendant and glinting directly into his eyes, momentarily blinding him.

"They're beautiful," he said, still too entranced by them to do much else.

"Is that it?" I asked, as I watched the officer stare at my earlobe.

"Ah, sure, go on," he said, waving us off in a dazed state of mind.

The spell worked! I knew La Llorona was real, but for her promise of magic to be real too was more than I had expected. I was so exhilarated by the realization that I did the most unexpected thing in the world. I listened to my inner nut and sped out of the *caseta*, leaving behind everything that was familiar and normal and full of life and crossing over the threshold into the darkness of a dead man's life.

We drove the few miles across the international bridge with the windows down, the wind whipping our hair around our faces, until we slowed down and drove into the *aduana*, the Mexican customs station. I pulled into the center booth and waited for the officer to come over to speak to us.

The Mexican official was scary. He was a big fat man, older than the moon, with huge, bulging eyes that devoured our female frames. When he saw that our "father" was asleep in the backseat, he looked from one pretty girl to another and licked his lips like an iguana. I wanted to sink the gas pedal into the floorboard and peel out of there, but he had other ideas. He looked at my small chest for a long time, and then he smiled knowingly at me.

"Where are you young ladies going?" he asked.

"We're going to Chihuahua," I lied in perfect Spanish, a task that was not difficult, since Spanish was our first language.

"We're taking him home to—" Pita interjected.

"Our grandmother!" Juanita exclaimed, smiling nervously. "We're going to go see our grandmother in Chihuahua."

The girls' lies cut through me with the sharpness of an obsidian knife. The mention of our grandmother made me physically jerk in my seat—it was so reminiscent of what La Llorona had said I should do. I turned around and whispered, "T.M.I.," with an *I could kick you* look on my face. Inside, I was fighting the urge to cry. The thought of going right up to my paternal grandmother's residence, sitting down at her table, and tasting her cooking more than saddened me. I wondered how she would receive us after only having seen us twice in her lifetime? Would she even know who we were?

"It's our birthday. Me and my twin's," Delia continued, pointing at Velia.

"My grandmother's throwing us a party," Velia said, batting her long eyelashes.

"There's going to be a live band, *Los Coyotes*," Delia invented, showing her perfect teeth as she smiled. "You can come if you want."

Where are they coming up with all this? I asked myself as I watched them lie shamelessly to the dirty old man. The more unsolicited information we provided, the more he might suspect something.

"He can't come. He has to stay here and take care of business," I said, turning to give them a look like the one Mamá gives us when we're being bad. The look worked, because after that they just looked at him and pouted in mock disappointment.

"Your big sister's right," the old officer said, laughing. "I have too much work."

"You see. He can't come," I concluded, staring straight ahead.

"But thanks for inviting me," he said. "You girls have fun. Maybe I'll see you on the way back." And with that, he winked, an act that turned the sandwich I'd had the night before into a revolting slime that churned and festered in my stomach.

"Bye! Bye!" Both Velia and Delia waved at the officer as we drove off past the *aduana* and into Piedras Negras. My heart was racing and my head was hurting, but the girls were whooping and hugging each other in the backseat. Juanita just sat back and looked at me smugly, a tiny bit of sisterly pride glinted in her brown eyes, but I didn't acknowledge it. I stared at the road ahead instead.

"We did it!" Velia yelled. "We got through the freakin' border!"

"Don't celebrate yet," I told them as I veered around the plaza. We circled around El Santuario de Nuestra Señora de Guadalupe and promptly crossed ourselves at the sight of the old church. We may have been wild and rebellious, but our mother wasn't raising complete heathens.

"You might want to go in there and pray," I continued. "We have a long, challenging road ahead of us. We'll be lucky to get past the checkpoint outside the city limits. This guy was the least of our problems."

"Hey, if we can get past that fat *bobo*," Juanita said, "we can get past the checkpoint."

"Whatever," I mumbled under my breath. They had no idea how much of an effort this was going to be, but I figured they'd find out soon enough. No use bursting their *sopapillas* quite yet.

5

El Mundo: "*El mundo pudiera estar parado y nosotros bien mareados.*"

The World: "The world could be standing still, and we'd all be just as dizzy."

We drove around Piedras Negras, getting a few more things for the road. Except for the initial shock and anxiety of seeing so many *sospechosos*, idle young men, conspicuously posted outside prominent buildings or lounging on stone benches in the plaza, we felt confident enough to go about our business. Although we did our best to make it fast. We didn't want to call attention to ourselves in case they were members of any of the border gangs, who had been abducting people along the *Frontera*, the border between Mexico and the US.

I bought a huge bag of tortilla chips, some peanuts, and some water bottles from a street vendor. Velia and Delia purchased piping hot ears of corn on a stick, wrapped in their own leaves and enveloped in newspapers to keep them warm. Juanita bought some *raspas*, icy fruit-flavored treats, to cool us down. I drove with one hand while I ate mine before it melted.

This time the girls were right—getting through the checkpoint outside Piedras Negras on Highway 57 was easier than getting past the old officer at the *aduana*. The guard at the depot didn't ask us where we were going or what we were doing in Mexico. We gave him the same story about our grandmother, but he seemed uninterested.

Actually, the officer, a young skinny guy in his early twenties, was more about making a buck than doing his job. When he asked us for our travel permit, he rubbed his fingers together and rested his right hand just inside the door as he looked away toward the road behind us. Velia, Juanita, and I looked at his hand dumbly.

"Ahem," Delia cleared her throat. We turned to look at her. The dead man's hand was propped back on the headrest of my seat, holding a crisp, neatly folded twenty dollar bill between the index and middle fingers. "The permit is in the glove box, remember?" she continued, arching an eyebrow to emphasize her point.

"Oh!" Juanita's eyes sparkled with understanding. Then she searched the glove box and pulled out a piece of paper. She looked at it for a moment, then offered it to me. I stared at it dumbfounded.

Velia took it, reached over me, and pressed the money and the paper into the man's hand and smiled at him. I'd seen Papá do this many times before, but it would've never dawned on me to try it. If it had been left up to me, we would have gotten hauled into a Mexican jail that day.

The skinny officer took both items. He pretended to read the piece of paper as he discreetly stuffed the twenty dollars into the cuff of his long-sleeved shirt. After a few seconds, he handed the "permit" back to me and waved us through. I handed the paper to Juanita and drove off. The whole incident took less than two minutes, but it was the longest, most stressful two minutes of my life.

"Ah, the power of moo-lah," Juanita said, resting back against her seat and laughing out loud as we drove off.

"I can't believe we pulled that off," I said, letting out a long-held breath. "What was that? What did you show him?"

"I don't know. An old receipt of some kind," Juanita said, looking at the piece of paper in her hand. "Doesn't matter. It could have been my Christmas list for all he cared."

After driving for hours in the hot morning sun without stopping, past Nava, past Allende, past Nueva Rosita and Sabinas, we hit a long stretch of open road. The day was hot and sticky and we were drenched down to our socks. The old Nova's air conditioner had never worked, so our only source of comfort came from the open windows. At the first signs of civilization, we veered off the road and stopped at an old gas station just south of Monclova.

Juanita went into the convenience store to pay for the gas. I kept an eye on her as she looked around for goodies to bring back to the car. The peanuts were running low, and the water and chips were long gone. After I finished pumping the gas,

I went in to hurry her along. I wanted to make sure we were on our way before other travelers showed up and saw the dead man propped up against our back window.

"Let's go," I said, as she picked through the bottles of Mexican fruit pop in the beverage cooler. "Papá is getting upset."

"Stop telling me what to do," Juanita ordered. "Can't you see I'm busy here? Man, you made me lose count . . . three, four, five. There. We can go now."

I picked up a pineapple soft drink. "Six," I said, handing it to her.

"No," she insisted, putting the bottle back in the open cooler. "We don't need so many. There's only five of us."

"No," I corrected her. "There are six of us."

Juanita lashed out at me. "You always do this, Odilia. You always think you know what you're talking about, but you don't. You're just a big fat bully who doesn't know anything. Count 'em! *¡Cinco hermanitas!* Five. There are five of us!"

"Don't forget Papá," I said, nodding to the shop owner and his wife staring at us from the counter.

"Oh," Juanita said, her ego deflating like a tire. "I forgot about Papá. He's probably dying of thirst. Here, let's take two for him," she said, picking up a seventh soft drink.

"Whatever," I said, walking away. "Let's go. You're making us late."

When we got back to the car, Velia had Pita in a fierce headlock. Our baby sister was squealing like a piglet, but Velia had her hands over Pita's mouth to keep her from crying out too loud.

"What's going on here?" I asked, hauling the door open and jumping in the front seat. Pita was crying silently, her body shaking.

"Little Miss Tattletale here was going to call Mamá," Delia hissed through clenched teeth. "She had a handful of change and she was trying to leave the car. She said she was tired and hungry and she was going home."

"Start the car!" Juanita demanded, dumping out the sodas on the floorboard and jumping in the front seat. "Hurry! They're looking at us. Let's get out of here before these two get us in trouble."

I didn't have to ask who was looking at us. The middle-aged woman and her husband were peering out the shop window, watching us. Juanita reached down for two sodas. She handed one to Delia and they made a show of opening them. As we pulled out of the gas station, Delia put on a bright, happy smile on her face and waved good-bye to the couple as Juanita guzzled down her soda enthusiastically.

"*¡Chiflada!*" Velia hissed, letting go of Pita and pushing her aside.

"Guys, you've got to stop tormenting each other," I said, as we made our way down the highway. "We're about to hit Castaños, and I want us to stop and eat a real meal, but not if you're going to act like this. I can't have you turn on us, Pita. We're in this together, remember? And Velia, you can't treat her like she's an animal."

"It's her fault," Velia spurted, her hazel eyes burning with resentment. "She bit me, the little mongrel."

"What?" I asked.

"I tried to keep her in the car, but she bit me. See? My arm is still bleeding." Velia held out her slim arm and I assessed the damage.

At the sight of purple teeth marks on Velia's forearm, I lost it. "That's it!" I said. "We're not stopping in Castaños. We're driving straight through. We'll stop to rest in the woods. You guys are just going to have to wait for me while I go back and get us some real food from a restaurant. It's a shame too, because take-out food doesn't taste nearly as good as when it's served warm. You're just going to have to eat your tacos all cold and stiff."

"I don't care!" Pita kicked the backseat. "You can keep your stupid tacos. The first chance I get, I'm telling—I'm being kidnapped!"

Juanita's head turned back faster than you can spin a top. "Kidnapped?"

"You heard me. I'm turning you in!" Pita insisted, crossing her arms. Tears were rolling down her face, her eyes were red orbs of anger, but she wasn't making so much as a whimper, which was unusual for her. She usually wails louder than a smoke alarm.

"I told you we should've left her behind," Delia told Velia.

"Yeah? Then she would've told Mamá where we were going, and they would've found us by now."

"True," Delia whispered as she turned to face forward. For the rest of the ride, we all ignored our disloyal little sister. Pita, her face scrunched, cried that she was hungry, so I assured her we would be stopping soon. After we passed Castaños, I took the nearest country road to the left and drove into the woods. We found a small clearing where we all got out to stretch our legs and catch our breath. We'd been on the road for at least four hours and my body felt numb. None of us were used to sitting around too long.

"I'm going back into town," I said after a while, and nobody complained. Juanita, Delia, and Velia unpacked some of the blankets and backpacks from the trunk. I left them there, resting sedately under the shade of a tall ash tree, far off into the woods, out of sight of anyone driving by.

Castaños was small—deserted. I'd noticed that on the way through, which was what made it the perfect place to stop. The less people saw of us, the better. The only street vendor I found was stationed at the edge of town. I got out of the car and bought some tacos and more sodas to go. The vendor pretended that he couldn't break the twenty dollars I handed him, so I made him give me the change in sodas, an act he did not like, but I didn't have time to make change anywhere else, and I was not going to tip him ten dollars. I was in a hurry to get back to the girls.

As I drove out of town, I saw an ancient woman standing in a blighted field. She stood watching me, her long gray hair caught in the wind like wisps of silver thread. I couldn't see the details of her long tunic dress from this distance, but I could tell it was old and graying.

"Llorona?" I whispered, slowing down to get a better look, but as I did, the mysterious woman turned away from me. I watched the road ahead for a good place to turn around, but when I looked back, the woman was gone. Disappeared, like she'd never been there.

As I sped away, I had a suspicious feeling that I was needed back at our secluded rest stop, and I was right. As I drove off the road and up to our hiding place, I saw that Delia and Velia were lounging together under the tree. They looked like bookends, sitting right up against Pita, who was tied and gagged between them like a giant *tamal* rolled up in her own blanket.

"What in the world . . . ?" I asked as I stumbled up the hill toward them.

"She tried to run away," Juanita explained. "We had to run after her, knock her down, and drag her back here. She did it again and again. A hundred times. It was getting ridiculous."

I handed Juanita the plates of food and shoved Delia away from Pita. "More ridiculous than this?" I asked, staring at them in disgust. If we hadn't been two-thirds of the way to El Sacrificio already, I would have shoved them all back in the car and taken them back home.

"They had no other choice," Juanita whispered, defending her sisters. "She's crazy."

Velia pushed Pita toward me and got up to stretch her long,

coltish legs. "Yeah, her brain is fried!"

Delia joined her twin to shake her legs out and kicked at Pita in the process. "She's got mad cow disease!"

"Don't kick her!" I knelt down and removed Pita's gag. "How could you do this to your own sister? This trip is supposed to help us get closer. We have to stick together, be nicer to each other from now on."

Pita squirmed miserably beside me like a cocooned butterfly trying to break free. "My arms are asleep."

"What makes you so righteous all of a sudden, Miss Know-It-All?" Velia taunted.

I ignored Velia's comment and started to undo the knots that held the blanket together around Pita's body. "Get away from her. What's the matter with you? She's not a goat. She's a human being, a child who's obviously afraid."

"She's a narc," Delia started. "She won't stop trying to turn us in."

"Are you okay?" I asked Pita as I removed the blanket and freed her completely.

She nodded and threw herself into my arms, bawling. "I'm not a narc," she wailed, clutching at my shoulder. "I just want to go home. I miss Mamá. I miss our *Lotería* games. I miss the *mariposas*!"

"I know," I whispered, holding her tightly. "I know, *mamita*, I know. But we're almost there, and after we deliver this man to his family, we can all go home. I promise. You'll get to sleep in your own bed tomorrow night. Can you just hang on for a few more hours? Maybe?"

"Yes," she whispered, worn out from her tearful release. "I think I can."

"Good," I kissed her forehead. "Are you hungry? I brought you some of those baby taquitos. The little red ones you like, with guacamole. You want some?"

She shook her head and buried her face in my shoulder. "No."

"You tired?" I asked her, feeling my heart twisting painfully within my chest. "You want to take a nap?"

"Yes," she whispered, snuggling her face into my neck.

I fluffed a couple of pillows and laid them down for us. "Well, why don't you lie down here with me and rest," I invited. Pita lay down and I put my right arm around her. Delia and Velia snorted in disgust. They turned their backs to us and opened up the containers of food.

They started to eat the tacos. After they'd had their share of the food, they slid a tray over to our end of the blanket, their faces contrite. It was their way. They were often hotheaded but also fast to regret their harsh words; this was their peace offering of sorts. Juanita and I coaxed Pita to eat before taking a nap, which she finally did, with delight.

After we ate, we all lay back down in the blankets and waited for the afternoon sun to burn itself down. When we awakened at dusk, we were covered in *mariposas*. The snout-nosed butterflies were everywhere, flittering in the air, resting on our bedclothes, even tangled in our hair.

"They found us!" Pita shouted, jumping up and spinning around on the blankets like a ballerina. "I love you! I love you!" she kept chanting to the butterflies. The *mariposas* swirled and twirled around us like dark snowflakes in the surreal light of dusk, making the moment almost magical in its beauty. Little by little, the butterflies drifted away. Onward and forward they went, moving toward the car, with Pita dancing in their midst.

I looked at the sun looming low in the horizon. "I think it's time we moved on. It's about to get dark, and I don't want to see what kind of wild beasts roam these woods after dark."

"I think you're right," Juanita agreed. She got up and together we shook out the blankets and rolled them tight. Velia and Delia packed up our gear and we headed out again. We left the afternoon's shenanigans far behind us as we drove farther and farther away from home. Our more sisterly mood had returned, at least for now.

"What do you think his wife will say when she sees him?" Juanita asked in the darkness of the car. We had been driving for almost an hour under the blanket of night, and by our calculations we were about to hit El Sacrificio within the next few miles.

"I don't know," I said. "But it's too late to turn back now. Besides, I think we're doing the right thing."

Juanita reached over and patted me on the shoulder. "We're doing more than the right thing," she said. "We're doing something honorable here. We're making sure this man receives what's coming to him."

"And what's that?" Velia asked.

"A proper funeral, of course," Juanita informed her. "Being laid to rest in his own hometown, surrounded by his family and friends. Everyone deserves that. This is an admirable thing we are doing. They'll thank us for this. His wife and his family will be eternally grateful to us. We might even end up in the news after all, but in an even greater light. We'll be heroes."

"Heroines," I corrected proudly.

"In the news?" Delia asked. "Are we ready for it?"

"Well, at least we're better dressed!" Velia retorted from her seat in the back. I didn't know that I agreed with her—we'd been driving all day in the hot summer sun, and we hadn't bathed since before our swim yesterday.

Delia squealed, as if the concept had finally sunk in and she couldn't believe it. "We're going to be celebrities!"

"We'll be in all the papers!" Juanita chimed in, turning to look at the twins in the backseat. "People will want our autographs."

"We'll be famous?" Pita asked, her eyes full of wonder, as if they were starting to wake up to the seriousness of our situation.

"There's nothing to be nervous about," Velia whispered. She wrapped her other arm around Pita's shoulders and pulled her in close for a hug. "Being famous is like eating the best flan in the world. It's so good, you can never get enough of it. Trust me, you're going to love being in the spotlight."

In celebration, Juanita turned on the radio. Our favorite songbird, Selena, was singing happily about something fun and exciting, a song about love at first sight.

"Bidi, bidi, bom, bom," she sang. "Bidi, bidi, bom, bom." Her voice on the radio was so exhilarating, so full of life, that, suddenly we were all singing. Our voices drowned out Selena's, but we didn't care. It wasn't about listening to her, it was about singing along with her, about being in the moment with her. For a brief and joyful instant, she brought us closer together and made us enjoy each other's company. She made us sisters again.

6

La Mano: *"Dame la mano, hermanita, que no tengo hermano."*

The Hand: "Give me a hand, little sister, for I don't have a brother."

It was almost ten at night by the time we finally arrived in El Sacrificio. The town was smaller than we'd expected. In fact, it wasn't really a town. El Sacrificio was no more than a few dozen houses clustered around the country road we'd been traveling on since we'd turned east on Highway 57. At a *puestecito*, a corner store about to close down for the evening, I got out of the car and asked an elderly man who was sweeping the storehouse porch if he knew how to get to the dead man's home. The old man squinted and looked toward the car before he answered.

"He would have been better off staying gone," the old man said, pointing to the car with his chin.

"What?" I asked.

He opened the door and placed the broom against the inside wall. "He has no business being here today. What does he want to do? Ruin that poor girl's day?"

"What do you mean?" I asked, confused. "Do you know him?"

"Of course I do. Everyone knows each other around here," the elderly man said as he took a rag out of his apron and began to wipe down the metal domino tables folded out by the front door. "He's a good for nothing. *Un vago*. But that's none of my business—flour from a different sack, as far as I'm concerned."

"Well, do you know how to get there?" I asked again. But instead of answering me, the store owner turned away and left me standing there. Then he went into the tiny depot, closed the door, and came to the window to pull down the shade. A moment later the porch light went out and I stood there, wondering what I had done wrong.

"You're almost there," a woman's voice whispered from the darkness. I turned around and almost jumped at the sight of a female figure coming out of the shadows from behind the storehouse, like a ghost.

"God, you scared me," I said, holding a hand to my chest as if to stop my heart from fluttering out of it.

"You've come a long way," the woman whispered as she inched her way toward me, never really leaving the shadows of the porch, but getting closer and closer to me, until I could finally see her face. "I'm proud of you, Odilia."

"Llorona," I whispered her name in grateful recognition.

"You're almost there," she continued. "Just follow the sound of the whispering moon, listen to her sighs. It's a small pink house. You can't miss it tonight."

"Wait," I said, as she started to drift back into the shadows. "Is this part of your destiny? To watch over us, help us when we need you?"

"I will be watching you as you deliver him, and afterward too," La Llorona said. "But I cannot interfere with your journey. There are rules that must be followed, and I will not be able to break them. There is only so much I will be able to do. The rest is up to you. You must face your own fears and fight your own battles as you go along. That's why I gave you the ear pendant."

"Fight my own battles?" I asked. "What are you talking about?" I'd battled too much with my sisters on this trip already. I was ready for some peace.

"I've said too much. It is not for me to explain," La Llorona whispered. She turned away and disappeared into the darkness, leaving me alone with her cryptic words. But I didn't have time to decipher their meaning. I had to get out of the night air. *El mal aire* can kill you if you linger in it too long. So I turned away from the *puestecito*, got in the car, and drove on, trying to finish what we'd started that morning. As we left the cluster of houses behind, I looked up at the moon and tried listening to her sighs. I wasn't sure it was the moon that sighed, but I could hear something, a wisp of music, a whisper of song.

"What's going on?" Juanita asked when I stopped the car and poked my head out the window, trying to hear where the soft sound was coming from.

I held my hand up with my palm out, signaling Juanita to

stop talking. "Shhh. Listen," I said. "It's coming from over there."

La Llorona had been right; there was no way of missing the pink house, not with a party going on in the front yard. A small mariachi band was playing in the background, and people were either dancing on the lawn or sitting at folding chairs at small round tables, which had been draped with white linens and decorated with white floral arrangements.

Juanita leaned over me for a closer look out of my window. "What do you think's going on?"

"I don't know, some kind of *fiesta*," I whispered. I passed the house and inconspicuously parked next door, just in front of their neighbor's fence, away from the lights strung on trees and all around the dead man's yard. The dimness of the night hid us from the guests, and we sat quietly inside our vehicle observing everything from a dark, safe distance.

"I think someone's having a wedding." Velia pointed. "See, there's the bride sitting at that long table by the band."

"That's not a wedding dress," Juanita said. We all peered out of the car without making any attempt to get out. I don't think any of us had the courage to crash a party by delivering a dead man to it.

"It's not?" Velia asked.

"No," I said, suddenly understanding. A cold chill went up my spine as I realized what was going on at the drowned man's house. "There's no groom."

"Then why is she wearing a white dress?" Pita's voice from

the backseat was small and innocent.

"Because it's her fifteenth birthday," I whispered. "It's a *quinceañera*."

"Whose *quinceañera*?" Pita asked.

"The girl in the picture," Velia whispered.

"The little girl in the picture?" Delia asked, horrified. "You mean . . . she's not little anymore?"

We were all dumbfounded at the realization that the dead man's daughter was not a child anymore, but a young lady my own age. How could we proceed with such a different reality from the one we'd imagined? It was like our dreams were shattered. The girls looked disillusioned. I was more than shocked; I was dumbstruck. Presented with the current situation, I didn't know what to do, how to proceed.

Juanita pointed to the celebration taking place in the dead man's front lawn. "We have to get out of here. We can't ruin her special day!" she said, shaking me out of my stupor.

"Shush. Keep it down. We don't want to call attention to ourselves. Not yet, anyway." I bit my fingernails and tried to figure out the best way to handle the situation. We could leave, of course, but where could we go? What could we do that didn't involve taking the dead man with us?

"We have to do something. We can't just sit here and eat our hands," Velia said, knocking my hand away from my face. She was just like Mamá, who didn't believe in biting your nails, no matter what the circumstance.

"I don't know," I admitted. Going up to the house at this time would be more than inappropriate. It would be downright mean to ruin someone's debut.

"I think we should get out first," Delia said.

"No. We need to talk first," I said, turning around to look right at the twins as I spoke. "Listen. When we get in there, they're going to have lots of questions for us. But we have to be smart and have each other's back. We can't just blurt things out anymore like you did at the bridge."

Juanita turned around in her seat and looked at Pita specifically. "Yeah. We've come a long way. We can't afford to blow it now. So you guys have to follow the rules of the *cinco hermanitas*. Let Odilia and I do all the talking and don't contradict anything we say. And for God's sake, don't improvise. Too much cream spoils the tacos, so just keep it simple. Okay?"

"Fine. Whatever," Velia said, flapping her hand dismissively in front of Juanita's face. "Can we get out now? I really have to pee. Does anyone else need to pee?"

"I have to pee," Pita piped up, squirming around in the backseat.

"Stop fooling around. You can't just go up there and ask to use their restroom. They don't know us from Adam," I whispered. Their commotion was only going to draw more attention to us.

"But I do have to pee!" Pita started rocking back and forth, like she couldn't hold it for one more second. I rolled my eyes and ignored her.

"Stop whining and be quiet," I said after a few seconds of further complaints. "I need to think, and we should keep a low profile until I figure out what to do."

"Maybe we should just drive away," Delia whispered behind me. "Come back later, when the party's over. We can find a store where we can use the restroom."

"Are you kidding?" Velia hissed. "We're in Mexico and those are real Mexicans in there. These people can party till dawn." Not to mention the stores we'd driven by had been dark, locked up like the *puestecito*. And our last resort would be to go in the woods. For this one single thing, the twins just wouldn't rough it. So we always rode up to the nearest gas station to use the restroom when we were swimming.

"Well, we can't sit here all night waiting for the party to end," Delia told her twin. "I don't know about you, but Papá here is stinking up the car. Seriously—he's giving me a headache."

"I don't smell anything," I said, and to prove it I took a deep breath. It was all I could do not to gag. The smell of death had been festering in the afternoon heat, and now it was unbearable.

"I say we find a place to park it for the night, and by that I mean get a room somewhere," Velia said, reaching over the front seat and touching my shoulder for a sign of concession.

"Yeah. Like that's gonna happen," Juanita said. "Did you see the size of this place? They don't even have a gas station here. We'd have to go back out to the highway if we wanted to find a motel." She turned around to look at Velia in the backseat. "And how would we move the body into a room without calling attention to ourselves? It's not like we can leave him in the car all night in the parking lot. Let's face it, going to a motel is out of the question, and nothing else is open this late. I think you're stuck sitting next to him until this party's over."

"He doesn't smell so bad," Pita said, pinching her nose. "I think the perfume's working."

I had to admit it. "Juanita's right," I said. "We can't get a room. Not until after we've delivered him."

"We could go back to the woods, camp out, wait until morning," Juanita suggested as she stifled a yawn, laid her head back, and closed her eyes.

"I am not going to sleep in the woods at night. I'm not a goat," Delia retorted. "Next thing you know, you'll be expecting me to sleep in a barn with horses and hay and God knows what else."

"And *lechuzas*? You want those evil owls climbing all over you while you sleep, pecking your eyes out?" Velia teased Delia in the backseat.

"Shut up!" Delia retorted, pushing at her twin's shoulder. "I don't believe in that stuff."

"Of course you don't," Velia continued. "How about vampires and werewolves, you believe in those?"

As if on cue, an enormous animal ran up to the car and jumped up onto the driver's door. He stuck his gigantic head in through the window and barked wildly. Delia and Velia screamed. I jumped in my seat, throwing my left arm out to protect my face.

The drooling, long-eared beast sniffed me and then yelped and clawed his way inside through the driver's side window. I couldn't see all of him at once, that's how enormous this beast was. He had to be as big as me, but much heavier. His huge paws dug into my arms and thighs, his claws painfully cutting through my skin. He was so excited, he punched me in the stomach with a mammoth paw as he pulled the rest of his enormous body into the car. I would have doubled over in pain, except that his weight was plastering me against my seat.

"Get him off me! Get him off me!" I screamed, but nobody could help. Juanita, in the front seat, was busy trying to get away from the beast—a Great Dane. In his excitement, the dog sniffed our clothes and licked our faces so frantically you'd think the frenzied creature had three heads. Finally the beast made his way over me and jumped into the backseat, which by that time only held the drowned man because fear had set the rest of my sisters into motion. They had all vacated the car long before I was free from the dog and able to open my door and crawl out.

As I stumbled up to Juanita, Pita scooted over to me and clung to my waist, trying to hide behind me. We stood against the chain-link fence in front of the dead man's neighbor's house watching the gargantuan canine panting and licking his chops and whining inside the car. He sat next to the drowned man with his enormous paws neatly propped together on the dead man's lap, his tail wagging a mile a minute.

"Great. So much for keeping a low profile! Now I'm going to

smell like a wet diaper," Delia said, mopping over her saliva-slathered hair with the hem of her T-shirt. Her actions reminded me of my own condition, and I wiped at my face with my shirt-sleeve. It was disgusting.

"Do we have any of that perfume left?" I asked.

"Yeah," Juanita said, without looking at us. "But it's in my bag, next to Marmaduke's evil twin. You wanna get it?"

"Serberús!" The voice and a pitched whistle produced by the tall figure of a young man at the gate of the drowned man's house made the mammoth canine stiffen in the backseat.

"Go home, Serberús!" the young man commanded.

"Serberús? Like the three-headed dog from Hades?" Delia asked, looking at me. "Well, he's right about one thing. He's got a Hell of a personality. But I'm not so sure he's fierce enough for that name."

"I know. He's nothing more than a big spoiled puppy," the young man said, stepping forward. As if he'd been a circus beast trained to behave like a domesticated creature, the mammoth dog left the dead man's side and slipped out of our car through the opposite rear window. He came around the car and sat docilely by the young man, waiting for his reward. The young man patted his forehead and pointed up the street, saying, "Go home, Serberús!"

To our surprise, the dog trotted off into the darkness.

"Are you okay, ladies? Sir?" the young man asked as he peered at the body of the drowned man sitting propped against the glass of the back window.

"He's fine," Juanita jumped in.

The dog owner stepped up to the car and reached for the back door. "What's wrong with him?"

"He's not feeling well," Velia explained, getting between the young man and the car door just in time to prevent a catastrophe.

"He's dead . . . tired," Delia interjected. She laughed nervously and shuffled her feet around.

This wasn't the time to blurt out the real reason behind our arrival at the house. "It's been a long trip," I said, trying to deviate the conversation away from the drowned man.

"Forgive me. I am being rude. I have not introduced myself. My name is Efraín Pérdido. I am sorry about my *abuelito*'s dog. He meant you no harm," the young man said. "Excuse me, but I didn't catch your names. Are you friends of Beatriz?"

"Beatriz?" Juanita asked, looking toward the house.

"*La quinceañera.* She is my little sister," Efraín explained, putting his hand on his chest and bowing his head slightly as a form of introduction.

I looked closely at the wide-set eyes and squared jawline of the young man. He looked vaguely like the little boy in the picture in Gabriel Pérdido's wallet, which weighed me down as I thought of the distressing news we were bearing. Dressed formally as he was, in a black tuxedo, it was obvious that he was part of the debut court, the escort of one of the birthday girl's attendants perhaps. It became very clear to me that we couldn't finish what we'd started that morning, not yet anyway.

"We're more like friends of the family," I started. "But we've come at a bad time. We'll be back tomorrow."

"Nonsense," the young man said, raising his arms in exaggerated welcome. "A *fiesta* is the best time to greet friends of the family. My sister's *quinceañera* is turning out to be quite a reunion. We just met some cousins from Sabinas today. But you have not told me your names."

"We are the Garza sisters," Juanita began. "This is Odilia. She is the eldest, and this is Delia and that's Velia. They're twins. This little one is Pita, and I'm Juanita. Listen, can we use your restroom? We've been holding it for a while."

"Of course, of course," Efraín said, extending his arm and stepping aside so that we might pass into the front yard. "You are welcomed at our festivity. Tell me, how do you know our family?"

"Well, we don't know anyone else. Just him," I said, pointing at the drowned man and then looking back at the girl in the white dress. She was walking around with her mother, clinging to her arm, happily greeting the guests.

A voice from the darkness spoke. "Efraín, who are you talking to?"

We all turned around to see an older man coming toward us. He was wearing black jeans, a nice pressed shirt with a bejeweled bolo tie, and a cowboy hat. He was too old to be part of the debut court. He was obviously not a *chambelán* or escort, but the authority in his voice made me think he was someone of importance.

"These girls just arrived. They're from your side of the family, I think, *abuelo*," the young man said, turning around to face the other man.

"Really?" the older man said. "Let me see. You look like my nieces from Nava, but I haven't seen you since you were bitty little things. Is that my *compadre* in there?"

Before we could stop him, the older man was stooped over holding onto the front door window, looking into the backseat of our car. He started to say something, and then suddenly, he stopped.

"Well?" the young man asked.

"¡Madre de Dios!" the older man whispered, still looking into the backseat of our car. "Gabriel, is that you?"

"Gabriel?" the young man in the tuxedo asked, leaning forward to peer into the car again. "It can't be!"

"Inés!" the old man turned around and started shouting toward the house. "Inés! Inés! *¡Hija mía!*"

We stood huddled by the fence, dreading the inevitable as we watched both the *Quinceañera* and her mother freeze in their tracks. The music stopped and both mother and daughter turned around to look at the old man as he yelled, "Inés, my daughter! Listen to me, *m'ija*. Gabriel is home! Inés! Your husband is home!"

As if we were in a B-rated movie, time seemed to stand still. I froze, unable to think. How could I warn them without making it worse? To my horror, everyone stopped talking and looked at the mother of the birthday girl. She stood rigidly holding her daughter's shoulders with both hands as if to stop herself from fainting.

Then silently, slowly, Inés Pérdido, wife of Gabriel Pérdido and mother of his two children, walked quietly past men, women, and children as if she were in a trance. She made her way toward our dusty old car with her daughter trailing behind her.

The older man held out his arms to her, and Inés went into them instinctively. Efraín, the young man in the tuxedo, took the birthday girl in his arms and they all stood looking expectantly at the car door, as if waiting for the past to hit them in the face when it opened. The guests, who had left their tables and chairs to follow Inés and her daughter out to the car, crowded behind the fence, quietly waiting for the night's drama to come to a head.

"Is it really him?" Inés asked, her voice small and faint.

"*Sí, m'ija.* It's him." The old man held his daughter against his chest and nodded. She sucked in a breath and smothered a whimper.

"No llores, m'ija," the old man said, stroking her hair as he begged her not to cry.

Efraín's voice quivered with emotion. "Mamá? Is it really him? After all these years. Is that really Papá? It doesn't look like him."

"Papá?" the birthday girl whimpered. "No. No. He can't do this to me. Not now. Not tonight."

"Beatriz, *m'ija,*" Inés started, her voice quivering with emotion.

"It's just like him, isn't it, Mamá?" Beatriz continued, anger streaking her face with tears. "Just like him to ruin everything!"

"Beatriz, *por favor*," Inés begged, reaching out to take her daughter into her arms.

Beatriz fought off her mother's embrace. "He should have stayed gone!" Beatriz sobbed. "I hate him, Mamá! I hate him! Please, make him leave. I hate him!"

"Beatriz," Inés continued in her quivering voice. "He is your father. He has a right to be here. Please don't deny him that." Ines finally gathered her daughter in her arms, visibly trembling herself now. She looked at the car again, her eyes narrowing. "Why doesn't he get out? What's wrong with him?"

"He can't," I said from my place at the fence.

"It's not that he can't. He won't. He's a coward," Efraín spit out, clenching and unclenching his hands.

"Listen," I started. "There's something you should know." I stepped toward Efraín, but he was faster than me.

"Get out, you coward!" Efraín Pérdido screamed at his father. Then without hesitation, he lifted the door handle and yanked the door open.

"No!" I screamed.

"Don't do that!" Velia and Delia finished my thought, but they were too late. To everyone's horror, the pillow cradling the drowned man's head slid down the glass and Gabriel Pérdido's body tipped over sideways, falling onto the cement sidewalk with his arms outstretched before him in full rigor mortis.

The birthday girl's head fell back and her body went limp. The crowd behind us gasped, and Pita screamed. Several of the guests moved quickly toward Beatriz, but her grandfather reached her just in time to stop her from hitting her head on the edge of the curved driveway.

Efraín helped his grandfather carry his sister into the house with Inés and a slew of gabbing *quinceañera* attendants following close behind them. My sisters and I waited by the fence with the rest of the guests, who stood around the body speculating about Gabriel's return.

While everyone around us talked about the tragedy and asked themselves where he had been, the old man came back down the driveway to inspect the body of his daughter's estranged husband.

When he was done his face looked pale and drawn. He stood on the sidewalk and looked at us with haunted eyes. After a moment, he said, "*Compadres*, please, help me get my son-in-law into the house. He must be given his own measure of respect. It appears that our birthday celebration has turned into a wake. Please, if you could help me, *amigos*."

"Of course," a man said, as he stepped out of the crowd to help.

"*Claro que sí*," another whispered as he too stepped forward.

"At your service," came the replies of several male guests as they stood beside Inés's father.

As six men lifted the body of the drowned man and started to carry him toward the house, the people around us started asking us questions. How did we know Gabriel? Why did it take him so long to return? Where had he been all these years? Was he involved with our mother, our aunt, our sister? In response to the last question, we shook our heads. But other than that, we kept our mouths shut. I was glad the girls were heeding my advice not to embellish because at that moment nothing we could have said would have made things better for them.

Instead of talking to the guests, we walked up to the porch and stood waiting to hear from the family. They would probably have more questions for us than the guests, and it would be rude of us to leave without filling them in on what little we did know. Besides, we were in a foreign country, and we needed help finding a place to stay for the night.

It seemed like an eternity before anyone came out of the house. In the meantime, Juanita and I sat on an old bench with Pita between us, while Delia and Velia clung to a pillar, trying their best not to wet their pants. Eventually, the old man came out of the house and spoke to everyone.

"*Amigos,*" he said to the crowd. "It is my sad duty to inform you that the festivities are over. Inés and I have some delicate business to attend to. Gabriel's body must be prepared for burial. You may return in the morning for the *velorio*, the viewing, which we will hold here. Please, feel free to take home as much of the food as you like. You are welcome to it." Then he turned around and spoke to the mariachi on the other side of the yard. "*Señores músicos*, thank you for your service. You are free to go. *Señoritas,*" he said, turning to address us. "If you will follow me. My Inés would like to speak to you."

The body of Gabriel Pérdido was laid out in full view on top of the dinner table surrounded by the soft glow of dozens of gloomy candles. We peered at it as we were escorted into the house. Inés Pérdido was sitting up primly on the edge of a cushioned chair in the parlor area directly across from the dining room next to an older woman who looked a lot like her. Inés's hands were clasped in front of her, clutching a rosary. She had taken her pink party dress off, and was now wearing a modest black sheath that covered most of her body, except for her forearms, hands, and ankles. She'd looked prettier in her party dress.

"I'm sorry, we haven't been properly introduced," Inés said, as she extended a hand to us. "I am Inés Pérdido, and this is my mother, Zaragoza."

We all shook hands. "Glad to meet you," I whispered as we sat down before the two women. "If we'd known about the *quinceañera*, we would have waited."

"We're so sorry," Velia began, but Inés waved the apology away. She pressed an embroidered handkerchief against the corners of her eyes and looked away.

"Where has he been?" she asked, when she had composed herself enough to manage the words.

"We don't know," I said. "He was already dead when we found him."

"Floating in the river," Delia interjected.

It only took a few minutes to tell Inés everything we knew. After she heard the extent of our story, she sat still, quietly blinking away the tears, a lifetime of pain running down her pretty face.

"He sent a letter," she finally said, her voice low and deep with emotion. "Many years ago, saying he wouldn't be back."

"I'm so sorry," I said. "We didn't know."

"I sent him a letter too, begging him to come home—for his children's sake. They missed him so much. But he never wrote back. For a while, I thought maybe he had married again, like so many men who go up north do," Inés whispered, looking down at her hands as she spoke, as if the memory of it was too painful to speak of in a normal tone of voice. "Then the authorities came. They said they had found the remains of a body in his vehicle in the Chihuahuan desert. They thought it might be him, but they couldn't be certain. The car was registered in his name and there were other signs—a gun and two rifles he had bought several months before which were in the trunk. I don't know who that man was, but it never felt right, them declaring Gabriel legally dead when they couldn't identify his body."

"At least now you know he is gone for sure, *m'ija*," Inés's father said as he stepped into the room.

"Gabriel was never really here," Inés continued, in her trance-like voice. "He was always roaming, always wandering. I think some men are just meant for the road. They have no sense of place or belonging, no concept of family. Anyway, he's home now, finally, and I thank you for that."

"I'm sorry we ruined your daughter's special day," Juanita

said, hanging her head and looking down at her hands.

"Don't be sorry," Inés said, patting Juanita's hands. "You have brought peace to my home."

Peace—exactly what we had hoped to bring. Her words confirmed it, but her face denied it. And we could all see it. She was miserable.

PART II

THE INITIATION

How my sisters and I had to leave the house of the drowned man in a hurry. How we were enchanted, and with La Llorona's help, were able to flee from the sorceress Cecilia, and sought advice from the old fortune-teller, Teresita. How we were warned about, encountered, and escaped from the clutches of a wily *nagual*, a coven of scheming *lechuzas*, and a blood-thirsty *chupacabras*, to end up at the hacienda of our paternal grandmother—a grandmother we hadn't seen more than twice in our lifetimes.

7

El Árbol: *"Debajo de un árbol reposan mis lindas mariposas."*

The Tree: "Under a tree rest my beautiful butterflies."

We'd wanted to stay at a motel, but Inés and her family insisted on boarding us for the night. In the small kitchen at the back of the house, we ate traditional birthday fare. Inés and her mother served us plateful after plateful of *enchiladas de mole.* The chocolaty sauce of the chicken enchiladas spilled out of the rolled-up tortillas and mixed in with the rice and beans, making the dish extra delicious. We gorged ourselves till we thought we'd pop. Then for dessert the women brought us generously cut slices of pearly white cake. It was moist and creamy and absolutely too much for our already bursting stomachs, but it was scrumptious. So we had two slices each.

During the meal, however, the Spanish Inquisition began. We had to think of some quick answers because even though we'd expected a full-on interrogation, we hadn't planned anything that came out of our mouths.

Luckily, the girls remembered our little talk about having Juanita and I "explain" things without giving out too much information. For the most part, they remained silent and didn't contradict or add anything to whatever we said.

"But where is your Mamá?" Inés's mother asked as she passed out the frothy white cake slices.

"She's at home," I said, putting a forkful of cake in my mouth to stop myself from having to give out any more details than were absolutely necessary. Our number one rule about answering inopportune questions from strangers was "don't add too much cream to the tacos." In other words, keep the answers simple and plain. Like Mamá always says, nobody needs to know all of our business.

"At home?" Inés's mother crinkled her eyebrows together, and I concentrated on my next bite of cake.

"Working," Delia said, acting nonchalant. "She's married to her job. She hasn't been able to take a vacation in years."

"So who takes care of you?" Inés asked, turning her attention to Delia. "Who drove you here?"

"I did. I'm old enough," I said, quickly jumping in before anybody else said anything too outrageous.

"*Sí*, of course." Her eyes said she didn't believe me.

"And how old are you?" Inés's mother asked. "You don't look older than fourteen."

"I'm actually eighteen," I said, concentrating on my cake again. "The women in my family look younger than we actually are.

We take after my grandmother. She's seventy-one years old, but she doesn't look a day over fifty." Not that I'd seen my *abuela* since I was ten, but it was the only justification I could think of.

"I see," Inés said, looking to her mother again. "And where does your *abuela* live?"

I yawned and stretched and made a show of being ready for bed. "Not too far from here," I mumbled.

"Really?" Inés's face changed then. She looked more interested, more alert, like a squirrel when she lifts herself on her hind legs and sniffs the air with instinctual intelligence.

"Yes. We'll be seeing her in the morning," I said without really knowing why. Maybe it was nervousness that made me say it, or maybe the decision had already been made and it had just been sitting there in my mind, in my heart, waiting to be put into words. I didn't understand how or why, but somewhere between the enchiladas and the birthday cake I'd decided to honor La Llorona's request, to run the course of our journey and try to find true happiness for my sisters and myself. And that meant going to visit Abuelita. It seemed to me that we had been through too much to not finish what we'd started.

Around the small round table, every one of my sisters stopped eating, stared, and then smiled at me. Their joy was evident in the way they nodded and grinned while they resumed shoving cake into their mouths with reckless abandon.

Zaragoza made her way around in the tight little kitchen to sit between me and Inés. "Oh?"

"Yes," I said, thinking on my feet. "Mamá told her about the body we found and she wanted to help. After they talked it over, Abuelita told us how to get here. It was really very easy."

"Super easy," Delia interjected, shoving another forkful of cake in her mouth.

"Well, we should call them and thank them. Let them know you arrived safely. We don't want either of them to worry," Inés's mother said.

"She doesn't have a phone," Velia said, joining the conversation with the same conviction as Delia and I. "I mean, my mother does, but . . . "

"What she means is that our mother doesn't answer her cell phone at work, and she's on the night shift right now," I interrupted, coming to Velia's rescue. She was always the worst at keeping things from strangers. She was just too candid. "It will be all right," I continued. "We'll call them tomorrow, after Mamá gets home from work and Abuelita is awake."

"I think we should try to get in touch with someone tonight," Inés insisted. "Don't you, Mamá?"

"No!" I said emphatically, hoping they would listen to us.

"Why not?" Inés asked.

"Because . . . because . . ." I tried to think of something else to say, something totally convincing, but nothing came to mind. I started to panic, and I realized I was holding my breath. Then, remembering La Llorona's words and the effect the ear pendant had on the duty officer at customs, I reached up to my left ear and flicked my index finger against the nestling orbs. They tinkled lightly and I could feel them twirling around each other, humming against my cheek. I turned my face slightly toward Inés and her mother to call attention to the spinning *argollas*, as I whispered the enchantment. "Aztec queen, Tonantzin, Holy Mother of all mankind, give us your magical assistance. Make these women believe and help us leave!"

"What is going on?" Juanita leaned close to me to look at my whirling ear pendant. The rest of the girls did the same from around the table. "Why is your earring spinning? And what was that you said?" She reached over to touch La Llorona's magical gift.

"Don't touch it," I whispered. "It's a prop to help me hypnotize them."

"Since when do you know how to hypnotize people?" Delia asked, a frown of disbelief furrowing between her brows.

"Who cares? It's working," Juanita said, putting a finger over her lips. "Look at their eyes. They look like cats."

"I like your earrings," Zaragoza said, reaching for them. "They look very old, like something the ancient *Aztecas* used to wear."

"They were a gift," I said, trying not to deviate too far from the original lie I'd told the border patrol agent early that morning.

Zaragoza took another sip from her coffee. "Oh, who gave them to you?"

"Abuelita Remedios," I lied, relieved to see that the women had dropped their concerns. "She's very generous."

"Of course." Inés's pupils were perfectly dilated, giving her a dazed expression. Her mother's pupils were dilated too. The spell was working. "I'm glad you're going to a relative's house. It's not safe for you girls to be traveling in Mexico alone."

I kept my voice even, willing the spell to keep them charmed by our lies for as long as we remained in their house. "Well, like I said, our grandmother lives down the road, about twenty miles away, between here and Ejido la Paloma. This was more like a quick stop along the way."

It wasn't a total lie either. Hacienda Dorada was technically located somewhere in the wilderness between El Sacrificio and Ejido la Paloma. There were a series of unmarked roads that led to Hacienda Dorada from El Sacrificio. Papá had outlined them on his road map when I was ten years old, to show me where we were going the last time we visited Abuelita Remedios. Juanita had looked it up while I was driving earlier today.

"So, you're going to visit your grandmother. That's nice. I bet you're excited about that," Inés's mother exclaimed. She smiled at Pita, who was shoveling cake into her mouth without saying a word. Pita was all bug-eyed and big-eared, nodding like a *ratoncita*, nervous as a little mouse sitting precariously on the edge of a wooden trap.

By the time we were done eating and answering questions, it was almost midnight. We sat at the table yawning in front of our hostesses, who were cleaning up after the party. When they saw us practically falling out of our chairs, Inés insisted that we follow her down the hall.

"First, we'll get you all cleaned up," Inés began. "You can take turns showering. Your little sister can go first. I suggest you don't take longer than five minutes each. Otherwise you'll run out of hot water."

"Oh, we don't want to use up all your water," I said, feeling more and more like we should just get out of the house, maybe go find a cheap motel room in the nearest town.

"Well, let's not worry about that," Inés said, as she put her arm around my shoulders and walked me back down the hall. "The water will be warm again in the morning."

Half an hour later, Delia was busy combing out Pita's wet hair. Pita looked refreshed with their hair slicked back. The twins looked revitalized too. Their hair was still wrapped in thick towels, and they were wearing their long shirts from home. Their legs were long and slim, and I wondered why they weren't cursed with the big-boned frames Juanita and I had inherited from Mamá.

"Are you almost done in there?" I called to Juanita, who was obviously taking her time in the shower. I was dying to scrub the grit off my arms and face. "I'm so dirty, you could take a spatula and scrape the filth off my skin."

"You're telling me," Delia said, looking at me with disgust. "You smell like a *chiva*."

"Thanks." I lowered the toilet lid and plopped down on it, upset at the idea of smelling like a billy goat. "I love being one of your analogies."

"It's a simile. I didn't say you were a goat, I said you smell *like* a goat. Didn't you learn anything in English class?" Delia pulled the towel off her head and started finger-combing her hair absently.

Delia pushed Pita toward the door. "I'm outta here. Let's go to bed, *Papita Frita*. Looks like we're sharing *piojos* tonight."

"Stop calling me that!" Pita pulled away from Delia and grabbed the side of the sink to anchor herself. "I'm not sleeping with you. You're mean!"

"Suit yourself, but there's only one bed, and I'm calling the left side."

"There's only one bed?" I asked, watching Velia pull her right eyelid down to check her eyes in front of the mirror.

"Yup," Velia said. She opened her mouth and stuck her tongue out to look at it. "I'm sleeping on the window sofa. Inés said I could. It's just long enough for one person, if I curl up real tight. Besides, I'm too tired to share a bed with Pita. She kicks like a wild horse."

"I know," Juanita chimed in from behind the shower curtain she was using to cover up while she dressed for bed. "I'm taking the blankets out of the car and sleeping on the floor."

"On the floor?" I asked, mortified. My back ached just thinking about it.

"It's better than being all crunched up in that bed with the three of you."

"I guess the floor's not so bad," I admitted. "I mean, compared to having Pita punching and kicking at you all night long."

"Do whatever you want. Shower's all yours," Juanita said. Then she pushed back the curtain and stepped out of the bathtub in her pink pajamas—she had dressed in the shower because she was much more modest than the rest of us.

"There's probably enough room for three of us on the bed," I said hopefully.

I couldn't have been more wrong. By the time I got out of the shower and dressed, Delia and Pita were asleep, fully stretched out on what would have been my side of the bed. Delia was awake, but just barely. I tried to shake her, so she could give me some room, but she moaned something that sounded like, *"Lotería!"*

"Odilia, it's not very comfortable, but you can sleep down here with me," Juanita whispered from her place on the floor by the window seat. "Velia and I are awake."

"I wish we had more cushion down here. Why didn't you take the comforter from the bed?" I asked.

"Delia called it, and she wouldn't give it up. But that's okay. I have my San Marcos blanket. It's not so bad. You'll get used to it."

Suddenly angry, I grabbed the edge of the comforter and yanked it off of the girls on the bed, leaving them with only the thin blanket underneath. Pita whined out an incoherent sound, and I smiled as I walked away with it without feeling even a little bit guilty. They were lucky I didn't push them off the side of the bed—selfish brats.

"So what's the plan for tomorrow? When do you want to take off?" Juanita asked in the darkness. I settled in beside her on the floor by the window seat, and we snuggled under the comforter together.

"I don't know what time the family is going to wake up." I took a deep breath and let it out slowly. "But we should hit the road as soon as the sun comes up. This whole thing has gotten too complicated for my peace of mind."

"I know," Juanita said. "Today didn't turn out the way we pictured it at all, did it?"

Velia turned over on the window seat to face us in the dark. "Who would've thought this guy had abandoned his family?" she said, joining our conversation. "He looked so happy in the picture. I thought for sure they'd be waiting for him."

"Nothing's ever the way it seems, is it? I mean, look at Papá," Juanita whispered at no one in particular. She sounded distant, sad.

I hated hearing the pain in their voices when my sisters remembered our missing father. "Let's not talk about him," I said.

"Okay. But I'm very disappointed," Velia continued. "I thought for sure this guy was different. I thought he cared about his family."

"I thought they'd be happy to see him, and us." Juanita pulled the comforter up and covered half her face with it. The thought of Papá had made us all gloomy again despite the refreshing showers.

"You're telling me," Velia whispered. "I thought we'd be heroes. Instead, I feel like the grim reaper. You were right, Odilia. We should have left well enough alone."

I turned away from Juanita and settled into a comfortable position on the floor. "Well, what's done is done. No use lamenting it. Let's get some sleep," I said, yawning. If I had been more like Juanita, I might have said, "I told you so," though.

"Odilia, are we really going to see Abuelita tomorrow?" Velia's voice was quiet from her spot on the window seat, as if she was afraid to ask the question. "Please say yes," she whispered.

"Yes," I said, and to my surprise the rest of the girls on the bed sat up and hollered with happiness.

"Yay! Yay!" they hollered. I shushed them and reminded them we weren't at home.

"People are mourning here," I chastised them. "Now settle down and go to sleep before I change my mind."

After the girls fell asleep, I lay awake for some time listening to their soft breathing, thinking about going to Abuelita's house and what might happen once we got to Hacienda Dorada. There were so many scenarios running through my mind, I was completely overwhelmed by them. Would Papá be there? And, if he wasn't, would Abuelita know where he was? Would she even recognize us?

The truth was, I didn't know what to expect. After the day we'd just had, I realized we had no way of knowing what tomorrow would bring. What if Abuelita wasn't home? How could

I keep the girls from getting their hearts broken if she didn't even live there anymore? Worse yet, what if she had passed away and nobody had bothered telling us?

I went to bed feeling utterly conflicted and, for the first time in years, I was scared for us. But even as bad as I felt that night, it was nothing compared to the shock I received the next morning.

It all started well enough, with us waking up to the aroma of homemade flour tortillas wafting through the house. As we rolled out of our makeshift bed and looked around the sunlit room, we found our clothes washed, neatly pressed, and laid out for us. We scrambled into them gratefully, and as we entered the kitchen, our hostess turned to smile at us.

"Good morning, *señoritas*," Inés said, her smile curling over her lips and creasing the corners of her eyes. "Would you like some breakfast? I can make some *chilaquiles*. It will only take a second."

"That would be amazing," Velia and Delia sang out, simultaneously, even as they scrambled into the nearest chair.

"Odilia, would you do me a favor?" Inés asked, as she turned on the stove and put a black iron skillet over the bright blue flame. "Can you please run down to the *puestecito* at the corner and get me today's paper? Just tell Don José to put it on my tab."

"Sure," I said. But as I left the house, I told myself I should be quick with the errand. We really needed to get out of El Sacrificio before the spell was broken and someone decided to call the authorities.

At the store, I picked up some chips and sodas for the road, walked up to the counter, and laid everything down in front of the cashier. The newspaper fell open before me, and I froze as I read the headline over the top of the front page.

¡DESAPARECIDAS!

The one word said it all: MISSING. Plastered across the width of the paper was a giant picture of us—my sisters and I huddled together under last year's scrappy little Christmas tree, happy as *mariposas*, our bright smiles belying our alleged situation.

We were officially missing children.

8

La Sirena: *"¡La Sirena—la mujer que se quiere llevar a tu Papi! ¡No! ¡No la dejaremos!"*

The Mermaid: "The Mermaid—the woman who wants to take your Papá away! No! We won't let her!"

It wasn't easy getting out of Inés's house without letting her know what was going on. First, I had to buy all the newspapers at the *puestecito* and put them in the trunk of our car so nobody else would see them. After I got back to the dead man's house, I told Inés they were all out of newspapers, then we ate breakfast in record time. We split before any of the neighbors had shown up for the wake, leaving behind most of the dead man's money inside the container of sugar on the table, tightly wrapped in its plastic bag, like a great big tip for our hostess. I only kept enough for us to buy food and gas for the trip home after visiting with Abuelita.

"We're in trouble. Big trouble," I told Juanita and the twins once we got down the road in my father's beat-up Nova.

"What do you mean?" Juanita asked. She was sticking her head out the window, admiring her new hat in the side mirror.

Inés had given it to her at breakfast, when Juanita had complained about how much her skin hurt because she'd gotten too much sun on the way down to El Sacrificio. It was one of those fancy white summer straw hats you see brides wear at their wedding receptions. Only this one wasn't so fancy, with a clump of saggy old silk flowers hanging off to the side. It was so big on her, Juanita had to hold it on with both hands. But she didn't care that it was old. In fact, she loved it.

"Here," I said, keeping an eye on the road as I reached under the seat to pull out a copy of the day's newspaper. "Look for yourself. We're all over the front page. I bet by now every channel on TV is running the story about our abduction. '*Cinco hermanitas,* the Garza girls, taken from their home in their own father's car.'"

"Where did you get this?" Velia asked, snatching the paper out of my hands and sharing it with her twin in the backseat. Juanita turned around and leaned over the front seat to read along.

"'*¡Desaparecidas!*' *¡Ay, Dios mío!* What are we going to do?" Delia pulled at a corner of the paper to get a closer look.

"We have to go home," Velia whispered, horrified. "Poor Mamá. She must be worried sick about us."

"I'm sure she is," I said, keeping my hands on the wheel. "But Mamá's got problems of her own."

"Is she all right? What happened to her?" Juanita's voice trembled almost as much as the sad-looking flowers on her hat.

"*Cálmate.* She's all right," I said. "Nothing's wrong with her, at least not physically."

"Oh, thank God!" she said, putting a hand to her chest and breathing out gratefully.

"You know, I can't take you seriously with that ridiculous thing on your head," I said, looking sideways at her. "You look like the Mad Hatter."

Juanita took the frumpy hat off and threw it out the window. "I don't care about the stupid hat. What happened to Mamá?" Behind us, the hat spun out into the morning air in a white blur, like a miniature flying saucer, and landed right smack in the middle of the highway.

I watched it get smaller and smaller until it disappeared from sight in the rearview mirror. "Litterbug! You know that's against the law, don't you?"

"Stop stalling!" Juanita ranted from her seat at the far end of the car. "What's going on with Mamá? Why did you say she's got problems of her own?"

"Mira." With one hand on the wheel, I took the paper from Velia in the backseat and handed it back to Juanita, pointing at the newsprint at the bottom of the front page. "It says it right there. She is a person of interest in the investigation of our disappearance. As of last night, she's not allowed to leave the country, so she can't come to Mexico to look for us. Papá's in trouble too." I'd never seen a newspaper back home say such things about people possibly involved in crimes who hadn't been arrested, but Mexican papers were quick to report speculations. They took information from anyone willing to talk and didn't hold back

crucial details the way US papers sometimes did.

"Papá?" Delia and Velia asked simultaneously, looking at me in the rearview mirror. "What's he got to do with this?" Velia continued.

"He's a person of interest too," I explained.

"How? Why?" Juanita inquired, her eyes widening in disbelief.

"Read the story," I said. "It's right there in the second to last paragraph."

Juanita unfolded the paper and began to read. "The authorities are looking for Ernesto Garza, the father of the missing girls. He is wanted for questioning in the unexplained disappearance of his daughters. Local police are also hoping to recover Garza's vehicle, as it might provide crucial evidence as to the whereabouts of the girls."

"They think we're dead," Velia said, "and that Papá had something to do with it."

I adjusted the rearview mirror so I could make eye contact with her. "Not necessarily. They always investigate the parents first."

"Look at this," Juanita said, after flipping through the paper. "There's a story about Papá on page two."

I glanced at a picture of Papá but had to keep an eye on the road, so I couldn't read the article beside it. "What does it say?"

"Local singer wanted for interrogation in the case of missing children." Juanita showed the paper to the twins in the backseat.

"They used his publicity photo. The one of him in his mariachi suit. He's going to hate that!"

"Nah. He'll be glad they used that shot. It's a good picture of him," Velia said.

Delia leaned in to look at the picture. "I forgot how handsome he is."

"Oh, he's handsome all right," Juanita's tone of voice told us exactly how she felt about him. She didn't need to explain what she meant with that comment, but she did anyway. "*Muy guapo*, and he knows it too. Look at him mugging for the camera, like a possum with a mouthful of worms. Funny how I never noticed before how conceited he really is. Do they know where he is?"

"No. But they'll find him. Now that the FBI is involved," Velia said after reading silently to herself for a few minutes.

"The FBI?" Delia whispered in disbelief.

"Yup. According to this, the National Center for Missing and Exploded Children is looking for us," Velia continued reading on.

"Exploited," I corrected.

"What?" Velia asked, looking at me like I was confusing her.

"Exploi-t-ed, not *exploded*," I explained. "The National Center for Missing and Exploi-t-ed Children."

"Whatever," Velia said.

"So what are we going to do? Turn ourselves in?" Juanita asked. She took the newspaper from the twins and took her turn reading it.

"Well, we have to get back as soon as possible," Delia told her. "To get Mamá out of trouble."

Velia slumped back in her seat and crossed her arms. "It's our fault. We should have left her a note or something."

"Too late for that," Delia said. "The best thing we can do now is get to Abuelita's house and call her from there. If we don't call home soon, they're going to arrest her because I bet you a million dollars they're not looking for us down here."

"Oh, yes they are," Juanita said, shoving the paper at Delia. "It says here the FBI is working with both the border patrol and the Mexican Federales to try and find us."

The girls had the right idea. Calling Mamá and telling her we were alive and well and visiting with our *abuelita* would solve her problem. But there was still getting there. The way I figured, we couldn't be very far—somewhere between twenty or twenty-five miles off.

If I could find the exit.

The biggest challenge was there was no official marker on the country road that led to Hacienda Dorada. We just had to follow an unpaved road beyond El Sacrificio, travel about twenty minutes, watch for the crooked fork in the road, and turn into it. From there, it was another fifteen miles on a dirt path—a straight shot to Hacienda Dorada.

"Why are they going to arrest us?" Pita asked from the backseat. "I don't want to go to juvie. That's a really bad place."

"They have no reason to arrest us," I told Pita, making eye

contact with her through the rearview mirror. "We haven't done anything wrong, so we have nothing to worry about. At least not so far."

"We found a dead body and didn't report it," Delia whispered, more to herself than to the rest of us. "We should have reported it, saved ourselves and Mamá a lot of trouble."

I pulled over on the side of road, reached up, and pulled Papá's road map off the visor. Unfolding it over my lap to read it better, I glanced at the mileage gauge and made a mental note to use it to measure our progress. If we traveled more than twenty miles ahead and we hadn't found the exit, we'd most certainly passed it. I'd have to turn around and look for the fork in the road again.

"We took Papá's car without permission," Velia said, looking over at me.

"Well, if he was so interested in the car, why didn't he take it with him?" Juanita wanted to know.

"He didn't take it because it's older than dirt," Delia said. "I'm surprised the thing still runs."

"We should turn ourselves in," Pita said, touching my shoulder from behind to get my attention. "We wouldn't go to jail, would we?"

"None of those things are bad enough to get us arrested. Trust me, we've broken plenty of laws, but I don't think we've done anything that would make us go to jail," I said, maintaining a normal tone of voice with the hope of reassuring them. "The best thing we can do right now is get to Abuelita Remedios's house as soon as possible and ask for her help. I think it's about time we let an adult handle this." We knew last night we'd gotten in over our heads when we'd crashed the *quinceañera*, but with the police and the FBI thinking we were kidnapped or dead, I wasn't sure we weren't in big trouble.

I started the car and got us back on the road, but my mind kept churning it over. Juanita had first noted it before we left, and Delia had reminded us—failing to report a body was punishable by law. The question was, who would they punish, us or Mamá? Adults had a funny way of seeking justice. Would they go after Mamá? Could they make her responsible for this? If our actions had damaged our family in any way, I would never forgive myself.

Juanita's thoughts seemed to be on the same track as mine. "We took the drowned man's money," she admitted quietly. Then she put her hands over her face so we wouldn't see her crying.

"But we returned it. Most of it, anyway," I said, keeping my eyes on the road.

Velia pulled out a small wad of folded bills from her pocket and handed it to Juanita. "Yeah, but we still have some of it, and who knows where it came from. Who it really belongs to."

Juanita threw the cash on the dashboard and turned away to look out the window at the tall desiccated trees that seemed to loom over us as we drove on. "It's probably blood money."

Her words silenced everyone in the car, and for a while nobody said anything. I thought about La Llorona then and wondered if she knew how much trouble this journey would cause. She was from another place, another time. What made sense in her world did not make sense in ours. Why had I listened to her? I should have thought this thing through.

As apprehension spread into every pore of my being, I did the one thing I could to quiet the guilt in my mind. I turned the radio on. But even with the sound of loud music reverberating through the car, I could still hear my conscience nagging at me. *You could have stopped this, all of it,* it whispered. *This is more your fault than anyone else's. You're the eldest. You should have known better.*

Disgusted with myself, I quieted my thoughts and concentrated on driving the car. The sun was in full bloom, blinding me as I tried to look for a crooked fork in the road ahead. To make things worse, the air was hot and blistery, burning our cheeks as we drove on.

We drove like that for a few more miles, everyone keeping her thoughts to herself, when suddenly I smelled something humid and foul. Actually, I tasted it before I smelled it. But then I saw it: the white smoke puffed out of the front of the car and crept in through the vents on the dashboard, penetrating my lungs and causing me to cough uncontrollably.

"*¿Que diablos?* What the hell-icopter is going on?" Velia sat forward in her seat and stuck her face out the window to get a better look. The whiteness of the smoke was blinding. I could barely see the side of the road and nothing ahead.

My first reaction was to press down on the brake with all of my weight. The car screeched to a stop on the side of the road, and I flipped the gearshift into park. But even without raising the hood of the car, I knew what was wrong. When water started pouring from the front of the car onto the pavement, creating a buzzing puddle inches away from our feet, I knew we were doomed. I'd seen this happen to Papá before. The radiator was busted.

"What do we do now?" Pita asked. She was standing next to me, while the others stood back behind me, fanning the smoky steam out of their eyes.

I looked at the mileage gauge. We were only about fifteen miles down the road from where we'd started in El Sacrificio, but it was far enough that going back there wouldn't be too smart. It might call more attention to us, the missing children, and fifteen miles was a long, long way to walk. Longer than just walking the rest of the way to Abuelita's. At least, I hoped it was.

"We walk," I said, fighting the sense of despair that was slowly seeping into my heart. "Because this piece of junk isn't going anywhere without a mechanic."

"Walk where?" Velia wanted to know.

"We're in the middle of nowhere," Delia finished her twin's thought.

I looked around and saw nothing. There were no houses, no animals, no major roads. Stretched before us in every direction, there were only miles of mesquite and huisache trees and tall brown grasses too dry and thin to feed to animals. If we turned around now, it would take us more than half a day to walk beyond El Sacrificio and up to Highway 57 on foot, but that's where the nearest gas station was. I didn't even know if that gas station had a tow truck, though we could use the phone there. It was better to just keep moving forward, since by my calculations, we were closer to Abuelita's house. The trek was going to be hard on us, especially without water to fight off the searing heat that was already burning through my clothes. I wished I'd thought about getting water instead of sodas at the *puesticito* before setting out this morning.

"To Abuelita's," I said. "Take whatever you want out of the car and let's get a move on. No use standing around here. We have a long way to go before we reach Hacienda Dorada."

I dug Papá's map and the envelope with my earrings out of the glove box and stuffed them into my bag. With our backpacks, purses, and the few provisions we still had in the car in tow, we started down the road heading east. We left the blankets behind because we didn't want to exhaust ourselves with too much to carry. Mamá would probably want to kill us for leaving them, but there was no other option. Perhaps we'd be able to return for the car and the rest of our things with Abuelita's help.

The morning sun grew hotter by the minute, and we were sweating profusely within half an hour. Several times along the way, Pita cried that she was either tired or thirsty and we had to stop and sit on the side of the road under a mesquite or a huisache tree, trying to make the trek without succumbing to heat exhaustion.

Two and a half hours later, we were huddled together on the side of the road, shoulder to shoulder under the full shade of a large cluster of scraggly trees, when we heard it—a woman's voice, sweet and melodic, coming from the brush behind us. She sang of flowers and gardens and sweet, sweet nectar oozing from every petal and leaf.

"What's that about?" Juanita asked, turning to look at me.

My heart quickened. *"Never talk to strangers."* Mamá's warning rattled around in the back of my head. We hadn't seen any houses along the dirt road.

I scrambled to my feet and stood listening for a moment. The woman's voice was engaging and lovely. She sounded nothing like La Llorona, and my apprehension began to subside. "I don't know. But we should be careful."

Ignoring Mamá's rule, the rest of the girls scrambled to their feet and ran to see where the enchanting voice was coming from.

"Hello!" Velia hollered into the dense thicket. She squeezed between the trunks of two mesquite trees in an attempt to avoid going around.

"Hello!" Delia chimed in, louder and more desperately than her twin sister. She had been complaining about being dehydrated for at least an hour and human life meant the possibility of water.

“Who are you? Who’s there? Who’s singing?” My sisters all hollered in the general direction of the woman’s voice.

“What are you girls doing out here?” the woman’s voice asked from somewhere behind the brush. The lady who emerged was lovely and petite. She wore a flowing, bright yellow dress, and her blonde hair was perfectly coiffed in a thick chignon.

“Our car broke down,” I said as she came closer. “Can you tell us how far it is to the next town?”

Immediately, the enchanting woman began doting on us, like a tiny yellow butterfly, fluttering about. Her words flittered up and down and all around us as she fretted, taking our reddened faces in her hands and looking into our eyes, inspecting each of us in turn for signs of heat stroke. “Where did you come from? *Ay, María purísima*, but you look dreadful. You must be absolutely parched, melting away in this heat.”

“We need to get to Hacienda Dorada as soon as possible,” I said when she pulled out an embroidered handkerchief and swabbed at Pita’s small face in a concerned, almost motherly manner. “Can you give us a ride?”

“I wish I could,” the woman said, “but I don’t have a car. Oh my, but you must be parched by now; you look like wilting flowers. You need something to drink. Come with me, I have just the thing.”

She invited us onto her property, a desolate piece of land we would have never imagined was inhabited, set far enough back from the road that we hadn’t seen it through the trees. I was so relieved to see someone, anyone, that I didn't question her sudden appearance. She was a godsend; I was grateful for the sight of her. Besides, she didn't look like she could be part of a gang or some kind of kidnapper ring, so we followed the sweet-voiced woman as she led us deeper and deeper into the brush.

Past a wasted field and through a graveyard of fallen mesquites we went, listening to her melodic words as she led us away, until we came to what can only be described as an oasis in the desert. Whereas the land we'd just crossed had been populated by huisaches and scrub, her house was large and impeccably landscaped, like the houses in the more affluent neighborhoods of Eagle Pass, with a beautiful garden of flowering plants and herbs. I recognized the orange bursts of Butterfly Weeds and the tall red Indian Paintbrushes, but there were so many beautiful plants in the garden all I could do was smile with joy and serenity. The woman's house was beautiful too, with wide, resplendent windows reflecting the daylight on every side, making it glitter and shine majestically. I thought for a moment we were in a fantasy world—a magical land, a dream come true.

The vivacious woman took us through her spacious living room and into a splendid, sunlit kitchen where we were asked to sit at a long mahogany table while our hostess poured us glass after tall glass of ice-cold lemonade. When she had quenched our thirst, she brought us platters full of sweet bread: pumpkin *empanadas*, *pan de huevo*, *cuernos*, and the most delicious *marranitos*—dense pastries shaped like piggies made with sweet molasses and full of spicy richness in every morsel.

We ate so much sweet bread and consumed so much tart lemonade, we felt gluttonous, but sinfully content. We listened to the lady of the house as she entertained us with her life's story feeling delightfully blessed.

Our enchanting hostess was named Cecilia. She was a *viuda*, a long-suffering widow. Her husband had been a police officer, a detective, who had lost his life in the line of duty, she said as she served us more and more of the delicious sweet bread. She was glad for our company because she lived too far from the nearest town to entertain visitors. Since she was self-sufficient, relying on her garden and animals for sustenance, she didn't know anyone in town. Having no other family to speak of also meant she hadn't had visitors since the days of her marriage. Her only contact with the outside world was her supplies delivery once a month.

Our long hot day in the sun was too much to contend with, and soon we felt sleepy and tired. We'd made pigs of ourselves. Now we wanted nothing more than to take a nap in the afternoon heat.

"You look tired," Cecilia said, pulling the trays of pastry off the table and placing them back on the counter behind her. "Perhaps you should rest awhile."

I watched her with half-closed lids as Cecilia moved about the room with slow, gentle movements that mesmerized me. "We should go," I whispered, more to myself than to her.

"Come on now," Cecilia said, as she turned off the lights in the kitchen. "I have the perfect spot for a nap. My husband built this cozy little den just for me. Come on. It's right through here." Being so happy to have us in her home, Cecilia made us comfortable in a small nook just off the kitchen, away from the sun and the heat of the day. Like a fairy godmother waving a magical wand, she tapped open cabinet doors and pulled out extra fluffy pillows so that we might rest comfortably on the sofas and recover from our arduous expedition.

Those hours resting went by very fast. We slipped in and out of wakefulness, wincing at the soreness in our muscles, and thirsting for more of that tart lemonade. Finally, we slept so deeply, that we were shocked when we awakened to find the landscape outside the windows in complete darkness. It seemed we had slept the day away and nighttime had descended upon the spacious house like an unexpected guest.

"What happened?" Velia asked, yawning as she stretched on a satiny divan chair.

Pita's face was illuminated by the light of the moon from an open window. Her cheeks were flushed a bright crimson, sunburnt from our walk this morning. "Where is she?"

"Do you think she knows who we are?" Velia asked as she got up and went to peer through the open door into the darkened kitchen. I wondered myself if she got the paper all the way out here.

"I hope she doesn't get us arrested," Pita whined scooting over to sit next to me on the plush sofa. Suddenly, the familiar pangs of guilt hit me again, and I winced. I hated seeing them so concerned. They were little girls. They should be at home, fashioning bracelets out of old aluminum cans or just sitting at the kitchen table playing *Lotería* with Mamá.

Juanita pushed herself off the couch and stood looking out the window at the darkness outside. "Do you think she's gone? She wouldn't have left us here alone, would she?"

"Girls? Are you awake? Come in here!" Cecilia's musical voice made us all jump, startled. We followed her voice into the living room, where she was sitting before a giant old-fashioned television that must have been brought in from somewhere else in the house because it was so fat and bulky, there was no way we could have missed it when we first entered.

"How was your nap?" she asked, lifting a silver platter full of tiny, delicately decorated sweets.

"Whoa! What are those?" Pita's eyes sparkled with delight; she was all but devouring the baby cakes on the platter.

"Petit fours," Cecilia said, smiling indulgently at the expression on Pita's face. "Try a chocolate one. They're my favorites."

I thought about asking Cecilia if she had a phone we could use, but the reporter's somber face on the television screen caught my attention. "What are you watching?" I asked. I popped a creamy petit four into my mouth. It melted away too quickly, leaving a soothing minty aftertaste that made me want more.

"Oh, listen to this. It's coming on again." Cecilia turned up the volume on the television. "They've been running your story on the news all day."

At her words, the girls abandoned the tray of petit fours and scrambled to sit in front of the television set. I fell onto the nearest couch and listened as the words "STORY IN DEVELOPMENT" scrolled across the screen in Spanish and an ominous tune began to play in the background.

The first segment of the news was an interview with Inés and Zaragoza. Both women seemed horrified at the idea that they had been deceived by the five little sisters who seemed to be so generous and pure of heart. They kept telling the reporter they didn't know why they believed us that our mother knew where we were, and felt terrible for not calling the authorities or at least getting in touch with our mother. They talked about the dead man's return and the bride's hat they had given one of the girls as a token of their appreciation. But most of all, they worried about our safety and hoped we would be located soon.

Feeling the blood rushing from my face, I looked around for a phone in the room, but I couldn't see one. I was just about to ask Cecilia if she even had one when the tray of petit fours started making its way around the room again. I took two and ate them absently. I knew I had to do something, call someone, but my mind was suddenly blank and I couldn't think what it was I needed to do. I couldn't even talk.

In the second news segment, after a brief commercial break, a female reporter pointed to a wide-brimmed hat stuck on the branch of a tall mesquite while she informed the viewers that the missing girls' broken-down car had been abandoned less than a mile down the road from the location of the discarded hat. She reported that at that time, only terrible conclusions could be reached because there was no sign of the sisters. Our previous plan to return for Papá's car evaporated when we saw it being towed away on television. According to the newscaster, it was being taken in for forensic analysis.

The third segment of the story was a previously taped interview with our mother. On the screen, Mamá was crying and blowing her nose with a tissue. She wasn't making any sense, but she kept repeating the same thing in Spanish. Over and over again, she begged, "Please, please, if you have my daughters, please let them go. Let them come home. They're all I've got."

At the sight of Mamá completely undone on the news, Pita broke down and started crying silently.

"Oh, I know you miss your *mami*," Cecilia cooed as she reached out to pull Pita beside her on the couch. "Come here, darling. Everything's going to be okay. I promise." After Pita settled down and stopped crying, we were all able to concentrate on the rest of the news broadcast. The fourth and final segment of the "Story in Development" was a live interview with the chief of police in Piedras Negras. Arnulfo Jiménez disclosed that the drowned man, Gabriel Pérdido, was a known drug dealer and fugitive. The Federales were investigating his death and the culprits behind it. Chief Jiménez speculated that the girls might have been abducted by the same individuals who killed Gabriel Pérdido. They believed the suspects were operating under the assumption that the girls knew more than they really did about the dead man's drug dealings. They suspected the abductors were manipulating the girls' actions as they traveled through Mexico to return the body to his family in El Sacrificio.

"The kidnapping might have all been part of a ploy to flush out Gabriel's cohorts. We don't know for sure. Anything is possible," Chief Jiménez said, claiming it was imperative they find the missing girls and bring them home safely. He assured the reporter that his men were working night and day on this case, and he was positive justice would prevail.

By the time our news story ran through, the local newscast was over. They had dedicated an entire show to us, a fact that mesmerized us into complete and utter silence.

"Don't believe everything you hear," Cecilia said, shutting off the television set with one click of her remote control. "That Jiménez is a corrupt anaconda. His position on the force is just a front. He's suspected of being in business with the mafia. Only, he's so cunning, so sly, no one can connect him to any of their crimes. But everybody knows he's working both sides."

"I don't understand," I whispered. "If he's such a bad guy, how can he say he wants to bring us home?"

"Of course he wants to bring you home," Cecilia said, leaning out over the coffee table to be close to us. "Don't you see? He wants to find you because he thinks you know more than you should about the drug dealer you brought home. It's a trick. You should avoid him at all costs."

"I'm scared!" Pita slid off the couch and scooted over to me on the floor.

"Oh honey, don't be scared," Cecilia said, leaving the comfort of the couch to slide down on the floor between Pita and me. "He can't hurt you. Not as long as you stay with me. I promise. Why—you're trembling! Here, have some more petit fours, sugar for my sweet one. There you go. Feel better?"

Pita bit into a tiny sweet morsel of cake and nodded even as she sniffed back her tears. Noticing the twin's fearful faces, Cecilia slid the tray of petit fours toward them. Soon, we were all sitting on the floor, sharing the enormous tray of petit fours. Funny how distress takes away one's appetite for real food, but when sweets are involved, all bets are off. Or maybe it was just us, because we sat there and ate every last petit four offered to us as we looked guiltily at each other for eating so greedily while everyone worried about us back home.

"At least Mamá is home and not in jail," Velia whispered close to my ear, so the others wouldn't hear.

"I'm not sure that's any comfort to her right now," Delia said from the other side of the coffee table. "She looked pretty torn up. Maybe we should call her."

"I've been meaning to ask you if you have a phone we could use," I said, turning to look at Cecilia.

"Freedom is always a comfort," Cecilia said, ignoring my request and thrusting a chocolate petit four into my hand. "Your mamá is lucky to be free, after neglecting you all the way she did."

"What do you mean? Who says she neglected us?" I asked, suspicion creeping into the corners of my mind even as I put the chocolate treat in my mouth. I shook my head, trying to remember if any of us had spoken rudely about Mamá, but my thoughts were cloudy, eerily void of memory, a fact that stupefied me. Biting into a tiny sugar-covered cake, I gave each of the girls the evil eye, letting them know Mamá was not a topic that we needed to discuss, not with a perfect stranger like Cecilia.

"I mean, I don't know exactly what's happened or why you are traveling alone," Cecilia started, blinking nervously as she spoke. "But I know if you were my daughters I'd never part with you. If you were my daughters you'd be safe at home, eating delicious things I'd baked, and wearing nice, beautiful clothes I'd made. I sew the most exquisite dresses. If you were my daughters, I'd dress you up like pretty little China dolls."

"Well, we're not the dress-up types," I said, picking up another sugary petit four and biting into it to stop myself from defending Mamá's honor to the point of being rude to our hostess.

After we ate, we started to drift into a sedate sleepiness again. All I could think is that we were so emotionally drained from listening to the news and worrying about Mamá that even sugar wasn't able to pick us up, and so we drifted into that deliciously dreamy stage before falling completely asleep. Seeing us lolling our heads like droopy violets, Cecilia told us to go upstairs and pick out a bedroom to sleep in.

"Go on now," Cecilia insisted. "You need your rest."

"We really need to get going," I said, my eyelids resting heavily over my eyes. "We need to get to our *abuelita*'s house."

"What you need is a long, relaxing bath. Come on. It will clear your heads." Cecilia got up and started for the stairs.

We bathed in luxury. Cecilia, singing harmoniously as she went, filled all three tubs in the upstairs bathrooms with bubbles. We dozed blissfully in the scented water until we looked like prunes, and then, because we could hardly walk from the drowsiness brought on by those hot, delicious baths, we headed right to bed. Pita slept with Juanita in a lusciously decorated pink bedroom, while the twins shared a sunny yellow room. I picked a heavenly blue master bedroom with a king-sized bed and French double doors. All those little windows in the French doors allowed the shimmer of moonlight to come in and kiss everything in the room with a glittering silver dust.

After my bath, I slipped between the soft, crisp bedsheets, happy and content. And for the first time in a long time, I didn't pray for Papá to come home. I didn't pray for Mamá to start paying attention to us either. I didn't even pray for my sisters, because somehow, I knew we were all going to be all right. For the first time in a very long time, I thanked God for a warm, comfortable bed in a nice, safe home.

I awakened in the middle of the night. Moonlight streamed in through the window, and though my vision was hazy, I could see the curtains billowing back and forth as the *mal aire* came into the room in mischievous gusts of wind that toyed with my senses as they entered my lungs and played with my sanity.

"Going . . . never again . . . home is an illusion . . . home is where you've never been . . . never again . . . never again. . . ." *el mal aire* said as it spoke to me, whispering and sighing, murmuring incoherent things, jumbled words, rambling thoughts I could not understand. Remembering where I was, I tried to get up to go look for Cecilia, but I couldn't focus, much less keep my eyes open. When I tried sitting up, my head spun and I fell back on the bed, dead weight on my pillows. That's when I finally understood what was going on.

"Something's wrong," I whispered. I went through the events of the day in my mind and realized that Cecilia never promised she would help us get to Hacienda Dorada. She'd acted so kindly toward us, but her lack of interest in our plight, our need to get to Abuelita's house, frightened me. But wasn't it a given? She knew what we were going through—she showed us the TV news. Right?

I tried to clear my head. "Wake up. You have to get out of here." But my voice sounded like a distant storm dying, waning in my ears. I tried to pick up my hand, to touch my head, to reach the ear pendant. But my hands were made of lead. My arms were wooden.

"Llorona?" I called out in a breathless voice. "Can you hear me, Llorona? Something's wrong. Llorona . . . please . . . help me . . ."

9

La Araña *"Una araña entre más hermosa más ponzoñosa."*

The Spider: "The prettier the spider, the more poisonous it is."

I passed out even as I called out to La Llorona. She awakened me what I guessed to be a few minutes later, not with ghoulish wails as might be expected, but as a mother would wake up her beloved child. She sat at the edge of the bed and called my name softly, gently, as she stroked my hair.

"Odilia, wake up, *m'ijita*," she whispered with maternal warmth.

"I can't," I said, opening my eyes slowly. They felt heavy and swollen with sleep.

"You have to," she said softly. "It's important that you get up and purge yourself from this sweet emptiness."

My stomach was aching dully, and my head felt like it was wrapped in layers and layers of gauze. "Something's wrong. I don't feel well," I complained. Everything around me looked foggy and dark.

"Odilia, I need you to drink this." La Llorona lifted my head off the pillow and put a warm glass to my mouth. "Drink, child, your life depends on it."

It took all of my strength to open my mouth and sip the warm liquid in that glass. It was bitter and tasted like rancid grapefruit juice. Cringing, I started to spit it out, but La Llorona coaxed me until I swallowed the rest of it down.

Suddenly I felt it, the need to puke. I flipped the sheets aside, jumped out of bed, and ran into the adjoining bathroom. My rubbery legs almost giving way under me, I reached the toilet just in time to empty the vile contents of my stomach into it.

"What did you give me?" I asked. I turned on the bathroom light and rinsed my mouth in the sink. I was so weak, I had to rest my upper body on the vanity. "I've never been so sick in my life." I felt like something ill was festering in my stomach, and my head felt like a piñata stuffed with cotton balls.

"It's Cecilia's sweetness," La Llorona explained. "It took control of you. The goddess sent me to give you a little bit of help to make you expel it."

"We need to wake my sisters." I made my way back to the bed and sat on the edge because the room was still spinning a little. "Where can I get more of that stuff you gave me?"

"Come, follow me," La Llorona commanded from the doorway. Now that I could notice more than my own sickness, I saw that her hair was not white anymore, but dark and just as disheveled as it had been when I'd first seen her on the riverbank. Her eyes were deep hollows, and her cheeks were gaunt, but she wasn't scary. She just looked like a tired woman again. With a wave of her hand, the door opened and La Llorona went through it. She was the only one who could help me now, so I followed her out of the bedroom.

She walked down the stairs without making a sound. My own feet felt as light as feathers as I stepped over the floorboards, and I wondered if it was her miraculous tonic making me feel so weightless and swift.

Quietly, we made our way through the spacious living room and past the formal dining room, guided by the bright light coming from the far end of the house. La Llorona stopped just short of entering the kitchen. We stood hidden in the shadows of the hall, La Llorona in front of me, with me looking over her shoulder.

Someone was moving around in the kitchen. "Who's that?" I asked quietly, so as not to be heard.

"Cecilia, *en su gloria*, in all her spectral splendor," La Llorona whispered as an ancient, haggish woman walked into view. "This is her true form. The woman you see by day is an illusion reflected by the sunlight. It is created by the potions she mixes in this kitchen and then secretly adds to her special treats."

It seemed unreal to me, but the woman in the kitchen was wearing the same clothing Cecilia had worn that morning. Her hair, however, was as gray and dusty as moth wings, and her sagging wrinkled skin almost hung off her face like a worn leather sack. She was grinding out something hard in a big black three-legged mortar. The *molcajete*'s legs kept thumping against the table, making an ominous rhythmic sound. Her discolored tongue poked in and out of her prunish mouth, and she puckered and twisted her craggy lips as she ground a coarse white substance into powder with a big fat pestle just like the one Mamá uses to make her homemade salsas.

"What is she doing?" I asked.

"Getting ready for tomorrow," La Llorona whispered, pushing me deeper into the shadows of the hall. "Cecilia is baking for you and your sisters. You have become her special pets."

But that wasn't any ordinary baking Cecilia was doing in there, because unlike Mamá, she wasn't swallowing any of the powdery concoction herself as she tasted it. Instead, every so often, she would test its consistency by rubbing a pinch of it between her thumb and forefinger, put a little on the tip of her tongue, and immediately spit it out. When she was done grinding the unusual ingredient, she spooned its fine white particles into a miniature sieve and dusted the top of four freshly baked pies with it.

"What is that? Some kind of sugar substitute?" I asked, touching La Llorona's shoulder to get her attention.

"To be sure," La Llorona whispered, turning to look at me. "Its sweetness comes from the seeds at the heart of the *chinchontle* plant. It is a sedative more potent than any sleeping pill you can buy at a *farmacia*."

"Do you mean—" I started.

"Yes, Odilia," La Llorona whispered more quietly than before. "She is medicating you and your sisters, sweetening your thoughts, dusting your dreams with a sugar sedative so sweet and satisfying you'll never want to wake up for fear of never feeling this happy again. Those pies are meant to keep you here forever."

"Oh my God," I whispered. I couldn't believe it. I had put my sister's lives in the hands of a witch. It was like something out of a storybook, like Hansel and Gretel finding the gingerbread house in the woods. I should have remembered Mamá's advice and been more wary. I should not have accepted food from a perfect stranger. But in this day and age, who would have thought fairy tales could come to life? Even those tales of razors in Halloween candy are just urban rumors. No one would have suspected Cecilia, not Mamá, not me, but especially not my sisters. They relied on me to keep them safe, and now I had to do just that. "We have to do something. We can't stay here."

"For now, all we can do is wait," La Llorona said. "She will be done soon. Come, we must hide and wait for her to leave."

We hid behind the French panels in the living room and waited. La Llorona was right, Cecilia was done within minutes. She turned off the lights and left the kitchen. When she was gone, and we were sure she couldn't hear us, we crept into the kitchen.

La Llorona removed the lids from the footed pie dishes, picked two of them up, and pointed to the others for me. I took the third and fourth pies, and we snuck outside quickly. Quietly, we walked across the lawn, all the way to the back of the yard, past an old orchard, where we came across a long row of pig pens lined up behind a small, weather-beaten barn.

"Pig slop," she said as she emptied the pie dishes into the trough inside the first pen. "Go on. They won't bite."

"Won't they get sick?" I asked, still holding the pies in my hands.

"Not any more than you did. The potion's not meant to kill, just keep you loopy and happy all the time," La Llorona whispered, taking the pies from me and throwing them next to the others herself. "The worst that can happen is they'll sleep through the day tomorrow. Now, about your sisters. They're going to be groggy in the morning, and probably won't want to get up. You'll have to give them some *jojotle* juice."

I followed La Llorona along the garden paths that meandered around the backyard, winding in and out and around each other. "That bitter stuff that made me throw up?" I asked.

"Sí." She bent over to examine a dark, spidery plant growing along the fence to the left of the house. "You only need a few leaves, this much. You'll have to soak them in warm water for an hour. Then, when the water turns purple, you take the sprigs out and make your sisters drink the potion. They only need a few sips. It's a strong remedy, so don't let them ingest too much."

"But what if I do it wrong?" I asked. "Why can't you stay and give it to them yourself?"

"You have to have faith, Odilia," La Llorona said, putting her hand on my cheek in a motherly caress. "You come from a long line of *curanderas*, healers of the people. Your Abuelita Remedios has been using her gift all her life. When the time comes, you'll know exactly what to do with this."

"Abuelita Remedios *is* a *curandera*! I remember now. She showed me her garden once," I said, taking the sprigs of *jojotle*, turning them over in my hands, and bringing them up to my nose for a quick whiff. "This looks like *yerbabuena*, only it's darker and more potent by the smell of it."

"Yes," La Llorona said, smiling at me. "It's a primitive herb, dating back to an ancient time, before the fall of our beautiful Tenochtitlan," La Llorona said. "It is what we gave our *escuincles*, our little ones, when the *mal aire* had crawled in through our windows at night and bewildered them. But that was before the river ate my children, before the arguments with Hernán, when we used to be a family."

"I'm sorry," I whispered. My heart suddenly ached for her, and I wondered if this sadness, this pain that seemed to overwhelm La Llorona, was what Mamá felt after Papá left, when she went to bed at night and cried alone in the dark. Did she miss having a family then? Was it the family and not Papá she had mourned? Had we misjudged her sorrow? I knew she was missing us now, afraid she would never see us again. The guilt of it stabbed at my heart as I considered all these new facts, and I felt a great pain in my chest. Standing next to La Llorona in the darkness, I suddenly felt ashamed.

"Come," La Llorona said, rubbing my arm with her cold, dead hand. "There is no time for regrets. The beautiful dawn, *la aurora*, will be here before you know it. You must prepare yourself for the confrontation that will ensue with her arrival. It will take more than cleverness—it will take courage to get away from the sorceress."

La Llorona walked away from me then, and I watched as she disappeared into the darkness. Suddenly cold, I ran back up to the house and tiptoed upstairs to the bathroom in my room. I put the sprigs of *jojotle* in a glass of warm water, hid it under the sink, and then slipped back into bed in the blue room.

I didn't go to sleep though. I stayed wide awake, staring up at the full moon outside the wide, arched windows next to the bed. I'd never noticed it before, but the silhouette of a woman was outlined in the brightness of that moon. Her hair was flowing in the wind, and she appeared to be looking back at something or someone behind her.

I felt I could learn something from the woman in the moon. From now on, I would look over my shoulder at every turn. I would make sure I knew who or what was lurking around me, waiting to harm us when we least expected it. For many people in this world were not who they claimed to be, and evil dwelled where you least expected it. It had certainly been that way with Cecilia, the beautiful butterfly who had turned out to be a poisonous wasp.

The moon made me think about Mamá too, looking over her

shoulder, crying for her loss, waiting for the day when she would see us walk through the door again. I knew she was frightened for us, because even with as much crying as she had done over Papá the last few months I could tell this crying was different. When she looked into the camera in that interview and begged for our safe return, I could see how much not knowing where we were or if we were even alive was killing her.

"I'm sorry," I whispered to the moon before I closed my eyes and cried for Mamá as I faced my guilt.

A few hours later, when the dawn started breaking over the horizon outside my window, I did as La Llorona advised. I tried waking up the girls, but they were dazed and disorientated and wanted only to be left alone, to linger in bed a little longer. I forced them to drink the *jojotle* juice. They coughed and complained about the bitter taste before they ran one by one into the restroom and threw up the nastiness in their stomachs.

After the initial side effects wore off and they had stopped cursing my name, I told them what I had discovered the night before. I made them promise not to listen to anything Cecilia said to them. Then we all got our things together and made our way downstairs to face the *bruja*.

Cecilia, looking like a vibrant *mariposa* in a purple tunic, her hair blossoming with sprigs of lavender, was fluttering about the kitchen looking confused and agitated.

"What's the matter?" I asked, as if I didn't know what was wrong.

"Oh, nothing," she said, smiling nervously. "I woke up late, and I just don't know what to make you for breakfast. How about some more of that sweet bread from yesterday? I think there's still some left."

"No, thank you," I said, trying not to let my emotions show on my face. "We have to get going. Our grandmother is waiting for us."

"Here it is," Cecilia singsonged as she pushed a tray of day-old sweet bread across the counter.

Delia pushed the tray back toward Cecilia. "We're not hungry."

"Here Pita, have a piggy. It's delicious," Cecilia said, picking up the front end of a piggy and waving it in front of the girls while she made cute little snorting noises. Pita tried to step back, but she faltered in her resistance. Cecilia took her face in her hand and tried forcing the sugary treat into her mouth. Pita flayed her arms and grunted from behind clenched teeth, resisting the witch's poison.

"Let her go!" Velia screamed.

"She doesn't want any!" I shrieked, pushing the tray of sweet bread off the table. It clattered to the floor, startling Cecilia, who turned around to look at the mess with wide-eyed amazement.

"Now look what you've done!" Cecilia's voice suddenly changed. It was no longer sweet and melodic but menacing and intimidating. I had a feeling the rest of the girls were about to meet the real Cecilia, and it wasn't going to be pretty.

Pita ran into Juanita's waiting arms, and we all stepped back.

I stood in front of the girls, ready to protect them from the witch's rage.

"You've ruined everything!" she screeched as we huddled together in the corner of the kitchen closest to the door. "Now pick it up and eat it! Or else!"

"Or else what?" I asked. "You'll put us under a spell? Do you have some magical words, some curse you plan to use on us now that we won't eat your medicated sweet bread?"

"Are you crazy?" Cecilia asked innocently, her face twisted into an indignant expression that was too fake to be effective.

"That's right! We know what you're doing," I said, my voice cracking momentarily. "But we're too smart to be lulled to sleep by your lies anymore. I saw you baking last night. I saw what you put into those pies. But we're wide awake now and we're not going to eat anything you try to feed us. That's why we gave those *tortas* to the pigs. You don't believe me? Go see for yourself. Your pigs are probably snout down in the mud by now."

"You're being ridiculous," Cecilia scoffed. "I didn't put anything into the sweet bread. Now clean it up, before I get really mad!"

"No! You clean it up! We're not your slaves!" Juanita yelled.

Cecilia lifted her left arm with her palm wide open, ready to slap her.

"What, are you going to hit her?" I asked. "Not while I'm alive!"

Then, to make my point, I unsheathed a butcher knife from its marbled stand and wielded it in front of her face. "Now listen carefully, and don't interrupt me. If you don't help us get home, we'll go straight to the cops when we leave here and make you wish you had. You see, Pita here is very good at crying. She can make anyone feel sorry for her. Not that she would be pretending to cry. She's scared enough as it is." Pita was sobbing even now into Juanita's embrace. "And there's enough evidence in this house and in our veins to prove that you were drugging us."

Braced against the counter, Cecilia eyed the knife and then us, taking in our determined faces. She slumped back, defeated. "What do you want me to do?"

"We need the keys to your car," I demanded.

"I don't have—" Cecilia began, but I didn't let her finish her thought.

"Don't mess with me," I threatened. "This is a very nice house you've got here. Too nice to belong to a lowly police officer. Your husband had money. So I'm sure there's a car parked somewhere."

"And if there isn't?" Cecilia's eyes were brimmed with tears, and suddenly she looked ancient. I resisted feeling sorry for her. What if this was another of her tricks?

"Like I said, we'll call the police. We'll tell them we were abducted and brought here where we've been fed *chinchontle* powder until we were almost out of our minds."

"I'm sorry," Cecilia said, hanging her head. "I didn't want to hurt you. I was only doing it because I have no family, no husband, no children to play with. It was my dream to have daughters, many of them. But things went wrong for us long ago. My husband angered the ancient ones and I've been paying for it ever since, doomed to dwell in this empty shell of a house. When you leave, you will see it for what it really is, a ruin from the past. As for a vehicle, I don't have one. Really, I don't. I don't have any money either. Everything I need, everything I have, I have carved out of the dirt with these tired old hands."

"She's lying!" Velia said from behind me. "Don't believe anything she says."

"Let's just go," Juanita said, her jaw firm. "She's not going to help us anyway."

"Oh yes, she will," I said, reaching up to spin La Llorona's ear pendant almost violently before Cecilia. "Aztec queen, Tonantzin, Holy Mother of all mankind, give us your magical assistance! Make this witch tell the truth so we can get to Abuelita's house!"

At my words, Cecilia fell under the spell of the spiraling circles of the earring. Her pupils were so dilated that her eyes glittered and shone, becoming giant orbs of darkness.

The witch's eyes and head bobbed side to side, following the light emanating from the ear pendant much like a cobra follows the movement of a charmer's flute. "That's some talent you've got there," Velia whispered.

"I just hope it works," Juanita said, pushing the twins back. They all backed up, widening the space between us and Cecilia, and I advanced on her.

I turned my head to the side so that the revolving rings could work their magic to their full potential. "Tell us how to get back home," I demanded of the witch.

"I can't help you," Cecilia said. "The ancient ones have decreed it. I cannot leave this place. I am to dwell on this island in the desert for the rest of time. It is my fate, my doom. But I know someone who can help you. The old fortune teller, Teresita. She lives up in the *cerro*, the hill behind the house. She has the gift. Even though she has cataracts, she can see beyond our limitations."

"Is this a trap? Are you sending us to another sorceress? Is she evil, like you and your kind?" I pushed the tip of the butcher's knife against her jugular vein. The movement felt foreign to me, but we needed to know. I didn't like the harshness in my voice, but I was desperate to save my sisters, and the faster we got out of there, the better. "Tell the truth, old witch, or I'll cut your throat and then you won't have to *dwell* here anymore." Even as the cruel words left my mouth, I felt terrible about their callousness.

"No. It isn't a trap. The best thing you can do is see her. Teresita won't hurt you. She works only for good. It is her wisdom that finds the lost and turns the wicked."

"If she's a witch, how can she help us when you can't?" Delia asked.

"Teresita is not a witch," Cecilia protested. "She is a prophet, a seer. She'll know what to do. If anybody can help you, she can. You must go, take the white goat in the barn, the young *cabrito*, as a gift for her troubles. She will be glad to receive it. Walk along the empty bed of the dry creek; her house is two miles beyond the crest."

There was a moment, just after we'd tied a rope around the

goat's neck and were pulling it out of the barn, that I wondered if we wouldn't be better off just walking to the next town. Sure, it was hours away, but then we'd be sure we were in the real world and not some wacked-out fairy-tale wormhole. Nevertheless, this felt right to me, like I was taking the path I was meant to take to bring my family together, the one La Llorona had told me about just two days ago at the river. I don't know how I knew it, but I was sure of it.

Cecilia didn't lie about one thing, at least not after I "hypnotized" her and forced her to tell us the truth. When we walked away from her house and started to climb the hill with the goat in tow, we dared to turn around and look back at it. What we saw was not the same house we had believed we had inhabited if only for a day. The dwelling at the bottom of the *cerro* was an old shack beyond repair. Just a few dry, weather-worn boards leaning haphazardly against a crooked frame, showing daylight through to the cracked furniture within.

For a moment, I felt sorry for the old, broken-down woman whose loneliness had turned her into a *bruja*—a fate worse than death, a fate I wouldn't wish on anyone, least of all Mamá. But then the earring's spell must have broken, because Cecilia, looking as old and wretched as her house, hobbled out of her shack. Thrusting a fist to the sky, she screamed that we would pay for threatening her.

"What happened to her?" Velia asked, pulling on Delia's arm and pointing at Cecilia.

"Whoa! Someone got a wicked makeover!" Delia said, bursting into peals of laughter.

Cecilia let out another horrific scream before she yelled back at us, "Don't laugh at me! You horrible brats! You have no respect for authority! But don't think you're going to get away with this!"

"Shut up, you nasty old witch!" Juanita screamed back, bending over at the waist to shout as loud as she could. "You deserve everything you got!"

"Run, run, as fast as you might!" Cecilia yelled at us. "But you won't get far. No one leaves here without my permission! And no one—absolutely no one—is allowed to mock me!"

"Oh, we're so scared!" Velia and Delia taunted. "A craggy old witch is after us! Whatever should we do? Wherever should we go?"

La Llorona's words of warning echoed in my ears. *"You and your sisters must remain pure of heart on this journey, Odilia. Be courageous but remember to also be noble and everything will be all right."* I hope it wasn't too late for me to heed her warning. I had to minimize the damage we might have already done.

"Stop it!" I said, grabbing each of the twins by an arm and pulling them back to follow me. "There's nothing she can do to harm us now. She's a broken old woman. No need to torment her."

"Come on, old woman, what are you waiting for?" Juanita yelled from behind me, to which Cecilia responded with a bloodcurdling wail that made us all stop. "Come on, give it your best shot!"

"Children of the dark, children of evil! Your mother has been humiliated! Come to me now, come back home. Punish these insolent girls! Unleash your wrath upon them! Make them suffer! Avenge my wounded pride!" Cecilia hollered. She lifted her arms to the sky and screeched. The act made thunder explode in the distance and lightning flash all around us as sinister black clouds began to swirl directly overhead. It was enough to make us all run away as fast as we could, up the hill without looking back, for fear of the evil Cecilia had set upon us.

10

La Garza: *"Parada en una patita, la garza mira y admira a mis gemelitas."*

The Heron: "Standing on one leg, the heron watches and marvels at my twins."

By the time we arrived at Teresita's house, towing the bleating goat by a *mecate*, an old rope, tied in a sailor's knot around its neck, the sun was completely out. I figured it was eight or nine in the morning. Already the heat blazed down on us with a vengeance, and we were so dehydrated our tongues felt like thick, dry parchments in our mouths.

We didn't have to call out. An old man with a sun-weathered straw hat and faded overalls unbent himself from his chores in the garden to nod our way as we walked up to him. We couldn't talk, we were so winded and fatigued from the long trek. Seeing our state, the old man walked over to a well, unhooked a tin pail, and dropped it carefully down into the water.

"You look dried out," he said, as he pulled the pail back up by the cord attached to the handle. "Come have some water. This is the best well in all of Mexico. It's so cold and fresh, it could wake up the dead."

For a moment, I was wary of the old man and didn't take the cup of fresh water. Instead, I looked down the well and saw nothing but the dark river water flowing freely, appetizingly on its way to some unknown destination.

With my sisters standing a few feet away from us, looking scared but hopeful, I took the cup of water and sniffed it. It smelled like nothing and everything. It smelled like the freshness of spring and all the joy that it could bring. It smelled like a promise. Gingerly, I tasted it, letting the coolness of the water sit on my tongue while I decided if it was okay to let the girls have some. It tasted better than it smelled. It tasted like summer, like fun, like innocence in the Rio Grande; so I swallowed, and the purity of it was divine.

We drank greedily from the pail, not bothering to talk or even look up at the old man, who seemed to be enjoying the scenery while he waited for us to get our fill.

"That will do you," he said, dumping out the rest of the water into the cement trough attached to the well. The splash scared off a scorpion who'd been sunning himself in the morning light.

"We're the Garza girls. We're here to see Teresita," I said as I wiped my mouth with the back of my hand. "Is this her place?"

"What took you so long?" he asked, waving to the front door of the shack. "Come in. She's been waiting for you for ages." Teresita was not who we expected. For starters, she didn't look like a woman. She looked like an old man dressed up like an old woman. There was just nothing feminine about her. Her floral print cotton dress hung on her rail-thin body like a discarded flour sack. She looked like a praying mantis, bent over, sitting at her table, rubbing her hands together. When she waved us in, we saw that her hands were big and bony with huge knuckles. The tips of her fingers were blunt, squared off, and tapered like those of a working man. Her nose, too, was unusually masculine. It was big and swollen and riddled with crevices and white, scarred blemishes. It hung like a bulbous mushroom in front of her face.

But that wasn't the worst of it. No, the worst of it was her small, naked head. Except for a few gray strands of hair, she was as bald as a baby pigeon, which gave her the appearance of being a very old man with enormous, wide eyes. The only feminine thing about her was the huge pair of silver earrings, which hung so low on her thin, elongated earlobes, they touched her shoulders.

"Come here. Let me look at you closely. My eyes are not as good as they used to be, thanks to these miserable cataracts," Teresita said, her skeletal fingers waving us in, urging us closer. As we neared the table, we saw what she meant. Her pupils were clouded over, opaque, and she seemed to not know exactly where we were standing in the room.

"Cecilia said—" Juanita said, pulling the bleating goat behind us.

"I know," Teresita said, a genuine smile lifting the sides of her thin, shriveled mouth.

"We brought you this *cabrito*. For your services," I said.

"Sí, sí, gracias," Teresita said, taking the goat and untying the knot at its throat. She picked it up, stroked it, kissed it, and then let it go. The goat ran off and made her way out the open door, bleating happily the whole way. "Sit down, sit down."

I sat down on the only other chair at her little table. Juanita scooted in beside me, and the rest of the girls huddled behind us.

"You want to know how to get to your *abuelita*'s house," Teresita said, picking up an old deck of cards with unusual images on them.

"Lotería!" Pita cried, exultantly. "Oh, goodie. Can I play?"

"Not quite," Teresita said, waving the cards in front of us before shuffling them expertly in her manly hands. "These cards are more ancient than your *Lotería*. More powerful. They will help you reach your destination, the home of your ancestors."

"Our car broke down," I said, being careful not to divulge too much information.

"I know," she said, leaning forward and looking at the deck spread before her. "You're going to have to travel by foot the rest of the way." She picked up a card and almost pressed her globular nose to it to look at it closely. Then she did the same with five other cards before she straightened up and sighed.

"How much farther is it?" I asked.

"It is a difficult road you've taken, one riddled with hardships and painful ordeals, but then again, you are difficult children." She smiled as she said it, pointing a crooked index finger at us.

"Unfortunately, the road ahead is full of trials and tribulations. You have angered the witch and now you must pay for your transgressions."

The doom of her words dragged me down, anchored me in misery at the knowledge that I could have avoided what was coming. "Pay?"

"Yes," Teresita said, looking at me closely now. "But then again, you knew that already, didn't you?"

"Knew what?" Juanita asked, turning back and forth between me and Teresita, waiting for answers that we were both reluctant to disclose.

"Cecilia has called upon evil to plague you," Teresita proclaimed, putting her hands over three of the cards on the table before us. "They are coming this way, the children of the night, traveling forth from the ancient world, coming from far and wide to avenge their mother."

"Cecilia has children?" Velia asked, leaning down to look at the cards. "But she said she didn't."

"Not children like you." Teresita turned the three cards on the table upside down and leaned over to get a better look at them. "Adopted children. Immortal children crafted by the devil himself and loosed upon this earth to aid in its destruction. Cecilia is a crafty, skillful sorceress. She has survived through the ages by cultivating that which lives and breathes in the darkest part of our fearful minds. In her greed, her need for power, she has cultivated three of our greatest nightmares, nurturing their dark souls and sustaining their evil spirits by feeding them only malevolence and sin. In a way, she is more their mother than their own creators, and that is the problem. Your arrogance and conceit has called upon her wrath and now you must face that which she has beset upon you, the Evil Trinity."

Velia put her hand on my shoulder to get my attention. "And you knew about this?"

"Why didn't you warn us?" Delia demanded.

Petrified in my seat by Teresita's horrible prediction, I could only blink away my fearful tears. "I didn't know she was real," I finally admitted. "I met La Llorona at the river. She warned me about all this, but I was too skeptical to believe her."

"Wait a minute. La Llorona is real?" Juanita asked.

"Yes, but she's not evil. She's actually trying to help us," I continued. "I tried telling you about it, but you didn't believe me. So I dismissed her warnings—until this morning, when you started taunting Cecilia and I heard her curse us. I'm sorry. It's my fault. I should have told you everything from the start."

"I wanna go home," Pita cried, reaching for Juanita, who took her in her arms and kissed her forehead like Mamá soothes us.

"You can't run away from this," Teresita said, touching the cards and looking at the ceiling blindly. "This time you have to face your nightmares."

Teresita was right. If only I'd warned my sisters of La Llorona's caution to be humble and good, we wouldn't be in this mess. Now it was up to me to contend with whatever evil I had brought upon us. I had to protect my *hermanitas.* "Isn't there anything we can do to stop them? La Llorona gave me this amulet, these earrings. She said I could use it five times, once for each circle on its orbit, but I've already used it three times."

"What Cecilia has beset upon you is just the beginning. You must save the ear pendant's remaining gifts. Use them sensibly, for there is so much more to life than nightmares and demons in the dark. In order to go home, to be truly happy again, you must face the worst enemy of all, the monster that lives among you. But you'll need your magical gift to get there, so save your good fortune—use it wisely."

"Can't you help us?" I peered across the table trying to get a better look at what was coming after us.

"I can't stop them," Teresita said. "It is not within my power. All I can do is perceive and forewarn. But there are other ways I can help you. I can see into your future and advise you, caution you. Tell you how to defeat that which dwells in the mystical realm. Those are things I am familiar with, things within my sight."

Teresita went back to looking closely at the cards. I waited anxiously, signaling to my sisters to be quiet as she pondered.

She pointed to a card. *"El nagual."* Then she rested her fingertips on two other cards sitting close together on the table. "*Lechuzas*, lots of them."

"Witch owls?" Juanita cried out. "Where? When?"

"*¿El nagual?*" I asked. "What's that?"

"*Un brujo*, a devious warlock. You will meet him first, but he will not show himself as who he really is. He will come in disguise, asking for help. But don't be deceived by his helplessness; he is wily and ruthless. At first, you won't know it is him. But once you discover his evil plot, you must sing and chant. Sing the song of the moon and the cave, the song of the birds and the rain, the song of your childhood. It will invoke the Mother and he will be much afraid."

"But we don't know the song of the cave," I said, looking around at my sisters for confirmation of our ignorance. Their faces were as confused as I'm sure mine looked.

"The *lechuzas* will be more difficult to escape," she continued. "They are evil beyond compare. Their tongues are made of the fifth element, and their words are sharp metal talons that can cut through even the cleverest of men. To avert the paralyzing effect of their punishment you must pray seven *Padres Nuestros* and seven *Ave Marías* while you tie seven perfectly spaced knots on a silk thread. Only then will you be able to escape the flame in their eyes."

"Flame in their eyes? Are you kidding?" Juanita asked, the tone of her voice told me she'd had enough of Teresita's riddles. I had already met La Llorona and listened to her cryptic message, so my own dismay was not as great as that of my sisters.

"Juanita, please," I whispered, pinching her arm under the table.

"Well, what does she mean by that?" she asked, rubbing her

arm absently. "I mean, what kind of advice is this? Cave songs and knots on stupid strings?"

"Don't be rude." Juanita's lack of respect to the elderly Teresita embarrassed me. Teresita was only trying to help us get out of this mess unscathed. I thought. Of course, given our experiences with Cecilia, I wasn't sure I could believe everything Teresita had to say, so I kept my ears and eyes open for suspicious behavior from the old soothsayer. Even if Cecilia had been under a spell and forced to tell the truth, I couldn't help but worry about my sisters. But if she was telling the truth, she was giving us answers we needed to pay attention to, even if we didn't understand them right now.

"No. It's all right," Teresita said. "It is this girl's fire that will keep you safe as you face the last of the malevolent trinity—the wretched *chupacabras*."

"*¡El chupacabras!*" Pita wailed, terrified.

"There is no such thing! I'm outta here," Juanita exclaimed, jumping out of the chair and heading for the gaping door.

"Believe me, child," Teresita's husband said, stepping out of the darkness that suddenly seemed to overcast the room. He stood in front of the door, impeding Juanita's progress. "The *chupacabras* is very real. I saw it with my own two eyes, and I don't have cataracts."

The twins had started for the door too, but like Juanita, they stopped to listen to Teresita's husband. "Where?" Delia asked, crossing her arms in front of her chest.

"When?" Velia demanded, mimicking her sister.

"A few months ago, out there, at the base of the *cerro*. It was sucking the life out of one of my goats. It hissed at me, when I came upon it. Its prickly coarse hair stood up like a sharp razor along the length of its back. It snarled and flew at me, the scrawny little thing. But I wasn't scared. I picked up my rifle and shot at it."

"You killed it?" Pita asked, sounding relieved.

"No," Teresita's husband said, looking a little chagrined yet firm at the same time. "But I injured it. Shot it through its left eye. Bullet went right into its head. It howled like a rabid dog. I've never seen anything like it before or since."

"That's the good news," Teresita said, leaning in to grip my hand with her clawlike fingers. "It's been injured by human hands, so it will be wary. But don't be fooled by its meekness. Its heart is pure evil. There is no humanity left in him."

"But how . . ." I started, feeling completely overwhelmed by everything Teresita had said. Questions ran through my head. How would we recognize *el nagual*? Juanita had a point—what *was* the song of the cave? It felt as if Teresita had given us more questions than answers.

"Don't show the *chupacabras* any mercy," Teresita's husband advised. "Take the nearest tree branch and pound its head in."

"But what if it . . ." Pita started to speak, but fear devoured her voice and she didn't finish her sentence.

"It won't," Teresita assured us. "It is all in the spread of the cards. You can save yourselves, but only if you are brave and cunning and stick together through these nightmares. You must never falter in your faith. It is the only way you will make it alive to your Mamá's house. You were never meant to die on the way. There are too many demons yet to be faced, too many tears yet to be shed."

I wasn't sure I heard Teresita right. Was she trying to tell us that there were more demons waiting at home? If that was so, our journey was going to be longer and more worrisome than I'd been led to believe.

11

El Alacrán: *A los que pica el alacrán, el cuartazo dan."*

The Scorpion: "Those who get stung by a scorpion end up on the floor."

As Teresita explained how to get to Hacienda Dorada, her husband drew up a sketchy map of the terrain for us on an old piece of linen, a shortcut, explaining it as he went along. "I've circled the areas I know to be dark. You need to avoid those bad places. Now this square is an old abandoned barn. You can rest there, get out of the sun, if you must. You'll have to travel about twelve or thirteen miles up and down those hills today, but you can get there this evening if you stay away from those monsters," Teresita's husband said.

They gave us a sack with provisions: a dozen hard-boiled eggs, a hunk of goat cheese still in its thin cloth casing, a stack of flour tortillas, and water. Most importantly, Teresita gave us a short piece of silver silk thread.

As we trotted away, the old couple waved to us from their

door and watched anxiously as we took the worn path down the hill. We walked along the dirt path for miles in the heat of the morning, resting often and drinking from the three huge gourds of well water Teresita's husband had given us. Velia, Delia, and Juanita argued often, especially over the amount of water any one person should drink. Sometimes, they got so nasty with each other, I threatened to blister someone's behind with my *chancla* if they said one more mean word to each other.

By late afternoon, I had them walking in pairs, a good ten feet apart from each other. Pita did nothing but complain, even when we sat in the shade, so I paired her with Juanita since she couldn't seem to get along with anyone else.

By the afternoon we realized we needed to get out of the sun for a while, so we started talking about looking for a shady place to rest. It was while we were looking for a safe place to settle down that we saw it: A lame donkey harnessed to a dilapidated old wagon was making its way down the road toward us.

"Eeyore!" Pita screamed and started to walk toward the cart.

"That's not Eeyore!" Juanita said pulling Pita back by her sleeve.

"Well, I didn't mean the real Eeyore," Pita explained. "Just one like him. Look, he even has a ribbon on his tail."

"That's not a ribbon," Juanita corrected. "It's a dirty rag."

Pita ran up to meet the donkey, who had come to a complete stop before us. "Whatever. I don't care what you think."

The donkey hung its head, looking pathetic. As I got closer

to the cart and inspected the poor animal, I had to admit it did look a bit Eeyore-ish. It had big sad eyes and his lips turned down at the corners, like it was a little depressed.

"Don't touch it," I said, slapping Pita's hands away as she came up to pet the beast.

"He says he's tired." Pita stroked his neck and face. "And thirsty."

"And covered in fleas," Juanita interjected. "You're going to get *piojos* if you keep petting him."

I moved to examine the animal's head. Pita was making kissy-faces at the donkey and cooing at him. "I said not to touch it." I tried to pull Pita away from the beast, but she shook me off.

Delia came up and joined Pita in petting the donkey. "You two are weird. You'll touch a dead man, but you won't touch a living, breathing animal. Something's definitely wrong with you."

"I'll touch it if it's not all dirty and gross," Juanita said.

"All right, that's enough," I said, pushing them all out of the way. The donkey's foreleg looked swollen at the ankle, so I crouched to inspect it.

"Is it hurt?" Juanita wanted to know.

"I don't know," I said. "I can't tell what's wrong, but it was limping. I wonder who it belongs to?"

Pita shushed everyone and cocked her ear at the donkey, who was braying loudly. "Listen to him! He says he's all right. He's just tired and we should give him a little time to rest."

"You're nuts. You know that, right?" Juanita told Pita, who ignored her and turned her attention back to the donkey.

"Leave her alone," I said absently. I looked down the road, trying to figure out where the animal had come from. Maybe we had missed a *ranchito* somewhere along the way. It might be worth our while to backtrack a little and investigate, because we were running low on water.

"Well, she is," Juanita complained. "She's having a conversation with a donkey, for God's sake."

"She is not," I insisted. "She's just pretending."

Pita put her ear to the animal's mouth like she was listening to him speak. Juanita grabbed our little sister's arm and pulled her away. "Pita, don't do that. It could be sick, *mamita*."

I scrambled onto a boulder and looked down at the horizon as far as I could see. With my hand shading my eyes, I surveyed the circumference of the area looking for a dwelling, a farm or a ranch house where the donkey might belong, but there was nothing out there but brush and huisache trees. As far as I could tell, he'd come out of nowhere. I couldn't help but wonder what happened to his owner.

"His name is Charrito," Pita said, interpreting the beast's thunderous brays. "He says he'll take us to Abuelita's house. He knows the way. We should just wait a little while, while he catches his breath."

Pita's words, her conviction that the donkey could speak and she could understand him, made the hairs on the back of my neck stand up to alert. La Llorona's warnings, Teresita's reading, they all came back to me.

"So let me get this straight," Juanita asked Pita as my mind raced through the warning signs, trying to remember the things I should be looking for. "This is a talking donkey, and it wants to give us a ride. Is that it?"

"I'm all for that." Velia jumped on the rickety wagon and looked around for a way to navigate the newfound vehicle. "Odilia, do you know how to drive this thing? Where's the steering wheel?"

My mind back on the present, I hurried to the front of the wagon. "There is no steering wheel. And you should really get down from there." I reached up to help her get off the wagon, but Velia ignored me.

"He says you don't have to use the reins. He knows where we're going," Pita said, pressing her cheek against the animal's cheek and smoothing down the tuft of hair at his forehead.

"Sure. Whatever." Juanita looked at me and circled her index finger around her ear to show me what she thought of Pita's interpretations. Juanita paused and scrutinized the wagon. It was big enough to hold all of us, and though it was old, it seemed sturdy enough to take us all the way to Abuelita's house. "Listen. This might not be a real talking donkey, but using the wagon to get to Abuelita Remedios's house is not a bad idea. Okay, everybody up." Juanita suited her own words and climbed up herself.

"No, no, no," I said, taking the reins in my hands. Juanita reached for them, but I stepped out of her reach on the driver's seat. The other girls stood half-ready to climb up, but scuffed their feet in indecision at my vehemence. "We didn't agree on this. This animal should have an owner nearby. I mean, where's the driver here? Farm animals aren't tethered to wagons twenty-four seven. It's obvious something happened to its owner. He probably fell, or, worse yet, the donkey might have gone psycho and run off without him."

At that moment, something struck my core and Teresita's words came back to me. Slowly, quietly, they echoed in my mind. *"A devious warlock . . . he will come in disguise . . . asking for help."*

"Girls, listen to me," I pleaded, holding onto the reins and standing my ground. "Remember what Teresita said? What if this is him, the *nagual*?"

"Odilia," Juanita interrupted. "You didn't really believe everything that old lady said, did you?"

I leaned in toward Juanita, losing my patience. "Look, I'm not making this up. I really did speak with La Llorona at the river, and she said it too. This world is different. Here, things are not always what they appear to be. I have a bad feeling about this, Juanita. Something about this creature just gives me the creeps. Let's leave him here and get back on the way to Hacienda Dorada."

"I agree," Juanita said, looking down at me from her seat in the front of the wagon. "We should get back on the road to Abuelita's house. And this is the fastest and safest way to get there. So stop being so mulish and get up here. Come on, everybody up."

Delia, who had been wandering off toward the back end of the wagon, looked at me remorsefully for a moment and then climbed up next to Velia. Pita, being so attached to the donkey, was too busy petting it to climb up, so Juanita whistled at her and said, "You too, Christopher Robin, up on the wagon."

As I watched Pita climb onto the driver's seat, Juanita reached down and yanked the reins out of my hands. As soon as they were all aboard, the animal started walking, pulling the wagon up the road in the same direction we had been heading.

"I can't believe this," I shouted, trying to keep up with the wagon. "If Mamá were here, she'd be doling out the spankings by now. I just hope we don't end up paying for this in a major way."

I walked beside the wagon briskly, always keeping an eye on the donkey, looking for a sign that he was not what he appeared to be. I could only hope I *was* wrong about this, even with as looney as Pita was acting—she kept conversing with the beast as we made our way down the road. But at least we were traveling in the right direction.

After a while, the girls celebrated their good fortune by breaking into the provisions. Juanita passed out the hard-boiled eggs, cheese, and tortillas. I was still mad at them, so I refused to partake, but they fed like kings, throwing eggshells off the side of the wagon like they were gold coins meant for peasants.

After the feast, the girls seemed to settle down. They sat back and enjoyed the rhythmic ride, mesmerized into a weary silence by the fullness of their stomachs and the steady movements of the wobbly cart. I trailed behind them at a slow but steady pace. We traveled for about an hour before I stopped to catch my breath. The sun was beating down furiously on us and I was ready to pass out from heat exhaustion.

Juanita looked back to talk to me. "You sure you don't want to get up here?"

"I'm sure," I said. "I just hope we reach Hacienda Dorada before nightfall."

"Oh, we will," Juanita said, turning back to look at the road ahead of us. "It's so peaceful here. This is what life is all about. No cell phones, no iPods, no cars driving by polluting our lungs."

"I know. This is how our ancestors must have felt," I said as I sped up to walk beside the wagon. The sun continued making its way westward in the sky and was almost directly above us now. "Unhurried, relaxed, and grateful for what they had."

"Sure. No running water!" Velia interjected.

"No indoor plumbing!" Delia continued sarcastically. "No deodorant!" As if to accentuate their cackles, the donkey let out two lungs full of vociferous braying.

"He wants to know if we want to drink some water and rest," Pita said. "There's a running creek up there on the left. Do we want to stop?" She leaned over and almost tipped out of the wagon.

"Be careful, Pita!" I pushed her back onto the safety of the cart with all my might.

"You hurt me," she complained, rubbing her arm where it had scraped the side of the wagon.

"We're already in all kinds of hot water," I said, refusing to apologize. "I don't want to have to explain to Mamá how I lost one of her daughters."

The business with Pita took all of my attention, but I did

notice that the donkey had pulled the cart off the trail and stopped. I was grateful for it until he took off again, speeding up ahead of me, bearing left, crossing a field full of daisies and heading up a hill at a trot too fast for me to keep up.

"Whoa!" Juanita called out, pulling on the reins. In her distraction, Juanita had obviously given him too much rein. He must have been instinctively just going off in search of something good to eat—right? However, my fear that this was the *nagual* Teresita warned us about kept me on edge. I ran as fast as my legs would take me, keeping an eye on them as I went, and hoped the donkey wouldn't take them too far astray. I just worried that my legs wouldn't take me very far after all the walking we'd done today and yesterday, after the car broke down. And all the while, as I ran, I tried to remember the song Teresita said we must sing if we came upon the warlock—the song of the birds and the rain. But my mind was blank. I had no idea what the song might sound like. Not even a single lyric came to me as I dashed after the girls in the cart.

"Whoa! Whoa!" Juanita kept calling, but no matter how loud she called, the beast just kept cantering along, ignoring her. They pulled so far ahead I worried they'd disappear over the next hill and I'd never see them again. I considered the ear pendant, but there was nothing to use it on, and Teresita had said to save it for our most dire circumstances. I would have to use my wits. I kept running, but even as I ran I couldn't help but notice the beast was running awfully fast for a lame donkey.

Finally, after about five minutes, he slowed from a canter to a steady trot—slower, but not slow enough for me to catch up. It was also fast enough that none of the girls could jump off the wagon safely. Even though they weren't saying much, their faces reflected the horrifying recognition that even if this wasn't the *nagual*, they might be in great danger. When the donkey did finally stop, it was so abruptly that my *hermanitas* lurched forward and caught themselves against the rails in order not to fall off.

"Holy guacamole, that was a close one," Velia said, jumping off the back of the wagon and walking around as if her legs were going to give out from under her. My legs felt like soggy *fideo* noodles too from all the walking and running. After running almost a quarter of a mile, I caught up to the wagon and stood with my hands on my waist trying to catch my breath. I needed that breath so I could give the girls a piece of my mind.

"Where are we?" Juanita asked as she helped Pita off the edge of the old cart. We looked around and saw that the creature had brought us to the mouth of a small cave on the side of the hill. "What is this?"

"I don't know, but it looks scary," Delia said from her seat in the wagon. "We should keep going. This place gives me the creeps."

"Don't go . . . in there," I started, winded to the point of stuttering. "Stay away . . . from it. . . . We don't know . . . what's in there." Where had I put the map that Teresita's husband had given us, warning us of places to avoid? I had a creepy feeling this place was on that map. I searched through my pockets and found it, but before I could gather my thoughts, Pita interrupted us.

"Don't be silly," she said. "Charrito says it's a good cave, and we should rest here. Night's coming."

I looked up at the sky and realized that she was right. The sky was darkening, but the girls had been so content just letting the donkey pull them up the dirt path, and I'd been so distracted by having to keep up with them, that we hadn't even noticed dusk was upon us. A dark, foreboding feeling took hold of me then. I had failed to convince my sisters to stay away from the creature and now we were being invited into his cave. I could feel it—something terrible was about to happen. If only I could remember the song of the cave, but it was useless. I had no idea what it was.

"Don't be ridiculous," Velia said. "I'm not sleeping in a cave. There's probably vampire bats in there."

"Velia's right," I said. "We should get back to the dirt path and try to find the next mark on this map. Teresita's husband said the path led to an old abandoned barn. We could rest there."

"Listen to the child," a deep male voice said, and we all turned around to look at the animal, who turned around to look at us. I couldn't help but notice the bit was no longer in his mouth and he was not hooked up to the wagon anymore.

"Donkeys shouldn't talk," Velia whispered, stepping away from the beast.

"The barn's no good. The roof leaks and it's out too far." The creature's lips were moving and the words were coming out of its mouth as he moved toward us.

I pushed Pita behind me and shoved Juanita out of the warlock's way. "It's the *nagual*! Velia, Delia, get our things!" I said, slowly stepping away from the donkey. "Listen, whatever or whoever you are, we don't want any problems."

"Aramés, aramás, todavía nada más, ven aquí, ven acá." The donkey's words stirred up something fierce and feral in me and I grabbed the nearest stick I could find on the ground. It wasn't big enough, but I could wield it like a sword to the eye if I had to.

"Let's go! Move it," I told the girls as they cowered behind me.

"Let me go!" Pita squealed, as she squirmed inside Velia's locked arms. "You're being stupid. He wants to help us! I know he does. He told me so."

"Pita," I said, pulling her into my arms. "You have to stop being so childish. He isn't a storybook character. He's an evil man, a sorcerer, not a donkey, and he's trying to trick us. We have to get away from him before he hurts us."

"Aramés, aramás, todavía nada más, ven aquí, ven acá, aire frío, aire mío, aramés, aramás," the *nagual* continued, even as his eyes rolled into the back of his head and his long ears perked up and flapped loudly.

Suddenly, the last rays of sun disappeared from the horizon and darkness descended upon us like the shadow of malevolence. The night air grew thick and sulfuric around us. Our breathing became shallow, and I felt sick and lightheaded.

"We have to get out of . . ." I didn't finish my thought. My tongue was twice its normal size, and I couldn't make out the words.

"*Aramés, aramás, todavía nada más, ven aquí, ven acá, aire frío, aire mío, hazlas mías, cinco hermanitas, cinco estrellitas serán mías, aramés, aramás . . .*" The *nagual* kept chanting different verses of the same spell, and before we knew it we were all on the ground, weakly looking at the donkey as he shifted from animal back to his human form and stood—a dark-clad figure looming tall and menacing above us. Regret was the last thing we saw in each other's eyes before we all passed out.

12

La Muerte: *"Jugando con la muerte,*
nadie tiene suerte."

The Death: "When playing with death,
nobody has any luck."

It was dark in the cave. I tried moving but my arms were aching. Then I realized my hands were securely tied behind my back as I lay on the dirt floor in a corner of the cave. Juanita was still passed out beside me. Looking around, I saw that all of us were in the same predicament. Every one of my sisters was tied up on the floor beside me.

All around us, on the dirt, lying sideways over jutted rocks and tangled in the dusty threads of the *telarañas*, the webs of a hundred black widow spiders, lay the corpses of our beloved friends, the snout-nosed butterflies. Their delicate winged bodies, prone and limp, were snarled in the girls' hair, attached to their clothes, even stuck to their bare arms and legs, like dried pressed flowers.

No longer disguised as a domesticated donkey, the *nagual,*

dressed in a soiled black robe, was standing over a huge bubbling cauldron. His long, white hair hung from his face in a stringy disheveled mess along the sides of his lean, angular face. He moved slowly and hunched over the cauldron like he was a hundred years old. I watched him without making a sound as he chanted something vile and wicked, something that made my heart flinch in my chest.

"Well, hello. Welcome back, *preciosa*," the *nagual* said, showing his green-gray teeth as he grinned at me. "I see you're ready."

I rocked myself into a sitting position. My head was spinning from the effort, but I managed to sit up on my knees and face him. His eyes were two small, dark slits that glittered with amusement as he watched me struggle. His skin was so sallow and dry, he looked like an old rattlesnake. I half expected him to lick his lips with a forked tongue. "Ready for what?" I asked.

"This. The final stop on your journey," he said, stirring the contents of his cauldron so furiously that it spun like a whirlpool. The fuming concoction sent swirls of steam up to the cave ceiling, where bats flapped their wings, clinging upside down from their claws, and pit vipers uncoiled themselves from thick iron hooks.

"And what is that?" I asked as I tried in vain to loosen the ropes at my wrists.

"This? This is my masterpiece," said the *nagual*. "My own personal recipe, perfected over the last four centuries. A potion so strong, so powerful, you won't feel a thing as you perish. Once I put you inside and close the lid, you'll cook almost instantly.

Then you can take your place in my favorite collection, the lovely bones of a thousand children, sacrificed with Cecilia's blessing. Your death will release me from this curse. No longer will I have to dwell in a cave. No longer will I have to wander the earth in the shape of a beast. With you—*las cinco hermanitas, las cinco estrellitas*—as my sacrifice, I will become more powerful than that cretin Huitzilopochtli ever was."

As he said those final words, talking about someone with an ancient sounding name—an Aztec deity perhaps, the *nagual* reached up to caress the collection of bones, both long and short, thick and thin, hanging from the wall behind him. Horrified, I wondered why I hadn't noticed them before. Their shapes and sizes made it impossible to mistake them for anything else—they were obviously human remains. His fingernails tickled their dry ivory exteriors, making the bones clang against each other with a hollow sound that echoed through the cave. It was the sound of death looming over me and my sisters, who were still unconscious on the ground beside me.

I tried rousting them by leaning into them and whispering, "Velia, Delia, wake up. Wake up girls," but they were out cold, so I closed my eyes and prayed. And as I prayed, I thought about Mamá sitting outside looking up at that full moon, wondering where we were. I thought about Papá sitting somewhere oblivious of our misfortune. I thought about Teresita and her husband, who warned us about the *nagual* and tried to tell us how to get away. Why didn't we pay more attention?

What was it she had said? Sing the song of the rain, the song of the cave, or was it the song of the butterflies? I tried to remember if Mamá used to sing to us in our youth, but it was no use. Nothing came to me now. If only I could remember, everything would be all right.

I shut my eyes tightly and concentrated. The song of the cave, the song of the birds, the song of the rain . . . My inner voice repeated Teresita's instructions again and again, but nothing made any sense. My mind was empty of songs. I couldn't even remember if Papá, who was a *músico*, had ever put us to bed with a lullaby. *It must be a spell,* I told myself. *The nagual must have wiped my mind clean when we first met him.*

I watched the warlock move about the opposite side of the spacious rectangular cave. He ignored us as he inspected jars filled with dark disgusting liquids and dirty sprigs of herbs on the shelves behind the cauldron, deciding what else to throw in the concoction simmering within. And all the while I wrestled with the tight ropes at my hands, working them loose slowly, carefully, until I was able to free my right hand. I was about to peel the loosened ropes off my left hand when I felt the warlock's grip upon my shoulder. It was disarming how he'd disappeared from the corner of the cave only to reappear directly in front of me in the beat of a second.

"Oh no, you don't," the *nagual* said, using my elbows as leverage to lift me from the ground.

My head spun like a carnival ride, but I twisted myself out of his grip and pushed him away. He grabbed at my free hand, but I turned around and kicked him in the stomach with such force that he fell to the ground. He lay on his side entangled in his own robes, struggling to get up.

I spun La Llorona's ear pendant with a dramatic flick of my hand. "Aztec queen, Tonantzin, Holy Mother of all mankind, lend me your magical assistance!"

"Noooo!" the *nagual* screamed, reaching for me.

For a moment, I thought he might be casting another spell, but no power stopped me, so I called to Tonantzin. "Sing to me, Mother Queen, sing me the song of the cave," I chanted as the ear pendant quivered against my cheek.

At my words, the earring began to hum as it spun. The humming became louder and more rhythmic. I watched the *nagual*, fascinated by his inability to move. He lay on the ground helplessly paralyzed by the musical notes emanating from the pendant.

"Juanita, Velia, Delia," I called to my sisters, who were still lying prone on the ground around me. "Wake up, girls. Wake up and listen."

Suddenly, from within the fogginess of my mind, something resonated. A fragment of a chord, a familiar tune came to the front in the form of a tiny sequence of notes.

"Girls! Girls! Wake up," I begged ecstatically. "Wake up and sing our tune!" The hum grew louder, and I joined in to sing.

"Que llueva, que llueva,
La Virgen de la cueva,
Los pajarillos cantan,
Las nubes se levantan . . ."

As I sang the ancient tune quietly to myself, I realized it was the refrain Mamá had sung to us to soothe our nerves on dark, rainy nights when we were very young. The rest of the song came to me, and I sang it, quietly, almost whispering it. I heard my sisters stir beside me, muttering as they woke, and I knew it was working.

"Que llueva, que llueva
El cóndor está en la cueva
Los pajarillos cantan
Las nubes se levantan . . ."

Louder and louder I sang, and when my sisters shook the fogginess from their own minds, they sat up and joined me in the chorus of Mamá's lullaby.

"Que sí, que no,
Que caiga un chaparrón.
Que sí, que no,
Que caiga un chaparrón."

"Stop! What are you doing? Stop it! Stop singing!" the *nagual* was screaming. He sat up and began to retreat, crawling on hands and knees to the far end of the cave to get away from us, and so we kept singing. Louder and more forcefully we sang. And when I loosened the ropes from my sisters' hands, we all stood in the center of the cave, joined hands, and sang louder and with more delight than any group of young girls ever sang before.

"Que llueva, que llueva,
La serpiente está en la cueva,
Los pajarillos cantan,
Las nubes se levantan,
Que sí, que no,
Que caiga un chaparrón,
Que sí, que no,
Que caiga un chaparrón."

All around us the desiccated corpses of the butterflies glittered and shone. Their tiny bodies quivered in the dust. Their wings fluttered and wavered as they trembled back to life right before our very eyes. Then a celestial light illuminated the door of the cave. Its radiance entered the room and pooled before the wily *nagual*, who was cringing in the farthest corner of the cave.

As if newly emerged from their chrysalises, the butterflies gathered their strength and began to fly. They flittered up into the air, dancing around the light, thousands and thousands of them, fluttering together, dancing to our song.

There were so many of them joining in the dance that soon they moved as one. Their bodies became a collective, a tapestry of wing and wind that fluttered with life, transforming into the figure of a young woman with dark hair and dark eyes. She was dressed in a shimmering tunic of gold and green jade. She looked like an Aztec goddess, but her face was that of a Mexican girl, the face of our many friends and cousins, a teenager, like us.

"Who are you?" Delia asked, dropping Velia and Pita's hands and stepping forth to take a better look at the apparition.

"What are you?" Velia didn't move, but she let go of my hand too.

Juanita fell to her knees and bowed her head in recognition. *"La Virgen de la Cueva,"* she whispered as she pulled on the hems of our shirts trying to make us follow suit.

"Tonantzin! *Madre Santa*, forgive me," the *nagual* begged, as he cowered away from the radiance of the goddess. "I did not know they were under your protection."

"How could you not," the youthful goddess asked in her childlike voice. "*Cinco estrellitas*—five stars, five little sisters, traveling through my domain in the sky. A warning for all to see, to let them pass unharmed. You are not dumb. You are not blind."

"Oh but I am. I am," the *nagual* muttered, his lips quivering. "I wasn't going to harm them. I promise I wasn't."

"Then what spews from your cauldron?" the youthful goddess questioned. "A stew? Or maybe it's a special offering for us. Stir it, man, before it sticks to the pot."

"It is of no consequence, your holy . . ." the *nagual* began.

"Stir it, I say!" the goddess ordered. Her command was emphasized by the roar of thunder somewhere out in the distant sky. "Stir it before I take my leave. I want to make sure you do your job as well as I do mine."

"No, please," the *nagual* begged, inching along the wall. He reluctantly made his way toward the cauldron. Suddenly, as if in slow motion, he turned sideways and made a dash for the mouth of the cave. In his great haste, he tripped on the hem of his robe and ran right into the cauldron he had been boiling for us. Unable to stop, a victim of his own momentum, he fell into the roiling mess. The liquid in the giant kettle gurgled and splattered as it ate away at his flesh, and he screamed in what must have been excruciating agony.

Instinctively, I reached over to block Pita's sight with my hands, but she pushed me away and stood staring at the gore before us without so much as a single tear in her eyes. "You don't have to do that," she said. "I'm not a baby. Besides, I'm glad he's dead."

Within seconds, a foul stench thickened and permeated the cave. The rest of my sisters and I ran for the mouth of the *nagual*'s cavernous dwelling. The Great Mother had saved us, and we escaped without looking back. We ran like *venadas*, frightened deer, fleeing all the way down the hill toward the safety of foreign woods and eerie dirt paths. Juanita and I brought up the rear, making sure our *hermanitas* escaped ahead of us. I looked back, wondering if I should have thanked the goddess before we ran.

"What do we do now?" Velia asked when we finally stopped at the base of the hill to catch our breath and slow our galloping heartbeats.

"I don't know," I said. "Do you have that flashlight, Juanita? I want to look at the map."

"Yeah," Juanita said, pressing a hand to her side. "It's in my bag."

"What's the matter?" I asked.

"Nothing. I just ran . . . too fast. I'll be . . . all right . . . in a minute." Juanita got the words out between labored breaths, and I knew what she was talking about. I too had a nasty stitch pinching at my side.

I looked around for some kind of landmark. "The best thing to do is keep moving." We'd been passed out so long in the cave that night had fallen, but the woods were thick and the full moon was somewhat obstructed. I could barely see my hand in front of my eyes.

"I think I'm done with adventures. From now on, I'm staying as far away from Mexico as possible," Delia declared.

Mamá's rain song came back into my head, and, without knowing why, I started to hum it as I pulled the map Teresita's husband had given us from inside my pocket. "*Vámonos*," I told the girls. "Let's sing the song of the birds and the rain and stay away from the dark places on this map. With any luck, we'll get to Abuelita's house before dawn."

13

***Las Jaras:** "Qué precisas plumas tienen que tener las jaras para poder volar."*

The Arrows: "What precise feathers the arrows must have in order to fly."

To say that we found our way quickly would be to lie. It took us hours to get back on the right path, or at least, the path we hoped was the right one.

"Who was that, do you think? Another witch? A sorceress?" Delia asked as we plodded along the moonlit path.

"That was the Great Mother, Tonantzin," I said. "I've been using her amulet, this ear pendant, to call on her for help along the way. La Llorona gave it to me. She was right when she said we'd need it." I peered at the map in my hand by the flickering light of our waning flashlight. It was hard enough not being able to read the map without having to worry about missing the landmarks altogether, but with the moon hiding behind a cloudy sky, they were both impossible.

"You mean she's the one who gave you these earrings?" Velia

asked, reaching up to touch the ear pendant hanging against my right cheek.

"We have special protection," Juanita said as she ran up to join our conversation. "Isn't that cool?"

"Yes it is. But there's more. La Llorona said we have to remain noble and kind. If we do that, everything will be all right," I said, relieved that she finally believed me. Then, remembering La Llorona and all that she had done for us so far, I began to wonder why she had not been the one to come to our aid. Had the *nagual* been too powerful for her? If that was so, had she asked the goddess to help us herself? Was La Llorona ultimately behind our salvation?

"I wonder if Mamá knows what the song is really for," Velia said. Mamá had sung that to us so many times I couldn't count. Now that the fog of the *nagual*'s spell had lifted, I couldn't believe I hadn't made the connection sooner.

"She probably doesn't. I mean who would have thought that some supernatural being was going to show up and save us because we sang her a song?" Delia asked, stating the obvious.

"I always thought Mamá's lullabies were magical," Pita whispered. "When we were young and Mamá used to sing to us I felt special inside."

"I know what you mean," Juanita said, wrapping her arms around Pita. "Her voice was so sweet, so loving, I always felt like we were more than her children. I felt like we were her life. It's almost as if she knew someday her lullabies would keep us safe from harm, so she made sure she sang to us every night. It's a wonder we forgot that song."

"Oh boy, it's getting deep out here!" Velia said. "What makes you think Mamá knows anything about Tonantzin coming to save us? Because, I'll be honest, I didn't know what the heck was going on when the goddess showed up."

"Whatever," Juanita retorted, letting Velia's negative comments slide right off her back like cold butter off a warm tortilla. "All I'm saying is Mamá knows the song for a reason. Someone taught it to her. It's a lullaby, right? So it's been passed down from generation to generation. Mothers must have been singing it to their children since the time when Mamá's ancestors, the *Aztecas*, were overpowered by the Spaniards."

I folded the map and shoved it back in my backpack. "Well, the bottom line is La Llorona gave me the earrings to invoke her, and Teresita kind of let us know Tonantzin would come to our rescue, and she did. But now it's time we moved on." I pulled my backpack over my shoulders and started hiking through the thick brush of the overgrown path.

"That's not true," Velia complained as she began to follow me and Juanita through the woods. "Teresita never said anyone would help us. She just said we had to sing the song of the birds. I know. I was listening, and I have a photogenic memory."

"*Photographic*, genius," Juanita spit out angrily at Velia, who had caught up and was now walking between us. "It's called a *photographic* memory, and anyway, I don't see how that would help you remember what was being said since photographic memory deals with sight—not hearing!"

"Okay, stop it! Both of you. I don't want to have to separate you again," I yelled, moving between them as we made our way through the shrubbery and into a clearing.

"Well, Teresita didn't tell us we were in danger of being boiled alive in a cauldron. So forgive me if I don't put too much stock into what that old bag of bones had to say," Velia complained, hiking her backpack higher up over her shoulders before she stalked ahead of us.

"I have a feeling there's a lot Teresita didn't tell us," Delia said, stopping to take a swig of water from a gourd.

"She did warn us about the *nagual*. She just wasn't very specific," Juanita said, turning back to face the road ahead.

"Yes, but there was more," I said. They knew what I was talking about.

"You mean the coven of *lechuzas*," Juanita whispered, looking at me sideways.

"We've got to find a place to hide for the night, before they find us," Velia said, looking to either side of the dirt path.

"Well, what do you know. Ask and you shall receive." Delia punched my arm and pointed to the right of the path. I peered into the darkness, but all I could see was the faint outline of far away mountains against the dusky horizon.

"What is it?" I asked, giving up on my poor eyesight.

"A barn!" Pita screamed. She ran up in front of us and jumped up and down in place with excitement.

"Now hold on," I said, putting my hand on Pita's shoulder. "Settle down. Let's not get ahead of ourselves."

"What?" Velia wanted to know as she joined our united circle. "What's wrong?"

"Nothing," I said. "Nothing's wrong. We just need to make sure it's okay to go in there. We need to be cautious, that's all."

"Teresita's husband said we could rest here. Why do we have to be so careful?" Delia asked, joining us as we faced the barn.

"We just have to, that's all. Well? Who's coming with me?" I asked, looking around for volunteers. Not surprisingly, nobody said anything. "You guys are like *gallinas cluecas, puro guato*, a bunch of clucking chickens, all talk and no action."

I started across the grass, heading for the barn on my own. Although I was scared, I wasn't going to show it. I was the eldest. It was my job to bring them to safety. Of course, leaving them alone on the side of a dirt road in rural Mexico wasn't my idea of protecting them, but I didn't have much choice either.

"Wait!" Juanita ran after me. "Do you really think it's safe in the barn? I mean, what if the *lechuzas* are in there?"

"Don't be ridiculous," I said. "*Lechuzas* don't hide in barns at night. Owls are nocturnal predators. You should know that. You've seen every animal documentary on the Nature Channel."

"Oh yeah, ever heard of a barn owl?" Juanita taunted. "What do you think a *lechuza* is? It's an owl, genius. Try keeping up."

"Whatever, Ms. Gifted-in-Everything. I'm going to check it

out. Are you coming with, or are you going back to cower with the rest of the broody hens?"

"I guess I'm coming with—" Juanita said, but she didn't sound too sure of it.

"Good," I said, starting off again. "Let's get on with it. I'm tired, and judging from this humidity, it's going to rain soon."

Side by side, we hiked through the overgrown meadow off the beaten path. We had to be very careful because the field was full of burrs and sting weeds. So we traveled slowly, stomping the tall grass down as we went.

When we finally got to the barn, we found an old oil lamp hanging just inside the door. I jiggled the compartment in the underside of the tin relic and found two long thin matches. While Juanita held a flashlight over me, I lifted the filthy cobwebbed glass and lit a match. To my surprise, the wick lit right up and, after shaking it a bit, I could hear that there was enough kerosene in it to keep it going for a while, maybe even all night. That would help keep Pita from getting scared.

"We should conserve what's left of the battery." I turned off the flashlight and stuffed it back in Juanita's backpack.

Looking around the barn, we saw that it was most definitely abandoned. There were some old rusted tools lying about and some desiccated straw lined the far left corner, but half the roof was either missing or about to fall off. Nevertheless, we decided it was in good enough shape to offer us some semblance of security for the night, however pitiful it might be.

The girls were delighted to hear the news. Once inside, Pita walked around the poorly lit barn for a while, playing with an old rusty rake and a pitchfork she'd found in a stall. The rest of us emptied the contents of the backpacks and lay on several rumpled layers of clothing. Unlike Pita, who was still playing with the rake, Juanita, the twins, and I had no desire to expend any more energy than we already had. It had been a hot, tiring two days of walking since we'd left El Sacrificio, and our journey was far from over. If Teresita's husband's hand-drawn map was even sort of accurate, we hadn't covered half the ground we'd intended to today. We were just content to rest our feet and curl up in a semicozy place.

I got Pita to finally settle down beside me. But even after everyone else fell asleep, I lay wide awake, looking up at the stars through the wide hole in the ceiling. We had traveled so long and so far from that first night, when I had seen that series of stars fall from the sky like a meteor shower, that I wondered if we'd ever get back to that life again—back to those long, playful days without danger or witches or warlocks. At the thought of Mamá crying every day, fearing for our lives, tears started to prick at my eyes and I wiped them away. It was then that I saw several tiny figures flying in and out of my field of vision over the barn.

"Bats?" I asked myself quietly, sitting up to get a better look.

"No," Juanita whispered as she too sat up. "They look too big to be bats."

"I know," I said. Keeping my eyes on the creatures above, I shook the other girls awake.

"What?" Velia mumbled, half asleep. "Leave me alone."

"They're here," I whispered, because by then I had figured it out.

Velia sat up so fast she stirred Delia beside her. "Who?"

"Mamá?" Delia sprang up into a sitting position beside her twin, and her eyes went to the doors on the other side of the barn.

"No," I whispered, pointing at the creatures. They had stopped flying and were now perched side by side around the hole on the ceiling, peering down at us from the darkened heavens.

"*¿Lechuzas?*" Velia asked, searching the sky above.

"There's six of them," I said, nodding. "I counted them twice."

"Then it's not them," Juanita said, putting a hand to her chest, still scared but sounding pretty relieved. "You need thirteen to make it a true coven. They must be regular owls if there's fewer than that."

"Maybe the other seven are dead," Velia whispered.

"Or maybe," Delia interjected. "They split up and the others are on their way."

I remained frozen, unsure of whether a reaction would startle the *lechuzas* into an attack. "Regular owls aren't that big, and they don't travel in broods," I said. "No. It's them." I reached for my backpack slowly, trying not to show fear.

"Parliament," Juanita whispered from beside me on the nest of clothes.

"What?" I asked, confused.

"A group of owls is a parliament, not a brood," she explained. "That's chickens—hens, actually—"

"Oh, like that matters right now." I started to move my hand slowly, toward the tiny front pocket of my shorts, pulling the piece of silk string out of it without drawing too much attention to myself.

"Sorry," Juanita said. "Do you have the string?"

"Yes," I whispered. "I put it in a safe place as soon as Teresita handed it to me, but I need you to wake Pita up without scaring her. Once everyone's awake, you'll have to form a protective circle around me, so they can't get to me while I tie the knots."

"Okay," Delia and Velia whispered in unison.

I could hear the *lechuzas* whispering menacingly above me, up on the roof, but I couldn't understand what they were saying. I unzipped the tiny front pocket of my shorts as slowly as possible, trying not to draw attention to myself. But the minute I pulled out the piece of marked silk thread, the *lechuzas* launched themselves off the roof and flew into the barn, wailing and screeching.

Startled awake by the *lechuzas'* bloodcurdling screams, Pita sat up and screamed almost as loudly as the winged witches. From that moment on, everything happened very fast. The *lechuzas* descended upon us with all their fury. As they came at us, I saw that they were as big as vultures, and their wingspan was twice their length. Their long, scraggly hair streamed behind them like raggedy, moth-eaten capes as they flew at us. But the most horrific parts of them were their faces. They looked like dried up pieces of fruit, desiccated human faces—witches with metallic beaks for lips.

The coven of *lechuzas* squawked and screeched as they flew in and grabbed at us with steel talons, pulling out chunks of our hair, shredding our clothes, and scratching our arms, hands, and faces as they flew by. One at a time, they soared up into the rafters and swooped down to do it all over again. If they had been less aggressive, less calculating, we might have been able to defend ourselves. But they were so fierce and erratic in their attacks, we never stood a chance.

"*¡Niñas malas!*" said one in Mamá's voice.

"*¡Malcriadas!*" said another in La Llorona's voice.

"*¡Egoístas!*" said the one with Cecilia's voice.

"*¡Arrepiéntanse!*" said another in Teresita's voice. According to them, we were evil children, spoiled rotten and selfish. We should repent.

They kept chanting over and over again as they scratched at us with their sharpened talons. "Repent! Repent! Repent!"

"Stop!" Juanita screamed as she swatted them away with her hands.

"Stop! Stop!" we cried as we whacked at them. But no matter what we did or how much we begged, they wouldn't stop. If anything, their viciousness grew even more intense. As they started to abuse us, the rain we had been expecting started to pour down on us through the holes in the roof. There was no escape from the feathers and the rain. The wind picked up and I could hear thunder in the distance.

I remembered the piece of silk thread and realized I was still clutching it. But no sooner had I looked at it than one of the *lechuzas* clawed it out of my hand. I tried to hold on to it, but the evil bird was too strong. She flapped her wings in my face, slapping my head with her sharp, bristly feathers. I was tugging against her, holding on to the string for dear life, when one of her feathers pricked me right in the eye. An intense pain shot through my eye like a bullet, and I let go of the string.

Taking the string with her, the *lechuza* flew out of the barn through the hole in the roof, into the darkness and rain. And just when I thought things couldn't get any worse, Velia and Delia rolled away from the rest of us. Screaming, they made a mad dash for the door at the other side of the barn. With two *lechuzas* at their backs, they busted out of the barn as if their heels were on fire, never once looking back. Had they abandoned their *hermanitas?*

I looked at the barn doors noisily slapping back and forth with the force of the storm, and I couldn't help but feel powerless. The twins' desertion shattered any hope I had left of defeating the malevolent witches. And for the first time on our journey, I wanted to cry.

But there was no time for that. With the twins gone, the remaining *lechuzas* concentrated on the rest of us. Two of them dived so fast and hard into me that they knocked me over. One of them sat on my chest. Another one had Juanita pinned faceup against the pile of clothes we had used to make ourselves a nest. Pita was pressed against the wall, shivering, while a *lechuza* pecked gently at her head, as if it were picking nits out of her hair.

"You like eating sweets, don't you?" The *lechuza* with Cecilia's voice pulled Pita in close until their faces were almost touching. "That's because you're a piglet! A little piggy with a piggy nose and a piggy mouth and a piggy stomach. You're a chubby baby, but give me time. I'll put some real meat on your bones, thicken you up, and get you ready to be eaten. My sisters and I haven't eaten much lately. Your big brown eyes look delicious. I bet they'd taste sweet slathered with jalapeño marmalade."

"How do you like your adventure now, you arrogant little twit?" a *lechuza* with Inés's voice asked Juanita as she caressed her face with the bristly feathers of her left wing. "What? Do you think you're smarter than them? Well, you're not. You dragged them all into this mess with your self-righteousness." Juanita sniffed and hiccuped as she tried in vain to stop herself from bawling. "Oh, what's the matter now? Why are you crying? Are you sad? Maybe you should have listened to your older sister. Maybe you should have stayed home and cleaned and cooked like your mother, instead of thinking you've got brains."

"You think you can fool me?" the one with Mamá's voice asked me. She was sitting on top of me, kneading into my chest with her claws like a cat, laughing when I winced in pain. "Answer me!" she screamed. But instead of talking, I looked straight into her red fiery eyes with what I hoped was disdain.

"What's the matter? Aren't you afraid? Want to run away?" she asked, and when I didn't answer she dug her sharp talons deeper into my chest. The pain was horrendous, and I wanted to scream out, but I held my breath instead. "Of course you do . . . I know how much of a coward you really are. I know how irresponsible you can be. Who's the one who relinquished the piece of thread? Who's going to protect your sisters now? Who? Who? Who?"

She was shaking me then, grabbing me by my shirt collar and rattling me like she wanted to loosen the last breath out of my chest. I closed my eyes and started to pray, silently at first and then with more courage and conviction, but my prayers were useless against her. Instead of getting off my chest, she started to laugh, a deep cackling laugh that vibrated inside my head and made me lose my place in prayer.

"You, that's who," whispered the *lechuza*, her rotten breath caressing my neck like a dirty rag, penetrating into my every pore. "You! You! You!" she kept screaming in a parody of Mamá's voice, spitting putrid saliva on my face. "You dressed like me! You took them away! You left me crying! You lost the thread!"

Her words, spoken in Mamá's voice, pierced through my heart and I screamed in agony. "No! No! It's not true! It's not . . ."

Just when I thought all was lost, Velia and Delia burst through the barn doors wielding what could only be described as giant metal baseball bats. I don't know what kind of tools they were or where they came from, all I know is they looked absolutely dangerous.

"Die!" the twins screamed as they charged in our direction. The *lechuzas* screeched angrily, let go of us, and scattered themselves around the room. One by one they flapped their wings and took flight, soaring above us, cursing our names and threatening to take their revenge.

"You take the pitchfork. I call the rake," I told Juanita. I scrambled to my feet and rushed to the other side of the barn where Pita had abandoned the rusty old tools.

"You can't hurt us. We're the avengers. The devil's playmates," the one with La Llorona's voice screeched.

"You've caused too much heartache and pain. You disrespected Cecilia, humiliated her, and now you have to pay," the one with Teresita's voice yelled from the rafters.

"You'll never get away," the one with Mamá's voice screamed, as she descended upon me.

With all my strength, I batted at her with the brittle rake. She flew around me to avoid getting hurt, but she wasn't completely successful. I'd clipped her right wing and she screamed in rage—or maybe it was pain. I shook the feathers out of the rake and prepared myself for the next attack.

"Just draw her close." Velia whispered. She and Delia inched themselves toward Juanita and me.

"We can take these bit—I mean, witches," Delia announced.

"Watch your mouth," I warned out of habit. Although, this time, I had to agree with her colorful language. These creatures were more than wicked—they were downright malevolent!

"Repent! Repent! Repent!" the *lechuzas* screeched as they swooped down on us like a squadron of fighter planes. We stood side by side, all four of us, defensively holding up our weapons like ninja warriors, while Pita huddled behind us, defenseless without a weapon to wield.

Claws, feathers, and hair flew everywhere during the first onslaught. But through it all, we never quit. We batted and struck and clubbed and raked, and as we did, one by one the *lechuzas* flew off our weapons, hit the barn walls, and fell to the ground, squealing like stuck pigs.

When Juanita pierced through one of them with her pitchfork, it screamed out, convulsed, and then lay lifeless. So that's how we got rid of most of them. The twins and I clubbed and raked them until they were stunned and dazed, and Juanita finished them off by staking them.

By the time we were done, the place was a bloody, feathery, eerie mess. We stood side by side, looking past the settling debris, not daring to talk in case we were dreaming wide awake. I knew I should be shocked, horrified even, that we had just slaughtered a group of beings—not human perhaps, but living, breathing beings in their own right. But my blood was pumping furiously through my body, washing away any remorse I might have felt. Maybe it was the danger they had posed, or maybe I was just becoming psychotic, but I didn't feel guilty at all. I felt strong and powerful and vindicated as I kicked a blood-splattered feathery lump out of my way and headed for our nest in the corner of the barn.

"You did it!" Pita squealed and jumped for joy beside me. "You saved us!" She shook fuzzy remnants of feathers out of her hair and spat them off her face.

"Wow," Juanita whispered, still caught in a dreamlike state. "We killed them all. Can you believe it? We won. We defeated them."

"No, we haven't," I said, looking up to the hole in the ceiling above our nest. "The rest of them are back."

Up in the sky, behind the rest of the perched, cackling *lechuzas*, there was a tinge of pink on the purple face of night. Dawn was coming soon.

"The sun's about to rise," I said. "If we ever want to be able to sleep again without fearing for our lives, we have to finish them."

I'd lost the silk thread, though. How could we do what Teresita told us would defeat the *lechuzas?*

I was bemoaning our plight internally again when I saw Pita, disheveled in her best Sunday dress, and realized we'd had the solution all along. "Come here, Pita." When she came closer, I grabbed the tiny bow at her collar and yanked it off her dress with one hard tug.

"What are you doing?" she wailed. "Give that back!" I'd ripped it off cleanly, without damaging the dress. But that bow was the thing Pita loved most about that dress. She was understandably upset and reached for the bow.

I held it out of her reach until I could untie the bow and smooth it out between my fingertips. "I need it, Pita. It's silk," I explained, ripping it so I could pull out a single piece of thread.

Pita touched her collar and mourned. "This is my favorite dress."

"Shh! We'll get you a new one once we're back home! Watch my back," I whispered, stepping back to stand between Pita and Velia. Delia and Juanita closed the gap in front of me and stood wielding their farming tools before them, ready for the next attack.

"Padre Nuestro que estás en los cielos . . ." I started to say the Lord's Prayer in Spanish. Only this time, I was smarter about it. This time I held the thread tightly against my chest. Since there was no way of marking it, I would simply make every knot sit tightly against the last. Teresita hadn't said the knots had to be set apart by any particular amount of space. She only said they had to be evenly spaced. So putting them side by side was, in my opinion, perfectly spaced.

With every word I spoke, it seemed the rain began to wane. Less and less of it fell in through the roof. As the first prayer ended and I closed the first knot, the rain stopped completely and the rest of the *lechuzas* screeched in pain and flew into the barn. They soared over us, ranting and raving and angrily flapping their wings. They circled and circled, creating a whirlwind, a dirt devil of debris and dark moldy hay that swirled all the way up to the ceiling. The miniature storm swirled and stood before us like a charmed snake, flicking our hair into our faces, wrapping it around our necks, choking us—stealing our breaths. But all the time, I stayed focused and prayed. Knot after knot I tied. Prayer after prayer I prayed, seven Lord's Prayers and seven Holy Marys, and it seemed that each one of those knots took away just a little bit more of that whirlwind's strength.

Shorter and shorter it got, and slower and slower the *lechuzas* flew, until finally, as I tied the last of the seven knots, a whisper of daylight broke through the roof and the whirlwind died away. The seven remaining *lechuzas* fell to the floor, dead. Their eyes closed, their feathers dulled, and their faces had become clean slates. Then the *lechuzas*, all thirteen of them, vanished into thin air, leaving only downy feathers floating innocuously in the rays of the morning sun.

14

El Diablito: *"Nomás baila y brinca*
el diablito cuando anda alborotadito."

The Little Devil: "The little devil only
dances and jumps when he's agitated."

"I'm tired," Velia said, and she fell into the nest of clothes we had built ourselves the night before. It appeared to be clean despite our tussle with the *lechuzas*. There was no sign of the struggle or the mud of last night's rain.

"Me too," Delia chimed in, joining her in the nest.

"Listen, Odilia, I think we should rest," Juanita whispered, eyeing the twins, whose eyes were closed in genuine exhaustion.

I stared at them for a moment, debating. "Okay," I conceded. "But just for a little while."

"I don't want to go to sleep," Pita whined as she watched me and Juanita making ourselves comfortable on the bed of clothes. "What if the *chupacabras* comes to get us?"

"There's nothing to be scared of. It's daytime," I said, reaching for Pita. She let me pull her down and lay next to me, burying her face into my side the way she does when we're at home.

"That's right," Juanita said, rubbing Pita's back for a moment. "We'll take a short nap and then move on. See, look at the map. We're here and there's Hacienda Dorada. We'll be there before the *chupacabras* has a chance to get us. Because he only comes out at night, you know."

I watched as Juanita pointed at the short distance on the map. I didn't have the heart to tell them that an inch on the map was a lot of miles on foot and we might not make it there before nightfall. I'd been overconfident in our ability to walk so many miles at once in such rough terrain when we left Teresita's.

After the girls handed it back to me, I looked at the map more closely and I saw once again that there were no houses or farms between us and Hacienda Dorada. Teresita's husband had drawn many hills and even a creek along the crooked path, but no other signs of human life were depicted on the map. It was both disheartening and worrisome to know we were out here alone with no hope of coming across someone to help us.

"Odilia, are you scared?" Pita asked, lifting her head to look at me.

"Not right now. No," I said.

Pita rested her face on my arm and let out a long breath. "Me either."

"I don't think the *chupacabras* stands a chance," Velia said from beside Juanita. "We're a force to be reckoned with, you know."

"We are!" Delia chimed in, sitting up on her elbow to make eye contact with us. "*¡Cinco hermanitas!* Together forever!"

I flipped to my side and wiggled myself into a more comfortable position. “If we’re going to sleep, then we should go to sleep.”

Nobody said anything after that. Even though nobody was admitting it, I knew deep inside we were all still worried about the *chupacabras*. However, we were so emotionally and physically exhausted that we fell asleep almost instantly and slept for hours without stirring.

When I first opened my eyes, I didn’t have to look at my watch to know it was high noon. The sun was peering down at us from the center of the gaping hole in the roof. However, it wasn’t the sun that had awakened me. There was something else, something inherently evil had drifted into my wakeful consciousness, a bad dream of some kind—a warning, perhaps.

“Juanita,” I whispered, reaching for her.

“El chupacabras?” she asked, jolting up to a sitting position.

I listened to the distant sound. “I don’t know.”

“I hear bleating and singing,” Delia said, sitting up slowly. “It’s a boy for sure, and he has animals with him. A shepherd?”

“Or maybe a goatherd,” I said, shaking the others awake. Velia woke up right away, but Pita stretched out on the nest and groaned with her eyes still closed. “C’mon ladies, get up. Someone’s coming! Get up!”

Juanita and I clung to the wooden slat barring the barn door. She looked too afraid to open it, and after what happened the night before, I didn’t blame her. “Who’s out there?” I called.

“He can’t hear you,” Velia said, shoving Juanita aside and pushing up the wooden slat.

"What are you doing?" I asked, alarmed. "We can't let him in here. He could be dangerous."

"More dangerous than what we encountered last night? Please. He's probably a ranch hand from some isolated *ranchito* out there. He might even be from Hacienda Dorada," Velia said, and opened the door.

"He has goats!" I said. "It would be like baiting the *chupacabras*!"

Juanita got up and tucked her shirt into her shorts. "Hello. It's daylight. The *chupacabras* only comes out at night. Besides, if he has goats, he has water. Let's just hope he can spare some."

"And food!" Delia said, running to help her twin push the other tractor-sized door open.

Pita followed us out into the bright sunlight. "Oh, I do hope he has food! I'm so hungry I could eat a donkey right now!"

"Of course you could, *Pita-Chalupita*," Velia said. "Some things never change."

"Whatever. Make fun of me. I don't care," Pita retorted, shoving at Delia's back.

I took a hold of Pita's arm and pulled her behind me as Delia and Velia peered out into the sunlight. "I'm not so sure we should be making new friends right now. He could be dangerous."

"Don't assume the worst," Velia said as she poked her head through the doors. "He looks like a very nice boy. See?" I couldn't see what Velia was talking about at this angle. I needed to get outside now, before the girls rushed headlong into another nightmare brought on by a lack of caution. How many times would

Teresita's warnings have to come true before they believed the seer?

Once outside the barn, Pita stood behind me, staring at the sorriest sight we'd ever seen. A small, bedraggled boy was coming up the hill toward us with a small herd of goats following behind him. His threadbare clothes were filthy and shredded to the point that I couldn't tell what his T-shirt used to say. His hair was long and stringy. Whole sections of it were clumpy and clung to his head like matted fur, and the parts of it that hung over his eyes and covered both his ears were wispy. Looking at him, it was hard to believe he was a human being. He reminded me of a mangy dog. But he had been singing, and even though we couldn't see his eyes for his shaggy hair, his shy smile confirmed it for us: he was human.

"Buenos días, señoritas." The boy looked up at us from behind a lock of that fuzzy black hair, and then shyly looked down again.

"Hi," I said from a safe distance.

"Hello." The girls greeted him the way they would have greeted a stray dog, with trepidation.

"Cresencio Aguilar, at your service," the boy said shyly, pushing his hair aside to get a better look at us. The one eye we could see under all that matted hair, his right eye, was warm and friendly, and his smile was genuine, so the twins reached out and shook hands with him. I stepped forward to get a better look at him and regretted it almost immediately, because his hands were grubby and he reached over to offer me a handshake. At close proximity, I also noticed he had too much body hair for a boy who couldn't be more than twelve years old. His forearms were hairy, and he even had tiny hairs on his knuckles. This fascinated me in a repulsive kind of way, and I couldn't stop looking at his hands.

"We are the Garza girls," Juanita said, stepping forth and offering him a welcoming hand. "Glad to meet you."

"You can call me Chencho," the boy said, nodding in greeting to Pita, who eyed him from her usual safe place directly behind me. "What are you ladies doing out in this heat?"

"We're heading to Hacienda Dorada," Pita said with surprising confidence. She stepped out from behind me and met Chencho's gaze as she spoke to him directly. "But we're running low on water. Do you know how far the nearest creek is?"

"I would say you are about eight miles away from *ojito verde*, more or less. It's the nearest source of water in these parts. But you can have some of mine if you like," he said, looking sweetly at Pita, who had obviously caught his attention.

Pita took the canteen Chencho offered and drank from it greedily. Then she passed it to the twins, who took turns finishing it off.

At first, I thought it was kind of strange that Chencho seemed to be attracted to the youngest among us. Most boys reacted to the twins because they're so pretty, but watching Pita interact with him with such self-assurance made me realize she was growing up before my very eyes. Soon she would be getting taller, shedding her baby fat, and wanting to wear lipstick. She looked both like Papá and Mamá, but she seemed to have inherited the best features from both, so she would be beautiful some day. The image of her looking more and more lovely every day made my heart tighten in my chest and I had a moment of sisterly, almost maternal, pride.

But even as I marveled at my baby sister's potential, I couldn't shake the nagging feeling that something wasn't quite right with the boy in front of me. He was more than strange-looking, and his sudden appearance set off all kinds of red flags in my head. Looking at his hairy hands again, I suddenly felt the urge to get away from him.

Juanita shook the empty canteen, frowned disapprovingly at the twins, and handed it back to the boy. "Where are you from, Chencho?"

"Oh, I'm from Puerto Vallarta originally, but now that I'm all alone, I live out here by myself," Chencho said.

"You mean you live out in the woods?" Pita asked. Her eyes grew wide with shock, but a glint of admiration twinkled in their depths.

Chencho grinned shyly as Pita questioned him. "Oh, yes," he said. "There's all kinds of places to sleep in the wild. Out here, nobody bothers me and I don't bother anybody. I only go into town when I need to buy supplies. The countryside is the best place to be for someone like me."

"Well, thank you for the water," I said. "Sorry we can't stay and chat, but it's late and we have to get going." Then I turned around to talk to the girls, shutting him out.

"Why are you traveling on foot?" he asked. "Where are your parents?"

"It's a long story," I said, not bothering to explain. "Let's go, ladies."

"*Bueno pues*, you can travel with me if you like. I'm heading in that direction. I don't have a wagon, but I have plenty of water, two more gourds, and some bread and goat cheese. It's not much, but I don't mind sharing," the boy said, smiling that shy, genuine smile again. At close range, and with his choppers showing, I could see he hadn't seen a toothbrush in quite some time, perhaps maybe never. His teeth were beyond yellow. They were downright blackened, and I wondered how long he'd been out here "in the wild" without parental supervision.

Chiding myself for being so shallow, I concentrated on being polite. "Thank you. You are very kind, but we don't want to slow you down. It's better if you continue alone. We've got some business to take care of before we head out. Have a nice day," I said. Then I turned around and started to push the girls back into the safety of the barn. Pita started to go in, but Velia and Delia wouldn't budge.

"What's wrong with you, Odilia?" Velia demanded, glaring at me as I tried to push her into the barn. "You're being awfully rude, you know."

"I'm not trying to be rude," I said, gritting my teeth and

keeping my words low enough not be overheard by the strange little boy standing only a few feet away from us. "I'm just trying to keep us safe."

Velia yanked my hand off her arm. "You're being stupid right now."

"No, I'm not," I whispered. "How many more monsters are you going to invite into our lives before you learn your lesson? I'm tired of you putting us all in danger. Now, you either stay here with me or head out alone, because I'm not going anywhere until I'm good and ready."

"Listen to her, Velia." Delia leaned in and whispered in her twin's right ear. "She's got a point. We can't be too careful."

"Fine. Whatever. But I think you're both overreacting." Velia pushed me out of the way. Delia followed her twin sister into the barn, but not before she gave me an apologetic smile.

"Well, have a nice day," I repeated as I waved at the little goatherd. With Juanita by my side, I looked out to make sure the boy was leaving as I pulled the barn door shut. The disheveled boy waved one last time, looking confused, before he headed up the road. I slammed the latch down to lock us in.

Juanita helped me pick up the clothes from the barn's dirt floor. We shook the old hay off them, folded them up, and put them back in our bags. "You really think he was dangerous?"

"No telling," I said. "But I'm not taking any more chances. From now on, we do things my way."

I waited a full hour, keeping time on my thrift store watch, to make sure we were far enough behind the goatherd to not meet up with him again.

But all my efforts were for naught. As we made our way down the dirt path later that day, he called to us from a cluster of boulders by the side of the road. In a moment of weakness, I decided to let him join us as we continued on our journey. He was nice enough to the girls, offering us water from a different canteen than the one the girls had emptied earlier.

"Why is your goat tied to your wrist?" Pita asked him, as she sidled up to walk beside the boy up ahead of us.

"Oh, do you mean this halter?" Chencho asked. "See that bell on his neck? He's the leader. Wherever he goes, the others follow. But he's a wanderer, and if I don't keep him close, he'll take off on me. Then I'll lose the entire herd. I can't afford that. They're my source of food. So I keep him right here, by my side."

"You mean, you only eat goat meat?" Pita asked, scrunching up her face in disgust.

Chencho threw back his head and laughed. "No. I didn't mean that. I eat lots of things, but goats are my—well, they're my livelihood. They sustain me."

"Oh. But he's so big. Don't you get tired of pulling him along?" Pita asked, as she watched the boy tug at the goat.

"Yeah," Chencho said, laughing. "He's a billy goat. They're stubborn sometimes. But I'm a bigger mule than he is. Have as much water as you like. We can refill it on the way, when we get to *ojito verde*."

The girls had been passing the second canteen around, taking small, careful sips from it. But at his request, they drank greedily.

We walked all afternoon by the goatherd's side. He was quiet and shy, but he seemed to enjoy listening to Pita. She flittered around him like a pesky gnat, glad to have someone eager to listen to everything she had to say as she recounted our adventures on the banks of the Rio Grande.

Every now and then, Chencho would turn around to check on us. At those times, the rest of us smiled and let him know that we were doing okay. No, he wasn't going too fast, and no, we didn't need to stop. We had to get to Hacienda Dorada before day's end.

It wasn't until I saw the sun kissing the horizon that I realized we were in trouble. I looked down at the map anxiously and tried to make sense of it. My wobbly legs were telling me we had traveled far, but in actuality, the landmarks showed that we weren't even halfway there. Going up and down hills on rough terrain was taking a lot longer than I'd anticipated, which meant we still had about seven or eight more miles to go before reaching Abuelita's house.

Looking at the two hills to the left of us, depicted as twin fists almost touching each other on the map, I wanted to cry. The tiny space on the map between the twin fists and Hacienda Dorada told us we were close, but I knew better. Half an inch on paper meant we were not going to make it there before dark.

"We're going to have to stop and find shelter," I said, breaking Pita's joyful stride with my somber words.

"What?" Pita wailed. "But you said . . ."

"It's going to get dark soon," I continued. "And we need to find a nice, safe place to rest."

Juanita tore the map out of my hands and flipped it around looking at it from all angles. "No. We can't stop. We're almost there. It can't be that much farther."

Chencho tugged at the billy goat's rope. "Your sister's right."

"But what about the *chu—*" Pita started.

"Hush!" I said, frowning a warning at her. "We'll look for a cluster of trees or maybe an abandoned cabin. I'm sure we'll find a safe place to rest for the night."

"An abandoned cabin?" Chencho asked, stopping to look back at us. "I know a good place to rest, up in the *cerro*. It's an old sod house from the days of Pancho Villa. Of course, now it only has three walls, but it still has most of the roof. I sleep there all the time. Nobody's ever bothered me there."

"Three walls?" Velia's disbelief showed in her face and I sympathized with her.

Chencho's face suddenly turned red. "Well, it's old, a relic."

"Come on," Pita said, taking Velia's hand and giving it an encouraging tug. "It'll be like camping, only nicer because there's a roof. Well, except that we don't have our sleeping bags. But we can make another nest with our clothes like we did in the barn."

"We don't have any other options, do we?" Juanita asked, and the girls hung their heads, defeated.

I tried thinking of ways to get out of this. After all, we didn't know anything about Chencho. He seemed harmless, but I couldn't shake the feeling that his accommodating manner, his eagerness to help us, was masking something unpleasant, something more sinister in him.

He didn't look like the *chupacabras*. The *chupacabras* was demonic in appearance, not human, so he couldn't possibly be it. But my suspicious mind kept telling me not to trust him too much, to be extra careful around him. We'd already gotten into trouble too many times when we didn't heed Teresita's warnings. Did she say something I'd forgotten that might help us to ward off the *chupacabras*? Whatever he was, whether a demon in disguise or just a simple goatherd, it didn't matter. I vowed to keep my sisters safe from the evil *chupacabras*. I wasn't going to get any sleep that night.

Chencho's place was worse than expected. There were three walls all right; three broken-down sides to what must have been a stone house ravaged during *la Revolución*. The windows were gaping, crumbling holes. The place was infested with sting weeds and scurrying field mice. And to make things worse, spiders and scorpions peeked out at us from under jutting rocks and fallen pieces of roof. It's one thing to step on them or jump out of their way when you're walking by them, but it's a totally different ball game to have to sleep among them.

Velia and Delia went around kicking debris out of the way

with Chencho, who seemed to know exactly where everything was. He pushed aside an array of mesquite branches to reveal the furniture: remnants of a filthy old mattress, two metal stools, and an ancient, rusty pot-bellied stove.

He smiled and jiggled a spotted blue coffee pot. "Who wants coffee?"

"That sounds lovely," Velia said sweetly, sounding like a heroine in one of those historical pieces on the arts channel instead of a modern-day girl stranded in the ruins of the Mexican countryside. Chencho made a fire in the center of the sleeping area, to keep us warm after dark. The twins and I drank the coffee and we all sat among a herd of twelve goats and ate the loaf of bread with goat cheese, swearing it was the best darned cheese we'd tasted in our entire lives.

"It's nice to have company," Chencho said. He leaned back against the third wall, snuggled under his poncho, and smiled proudly at us as we huddled together on the mattress.

A lone coyote howled somewhere in the dark, and we froze momentarily. Several of the goats that had settled around us lifted their heads and listened to the coyote's call. Then, hearing it again, they bleated and inched closer to each other. We inched closer to each other too.

I looked at Chencho and wondered what had brought him here. What could possibly make him think this was a better life than the one he had before? "So tell me, why are you here all by yourself?" I asked.

Chencho's voice was small, quiet, like he was. "It's easier for me, being out here."

I couldn't help but think there were things he wasn't telling us, so I pressed on. "What happened to your parents? Don't you have brothers and sisters? Aunts? Uncles? Someone who could take you in?"

"No," Chencho said. "My mother died when I was seven years old. I'm all alone in the world now. Nobody wants to take care of an orphan and I don't much care for the street life. Sleeping on sidewalks, fighting for trash and scraps, that's no kind of life. I'd rather be out here, raising goats, camping out every night, sleeping under the stars. It's peaceful."

"Don't you get scared out here?" Delia asked Chencho, curling up closer to her twin sister.

Lifting his arm in midair, Chencho flexed his muscles and pointed to his puny right bicep. "There's nothing to worry about," he answered confidently. "Chencho's here."

"What about the *chupacabras*?" Pita asked.

Chencho didn't answer. Instead, he picked up the coffee pot and poured the last of the old coffee into the grass, turning away for a long moment. Finally he turned back to look at us again. "Oh, well, there is that," he said, sounding less sure of himself.

"Have you seen it?" Pita wanted to know. "The demon?"

"Seen him? Yes. We've had our—disagreements," he whispered. "Once or twice, to be sure." His words sent chills up my spine and I had the sudden urge to flee, to take my sisters and make a mad dash for it. But where? There was nowhere to hide from the demon if it were to show up here.

"Did he attack you? What does he look like?" Velia wanted to know.

Chencho threw another log on the fire before us and then looked at the twins sitting beside him. "I'll never forget him," he whispered, sounding more and more morose by the minute. "His eyes are the color of burning coals, and his fangs are bigger and sharper than a javalina's tusks. But his claws are just as dangerous. He can rip out your heart with them."

Pita leaned forward to peer into Chencho's face. "How do you know about his claws?"

"He took my eye," Chencho said, lifting the lock of hair from over his left eye to reveal a deformed eyelid fused together by thick scars.

At the sight of his missing eye, Teresita's husband's voice crept into my head, *"I injured it. Shot it through the left eye. Bullet went right into its head. It howled like a rabid dog. I've never seen anything like it before or since."* Suddenly spooked, I sat up to inspect Chencho's missing eye."The *chupacabras* has a missing eye," I said suspiciously. "A friend of ours shot him."

"That's great!" Chencho said. He put the empty coffee pot aside and sat forward, giving me his undivided attention for the first time since we'd met him. The bloodthirsty look in his right eye told me he was glad to hear the news and wished the *chupacabras* was just as dead as we did, and for that reason I started to believe he was who he appeared be. "I just wish it had been me who shot it. Oh, how I wish he'd disappear for good." Like us, he had reason to fear the *chupacabras*. That was probably why he'd brought us to this miserable place, to keep us safe from the beast.

"Is he really a bloodsucker? Did he try to bite you?" Juanita asked, leaning into our intimate circle from the other side of the campfire.

"He's like a vampire," Chencho said, patting his hair down over his deformed eyelid. "He's bitten my goats and taken several of my kids. He's a thief, a miserable beast, forced to suck on the necks of animals to satisfy his unnatural thirst for blood. Because of his sins against mankind, he will be hunted by humans for all eternity."

Velia's eyebrow rose. "A vampire?" she asked, disbelief edging her words.

Juanita stood up and paced around the fire before she came to sit between me and Chencho. "Well, if he's really a vampire we can kill him," she said.

"Nobody can kill it," Chencho said. "God knows I've tried."

"No, listen," Juanita put her hand on Chencho's shoulder. "We can do this. I read this library book once about vampires and werewolves. It was written by an expert on demons, and I remember everything it said about how to kill a vampire. All you need is holy water and a stake."

"Holy water and stakes?" Chencho looked astonished. "We don't have those things here! Besides, he can't be killed. The *chupacabras* is immortal."

"So were the vampires in that book," Juanita insisted. "I'm

telling you, we can do it. We can get rid of this demon for good."

"We have to at least try," Delia said. Velia and Delia jumped up to join Juanita at the foot of the mattress. "We can't just lie here, waiting for that beast to get us in the middle of the night. Not when we know how to kill him."

I wasn't as convinced that the *chupacabras* could be defeated with stakes and holy water. After all, a *chupacabras* wasn't *exactly* a vampire. But Velia took up where Delia left off, and the girls' confidence grew. "What was it Teresita's husband said? *'Don't be afraid, take the nearest branch and bash its head in!'* Even Teresita herself told us we could defeat it. She said all we had to do was stick together and be brave. Besides, we have you to help us now. That makes six of us. We can take him."

It didn't take long for everyone to jump up and join the twins in their resolution to kill the *chupacabras*. Even Pita, with her newfound courage, was up in arms. My skepticism remained, but to be honest, I figured their enthusiasm would wear out soon enough and they'd all fall asleep eventually. As for me, I would continue to keep vigil throughout the night, hoping, praying that the *chupacabras* wouldn't find us before dawn.

But before I knew it, our entire party was sitting around the campfire like a gang of renegades in an old Western. Chencho was keeping the fire alive by throwing another log in and poking at the base of it, but Juanita and Delia were carving away at branches with two small pocketknives from Velia's tool belt. Velia and Pita were pulling leaves and sprigs off the branches that were still to be made into stakes before piling them neatly next to the whittlers.

Juanita put the knife down and shook a cramp out of it in the semidarkness. "My hand feels like it's going to fall off."

"Here, I'll do it," I said, taking the branch out of her hand. I picked up the knife and sliced off sliver after sliver of wood until the rest of the branches had been whittled into weapons. After we had finished carving out as many stakes as we could, Juanita placed the finished ones strategically along the walls so that everyone had access to them.

It felt weird, preparing for what might happen to us in the night. I felt like we were in a different world, a magical realm, where everything was larger than life. Did I think we could really kill the mythical *chupacabras*? Normally, I would have said not on your life, especially since we weren't even sure if he was a vampire. But my skepticism had mostly worn off, because I figured this was as good a plan as any to protect ourselves. Stakes were weapons, and having weapons was better than being defenseless. Besides, there was something about being in those ruins in the Mexican countryside that made anything possible, because that night I believed in *us—cinco hermanitas, five little sisters, together forever. No matter what.*

We must have stayed up most of the night, putting log after log on that fire, waiting for the *chupacabras*. Velia and Delia huddled together on my left while Pita balled herself into a fetal position on my right. Juanita lay on the other side of the twins with a baby goat in her arms. I don't know exactly when it happened, but despite all their talk and my resolve to stay awake, we all fell asleep before dawn. I was dreaming something bizarre and twisted, but I couldn't wake up.

In my dreams, Pita lifted Chencho's hair and looked into his empty eye socket. I tried to stop her, but she pushed me away. Chencho's face around the missing eye was big and swollen as if it were infected. I smelled something vile and repulsive. And somewhere, far away from me, I heard a girl let out a bloodcurdling scream.

I turned around and around in a foggy, dreamlike state, looking for the source of that scream, but only darkness surrounded me. I was lost in the woods and I couldn't find Pita or Chencho anymore, but I could smell his putrid eye socket.

I ran, bleary-eyed and blind, searching the night for my absent sister and the boy with the missing eye, but I couldn't find them. They were lost to me. Then, suddenly, I wasn't dreaming anymore and Pita wasn't so far away but right beside me—screaming her lungs out.

I peered into the darkness and saw a red eyeball glowering at me. It was the *chupacabras*, clutching and sucking on Pita's right leg—right there, in front of me!

"Get away from her!" I yelled, flapping my arms, but the horrendous thing quivered with rage. The long, sharp quills running along its back stood straight up and it expanded its shoulders menacingly. Then it lifted its head, opened its bloody mouth, and hissed at me. Its breath was so potent, so toxic, and it swirled up my nose to make me gag. Pita screamed again. She squirmed and gripped my arm, trying to kick the disgusting thing away.

"Chencho!" I screamed for help, but as I looked around, I saw that he was gone. "He left us! Juanita! Delia! Get up!"

Beside me, the girls lifted their heads. They were groggy and confused, so I didn't wait for their help. I reached behind me, grabbed the nearest stake, and stabbed at the *chupacabras*. The spiked branch barely brushed over the long spinal quills quivering along his arched back, and in my haste I let go of the stake. The *chupacabras* let out a deep threatening growl before he bit down into Pita's leg again with his razor-sharp fangs.

Pita bawled in agony and clung to my arm. I reached for another stake. This time, I didn't drop it. This time I stood up and stabbed at his face with all my might. The stake went into his right eye, piercing through his glowering red eyeball. But I didn't stop there. As the *chupacabras* let go of Pita's leg, I shoved the stake deeper into his skull with the full weight of my body behind it. Wielding their makeshift weapons, Velia, Delia, and Juanita surrounded the *chupacabras*.

The beast grasped the stake, pulled it out of his eye socket, and cried out, a wounded, demented howl that raised the hair on the back of my neck. Seeing the glowing eyeball gutted out and spiked on a stake made the girls back away in disgust. Even I was horrified by my gory accomplishment.

Sitting up on his hind legs, the beast howled and threw the stake aside. His eye socket was gushing, and he clawed at it frantically. He shook his head and shrieked and clawed and hissed, but he was blind, so he couldn't see us.

Keeping another stake aimed at the *chupacabras*, I leaned down and inspected Pita's leg. The bite didn't look too bad. She had three bloody puncture marks above her right ankle, but there didn't appear to be any missing flesh. "Are you okay?" I asked, and she nodded.

"Be careful. He might be blind, but he's still dangerous," I told the girls.

They closed in around him again. Velia jabbed at him first, stabbing him in the back.

"Kill it!" Pita screamed from behind me. "Don't let him get away."

"*Por favor, señoritas*, don't kill me," the *chupacabras* cried out in a thick, animalistic voice. "Please, please, don't kill me."

"He can talk?" Velia asked, looking at me for answers. She didn't back down from her fighting stance.

I shook my head, confused. The pathetic creature knelt before us, quivering as he pressed his paw against his wound. I jabbed at his side with a sharp stake. "Who are you?" I demanded.

Juanita stabbed sharply at his arm with her stake. "What are you?"

"Please," the *chupacabras* said between sobs. "Please don't hurt me. I am Chencho, the boy who helped you. I am your friend."

"Chencho?" I asked. The beast shook as he transformed himself back and forth between his goatherd self and the grotesque form of the fiendish *chupacabras*. "Is that you?"

"Yes. It is me. Chencho," the semidemonic boy said. He rocked himself side to side trying to control his form, which was weakened one minute and strengthened the next, constantly shifting between beast and boy. "I beg you not to hurt me. It is not my fault. I am not myself tonight. Please, let me go. I promise. I won't hurt you again. I promise."

"Who did this to you?" I asked, poking him in the chest with the sharp tip of my stake.

"I don't know. I don't know," the *chupacabras* whined.

"What do you mean you don't know?" Juanita asked, poking him in the back. "How did this happen to you? Is it some kind of spell? Can it be undone? Tell us, maybe we can help you."

"Nobody did this to me," the *chupacabras* said, his voice low and pained. "This is just what I am, what I have always been. I try to control it, but sometimes the beast inside me takes over and I am overcome by the need to feed."

"Well, you weren't trying very hard tonight," Pita said. She pushed herself back with her good leg, scooting as far away from the *chupacabras* as she could get. I reached down to help her.

When she was sitting at a safer distance, I came back to the *chupacabras* and started circling him while my sisters kept their stakes at his throat and back. Taking a good look at the quills on his back, I ran my stake along them to test their sturdiness. The action made the *chupacabras* arch his back like a cat and he hissed again. "You lied to us," I said. "You told us you were an orphan. That your mother died."

"I didn't lie about that," the *chupacabras* said. He turned his head sideways, following the sound of my traveling voice. "My mother was like me, the only other one of our kind I knew. We used to live in the jungle, in a cave high up in the Sierra Madre, happily minding our own business, until a group of hunters tracked us down. They set a trap for her. The metal gear almost cut off her leg. I stayed with her until the last breath left her body. I wanted to go after them, to kill them, but she made me promise that I would leave the jungle. She wanted me to try to live a normal life, to control my beast and behave like a normal boy. But as you can see, that is easier said than done. "

"So you're some kind of wild animal?" I asked. "Why didn't the hunters come after you? Why didn't they kill you?"

Chencho shook his head and cried. His whole body trembled as he spoke and his quills quivered with his sobs. "I don't know. They didn't see me. I left before they came back for her," Chencho said, crying and covering his face with his hands. "Please, please, let me go."

Velia pushed a stake at the *chupacabras*'s throat menacingly. "What should we do with him?"

I put a hand on Velia's shoulder to stop her from doing something drastic. "We can't kill him," I said. "We're not murderers."

"We have to do something though," Delia said. "He's still dangerous."

"Please, please, let me go," Chencho begged as he crouched on the ground before us. "I am blind. I cannot see you, so I can't hurt you anymore."

"He attacked Pita. We have to kill him," Juanita said, lifting her stake high in the air, ready to deliver the final blow.

"No," I said, resolutely. "He can't hurt us anymore. Let him go."

"But—" Velia began.

"—we can't," Delia finished her sister's protest.

"Let him go!" I said, more firmly than before. "Look at him. He's just a little boy. Wounded and blind. The *virgen* wouldn't approve. We have to let him go."

"What about what he did to Pita? Doesn't that count?" Juanita wanted to know.

Remembering La Llorona's warning, I firmed up my resolve. I wanted revenge just as much as my sisters did, but my blood was cooling now, and I knew we needed to do what was right. "If he comes back, we won't have a choice, we'd have to kill him then, like the *lechuzas*. But for now, we have to let him go." I looked around, making eye contact with every one of my sisters.

Velia and Delia were shaking their heads in disagreement, but Juanita straightened her shoulders and lifted her weapon away from the beast. "Odilia is right. We're the Garza girls, *cinco hermanitas*, five little sisters under the protection of the goddess," she said, holding the stake in front of her with both hands and anchoring the sharp point of it on the ground.

"That's right," I said. I looked down at Pita, who was clutching her ankle, wincing. "Remember what I told you? La Llorona said we must remain noble and kind. We should grant mercy when it is asked of us. Besides, we're armed and dangerous. He knows not to mess with us anymore."

"Gracias, señoritas," the *chupacabras* said, looking more like Chencho the goatherd than the demon. *"Gracias."*

"Go!" I yelled, and without hesitation the *chupacabras* jumped up and ran off. We stood, side by side, four little sisters, holding our weapons at our sides ready to defend our baby sister as we watched him disappear into a new dawn.

15

La Dama: *"Una dama es dama en el vestíbulo y en el campamento."*

The Lady: "A lady is a lady in the vestibule as well as the campsite."

Things changed after our encounter with the *chupacabras.* Suddenly, my sisters and I became more focused. I used the water from Chencho's abandoned canteen to clean Pita's wound. I could see by the light of the campfire that her leg was obviously getting infected. The *chupacabras*'s *mordida* had left three ugly lacerations two inches above her ankle, on the outside of her leg, so both her ankle and calf were swollen to twice their normal size. I did my best to keep it clean by wrapping it in one of Pita's short-sleeved shirts.

Velia, Delia, and Juanita were too worried to sit around watching me treat Pita's wounds. Instead, they scurried around like little sugar ants, busy *hormiguitas*, gathering the materials to create a sturdy device in which to carry our wounded sister, because her leg hurt so much that she couldn't walk.

I was surprised at how helpful and cooperative everyone was with each other. Even the twins were being polite. I didn't mention how nice it was to see them working together or praise them in any way, for fear of breaking the spell. But I was proud of them nonetheless.

By sunrise, the girls had built a stretcher by tying old pieces of wood and broken branches with torn strips of cloth from a pair of Juanita's old shorts. It wasn't pretty, but it was strong enough to hold Pita.

Velia and Delia picked up the stretcher from the front, while Juanita and I took the back. With Pita gratefully resting on the makeshift gurney, we continued our journey toward Hacienda Dorada.

We traveled slowly, stopping often to rest because our arms were not used to carrying so much weight for so long. By the middle of the afternoon, we stopped by an *ojito*, a spring bubbling out of a rock wall, and drank water straight out of the spouting hole. Our sleep-deprived night could be seen in the circles under our eyes, and our stomachs rumbled with hunger, but we felt for the first time that our ordeal might soon be over.

"It won't be far," I said as I stood rubbing the pain out of my wrists.

"How much longer, do you think?" Juanita asked, looking at the map. "Because it looks like we should be right on it."

"Just over that big hill." I checked on Pita's leg. Carefully, I peeled back the dressing and saw that, although the wound wasn't oozing, her entire calf was purple now. Pita seemed to be in too much pain to talk, because she wasn't complaining anymore. Instead, she drifted in and out of sleep for the last leg of our trip. Her lethargy worried me, so I took her temperature with a thermometer in the twin's toolkit.

I was so afraid of Pita losing her leg, I considered using La Llorona's gift. I was sure its magical properties could do the job well, but I also worried about misusing the amulet's last gift when I knew that in less than an hour, in the time it would take to walk the last few miles of our journey, Abuelita would be able to take care of her.

Our grandmother was, after all, a *curandera*. She knew how to use natural herbs to cure almost anything. The memory of her treating a farmer's ulcerated arm the last time we visited her was still fresh in my mind, so I decided to wait and see what she could do for Pita's leg. The ear pendant would still be there if I needed to use it later.

"She's running a fever," I said. Juanita shook her head in dismay. Velia and Delia cursed under their breaths and knelt beside Pita. Delia touched her face and forehead and asked her if she wanted some of the water they'd been saving just for her.

"No," Pita whispered weakly. "I'll be all right. Let's just keep going."

"You heard her. Let's go," I said. Pita closed her eyes to the sun and rolled her head to the side as if she didn't care what we did.

We lifted the stretcher and started walking again. Up the hill we went, on and on, until our arms and legs hurt so much that we kept losing our footing. We walked so far and for so long, we almost dropped Pita a couple of times before we reached the crest of the *cerro*.

I knew it the minute I saw it from the top of the hill. The girls didn't recognize Hacienda Dorada, but I did. "Pita, we're here. You're going to be okay, *mamita*," I said as we stood staring down at our destination.

Pita lifted her head long enough to look down the *cerro*. "Oh, thank God," she whispered before she lay back down and closed her eyes again.

Exhilarated by the sight of our paternal grandmother's home, we walked hurriedly down the hill toward the pink stucco building within the corral-like fence, being careful not to jostle Pita too much in the stretcher. The lilac jacaranda tree by the gate, leaning backward over the fence as if the wind had made it laugh, was exactly as I remembered it. The abundant crepe myrtles and pink bougainvilleas that dotted the courtyard were also as beautiful and lively as I recalled.

"Look at all those flowers," Pita said, looking at Hacienda Dorada as if she'd never seen anything more exquisite in her life. She probably didn't remember playing there among the flowers the last time Papá brought us to see his mother so long ago.

"Forget the flowers," Velia whispered. "Have you ever seen so many *mariposas*?"

As we got close enough to see the multicolored array of butterflies flittering in the courtyard of our grandmother's house, Juanita answered, "Not so many different kinds in one place." The girls kept marveling at the sight as we neared the gate.

"Forget the butterflies," I said, interrupting their rapture. "Let's find Abuelita. Pita's leg isn't going to cure itself. How are you doing?" I looked down at Pita's face as we moved along. She was so flushed, I just knew she was getting worse.

"Fine," Pita closed her eyes and sighed. She was trying to be brave, but I could tell she was still in pain. "I'll be all right once we get inside."

"Hold on," I said. Velia and Delia banged on the gate with a stick and called out for help.

It didn't take long for someone to notice us. Looking up from their chores, two men dropped their garden tools and hurried over to open the gate for us.

"What is the matter? *¿Qué pasó?*" they asked.

"We are here to see Remedios Garza," I said, still holding on to the stretcher. "We're her granddaughters."

"From *los Estados Unidos*?" the first man asked. He took the front of the stretcher and the other man took the back.

"Yes, from the United States," I confirmed as I relinquished my end of the stretcher gratefully.

The younger of the two men hoisted the stretcher and began walking backward toward the main house. "Oh, what a great surprise," he exclaimed. "Your *abuela* will be very happy to see you, but she will not be happy that one of you is hurt."

The older man walked forward holding his end of the stretcher before him. "This way. Follow us, please."

Abuelita Remedios looked exactly as I remembered her. Her white-streaked hair was perfectly coiffed into a bun, and her blue eyes were sharp and fierce, centered over a long aquiline nose. Yet her mouth was wide and generous as she turned around and smiled at us.

"Dios Santísimo," Abuela Remedios crossed herself and kissed her thumb before she reached out for us, welcoming us. "Is that really you? *¿Mis niñas? ¿Mis nietecitas?"* she asked happily.

"It is us," I said, stepping forward to receive a hug. "We're all grown up now, Abuelita."

"*Sí.* I would say so! *Mira, pero* what has happened to you?" Abuela Remedios asked as she took hold of Pita's head in her hands and looked at her flushed face. "Arturo! Roberto! Take her inside, to the *sala rosada.* Quickly now! She has a fever!"

The two men, who looked too alike not to be related, hurried ahead of us. "Come in, come in," Abuelita said as we entered the house behind the men and followed them into a pink receiving room. "Have a seat. You look like the *zopilotes*, those nasty good-for-nothing vultures, beat you up and plucked every feather off your pretty wings."

Once inside, Arturo, the younger man, picked up Pita's limp body and transferred her over onto a cushioned wooden bench. Abuelita Remedios put one arm around me and another one around Juanita and gave all of us a group hug.

"We're okay," I told Abuelita. "It's Pita we're worried about."

"What happened to her?" she asked, inspecting Pita's leg as our sister lay with her eyes closed on the rustic bench.

"Something bit her," I said, not sure how much to disclose—not because I didn't trust Abuelita, but because I wasn't sure she'd believe me.

Abuelita's eyebrows furrowed with worry. "But this is not an ordinary dog bite." She knelt at Pita's leg to examine it closely.

"It wasn't a dog," I said, fighting the urge to go ahead and tell her what really happened. Having Abuelita think I was crazy would only complicate matters. "But it's infected," I continued, trying to provide a little more information without sounding like a lunatic.

"I can see that," Abuelita Remedios whispered. She turned Pita's leg sideways to get a better look.

Pita took in a sharp breath at Abuelita's touch. It looked like her leg was painful to move at this point. "It happened late last night," she said, wincing.

"It's not a snake bite either, is it, Roberto?" Abuelita declared, as she showed Pita's ankle to the older of the two men. "See here? Three puncture wounds."

Roberto crossed himself, horrified at the sight of Pita's leg. "*¡El chupacabras!*" Looking back at us, he asked, "Did you see the thing that bit her?"

"Yes," I said. My voice cracked as I tried my best not to cry, because for the first time on the trip I was worried about one of us not making it back to Mamá.

"It *was* the *chupacabras*," Velia exclaimed. "But he didn't get away with it. We took care of him."

"What do you mean?" Arturo asked, his dark brown eyes penetrating as he looked at me for answers. "You saw it?"

"Saw it? We did more than that. We blinded him. He won't be attacking anyone anymore," Delia said, sounding quite proud of herself.

"You did?" Roberto asked. "That's incredible."

"Odilia did it," Juanita said, looking at me with an appreciative gleam in her eyes. "She's fearless." She would have proceeded to recount the whole thing if I hadn't interrupted.

"Well, at least he's not likely to hurt anyone else. Not without his other eye," I said, trying to play the whole thing down a bit. Not only did I not like being the center of attention—that's a job better suited for the twins—but I also felt bad for inflicting pain on Chencho, even though I had been suspicious of him. But more importantly, I still worried about what he did to Pita. We didn't have time for stories right now.

"Unfortunately, the damage has already been done," Abuelita said as she checked Pita's pulse. "We have to treat her immediately. Arturo, get me my *bulto*, my medicine bag. It's in the hallway, in the broom closet, up high. Hurry! We don't have much time." Abuelita Remedios waved to the younger man, who ran out of the room in a fright.

"You mean she's going to turn into one of those demons?" Velia asked, her voice high like a scared little girl.

"No, of course not," Abuelita said, turning around and patting Velia's hands to reassure her. "That's not possible, not when you're dealing with the *chupacabras*. His bite is very dangerous, but he's not contagious. What I mean is that his saliva is tainted. It has contaminated her blood. She's fighting the infection, but she's so young, it's hard to tell how much damage it has done."

"I knew it," Delia said, tearing up at the terrible thought. "I knew it. We should have killed that rotten little mongrel."

I don't know what I'd envisioned, but Abuelita Remedios's medicine bag was nothing like what I remembered. The "*bulto*" was just that, a bulky remnant of thick, white cloth tied together at the top in a vagabond's knot. And when she opened it, I wasn't as surprised as I was curious. Inside, she had all manner of herbs, seeds, sprigs, and plant roots. The contents of Abuelita's *bulto* looked like it may have belonged to El Niño Fidencio, the famous *curandero* of olden times, and I watched in awe as she sorted the ingredients for Pita's treatment.

"Shouldn't we send for a doctor?" Juanita asked, eyeing the medicine bag suspiciously. "She needs antibiotics."

"What do you think these are?" Abuelita Remedios took her *bulto* to the coffee table and started to grind dried leaves and sprigs together in a miniature white mortar with a tiny white pestle.

"Herbs." I explained to Juanita. "Like the ones pharmaceutical companies use to make medicines in the United States."

"*Sí*," Abuelita Remedios said. "But regular medicines are useless when it comes to treating a wound like this. A bite from the *chupacabras* is ten times deadlier than any viper's. These, however, are the finest herbs in all of Mexico. People from all over the country come to my garden to harvest these medicines." Abuelita picked up a desiccated brown sprig between her fingertips. "This one is for the pain. This one is an anti-inflammatory, and this"—she said proudly, as she picked up a tiny blue glass bottle and shook it in my direction—"this is stronger than any anti-venom in the world. It is my secret potion, the power and the glory of potions, made from the blood of the lamb and *agua bendita*, sacred water from Texcoco Lake."

We watched in awe as Abuelita Remedios lanced, compressed, and flushed Pita's wounds one at a time before applying her concoction liberally to each laceration. Because she was heavily sedated, Pita slept through the lancing and compressing and didn't come back around until Abuelita Remedios was done wrapping her leg with a pale thin gauze.

"Am I going to die?" Pita asked when she regained consciousness.

I caressed her forehead and pushed her hair out of her face. "No. Of course not. You're going to be just fine. You just need to rest. Okay, *mamita?*"

"That is a fact," Abuelita Remedios said, feeling Pita's forehead and pinching her cheek affectionately. "You and your sisters all need to rest. You'll stay here with me for as long it takes you to get your strength back. It will give us an opportunity to get to know each other again. I'll call your mother and let her know you're okay. She will be glad to hear from us."

"We don't have a phone. I mean, it's been disconnected, so there's no way to reach her," I whispered. I hated myself for lying to my own grandmother, but I silently promised the *virgen* I would come clean soon. I just had to sit down with Abuelita tomorrow and explain why we couldn't afford to call the café and let Mamá know where we were yet. If Mamá tried to leave the country to come get us, she could get in trouble with the police, and that's something I couldn't live with. I hoped Abuelita would understand.

"Well, that's the least of our worries. We'll find a way to get in touch with her when the time comes." Abuelita waved her hand as if to dismiss the issue. "For now, I think we need to let your sister rest. Come. Let us go to the kitchen and get you all fed. You look like scarecrows who've lost their stuffing."

Because we hadn't eaten since the night before, sharing the cheese and loaf of bread with the *chupacabras*, we ate everything Abuelita Remedios put in front of us that afternoon. First, she brought out plates of spicy tamales and *borracho* beans, and when that was gone, she brought down a fruit basket. There were ripe, sweet figs and fleshy pears and a fragrant papaya that Abuelita sliced through and splayed out for us on a serving tray. We drank the most delectable *agua de tamarindo*, sweet-tart juice made from tamarind, and ate and ate and ate.

After dinner, Arturo pulled bucket after bucket of water out of the well in the courtyard to fill up the enormous bathing trough in the laundry room. While we bathed, Abuelita looked in on Pita and informed us that her fever was going down.

After our baths, we sat, all five of us, on an enormous carpet around Abuelita's bed telling her the tales of our adventures along the bank of the Rio Grande. She laughed at our jokes and teased us when we couldn't comb through the knots in our ratted hair. But she was kind and generous and braided our hair for us before we went to bed.

Eating, sleeping, bathing, laughing, talking, helping, and tending to Pita's every need, that is how we spent the next few days at Abuelita's house. In the mornings, Juanita and the twins helped Abuelita with the feeding of the animals. But when they went back in the house to take care of the household chores, I helped Abuelita in the herb garden. We watered the delicate plants and pulled weeds and Abuelita named each plant as we went along, telling me what they were good for: *yerbabuena* for a belly ache, *manzanilla* to soothe the nerves, and *milenrama* to heal wounds or stop hemorrhages. She described different features of each plant and explained the best way to remember them.

In the afternoons, however, we sat in the courtyard while Pita lay out in the sun on a wrought-iron bench, recuperating among the myriad of colorful *mariposas* that abounded in that heavenly place.

By the end of the week, Pita got up and hobbled about the courtyard of Hacienda Dorada, clapping and laughing at the girls as they chased *mariposas* around the wide, robust bougainvilleas. Abuelita Remedios walked over and took a good look at Pita's sparkly eyes and pink cheeks. She touched her forehead and a small smile made her thin lips curl up at the edges. *"Bueno,"* she said. "I think you're well enough to go home now. Girls, we leave at dawn."

As we sat cross-legged on the rectangular carpet in her bedroom the evening of the fifth day, Abuelita proclaimed, "It's time you got back to your Mamá, but before you do, we have to talk."

"Yes!" Juanita exclaimed. "There's so much more we want to know, so much you haven't told us yet."

"Like what?" Abuelita asked, pinning Juanita's long thick braid to the back of her head in a circular pattern.

Pita looked at Abuelita with adoration. "What was Papá like when he was our age?"

Her question startled me. We'd been so focused on our little sister's recovery that we hadn't given Papá a single thought since our arrival. The realization baffled me, since that had been primary on our minds when we left—the be-all and end-all of our journey, the reason for leaving Mamá's side.

"Your father hasn't changed," Abuelita Remedios said, pausing to look at us with much sadness. "As a child, he was exactly as he is today."

A long moment of silence followed. "We haven't seen him in

a while," I said. "He's been gone for a long time."

"I know," Abuelita whispered. "He left about this time last year."

As far as I could tell, none of us had divulged that bit of information yet. "How do you know that?" I asked in surprise. "Who told you?"

"He did," Abuelita Remedios whispered, her brows furrowed worriedly over her eyes. "He told me he'd left the last time I saw him. I urged him to reconsider, but he said it was already done."

My chest suddenly felt tight and constricted. I pressed my hand against it and let out a long-held deep breath. "So he's been here?" I asked, choking back the tears of relief and something else, something deeply rooted, something wounded and mad. "Well, at least we know he's alive. We haven't heard from him in so long, I was beginning to wonder."

"You were?" Juanita asked. "You never told me that."

I covered my face for a moment to stop the tears from coming, and when I uncovered it, Abuelita was leaning forward, looking into my eyes. She took my hands, kissed my knuckles, and then squeezed my fingers tightly between hers. "Oh yes. He's alive," she said, nodding. "At least he was a few months ago."

"A few months ago?" I asked, the anger within me growing as it devoured the hurt and the pain the knowledge was causing.

"Did he tell you why he left?" Juanita asked, her eyes narrowing intently.

"He did," Abuelita said. "But that is not for me to discuss. That is for your parents to explain."

"But why?" Pita whined. "Why can't you tell us? We told you everything. We even told you about the dead man's body and about La Llorona and the *nagual*. Why can't you tell us what's going on with Papá?" Pita started to sob softly.

"*Ay, mi niña*. Please don't cry," Abuelita Remedios said, wiping a runaway tear off Pita's cheek with her right thumb. "Listen. I'm not trying to keep secrets from you, and I'm glad you've been so honest with me. I needed to know those things. So I *am* going to tell you one thing. Your Papá left because he is selfish. It's our fault really, mine and your *abuelito* Reynaldo's, God rest his soul. You see, we spoiled him. We made him think that because he was so talented, because he could sing so well, he was more important than everyone else in the world, and for that, I am deeply sorry."

"You spoiled him?" Juanita asked, confused.

"And yet, he never spoiled us," Velia said.

Juanita reached over and smacked Velia's arm. "Yes, he did. He spoiled us all the time."

"When?" Delia asked indignantly.

"I don't remember that," Velia agreed.

"Spoken like a couple of spoiled brats," Juanita said, giving them the evil eye. "When we were younger, he wasn't performing, so he had a regular job in Houston and used to come home on weekends with his arms loaded with presents. It was like Christmas in April, or July, or August, or whatever month it happened to be. He always brought us presents when he came home."

"I remember!" Delia exclaimed. "He brought us dolls and

board games, and those little plastic jewelry sets with the giant rings and matching tiaras. Don't you remember, Velia? He even brought you a special present once because you saw a game on TV and called him begging for a basketball."

"Oh yeah, the basketball incident. You all hated me for that," Velia said, twisting her face with the effort of recollection.

"We had so many toys, we didn't even play with most of them," Juanita said, remembering how good life used to be before Papá stopped coming home regularly and only showed up every now and then.

"And now we have to make our own bracelets out of used aluminum cans. Way to go Papá!" Velia drew her knees up to her chin and stared off into space, pouting.

"I like *our* bracelets better. Besides, I'm not so sure Papá was spoiling us. I think he felt guilty, for being gone so much," I said. The picture of Mamá crying on the television because of us came to my mind, and my throat tightened. "And there are worse things than not having him around anymore."

"Like not knowing where your daughters are?" Abuelita asked as if she'd read my mind. "Or if you'll ever see them again?"

Velia sat up on her knees to face us. "I'm sorry, but am I the only one who thinks maybe Mamá deserves it a little? I mean, think about it. After Papá left us, Mamá literally stopped taking care of us. She didn't listen to us anymore. She didn't even know where we were half the time."

"Velia!" I exclaimed. "Nobody deserves this." I thought of what terrible daughters we'd been, how the cries of the *lechuzas* were not far off. We'd been bad too, and Mamá still loved us.

"I think Velia has a point." Delia intervened in a strangled voice. "The truth is Mamá was just as bad as Papá, *muy descuidada*, very neglectful of us."

"That's not fair!" Abuelita Remedios exclaimed. "I know your Mamá. She's a decent woman, with good morals and values. She's always been a good mother and wife. I want you to understand one thing. Your mother didn't do anything wrong. Your father left because he's a louse, a good-for-nothing who cares more about himself than his own wife and daughters. He's up to no good. Otherwise, why would he be trying to divorce your mamá?"

"Divorce Mamá?" Juanita asked, her eyes wide with sudden understanding.

I left the floor and sat up on the bed next to Abuelita. "Did he tell you why?" I asked turning my full attention to her.

Abuelita looked disgusted. "He wants to reinvent himself! He says he wants a new life. It's a common story. You hear it all the time around these parts: men go work up North, and after a while, they forget their families because they've started a new life *en los Estados Unidos*. But I never thought my own son would do this. Not to your mamá. Not to Rosalinda."

"He can't do that," Pita said, choking on her words as she wiped the tears from her eyes.

"I'm afraid he's already filed the papers. I probably shouldn't have told you, but you all are *señoritas* now. I think you can handle it," Abuelita Remedios said.

Juanita blinked, fighting back her tears as she looked up at us. "There's no hope, then. He's gone for good?" she asked. "Why didn't Mamá just tell us what was going on? Did she think we were never going to find out? How long did she think she could keep this a secret?"

Abuelita patted the mattress beside her, signaling my sisters to join us on her bed. She scooted back to let us all snuggle up to her. "I'm sure she thought she was protecting you," Abuelita explained, putting her arms around us as far as she could.

"Things are never going to get better, are they?" Juanita asked. "Mamá's never going to get over this. And there's nothing we can do to change it. Not if he's never coming back."

Abuelita pulled Juanita into her arms and held her tight. "Oh, that's not true. Eventually, your Mamá will get over him."

"But I always hoped that he would . . ." Velia trailed off.

"—come back and make things better," Delia mumbled, finishing Velia's thought.

Both girls looked absolutely crushed. Papá's slow, painful abandonment had wounded us deeply at first, but we had managed to get beyond it by telling ourselves we were free spirits and nothing could ever destroy us. However, looking around the room, I could see that wasn't the case at all. Apparently, I wasn't the only one who had never given up on him, because we were all openly crying now.

"Well, I can only pray he reconsiders," Abuelita Remedios said, looking at us like we were her own daughters. "Lord knows I tried talking some sense into him."

"But he hasn't done it yet, has he? He hasn't divorced her?" I asked, wondering how Mamá was able to keep her sanity with everything that was going on with us. How awful we had been to her!

"There is that," Abuelita said, reaching out to caress our faces one by one, listening to our unhappy sighs.

"Ay, *pobrecita* Mamá!" Juanita wailed, giving in to her tears. "What she must be going through."

Velia's eyes were suddenly full of rage. "Papá can be such a jerk!"

"I'm ashamed of being his daughter," Delia added.

"We have to get back to Mamá," Juanita whispered, looking to the rest of us for support. "Mamá is in a lot of pain right now. She needs to hear that we still love her. Think about it. When was the last time you reached out to her?"

"Well, it's hard to get close to her when all she does is yell at us or go to her room and cry," Velia said defensively.

"Well, hello? She's been abandoned!" I pointed out emphatically. "And what did we do to make things better for her? Were we concerned? Did we make things easier for her? No. We abandoned her too. We stole Papá's car and took off. No note. No phone call. No explanation." I paused, wondering if I should voice my previous thoughts aloud, then charged ahead. "Maybe . . . maybe Cecilia and the *lechuzas* were right about us. Maybe we are wicked children."

"We are. We took advantage of her state of mind," Juanita

concluded, biting her lip nervously.

"We stopped doing our chores and ran wild and did whatever we wanted when we should have been taking care of her," I pointed out with disgust.

"We should go home and ask her to forgive us," Velia whispered, hanging her head.

"For being as selfish as Papá," Delia finished her twin's thought.

"We should take her some flowers or something," Pita said, looking at Abuelita Remedios for approval. Her face was scrunched with wretchedness.

"Yes, we have to go home and find a way of making things right for Mamá," Delia concluded.

Delia wiped away her tears roughly with the back of her hand. "I think it *was* actually all our fault," she declared. "Papá left because we're *pesadas*, too much to handle. He left because we didn't listen to him half the time and we're always getting in trouble with Mamá. And, well, I think he was just sick of hearing about it."

Pita used the bottom of her shirt to wipe at her eyes. "You mean he doesn't love us anymore?" Pita asked.

"Would you? If you had *us* for daughters?" Delia asked Pita, looking at her sister resentfully.

That's when I realized the evil of what the *lechuzas* said about us. We had been bad, yes, but was what Papá did our fault? "Yes, I would still love us," I said, angry with myself for not realizing the twins had been blaming themselves for Papá's absence all this time. "The way I see it, we didn't fail Papá, he failed us. He's the adult here."

Abuelita reached into her pocket and handed Pita a handkerchief. Pita took it and blew her nose into it indelicately. "Now, you listen to me, *muchachitas*!" Abuelita Remedios's eyes darkened with emotion. "The truth is, adults don't always make sense. They don't always do what's right. Sometimes, they are like children themselves, doing whatever they want. *Cada cabeza es un mundo,* they have a mind of their own. Do you understand?"

"I think so," Velia whispered, nodding her head.

"Sometimes, men leave, for whatever reason," Abuelita continued. "Nothing you did or could have done differently would have changed that. So I want you to stop blaming yourselves or your Mamá for the choices your father has made. Instead, I want you to continue taking care of each other the way you've been doing so far. I'm so proud of you for standing up for your *hermanitas* against those evil creatures. I'm sure having to do that has taught you how important it is to stick together and love one another more than anything else in the world."

With those words, Abuelita Remedios gathered us closer around her. We went into her arms and let her hold us. She held us tight and said, "What's done is done. The best thing you can do is go home and let your Mamá know you're all right. You're all she cares about right now."

PART III

THE RETURN

How my sisters and I were trapped in Mexico, but with the aid of the ear pendant, we were transported across the border and were taken home by the FBI. How we encountered, rejected, and sent Papá away. And how we eventually gained happiness with Mamá.

16

El Nopal: *"Ay, qué nopal tan regio,*

coronado con tunas moradas."

The Cactus: "Oh, what a regal cactus,

crowned with purple prickly pears."

Shortly after breakfast the next morning, we stuffed our belongings into our backpacks and headed home. Abuelita Remedios was sitting at the table drinking coffee when we went into the kitchen. Sitting next to her hand, on the table, was a small pile of tiny homemade envelopes. She took them and placed them in my hand when I sat next to her. "Something to get you started," she said, closing my hand over them.

"What are they?" I took the sealed rectangles and turned them over to read the hand-printed labels.

"*Semillitas*—from my garden to yours," Abuelita said.

I looked through the assortment of seed packets she had put together for me and almost burst into tears. "I'm going to miss you, Abuelita Remedios."

"Me too," my grandmother said, pulling me close for a hug.

"I'm going to miss you too," Delia chimed in.

Abuelita let me go long enough to hug Delia. I put the seed packets in the left pocket of my shorts and wiped my eyes. "I wish we could have stayed longer."

Our grandmother pulled a handkerchief out of her dress pocket and dabbed at her eyes. "I know. Me too."

"Don't be sad, Abuelita." Pita squeezed in with us and put her arms around our grandmother's neck. "We love you. You're the bestest grandma ever. You are, Abuelita. That's why we love you so much."

Velia let out a disgusted groan and rolled her eyes. She looked down at Pita, and declared, "You're such a kiss-up!"

Abuelita smiled. "Oh, I know you love me, Pita, just like I know you love your mother. That's why it's important you get back there. She is going through a very difficult time right now; she needs you as much as you need her." She patted our cheeks, kissed our foreheads, and caressed our hair before she continued. "Besides, now that you know where I live, you can start visiting me more often—only maybe you can drive with your Mamá next time. You and your Mamá are welcome to come stay with me whenever you want, for as long as you want, especially at Christmas time."

"Oh yes! We'll bring presents, and eat tamales, and stay up every night," exclaimed Pita, not at all sounding like a kiss-up, but like her true generous self, the Pita that Mamá knows and loves and babies more than the rest of us.

“That sounds like a plan,” Abuelita Remedios said, hugging each of us in turn again. “We’ll do that then. Every Christmas. Every holiday. But especially in the summertime.”

I hated to break up this moment, but it was getting late. “We should get going,” I whispered.

Immediately after breakfast, Abuelita drove us in an old four-door ranch truck. She hadn’t driven in almost ten years, she said. Mostly, she kept the vehicle for emergencies. Everything that needed to be driven to and from the hacienda was taken care of by either Roberto or his son, Arturo, who loved to go into town. But today she’d decided to drive us to the border herself because there was only room in the pickup for six people. Her driving was a little rusty, which made for an interesting ride. Sometimes she’d veer out of her lane for a second or slow down so much, she’d be driving way below the speed limit. But all in all, I felt confident in her ability to get us to the *Frontera* safely.

During the ride, the girls were somber, almost distant, but Abuelita Remedios was full of spunk. She talked all the way up Highway 57, giving us advice about how to handle questions we might encounter about our adventures in Mexico. She didn’t believe in lying—was against it in fact—but she also didn’t feel we should go around telling people things that would make them think we were fibbing.

“Nowadays, people are too cynical and don’t believe in magic anymore,” Abuelita Remedios said as she drove us down the road.

"Best to keep all those supernatural experiences to yourselves. No use trying to convince people of things they can't understand, much less believe."

It was good advice, and we all agreed Mamá would be the only one who would ever believe us. Because to be honest, if I hadn't lived it myself, I wouldn't have believed it either.

Halfway up to the border, Abuelita stopped to buy us new outfits before we drove on. She said she didn't want Mamá to see us dressed like *limosneras* and think we'd taken to begging for food in the streets during our stay in Mexico. We slipped into our new clothes in the dressing room of a quiet little dress shop on the outskirts of Monclova. Pita was especially joyful to be wearing a new dress, although she rejected the one with a silky red bow at the collar, saying she was too old to wear *moños*.

We all smiled gratefully and thanked our grandmother when she pulled the tags off our new outfits, handed them to the saleslady, and said, "They'll be wearing these out."

After the morning's shopping, Abuelita Remedios bought us some lunch. We stood on the sidewalk on Avenida 4 in Monclova eating *taquitos* off an old vendor's cart. Looking around the busy streets with their modern buildings, I thought Mamá would be enamored of this place. Monclova looked as beautiful and as cultured as any large city in the United States. I relaxed and ate *jícama* dusted with chili powder from a tall fruit cup and told myself we could move here if Papá never came back and we lost the house.

Soon after that bittersweet moment with our newfound grandmother, we got back on Highway 57 North and drove straight through Sabinas and Nueva Rosita. We stopped in Allende for some *aguas frescas* at a *puesticito*, but other than that, we stayed on the road.

We arrived in Piedras Negras at three in the afternoon. The sun cast golden rays lazily upon the quieting city from its low point in the sky. Abuelita pulled over and parallel parked in front of the Santuario de Nuestra Señora de Guadalupe. She got out of the vehicle and stretched her legs as she looked around.

"Now who wants a *raspa*?" she asked, eyeing us with mischief in her eyes. "Well come on, don't be shy."

After Abuelita Remedios treated us to *raspas* and *campechanas*, those delicious puffed pastries we all loved so much, we walked back to the truck. We sat in the pickup and tried to enjoy our last moments with our beloved grandmother.

"Well, girls. It's time we say good-bye. I wish I had a green card, or even a worker's visa, but I haven't had much need for those things, not with my own place to run. So this is as far as I can go with you. You'll have to take a taxi across. Here," Abuelita said, reaching into her purse and handing me a small wad of American bills. "Where are your papers? We'll have to show them to the driver."

The question, like a hit to the temple, jostled something loose in my head, and suddenly my heart was in a panic. "Papers? Wait a minute! Did any of you bring your birth certificates? I know

I didn't." I'd run out of the house in such a panic to stop Juanita driving away that the thought never occurred to me.

"Yeah," Juanita said. "I got all of them. They're in Velia's backpack."

Velia put her hands on the bench seat beside Juanita and pulled herself forward in her seat. "No they're not."

"What do you mean? Where are they?" Abuelita asked, turning sideways to give Velia her full attention.

Juanita stopped eating her *raspa*. "What are you talking about? I gave them to you, when you were getting ready. I sat them right there, on your dresser, next to your clothes."

"Juanita," Velia whined. "I never saw them!"

"You mean you didn't bring them?" Juanita asked, putting a hand to her forehead and shaking her head in disbelief. "Oh my God. I can't believe this."

Velia slid back into her seat like a turtle trying to get back in its shell. "I'm sorry! We were so focused on leaving that I didn't even notice them."

I picked Juanita's backpack off the floorboard, unzipped it, and started pulling everything out of it. "Are you sure you didn't put them in here?"

"I'm sure," Juanita said, pushing her hair out of her face in frustration.

I unzipped every zipper and looked through every pocket of Juanita's backpack, making sure no documents were hiding there. "Delia? Pita? Did you bring anything else? Your school IDs, anything that might prove we are who we say we are."

"School IDs aren't going to help us. You need state IDs or birth certificates to get across," Delia said. "And, no, I didn't bring mine either."

I dumped Juanita's backpack onto the floorboard and sat with my back pressed against the truck's door, looking at Abuelita as I rubbed my forehead. Suddenly, I had a massive headache. "I can't believe this. After everything we've been through, and now we can't go home."

"Now hold on, let's not get melodramatic," Abuelita said. She pointed behind me, to the other side of the plaza. "All we have to do is go in there, to the *aduana* offices, and tell them everything. Well, not everything, remember what we talked about. None of that magical, mystical stuff. We don't want to lose credibility. Anyway, they'll get in touch with the authorities on the other side and someone will get a hold of your mother. It will take some time, but they'll sort it out. It's in their best interest to get the matter resolved as soon as possible, especially with all the media attention you've been getting, so I'm sure you won't be waiting too long. You'll be home sometime tonight. I'm sure of it."

Pita sat forward on her seat and poked her head over Abuelita to look at us. "Do you really mean tonight? Where would we wait while they cleared things up?"

"Oh, I'm sure they have some kind of facility where we can wait," Abuelita began.

"You mean like a detention center?" Delia's high-pitched voice echoed the horror in her wide eyes.

"Oh, I'm not staying in a detention facility on this side of the border," Velia said, shaking her head. "Cecilia said the police are corrupt, and you've heard the stories! People have to pay huge bribes just to see their family members when they're detained on this side of the border. Mamá can't even afford to pay the phone bill. There's no way she'd have the money to get all five of us back."

"Not all rumors are true," Abuelita said, a frown marring her forehead. "Not everyone is corrupt."

"Let me see that," Juanita reached back and pulled on Velia's backpack until Velia wiggled her shoulders out of the straps and handed her the bag. Frantic, Juanita rummaged through Velia's bag like her life depended on it. "Regardless, I don't think we should take any chances by going to the authorities. Even if they were to do right by us, the whole thing would create an international incident. The media would catch wind of it and things could really get out of control then."

She had a point. It was already bad enough that we'd gotten all the media attention we'd gotten so far. The police couldn't let that kind of thing slide if a reporter were to wonder who was at fault and maybe call for someone's punishment. "Child Protection Services would probably get involved," I said. "Mamá would definitely be in trouble then."

Juanita pushed her fists into the empty backpack on her lap, which deflated as she leaned over like she was going to be sick. "It's no use. They're not here."

"Wait a minute," I said. I opened the door to step out of the truck, looking up at the building we'd parked beside. "I can't believe it! The answer has been sitting right here all along."

"What are you talking about?" Abuelita asked, joining me on the sidewalk.

The rest of the girls left the truck to cluster around us. Juanita followed my gaze and stared up at the *santuario*. "What's going on?"

"This is it. The Virgin's sanctuary, her home," I said, taking in the beauty of the ancient cement building with its stained-glass windows and tall central tower.

"So what are you saying?" Velia asked. "You think we should pray?"

I turned to Abuelita Remedios, put my arms around her, and squeezed her with all my might. "Thank you!" I said. "You couldn't have brought us to a more ideal place. Ladies, we're going to do more than pray. We're going to go in there and ask for a miracle."

"A miracle?" Pita straightened her clothes as she stared at the church.

"Yes." I let go of Abuelita and started off for the wooden doors of the *santuario*. "Come on. I have one more spin left."

Inside the dark, empty church, I walked to the nearest pew, held onto the edge of the seat, dropped to one knee, and crossed myself. Then I turned left, intentionally passing the replica of the body of Christ. I touched the glass of the ancient display case and said a brief silent prayer as I continued to make my way to the altar of the Virgen de Guadalupe at the front of the church.

Like little ducks, the girls mimicked my every move until we were all standing in front of the virgin's altar, crossing ourselves, one right after the other. Abuelita reached into her pocket, pulled out a worn leather coin purse and deposited six coins into the slot of the metal box in front of the iron candleholder. Then she took a long wooden stick, borrowed flame from a burning wick, and lit a new candle. She passed the stick around and we all took turns lighting our own candles.

"Ready?" I whispered as I took Juanita's hand on one side and Abuelita's hand on the other. "Get in close."

I watched the rest of the girls take each other's hands until we were all standing in a semicircle, joined in prayer before the *Virgen de Guadalupe, la Madre de México*, our Holy Mother standing on a bed of roses.

"Here we go," I whispered. "Bow your heads and close your eyes."

Everyone did as they were told. I let go of Abuelita's hand long enough to give the ear pendant a spirited flick. It spun to life, humming a joyous tune as I took Abuelita's hand back in mine and started to pray out loud. "*Virgencita Santa*, Holy Mother, we have done as you asked. We delivered a man to his wife and children and tried our best to stay humble and kind and gave mercy when it was asked of us. Aztec queen, Tonantzin, Holy Mother of all mankind, lend us your magical assistance one last time. Please help us cross the Rio Grande, deliver us home to our Mamá."

At my words, the ear pendant whizzed and whirled like a top, sending thousands of tiny, exquisite vibrations to every nerve in my body. Then my body jolted and my eyes flew open, as if I'd been suddenly awakened from a nightmare.

Even as I blinked to focus in disbelief, I knew the vision before my eyes could not have been anything else but a dream. For we were all standing huddled together before a serene sky. A foggy mist swirled around us and before us lay a moonlit path that led straight up to the stars.

Pita opened her eyes and her mouth dropped. "Whoa!"

"What is in the—" Velia began to say something, but she was so shocked by her surroundings, she couldn't finish her thought.

"What is this?" Delia asked. "Some kind of hallucination?"

I put my foot in front of me and took a tentative step forward. My sisters moved around, prodding and testing the moonlit path with each footstep as they milled around. "No. It's real," I said. "Come on. This is going to make your *sopapillas* curl up."

As if mesmerized by the sound of some celestial being softly beckoning to us, we followed the moonlit path to the heavens, silently walking on stardust and moonbeams until we reached the summit of a hill and stopped. A brilliant dawn broke through the morning dew, caressed every shadow, and lifted the fog to reveal a floor of white clouds dotting an azure sky. Before us stood a giant cactus patch, each pad covered with budding prickly fruit that sparkled in the light, like tanzanites.

At the top of the hill, a youthful Tonantzin, the Goddess of

Sustenance, the girl who had saved us from the *nagual*, lifted her arms to welcome us, her beloved daughters. And when I looked around, I saw that a flurry of magnificent *mariposas* swarmed around us as we stood waiting on the summit of the hill, awed by the surreal beauty that surrounded us.

"Are we dreaming?" Juanita asked.

"Dreams are revelations," Tonantzin said, smiling down at us from her altar of cacti. "You have come far, my children. And I am proud of you."

"We shouldn't have come," I said, hanging my head. "My sister got hurt and we've put our mother in a bad position. She might never trust us again."

"The mother is the earth, the creator. Every part of her is alive," Tonantzin said. "She is the river, the flower, the bud. She is the regenerator. Her faith in her offspring is always alive."

"What did she say?" Pita asked, her face screwed up in confusion.

Abuelita put a finger up to her closed lips to show Pita she should be quiet and pay attention to what the *virgen* had to say.

"*Hijita mía*, youngest of my daughters, *la más pequeña de mis Mariposas*," the goddess said, turning her attention to Pita. "Do you have a question?"

"We all do," Velia interrupted.

Abuelita Remedios reached up and wrapped her arms around Velia and Pita's shoulders protectively. "Forgive them, Great Mother. They do not mean to disrespect you or question your judgment. They are good girls, but they are also curious—inquisitive to a fault. It's what makes them brave. But you knew that already, I'm sure."

The *Virgen* smiled at Abuelita, and her radiance shone brightly upon us as she said, "Yes. That is why I chose them."

"You said Mamá is a flower, so she is basically good to us," Velia said. "But what about Papá? Why did he leave us?"

Delia, upon hearing her twin sister's question, pushed her way to the forefront to stand between me and Abuelita. "Forget that. When's he coming back?"

"Your father is like the sun, splendid to behold, but he must descend and let darkness rule for a time."

"I don't get it," Pita said.

The virgen stepped down from her throne and touched Pita's face. "Without night there would be no rest, no room for growth. It is just the way things are," Tonantzin explained in a serene voice.

"You speak in riddles, like Llorona," I accused her. "I don't get it. If dreams are supposed to reveal things to us does that mean we're dreaming now? And if we are, then how come I'm more confused than I ever was?"

"I know you don't understand what is happening with your family," Tonantzin said gently. "But you will, when the time comes. A new dawn is approaching, but you are very clever, very brave. You will not be blinded by his light."

"So why did you set us on this path?" I asked. "What were we supposed to accomplish? Can you at least tell us that much?"

"Odilia, you are here because I needed your assistance," Tonantzin said, fixing me with her gentle gaze. "And you've been very helpful. You might not realize it yet, but you've learned many lessons along the way, about your Mamá and about life. However, there is one more thing you must do to complete your task. I need you to remind the mother that she is the flower, the bud, the giver of life. She needs to be honored with love and redemption."

I let out an exasperated sigh. "Honored with love and redemption? How am I supposed to do that when I don't even understand what you are saying?" I didn't want to disrespect the *virgen*, but this explanation just left me more confused.

Tonantzin placed her hands on my shoulder and suddenly I wasn't so overwhelmed. Her gentle smile, her luminous eyes, her rose scented perfume filled me with an inner calm, and I felt blessed. "Soon, you will understand everything."

Mesmerized by her glory, I reached out and touched the sleeve of her emerald gown. "Go on," the goddess said, extending her arm out to my sisters, who all touched the sleeve of her garment and oohed and aahed when it came to life, glittering at their touch, infusing us with sunlight and warmth. "When your journey is over everything will make sense and you will live joyful, productive lives. But first, you must pick the *rosas de castilla*," Tonantzin said, pointing behind me.

I turned to follow her hand and saw the clouds lifting and

the earth rising up to meet us. Up and up it came, until we were standing in our path in the woods by the Rio Grande. There, at the bottom of a hill, off the beaten path, amidst a cloud of glorious *mariposas*, a patch of rosebushes began to break through the ground, bursting to life one right after another, until the hill was covered in white rosebuds that bloomed in the morning light.

Tonantzin began to walk toward the rosebushes. We followed her down the path, and as we did, I noticed her feet were bare. But she walked without regard to burrs or thorns, for as she stepped forth the ground beneath her became carpeted with fluorescent rose petals.

"They're beautiful," Juanita whispered as we came upon the cluster of blooming rosebushes.

The *Virgen* reached over, plucked a perfect blossom from the bush and handed it to me. I took it and instinctively brought it up to my nose. Its heady perfume overwhelmed my senses and I felt dizzy for a moment. "Give the roses to the mother," Tonantzin said. "They will remind her of who she is, who we are, and what we are all meant to become."

"Roses," I said, trying to imprint her instructions into my mind. "On the hill. When we wake up. Okay. I can do that."

"They will bring light into her eyes," Tonantzin continued. "They will transform her."

"*The* mother?" Velia asked. "Is she talking about Mamá?"

"I think so," I said as Tonantzin turned away from us. We followed Tonantzin as she walked back up to her altar. She stood on the cacti, her feet unharmed by the prickly pears and thorns.

"So this is what it's all about?" I asked, as we stood before her again. "Giving her flowers?"

"She has earned them," Tonantzin said. "Paid for them with tears of gold. Give her the roses and you will bring her back to life. If you do this, you and your sisters will be blessed forever. You will look up at the sky and know that you played your part in creating new life in our universe. But to end, you must begin. It is time for you to go."

"Pick the flowers. Give them to the mother," I whispered to myself. And even as I said it over and over again, reminding myself of what had to be done, I wondered why Tonantzin kept referring to our mother as "*the*" mother. Her word choice seemed odd and old-fashioned, almost regal in a way. Ancient kings used to refer to themselves as "we" and "us," so it was probably common for the ancient goddess Tonantzin, the Holy Mother of all mankind, to use the word "the" to refer to other mothers in her care.

As I pondered this, the silhouette of the goddess began to change. The light that had surrounded us faded into darkness and Tonantzin slowly disappeared into the night. The stars began to shine all around us, and the path of stardust and moonbeams reappeared beneath our feet. We walked down the moonlit trail toward a dark and misty shore, a surreal place, a place somewhere between sleep and wakefulness.

17

La Chalupa: *"Lupe, Lupita, pasea a mi*
Pita chiquita en tu chalupita."

The Canoe: "Lupe, Lupita, give my little
Pita a ride in your little boat."

The marshy lake stretched far and wide before us was covered in a misty haze. The sky above me was a deep purple-gray, and on the horizon I could see the first rays of light pushing through, announcing a new day.

"Where are we?" Velia and Delia asked in unison.

"Not where, but when," Juanita said.

As we wandered along the shallow shore, the mist dissipated, exposing an entire community of canoes being steered by both men and women on the surface of the lake. Fishermen stood on their bobbing vessels, throwing nets across the dark, still waters. Native Mexican women dressed in pale tunics slid their paddles into the lake and rowed slowly, serenely across the water toward what could only be described as densely vegetated islands floating on the water. And as the sun's rays peeked out of the horizon, turning the sky into an amethyst haze, the canoe people sang in a language I'd never heard before. Their songs were filled with pleasure and warmth and life.

"What time is it?" Juanita asked. "It looks like the sun wants to come out but it can't."

Abuelita looked at the watch on her wrist, tapped it, put it up to her ear and shook her head. "I can't tell. This old thing's stopped ticking."

"Now what?" Velia asked.

"I don't know," I said. "Since we met La Llorona, I never know what to expect."

I was wondering what we were supposed to do when a young woman paddled her canoe to shore and docked it right in front of us. "You wish to go across?" she asked.

"Across?" I asked, looking at her canoe closely. It was not large, but it was big enough to carry us all together if we chose to go aboard.

"To the other side, to your worlds," she said, smiling. "The Great Mother has ordered it so. She has sent me here to help you. I am to take you back to your mother and your *abuelita* to Hacienda Dorada."

"Yes," Juanita said. "Yes. We all have to get home."

The beautiful woman moved a bouquet of calla lilies out of the way and placed it over a basket full of fresh tomatoes, squash, and *chiles* to make room for us. We all scrambled onto the small vessel. Then we watched as she anchored her paddle against the murky lake's floor and pushed the little boat away from the shore.

"My name is Ixtali," the beautiful young woman said as she

rowed us out toward the middle of the quiet lake. The sky above us was blushing with the promise of sunrise. My eyes had adjusted to the meager light and I could see details now. The men wore white tunics and pants that stopped at their ankles, with no shoes. The women wore tunics too, the length of dresses, but their hair was braided intricately and adorned with flowers and little stones I did not recognize.

"We are the Garza girls, and this is our Abuelita Remedios," Juanita said, pointing to the rest of us. "Ixtali, can you tell us where we are? Why are we traveling back in time?"

"You are not traveling back in time," Ixtali said. "You are moving forward, gliding across Texcoco Lake, where your mother's people made their home."

I looked at the islands of vegetation fenced in within the clusters of willow trees creating the illusion of a heavily forested swampland. "I've never seen so many little islands in a lake," I said.

"They are *chinampas*, the floating gardens that feed us. They provide us with everything we need to sustain our families. They are our livelihood. We are tenders, cultivators, nurturers. But this is more than a way to survive for us. It is our way of life."

I reached out and touched the end of a muddy wooden stick, a digging tool of some kind, sitting next to a small wooden hoe beside me on the boat. "So you're a farmer?" I asked.

"Yes," Ixtali said, rowing slowly, carefully, as she watched the other boats around us, making sure we were not in their way. "But I also harvest flowers, fragrant blooms to decorate the palaces, the houses of the nobles on the mainland." She lifted her paddle and used it to point to the left of us.

I followed the gesture and gasped at the sight of a beautiful city that seemed to be floating in the middle of the lake, encircled by a magical mist, bedazzling us with its towering splendor. Complex clusters of stone buildings, so tall and imposing they looked like gods rising out of the water, reached for the sky.

"Tenochtitlan," Abuelita said, looking in wonder at the great city looming over the swampy lake. "The Aztecs decided to build it here, on the lake, when they saw the sign—an eagle sitting on a cactus, eating a snake. It was the center of a great empire, the home of our ancestors."

I watched Ixtali row and row, taking us away from the city. "Why are we so far away from home?" I asked.

"This is the goddess's gift to you," she said. "A vision, to always remember who you are, where you came from, as you develop a better future."

As Ixtali rowed on, we passed a fisherman pulling up a turtle in his net and two women picking fresh vegetables from a floating garden. "It's beautiful, your way of life. Thank you for showing it to us."

"And for giving us a ride," Pita said, inching closer to me. I put my arm around her and pulled her in beside me.

"You are welcome," Ixtali said, as she rowed away from the city and toward shore. It didn't even occur to me to wonder what language we were speaking. We just understood each other.

We spent the next few minutes watching the fishermen pull up their nets in the subtle darkness before dawn. As I sat holding Pita close to me, listening to the soft songs of our ancestors working in the waters of Texcoco Lake, I wondered what time of day it would be when we woke up from this wondrous dream. A chilly breeze picked up around us, and I saw the rest of the mist lift off the water, exposing a familiar shoreline.

"Look!" Juanita said, pointing to the land coming closer and closer. "It looks just like . . ."

"Our swimming hole!" Velia and Delia jumped up in the boat with excitement as they finished Juanita's thought. The canoe rocked severely, and before Abuelita could pull the twins down beside her, it capsized. We all fell overboard, landing in the waters of our very own eddy in the Rio Grande.

"We're home!" Pita screamed as she tried to stand up in the water. Velia and Delia scrambled across the water to help her as Juanita, Abuelita, and I helped Ixtali drag her canoe to shore.

Juanita helped our grandmother out of the water. "I'm sorry about this," she told Ixtali, who was standing on the riverbank wringing the water out of her dress.

"Oh, don't worry," Ixtali said, looking up from her dress. "It'll dry out before I get home."

"Thank you. Thank you," the twins kept chanting as they held Pita up between them, her arms wrapped around their shoulders for support.

"Thank *you* for the pleasant company," Ixtali said.

As the girls helped Pita sit down on a huge flat rock a few feet away from the shore, I held my grandmother's hand in mine. She was looking at Ixtali's boat, and I could tell she didn't want to get back in it.

"One last hug," Abuelita said. Her voice cracked and quivered with emotion as she leaned down and hugged me tight.

"I'll see you soon," I said. At my words, Juanita, Velia, and Delia convened around us, trying to get one last hug out of Abuelita.

"We'll visit you soon!"

"We'll take the bus and come see you!"

"We promise. We promise," they all said as they hugged her. Even Pita from her place on the shore was calling out similar promises. Our grandmother leaned down and hugged her before heading back to join Ixtali in her little boat.

By the time she settled into her seat, Abuelita was crying so much she was rendered speechless. All she could do by then was wave at us.

"It has been an honor bringing you home," Ixtali said as she waved good-bye. Then she anchored her paddle against the bed of the river and pushed her *chalupita* off. They were gliding away as Ixtali said, "May the Great Mother be with you in all your travels, and don't forget to pick the flowers."

"The flowers? Oh, yes. The roses for Mamá," I yelled back. "Thank you. Thank you for reminding me."

We walked out of the water then, and stood on dry land

watching Ixtali row away from us until she and Abuelita Remedios were nothing more than a memory in the thin mist that still hung over the Rio Grande.

"Let's go, girls. You heard the lady. I have roses to pick," I said.

The twins shouldered Pita between them and they hollered and hooted all the way up the hill as we left the riverbank behind. Our bodies were worn out, but we didn't let that stop us. We hiked through the sparse woods, making our way carefully down the beaten path we had created that summer, the summer of the *mariposas*. Only there were no butterflies anywhere. Maybe they were asleep and would awaken with the sunrise, a sunrise that seemed to elude us as we walked along.

Pita looked more than tired. The twins were doing their best to steady her by hoisting her arms around their shoulders and bearing most of her weight, but she still looked like she was ready to keel over. We had been walking slowly, carefully, for at least twenty minutes as the woods became more dense, pushing the hackberry bushes and *hierba de zizotes* out of our way, when we saw light breaking over a hill to the left of us.

"Well, look at that, the sun's finally coming out," Delia said, stopping to admire the new dawn.

"No. That's something else." Juanita stepped forward to take a better look at the wooded area being illuminated. "I think it's your roses."

"Let's go," I said. I headed into the woods in the direction of the glow.

We were barely over the *cerro* when we saw them to the right of us, in a clearing, on yet another hill: hundreds of snout-nosed butterflies hovering over dozens of rosebushes. The rosebush clusters bloomed joyously, their blushing white crowns illuminating the darkness we had endured for so long.

The joy of finding the roses was short-lived as I realized all our belongings were still in Abuelita's truck, sitting in front of the Santuario de Nuestra Señora de Guadalupe, right where we'd left it before we were transported here. "I don't have anything to cut them with," I said.

"Oh. I do," Velia said, reaching into her pocket and unfolding a blade out of a complicated gadget that looked like twenty tiny tools in one. She handed me the small contraption. "Here you go. Can I come? I can hold them for you."

"Okay." I looked at the others and smiled. "This won't take long. I promise."

Juanita took me by the shoulders, pointed me toward the hill, and gave me a tiny push to get me going. "Go on. We'll wait here. Pita needs to rest," she said.

Velia and I walked all the way up the hill, the bright morning light illuminating our steps as we trampled through the brush. When we got to the roses, we both gasped. Their pale complexions blushed with an iridescent splendor that made them look almost magical.

Velia touched one of them, her eyes sparkling with admiration. "They're beautiful."

"Yes, they are," I said. "Come on. Let's not waste time."

Velia stood just behind me as I started to cut the roses. When I handed her the first one, she untucked her shirt and pulled it forward, creating a bed for the blossoms. I carefully pressed the thorns off their stems with my forefinger and thumb before laying them on the cradle of her shirt. Their wide leaves trembled delicately as they lay one on top of the other.

Velia folded her shirt over the ten roses I'd already given her. "You almost done there?"

I pricked my finger on a thorn and winced at the pain. "*¡Ay!* See what you made me do? Be patient. I'm almost through."

"*I* don't care if you take all day, but we don't have that kind of time," Velia continued.

"What do mean?" I asked, sucking on my throbbing thumb.

She tapped my shoulder and pointed down the hill. "I think our ride is here."

I turned around and saw them coming too, two border patrol trucks rolling up the hill with their headlights full force on us. "Oh, thank God," I said, relieved. "Now we don't have to walk."

"Well, I wouldn't be so happy right now. Or did you forget?" Velia asked, turning to look at me with a furrowed brow.

"Forget what?" I asked, annoyed. I wasn't sure what she was getting at.

"Hello!" Velia retorted. "We don't have our papers with us. And Pita is hurt. They're going to call CPS on us for sure."

18

El Corazón: *"Sin aliento y sin calor,*
un corazón sin amor no palpita."

The Heart: "Without breath or warmth,
a heart without love cannot beat."

The border patrol called the police, the police called the FBI, and they all sat in front of us at a small table in a nice little office at the International Bridge Customs Station. They asked us the same questions over and over again. The FBI agent was the nicest one. He was tall and well-groomed, but most impressively, he was Mexican-American. His name was Special Agent Gonzales, and the girls were in awe of him. They thought he was brighter than the moon.

They were very nice to us. However, no matter how many times they asked us the same questions, we always stuck to the same story; we found a body and went to Mexico to deliver it. On the way back our car broke down so we had to abandon it. We walked to Abuelita's house and she drove us back, but when we realized we didn't have our papers with us, we swam back across.

When they asked us how we made it across the river if grown men were known to drown in it, we said we were great swimmers. We'd been swimming back and forth across that river all our lives.

"Oh yeah." Special Agent Gonzales leaned in to speak to Pita directly. "So what happened to your leg?"

"A stray dog bit her, but she's all right now. Abuelita gave her some antibiotics and cleaned the wound for her," Juanita said, jumping in to save Pita from having to explain. Abuelita Remedios would probably forgive us for that one white lie, given that there was no other way to explain a *chupacabras* bite. When Special Agent Gonzales continued to question us, we all followed Abuelita's advice and stuck to the more realistic part of our story.

We hadn't been there very long before Officer Lopez, a young woman, came into the room and said, "Gonzales. The mother's here."

"Mamá!" Pita said, almost jumping out of her chair.

Juanita stood up and looked at the door behind the officers in the room. "You mean our mother?"

"Where is she?" I asked.

"Can we see her?" the twins asked, standing up to flank Juanita and Pita.

"Bring her in," Special Agent Gonzales said, nodding toward the door.

And so it was that on the twelfth day after our departure, we were finally reunited with Mamá. I'll never forget that moment when the door of the office first opened and Mamá stepped timidly into the room. One look in our direction and her eyes lit up like stars, and pure, unrestrained joy glittered and shone in them. She was more than happy. She was ecstatic. As soon as she saw us, Mamá ran around the table to reach us. Her purse fell out of her hands and hit the floor with a muted clank as she put her arms around Pita. Tears rolled down her face as she hugged and kissed us one at a time, again and again, like she never wanted to stop. She was so overwhelmed with such relief, such joy, she could hardly talk.

"I love you! I love you!" she kept saying as she kissed us repeatedly and held us tight.

"Please sit down," Special Agent Gonzales said, watching Mamá surrounded by the love of five grateful daughters. "Would you like something to drink? We have coffee. The girls had soft drinks while we waited."

"No. Thank you, I'm fine," Mamá said. "When can I take them home? They're drenched. I can't believe they swam all the way across the river."

Special Agent Gonzales smiled, a sincere smile that made his full lips curl up softly at the corners. I noticed that his eyes shone more when he made eye contact with Mamá, like he was genuinely happy for her. "We've asked the girls what happened so we can file our report. I'm sure Officer Lopez has already informed you of the details, but I can go over my report with you if you like. You'll get a copy of it before you leave here today, of course. But if you have any questions, any concerns, you can always call me."

Mamá turned around to look at Special Agent Gonzales without letting go of Pita. "I appreciate that. I'm forever grateful to you."

"Well, we didn't do much," Officer Lopez said, standing behind Special Agent Gonzales across the table. "The girls got themselves home. Oh. I almost forgot. They brought you a gift."

"Yes. We have roses for you," I said, turning to look at Mamá. "Officer Lopez was kind enough to put them in a vase so they would stay fresh for you."

Mamá took my hand and squeezed it, her eyes suddenly misty. "Roses? For me? Whenever did you find the time to get me roses?"

"They are a gift," I said, clinging to Mamá's warm, loving grip.

"Officer Lopez will get them for you," Special Agent Gonzales said, and the young officer left the room in a hurry. "Now, there's one more thing. The girls were concerned about Child Protective Services getting involved."

Mamá's grip on my hand suddenly slackened, and I squeezed it tightly, letting her know silently that we were not going to let anything happen to our family—that we were going to be there for her. "CPS . . ." Mamá's voice trailed off and she stood rigid, waiting for Special Agent Gonzales to continue.

"Yes," Special Agent Gonzales said. "It is procedure to report any incident involving children to them. Someone from their office will make contact with you soon. Now, I've explained to the girls that they should tell the CPS investigator exactly what they have told me. Personally, I don't see a problem here, not as far as you are concerned. But they have their own procedures to follow and my report will indicate that I see no evidence of neglect on your part. If you should need my assistance in any way or have any questions that I might be able to answer, I am here to help you."

As Mamá processed the information, Officer Lopez walked back into the room carrying the vase. "Here you go," she said.

I took the vase from her and speculated on the luminous white roses. The *Virgen* said they would transform Mamá, and I wondered how the change would manifest itself. Would the presence of others affect Mamá's transformation, or would it be instantaneous? Not knowing what to expect, I hesitated.

"These are for you," Velia said, taking the vase out of my hands and presenting them to Mamá, who gave us a watery smile and took them with great appreciation.

"Thank you. They're beautiful," Mamá said, putting her nose into the bouquet and smelling them. "I love them almost as much as I love you."

As the white rose petals caressed her face, I held my breath, waiting for that glorious moment, the moment when she would become more than ordinary, when she would be touched by the divine. However, the only thing that happened was that Mamá put the vase down on the table and turned around to wrap her arms around us again.

"Well, we won't take any more of your time." Special Agent Gonzales held out his hand for Mamá to shake. "Señora Garza, we thank you very much for your patience. If it would be okay with you, I'd like to personally escort you home in our unmarked units. It would make things easier, more private for you."

Mamá accepted Special Agent Gonzales's proposal and we were all driven home in a couple of dark sedans. The vehicles pulled up to our driveway and we jumped out and stood on the sidewalk waiting for Mamá to come in with us.

"I can't tell you how much I appreciate everything you've done for us," Mamá said, her eyes misting over again, as she stood just inside our fenced yard, shaking Special Agent Gonzales's hand.

"We were glad to help," Officer Lopez said, extending her hand to Mamá and then giving her a small, friendly hug. "And remember, if you should need anything, we're a phone call away."

No sooner had they left than the girls were all over Mamá. They clustered around her in the front lawn, pouring so much sugar on her that she looked downright mystified.

I walked up to the house and stood on the front porch holding Mamá's roses, waiting for them to start walking up the driveway. I rubbed a translucent rose petal between my fingertips, wondering why they had failed to transform her. Looking sideways at Mamá, I could see that nothing had changed about her. She looked as pretty as she ever was, but not in any way different, not enchanting, not bedazzling in her daughters' eyes, at least not in mine.

"Let's go inside," I said. "I can't wait to sleep in my own bed tonight."

"Mamá." Juanita stood in the driveway at the far right corner of the house, looking at something the rest of us couldn't see. "Whose car is that?"

"What car?" Mamá asked.

Juanita pointed toward the back of the house. "The blue Honda parked in the back."

Mamá walked over to look down the driveway. I stayed on the porch holding the roses with the twins and Pita around me, waiting. "*¡Ay, Dios mío!*" Mamá said, and she glanced around the neighborhood nervously, like she was expecting someone to step out of their house and attack us. Then she turned around, stepped onto the porch, and hurried up to the door, but she didn't open it. She just stood staring at it, blinking and looking confused, as if she didn't know how to open her own front door. "It's all happening so fast. I didn't see it coming, and on the same day—all at once."

"What are you talking about?" I asked, but Mamá's eyes were glistening with unshed tears and her hands were trembling as she held the keys in a tight grip.

"Girls. I have to tell you something." Mamá's voice suddenly cracked, and her forehead creased with worry lines. She took a deep breath and stammered on. "Things have changed. Nothing's ever going to be the same again for you . . . for me . . . for us."

"What do you mean?" I asked. "What's changed?"

Mamá let out a short, heavy breath, and she pressed her fingertips against the frown that puckered her brow together.

“Maybe we should just go inside,” she whispered, as if she were suddenly afraid the neighbors would hear us.

“Okay,” Juanita said, raising her eyebrows and shaking her head to let me know she had no idea what was going on.

As soon as I walked through the door, I set the vase down on the coffee table in the hallway to the left of the front door and turned around to hug Mamá tightly. I had missed her so much. She had been absent from our lives far longer than the twelve days we'd been gone, and I was thankful for the comfort of her love.

“I'm sorry,” I whispered into her ear as she held me in her arms.

Mamá squeezed me tightly. “It's okay. We can get through this. Whatever happens, I promise you everything's going to be all right.” Being in her arms gave me the feeling that everything *was* going to be all right. But just when I was beginning to feel at ease, the most startling thing happened.

We heard footsteps—cowboy boots, unmistakably loud and clear as they walked on the linoleum. Letting go of Mamá, I turned toward the source of the footsteps to see the figure of a lone man standing at the threshold of the kitchen door. Papá paused, then stepped into the hallway. We didn't react immediately. Instead, we stood there, all five of us, shocked at the sight of him after all this time.

“Papá.” The word left my mouth in a thin breath that barely touched my lips, because I couldn't believe he was really there.

Yet, as he waited there at the end of the long hallway, all the way past four bedrooms and a bathroom door, something small and fragile twisted inside of me, my tattered heart shrinking away from him.

We'd been so happy to see Mamá, so overjoyed at her loving, genuine reception, that we had, for a moment, forgotten we had a father. Being chased by witches and warlocks, battling monsters, even defeating demons, was nothing compared to the task of facing the reality of our father's abandonment.

Instinctively, Pita left our mother's side and wrapped herself around me, as if I and I alone could protect her from the stranger Papá had become. I draped my arms around her small shoulders and filled my lungs with air, waiting for his explanation. But instead of explaining himself, my father did the same thing he had always done when he'd come home from working out of town. As if his long, unexplained absence had been nothing more than another one of his trips, he took a small step forward, and with little fanfare, he opened his arms to us in a wide, welcoming arc and said, "*Chiquitas*, I am so glad to see you. Come, come, give your Papá a hug."

The minute she heard his words, Pita unfurled. Like a dandelion seed—*se desprendió de mí*—she pushed me off and flew at him, almost knocking him backward as he went down on one knee to receive her into his strong, protective arms.

I have to admit for a small, deranged second, my erratic heart jolted in my chest and I almost did the same thing. I almost ran into his open arms. But then I remembered what Abuelita had revealed to us and I knew Papá had not come home to be reunited with us. He was probably here to finish what he'd started when he first abandoned us. Maybe he was picking up the rest of his stuff. He might even want to know why we'd taken his car. But I knew, I just *knew*, he wasn't there for us.

"Papá! Papá!" Pita squealed, calling out to him over and over again. Her voice filled the room with a heartbreaking desperation not unlike the twittering of a nest full of orphaned sparrows.

"Delia. Velia," Papá whispered, his eyes imploring them to go to him, even as he hugged Pita to himself like she was his lifeline. "Please. It's been so long. Come give your Papá a hug."

The twins looked sideways at each other, but didn't budge. They turned to look at Mamá. Her eyes were brimming with unshed tears. But instead of saying anything, she pressed her lips together, swallowed hard, and looked away.

"Mamá?" Juanita stepped forward and put her hand on our mother's shoulder.

"What is going on?" Delia and Velia's words mingled together in the air. They touched Mamá's arm, and our mother did what I feared she might do under the circumstances. She waved her hand toward Papá as if to say, *"Go. Go. I give up."*

"Don't do it," I muttered as I fought the urge to scream, *"He's faking it!"*

"Papá? Please say—you're not leaving," Velia and Delia's plea ripped through my heart and I wrung my hands, wishing there was a way I could expose Papá for the wretch that I feared him to be before the girls got too attached to him again.

"*Mis cuatitas*, my precious twins. No. I won't leave again. I love you too much." At his loving words, the twins took a step toward him. I couldn't stop them, but I also couldn't keep my mouth shut.

"You've been gone for almost a year. Where was this love all that time?" I asked, tasting the bitterness as the words left my insolent mouth.

"Odilia, *hija mía*, love doesn't go away from one day to the next. Not a father's love. It clings to our hearts and holds on so tight, it keeps us awake at night. Please. Don't be so hard on your Papá."

Pita wrapped her arms tighter around Papá's neck and she kissed his cheek, while Delia and Velia stood their ground with their arms crossed over their chests. The twins' eyes were blank, cold. But not me. No, I was so enraged, I wanted to slap Papá hard across the face. I wanted to break him, make him beg forgiveness for having left us without letting us know where he was or if he was even alive. But instead of hurling myself violently at him, I did the only thing I could do. I questioned his devotion.

"Is that true? Or is it just a line from one of your songs?" My spiteful words delivered their poison, and my father flinched. He blinked nervously, and for a moment, he was at a loss for words. Pita let go of Papá's neck and turned to look at me, her eyes full of fear, and something else—doubt, I think.

"It's not a line. I don't even sing anymore. I left the band. I'm home for good," Papá finally answered, tightening his hold on Pita as if to mark his words. "Odilia, I am your Papá. I could never stop loving you. Ever. Your faces are embedded in my heart."

"Our faces? Really?" I moved slowly, deliberately toward Papá as I continued. Accusations roiled inside of me, swirling in my head like furling tornado clouds, until I thought I might explode if I didn't let them out. "What about our feelings, Papá? Did you ever think about what your disappearance would do to us? It seems to me like you think being gone for almost a year without even one phone call to let us know you're alive is perfectly all right—but it's not. It's not all right at all."

Mamá, standing behind me, was crying openly now. Her face was covered in tears, and her body shook as she hugged herself.

"Trust me, *muñecas*," Papá continued. "Delia, Velia, Juanita, I have never stopped loving you, any of you. Not even for a second."

His words were meant to charm, and the twins were wavering. Their lips were quivering. They were getting closer to each other in that connected way of theirs, as if trying to make up their minds. Then, suddenly, they broke the bond and rushed to hug Papá, who let go of Pita to hug them.

The twins huddled around him, towering over him. They'd grown so much in the time he'd been gone, yet they were still little girls, clinging to their childhood and their need for his love.

I wondered if I'd ever been that innocent. I felt numb inside.

"Come on," Juanita begged me, inching herself toward the familial scene before us. She grabbed my hand, but I shook my head. Something inside me was wounded. The pain speared my heart and the threat of tears blinded me, so I tightened my grip on Juanita's hand, fighting the urge to scream, to cry, to run away from it all.

Then, just as reluctantly as the last leaf of autumn falls off a desiccated branch, Juanita's hand slackened and fell away from mine. She walked away from me, leaving me alone with my anger and resentment. Papá's arrival had done what Cecilia and her Evil Trinity could not accomplish. His empty promises broke the code of the *cinco hermanitas*. We were five little sisters, together no more—*cinco hermanitas* torn completely apart.

"Just promise you'll never leave us again," Juanita requested, and hugged Papá. His eyes misted with love as he broke free of the others and took her into his arms as if she was the most beloved of his daughters.

"You are my family," he whispered, kissing the crown of Juanita's head. "I would never tear us apart. We were a family once, and we will be a family again. If it kills me, I will never again leave your side."

19

El Músico: *"El músico no es torero,*

pero sí sabe tocar y torear."

The Musician: "The musician is not a bullfighter,

but he does know how to play and deceive."

I listened to Papá's words with a suspicious ear. He seemed so sincere, so committed to us, that I almost put aside my reservations and allowed myself to be sucked into his whirlwind of affection. But I held back instead.

I couldn't put my finger on it, but something didn't feel quite right. Perhaps it was my intuition that kept me away, the suspicious nature I'd developed since our journey in Mexico. More than likely, though, it was that solitary figure of Mamá holding herself together, alone—apart from my sisters, apart from Papá, apart even from me, her firstborn daughter, the closest thing she had to an ally. I was pondering my resistance, when suddenly the twins' bedroom door flew open.

Papá froze, took a deep breath, and then turned to look at the door to his left.

"What's going on?" he asked, releasing my sisters to stand up.

Two pasty-faced girls walked out of Velia and Delia's room. They couldn't have been much younger than the twins, but they were shorter and very plump. Their dirty blonde hair was frizzled out, like unraveling kite strings dragged through too many hands, but they didn't seem to be concerned about what they looked like. They were too busy carrying a huge plastic sack between them.

"Daddy," one of them whined. "We don't know what to do with this stuff. It smells bad."

"Yeah, like cockroaches or something," the first girl blurted out, her muddy brown eyes settling on us for the first time.

"What in the *hell-icopter* . . ." Velia started.

" . . . were you doing in our room?" Delia finished her twin sister's thought, looking at Mamá for an explanation.

"Sarai!" Papá called out to someone who came rushing out of Juanita's bedroom to the left of us. Shock ran up my spine and jolted me into awareness as I watched a tall, narrow-hipped blonde woman walk past us in the hall like she owned the place. She went to stand next to Papá in front of the kitchen door and clung to his arm as if to show that she had possession of him now.

"Ernesto," the woman said, her eyes glittering with something like malice or spite as she looked at each of my sisters and then settled on Mamá. "There's no use dragging this on. *Por favor, diles*—just tell them what's going on and be done with it, *amor*."

Papá's eyes made contact with mine, and then he cast his gaze downward to the floor, as if he were embarrassed. "I thought we talked about this," he said quietly, almost inaudibly. "Now is not the time."

Suddenly, I understood everything: the arguments with Mamá, his inappropriate riddle for *La Sirena* the last time we had played *Lotería* as a family, the disconnected phones, his unexplained disappearance, it all made sense now. Papá had been having an affair with this woman, and now he had brought her here—*to our house*!

Looking at her dispassionate face, I wondered how Papá could've traded our sweet, loving Mamá for this cold woman. What hold could such a manipulating woman have on him?

Thick, molten hot anger welled up inside me as I waited for an explanation. "Now is not the time for what?" I asked Papá in a terse voice, barely suppressing the rage simmering inside me.

"Now is not the time for this." Papá pointed toward the woman's daughters, who were still holding the huge plastic sack between them. "We have to talk about the situation, let everyone get used to the idea," Papá snarled at the blonde woman from between clenched teeth, the way he always did when he was running short on patience.

"I know. I told them, but you know how they are," the woman whispered into Papá's ear, smiling slyly at Mamá, who put a hand over her mouth and shook her head in shock—or maybe it was disbelief or embarrassment. I couldn't tell which.

"Girls, please put that back," Papá asked.

"But we're cleaning our room. There's too much stuff in there," the little one said, pointing to Velia and Delia's room.

"What?" Velia said.

"You mean this is our stuff?" Delia demanded, reaching for the huge plastic sack and yanking it away from them.

The girls held onto the sack while Velia and Delia pulled with all their might. The tug of war ended almost before it began as the sack ripped and articles of clothing spilled everywhere.

"These are *my* clothes," Velia said. Disgusted, the woman's daughters threw the ripped sack on the floor in front of the twins. Velia gathered up an assortment of jeans, shorts and shirts, holding them in front of her like they were misplaced treasures.

Delia pointed to the sandaled feet of one of the girls. "Hey, those are mine! Why are you wearing my *chanclas*? Take them off, you fat little thief!"

"They were in my room, but you can have them!" The girl slid the pretty white sandals off and tossed them with her feet in Delia's direction. The sandals landed in front of Delia with a thud. Without taking her rabid eyes off the thief, Delia kicked both sandals aside. I could tell by the violent nature of that kick that she would never wear those *chanclas* again.

Juanita stooped down and picked up the rest of the clothes from the floor and handed them to Velia. "You can't stay here. This isn't a hotel!"

"Ladies," Papá said. He disentangled himself from the blonde woman and came to stand between the twins and the woman's daughters. "Let me explain."

"Yeah. Tell them, Daddy. This is our house now!" the older of the two sisters said, tossing her disheveled hair back with a flick of her hand.

"It is not! This house belongs to us!" Velia stepped behind the strange girls, threw her clothes inside her room haphazardly, and closed the door to her bedroom to punctuate her words. "Stay out of there if you know what's good for you."

"You have no right to be here," Delia said, kicking at the girl nearest to her. She didn't make actual contact, though, because Papá put his hand on her shoulder and held her at bay.

"Your house stinks like a lice farm," the older of the strange girls said. No sooner had she spoken, than Delia slipped out of Papá's grasp, and both Delia and Velia threw themselves on the invading sisters, who were knocked to the floor. Papá reached in to stop them, but the twins were too fast for him.

Raining blows, *como molinos*, Delia and Velia were two demonic *lechuzas* shrieking out their outrage in Spanish and cursing the intruders for their transgressions.

"Stop it! Stop it right now!" Papá yelled, taking each of the twins in turn and peeling them off the two other girls, who were wailing miserably on the floor.

Mamá, who up to now I assume had been too embarrassed to speak, was suddenly standing right in the middle of things. She was holding Velia and Delia in front of her, arms wrapped around them, securing them. "Girls, I've told you before. No matter how mad you are, fighting doesn't solve anything."

"They started it," Delia spat out, straightening her shirt.

"Yeah," Velia continued. "They mess with our stuff, they mess with us."

Mamá let go of the girls and made the twins turn around to face her before she spoke again. "Please apologize."

"I'm sorry," Velia mumbled to no one in particular.

"Sorry," Delia whispered halfheartedly as Mamá stroked her arm and held her and Velia close.

"Delia, Velia," Papá's tone of voice was downright stern. "You can't mistreat Alison and Ashley like this. They're going to be part of our family from now on, and we don't hurt our family."

"What are you talking about?" I asked. "What do you mean they're going to be part of the family? Are they . . . *yours*?"

"They're my stepdaughters, or they will be as soon as the divorce goes through," Papá said. He took the strange girls into his arms and hugged them to himself. His words, delivered so swiftly and with such disregard for our feelings, cut through me like the blade of a guillotine. My stomach lurched and tightened and lurched again. Abuelita said that Papá was divorcing Mamá, but she didn't mention that he had another woman and two other daughters. She told us he wanted to start a new life, but she neglected to inform us that he had a whole other family that did not include us.

"Now let's try this again," Papá cooed into the two pasty girls' ears as he kissed them and then turned around to look at us. "Ladies, this is Ashley," he said, placing his hand on the younger girl's head. "And this is Alison," he continued, referring to the older girl. "They are going to be your stepsisters, your *hermanitas*, and we're all going to live here together, so please, try to be nice."

"Live together?" Juanita's eyes sparked with derision. "Here? You mean you all, us, *and* Mamá? Who do you think we are, the freakin' *Brady Bunch*?" The whole thing was beyond ridiculous. Even the Brady Bunch only had one mother and one father.

The girls' mother stepped forward and reached for my hands, as if she and I could ever be friends. "I know this must be very hard on you girls."

"Hard?" I asked, feeling the boiling anger rising up in me again. I pulled away before she could touch me and moved back to stand next to Mamá, who had retreated from the familial scene and was standing by the front door, looking more and more like a ghost of a woman. "Lady, this is beyond hard. This is absurd. What did you think, that we were going to just hug and kiss and act like this is all right? No. No. It's not all right. None of it. Not the surprise reunion, not the home invasion, and certainly not the fake sisterly love. And what about Mamá? Where does she fit into this picture-perfect story of yours? Where is she supposed to live, Papá?"

"Well, we can't very well all live here," Papá said, looking at his new woman. The intimacy of that look made my stomach tighten again. They had secret plans—plans that didn't involve Mamá!

"You're such a—" I started, but then I had to stop because the tears were rolling down my face so heatedly that I was afraid I wouldn't be able to control myself. I needed to be in control of my emotions if I was going to help Mamá not get thrown out of her own home.

"Say it," Papá taunted, his fists at his side, as if ready to strike. "Don't be afraid to say it. I'm such a what, Odilia?"

"You're a jack-a— a jack-a—" Velia began, stumbling on the word, too upset or maybe too hurt to spit it out.

"A jack-o-lantern!" Delia yelled, her face stained with tears as she backed away from the scene. She stood with her back pressed against the paneled wall of the narrow hallway between her bedroom and the kitchen. "You have that big old grin on the outside, but inside you're all hollow and empty."

I was proud of the girls for not cussing, but I was even more proud of them for hitting the nail right on the head this time. "She's right," I said. "You have no heart."

Papá froze for a moment, and then he hung his head and shook it from side to side, as if to show his disappointment. But the twins were beyond caring. They were disgusted, and it showed in the way they looked at Papá, as if they wanted to shoot him.

"It doesn't matter what you say," Papá said, looking only half in control of his own emotions. He clenched and unclenched his fists at his sides. "I am the man of this house. I say who goes and who stays, and I say your mother has to go. You're my daughters, and as your father, it is my duty to do what's best for you. Her mothering has not served you well. Look at you all. You look like vagrants. Even street urchins are cleaner than you are. What have you been doing, Rosalinda? Sending them out to beg for *limosnas*? You ought to be ashamed of yourself."

We looked fine to me. We'd had a little dunk in the river this morning, but other than that, we were radiant. "You're the one who should be ashamed of yourself, coming here and acting like you have any right to us or to our home," I said, my voice trembling with pent-up emotion. "Tell me, did you ever have any intention of coming back here? If we hadn't gone missing, would you have returned to us? Were you ever going to tell us what was really going on?"

Papá stood perfectly still, his eyes cold, distant even as he held hands with his new woman.

"How long have you had two families? Is this your *Sirena*? *La mujer* from your riddles? The one who wanted to take you away? I thought you said you wouldn't let her," I taunted.

"That's quite enough!" Papá said, putting his hand out as if to stop me from going on. "What's done is done. The important thing is that I'm home now, and things are going to change around here."

"Change?" I walked over to him, blocking him from Mamá and the rest of my *hermanitas*, getting into his face. "We're not *tortas* you can take out of the oven and set aside to cool off while you dillydally with a whole other life. Families are supposed to be important, and that's one thing you never did: Make us important. And now you want to take away the only real parent we've ever had? Well, it's not going to happen. We're not going to let you get rid of Mamá."

I moved away from Papá and went to stand between Mamá and the twins. I took her hand in mine and held it tight. My *hermanitas* gathered around us, clinging to Mamá. "This is our house. You don't live here anymore. You never did. Everyone knows it. The whole neighborhood talks about it. You're a *desaparecido*, a vagabond, a lost cause. So why don't you do what you do best—why don't you just get lost!"

"Yeah, leave!" Velia said.

Delia crossed her arms. "We don't need you anymore."

"I thought you said they were nice?" Papá's woman said, turning her nose up at us as she reached for her two sniveling daughters and pulled them close.

"Oh, you haven't even begun to see just how '*nice*' we are, lady," Juanita broke in, her Amazonian frame blocking Papá as she stood in front of my sisters protectively. "But you're about to find out."

"Rosalinda!" Papa's voice was clipped, enraged. "Say something. I can't believe you let these girls act like this, *como demonias*. You're a disgrace as a mother."

"I might be a disgrace as a mother, but you're not winning any Father of the Year contests, either—*traidor!*" Mamá said, confidence creeping into her voice. "The girls have a right to be mad at you. You've done nothing but put them aside all their lives. And now you have the gall to bring this usurper into our home, to parade your new family in front of us like we were less worthy of your affection. How dare you!"

Mamá's eyes flashed, her nostrils flared, and her mouth was set into a straight thin line, like a she-wolf snarling fiercely as she protected her cubs. She was beautiful to me, everything we'd wanted her to be since Papá left.

"And what am I supposed to do, Rosalinda?" Papá asked, lifting his hands palms up, helpless. "Stay with you? I don't love you anymore."

Papá's words punched me in the gut. Instinctively, I turned to Mamá, half expecting her to cry. But to her credit, she didn't budge. She stared coldly at Papá like he was a stranger to her. Shaking her head, she smiled and spoke to him again in that strange, even tone she takes when she's dead serious.

"You heard them," she said. "Leave."

"Yeah," Delia and Velia said. "Leave!"

My sisters kept repeating each other's words, over and over again, as if once or twice just wasn't enough. "Leave! Leave! Get lost!"

"Fine. I'll leave," Papá said, turning to his woman and her children huddled behind him. "But don't come crying to me when you don't have money to buy groceries, and there's no food on the table."

"Ernesto!" Papá's woman balked at his retreat. "We can't go. You said we'd live here. That this house would be ours."

"But this isn't his house," I said. "And he has no claims to us. We are five little sisters, *cinco hermanitas*, together forever. No matter what!"

"And who's going to take care of you?" Papá's voice was deep now, regretful, almost. "Who's going to provide?"

What a question for him to ask, when he hadn't sent us anything for almost a year. I had a feeling that a court would make him pay child support. But even if the law didn't make him do the job he wouldn't do on his own, I knew something he didn't. "The *Virgen* will provide," I said, pointing at the flowers sitting in their vase on the coffee table beside us. "*La Virgen de la Cueva*, our Mother in Heaven, the protector of women and children, will take care of us. She has been with us all along, guiding us, protecting us. All we have to do is have faith and believe."

"You're as crazy as your mother!" Papá's woman said, pushing Juanita out of her way as she tried to get past us to get to the front door.

"Don't you ever lay a finger on my daughters again!" Mamá howled, her anger propelling her into action. Papá's woman didn't know what hit her—before she knew what had happened, she was flat on her butt on the floor in front of Mamá.

"Ernesto!" Mamá screamed. "Get this piece of trash out of here, before I drag her out *de las greñas*!"

"This isn't the way I wanted things to go," Papá warned as he helped his woman up. "But it's not the end of it either. You'll be hearing from my lawyer."

"Good," Mamá said. She went to the front door and opened it in a swift, determined pull. "I hope you have a good lawyer, because you've definitely got a fight on your hands. I've already filed for custody of the girls and the right to keep my house—the house that my father built for us, for *me* and *my* daughters, before he died. Rights? You have no rights here! Go on then! Go! Have a nice life!"

It took Papá less than a minute to move, to make his decision. But I could tell by the way he walked out, without looking back, that he wouldn't return.

20

La Rosa: *"Es muy bella y deslumbrante,*

Rosa, mi linda esposa."

The Rose: "She is beautiful and dazzling,

Rosa, my lovely wife."

It didn't take the media long to find out we were home and make a three-ring circus out of it. By Saturday afternoon, just two days after our return, Mamá had to call Special Agent Gonzales to come deal with the media crews. They had been spinning themselves into a frothing, famished frenzy, like blood-thirsty piranhas, in front of our house all morning.

It wasn't easy getting rid of them though. We actually had to give an official interview to get rid of the lot. One local news crew was allowed to set up their camera equipment in our living room. Special Agent Gonzales guided the discussion. Looking like he belonged in our house, he sat right next to Mamá on the couch, their hands almost touching as they answered questions about our disappearance and return.

Seeing Mamá acting so coy and proper on the sofa next to Special Agent Gonzales had been enlightening to say the least.

We'd never seen Mamá act so feminine with anyone else other than Papá. He probably wouldn't have liked seeing her act so demure. But what was even more surprising was finding Special Agent Gonzales waiting for us outside of the Sacred Heart Church the next morning.

I saw him before he saw us. Standing at the church door in his white pinstriped shirt, with his hands in the pockets of his gray slacks, he looked like a male model straight out of a Sears catalogue, sexy in an older man kind of way. Nothing any of us would have found exciting, but definitely someone nice and suitable for Mamá.

We were cutting across Williams Street at San Luis Elementary when he turned around and saw us. He waved, and Pita absolutely lit up as she waved back at him. He left the doorway to come meet us halfway up the sidewalk, and Mamá, looking beautiful in her blue Sunday dress with the ruffled neckline, seemed surprised to see him there. She took the hand he offered and shook it modestly saying, "*Buenos días*, God be with you."

Velia nudged me as we followed the crowd inside close behind them. "What's *he* doing here?"

"I don't know," I said, trying to keep my voice to a soft murmur.

Velia ribbed me again. "I guess he goes to church here now."

"I think he likes Mamá," Delia whispered.

I tried not to read too much into perhaps the most promising thing to happen to us in a very long time. "Maybe it's just a coincidence."

"A coincidence?" Juanita asked from behind us. "Maybe, but

quite fortuitous. Don't you think?"

"Speak English. I didn't bring my dictionary," Delia warned, turning to Juanita.

"Shush," I said, as we entered the church doors and took in the sights and the sounds of our local parish. We hadn't been to church as a family in a very long time, so it made sense that we didn't know Special Agent Gonzales was part of our neighborhood's congregation. Given our recent journey, and Mamá's assurance that we were indeed under the protection of the *Virgen*, we had a newfound appreciation for the religious relics that surrounded us, making the experience doubly profound for us.

Juanita, the twins, and I were especially drawn to the statue of the *Virgen de Guadalupe* displayed in a nook to our left. We left Mamá standing just inside the door, holding Pita's hand, chitchatting with Special Agent Gonzales. Together, we paid homage to the *Virgencita*, our Mother in Heaven, and our very own protector, by lighting five small candles, one for each of us.

Remembering the warmth and love she had bestowed upon us on the hill, I reached up and caressed the *Virgen*'s glorious blue garb, tracing the embroidered stars delicately with the tips of my fingers. She had done so much for us, but I suspected there was still unfinished business between us.

I knelt beside the twins at the cushioned pew before the *Virgen* and said a special prayer just for Mamá. It was then that I noticed them: the white blushing roses sitting in a clear crystal vase among an array of their colorful counterparts.

Red, yellow, pink, and orange roses, all in their own simple vases, were kept fresh by the older ladies of the neighborhood who spent their days at *misa* dusting the many altars and freshening up the flowers. But even with the knowledge of the special care those ladies took with the flowers, I could tell these white roses where not grown in one of their own gardens.

No, these roses were special. They were too crisp, too fresh, too pure and white to be anything but from the same rosebush as the ones I'd given Mamá. But they weren't hers. I'd touched the petals of Mamá's bouquet as we'd left the house that morning and marveled at how fresh and perfect they still looked even after three days of sitting in a vase at the kitchen table. No, someone else in this congregation had been blessed with these roses, and as a tribute, they had brought them here and presented them to the *Virgen*.

I stroked the petals of the white roses and wondered if this was what I was meant to do with mine. But it didn't make sense. Tonantzin had given me specific instructions to give my *rosas* to Mamá. It was important that I do it, because they were meant to transform her.

"I'm confused," I mumbled to myself. "Please, tell me what to do. Was there something more? Something I forgot?"

The twins stirred beside me, but they kept their heads bowed and their eyes closed in prayer. I lifted my head, and the *Virgencita*'s eyes met mine. Shocked, I turned to the twins, but they were too engrossed in prayer to see what I was seeing. When I looked up again, the *Virgencita*'s gaze was fixed again, so I bowed my head and prayed for inspiration. I needed wisdom to honor the *Virgencita*'s request.

Juanita shook me a bit as she stood up. "Let's go."

"Go ahead," I whispered, "I'm not done yet."

I must have knelt there for at least fifteen more minutes before mass started and I had to join Mamá and my sisters at their seats. I listened to the sermon and ran through all the procedures of mass, only half involved because I kept going back to the sight of those roses at the altar of the *Virgen de Guadalupe*, wondering what went wrong.

Outside the parish, we spoke to neighbors and friends, but only momentarily because Special Agent Gonzales came over to offer us a ride. When Mamá reminded him we only lived two blocks away, they both laughed about it a little too long. It was weird, almost awkward, watching Special Agent Gonzales and Mamá acting like teenagers around each other, but it was also kind of cute.

After we walked home, we spent the afternoon in the backyard. The girls helped weed out Mamá's vegetable garden and picked fat zucchini, ripened tomatoes, and spicy *serrano* peppers, which they bundled together in delicate netting to give away as gifts to Mamá's *comadres*. I spent my time planting the seeds Abuelita Remedios had given me in large ceramic pots. When I was done, I lined them up in a row along the edge of the back porch, where Mamá said they'd get the most sunlight in the mornings.

In the evening, we worked in the kitchen, a group of almost grown young women talking and laughing with their Mamá, cheerful and deliriously happy. We made *pollo con calabacita* for dinner. The chicken and zucchini casserole was so comforting and so delicious that we stuffed ourselves until we couldn't move.

Afterward, the girls entertained themselves by playing *Lotería* and watching *telenovelas* on the Spanish channel while Mamá and I cleaned the kitchen. We finally sat down with the girls to watch a rerun of the 1967 rendition of *Corazón Salvaje*. By the time the final credits rolled on the old movie, we were more than ready for bed.

"*Buenas noches,*" Velia and Delia said, pushing themselves off the couch and hugging Mamá.

Mamá embraced first the twins, then Pita, and finally Juanita. "*Buenas noches, muñecas.*"

The girls all filed out of the living room and made their way to their bedrooms. I sat on my knees on the floor in front of the coffee table as I gathered the *Lotería* boards and playing cards to put them back in their basket.

"One more game," Mamá said. "Just you and me."

"Okay," I said, rifling through the basket to find my favorite board, the one with *La Luna*, the moon, in the right corner block. "Which one do you want, Mamá?"

"You know which one," she said, her eyes twinkling, daring me to figure it out. I sorted through the thin stack of boards, trying to remember if I ever knew which one was her favorite, but I couldn't think of it.

I stopped to show her the board with *La Rosa* on the corner block. "Is it this one?"

The *Virgencita*'s roses were still on my mind. Only the solitary rose on the board was pink, not white, and there was no magic manifesting itself in this house, or in Mamá, and I worried that I had misused the great gift Tonantzin had given us.

"Come on," she said, with a soft, patient gleam in her eyes. "You know which one."

I let out a frustrated sigh and offered her the *Lotería* boards. "No, I don't know. Why don't you tell me, because I can't figure it out."

I realized I sounded curt, but I couldn't help it. The whole situation with the roses was really bothering me. I didn't want to disappoint the *Virgencita*. She'd given me the roses to give to Mamá and I had failed to deliver them in time, because somewhere along the line they had lost their magic.

"I'm sorry," I whispered, trying not to lose it in front of Mamá.

"What's wrong, *cariño*?" Mamá asked, leaning over to stroke my hair and lift my chin up. "*¿Qué pasa?* What's going on with you tonight?"

I rubbed a telling tear off the corner of my left eye with the heel of my hand and looked away. "I just can't figure it out that's all," I said. Before I could stop them, a shower of fat, ugly tears started rolling down my face.

"Can't figure out what?" she asked. "Because I know this isn't about the *Lotería*."

I clutched the wrong board card in my hands. "La Rosa," I said. "I thought that was yours. I thought roses were your favorite flowers. I thought roses always made things right."

Mamá pulled out the board with *El Corazón*, the human heart, in the corner block out of the basket and showed it to me. "Oh, honey. *This* is my favorite one," she whispered. Then she sat on the floor beside me to hug me close to her. "Roses are beautiful things. They are. But that's not what moves me. The most important things in life are not items people can give us. No. The most important thing in life is what's in your heart."

"So you didn't like the roses?" I asked, trying to figure out why they had failed to transform her.

Mamá took my hand in hers, kissed it, and rubbed my knuckles with her thumb. "No, I loved them. I really did. But it wasn't the roses that made my day. It was seeing your faces again, looking into your eyes, and knowing that you still love your mamá. The love in your hearts fills mine. It's what keeps me going. The roses were nice and very much appreciated, but it was you and your sisters, my children, that I needed to hold. Without you, I would be nothing more than a ghost of a woman, a spirit wandering this earth with no purpose, no direction—*un fantasma* with no one to love."

Goose bumps popped up on my arms and chills ran down my spine, shaking me to the core. "You mean like—La Llorona?"

Mamá crinkled her brow and looked at me like she wasn't quite sure what I was talking about. "La Llorona? I suppose so—yes."

"Oh my God—you're right!" I exclaimed. I hauled myself up and out of her arms. "Thank you, Mamá. Thank you for loving us so much!"

I ran into the kitchen, plucked the roses from the vase, and headed for the front door. "Odilia, *hija*?" Mamá called after me. "Where are you going?"

"I'm sorry Mamá, but I have to deliver these to the right person," I said. As I left the house, the screen door slammed itself shut behind me and I yelled, "I'll be back soon. I promise."

21

La Corona: *"La corona más grande y preciosa le pertenece a una reina humilde."*

The Crown: "The biggest, most precious crown belongs to a humble queen."

Telling a woman who had just gotten her daughters back not to worry was like telling the river not to roll, but I couldn't help leaving. I finally understood what I was supposed to do with *las rosas* Tonantzin had bestowed upon me.

There was only one person who needed to be reminded of who she was, and that was La Llorona. Her sadness, her grief over her lost children, overwhelmed her. Maybe the roses were a token from the *Virgencita*, a small light in her otherwise gloomy existence, a gift to brighten her spirits. Although how they were meant to transform her, I had no idea. All I knew is that she was definitely the only other mother the *Virgencita* could have been talking about. She was, by her own account, responsible for the death of her own children. If anybody needed a magical remedy for her plight, it was La Llorona.

As I pedaled my bike down El Indio Highway in the stillness of the dark summer night, I could feel the magical power of the roses propelling me toward the Rio Grande. Lying sideways within the basket attached to the front of my bike, the *rosas* shimmered in the moonlight like fallen stars, and I took special care not to ride too fast for fear of having the roses fly off or fall onto the road.

I pedaled down our soft dirt path through the woods, all the way down to the river's edge, where I hoped I might find her. I stopped, still straddling my bike, and at first all I could hear was the river, its waters churning out an eerie lullaby. Then, as the reverberation of my own heartbeat stopped hammering loudly against my eardrums, I heard her. Hers was a distant, unending sob echoing the mournful song of the ancient river as it passed by.

I picked up the roses and dismounted my bike, letting it fall to the ground as I walked toward the water. My legs felt like thin *fideo* noodles from pedaling so hard, but I didn't let that stop me. Slowly, I made my way through the brush toward the place we'd met that first time. There she was, a spectral figure illuminated by a sad, wavering light.

"I think these are for you," I said, holding the roses toward La Llorona.

"*¿Rosas?*" she asked, bemused by the white, blushing petals glowing magically in the dark. She didn't reach for them. "For me?"

"Yes," I whispered. "A gift from the *Virgen de Guadalupe*, for all you've done for us."

"I was only honoring a request," she whispered, still not taking the roses. Her longing was almost palpable. "I was merely following orders given by One who is wiser than you or I. It is part of my penance."

"You were following more than orders. You were following your heart." I deposited the roses into her arms. She took the bundle and cradled it lovingly in her embrace, as if it were a fragile baby.

"Gracias," she whispered. The thin rivulet of a tear fell quietly down her pale cheekbone, disappearing into the darkness.

"You deserve them." The tearstain on her cheek began to glisten. The shine spread across her skin inch by inch. Then right before my eyes, her tired middle-aged face regained a bright, youthful complexion. The skin of her bare arms and face glowed with health and vitality, but her skin was not the only thing transformed. Her entire facade changed, until the ghostly La Llorona became as radiant and alive as a young woman bronzed by the sun.

Behind her, a newly emerged brood of tiny snout-nosed butterflies crawled out from under the spiny hackberry bushes and began to creep upon her. They fanned their wings in slow motion as they made their way up her long, pale dress from the hem up to her neckline, forming an intricate floral pattern. Once in place, they sat perfectly still for a moment, and then the fabric of her gown came alive. Delicate silver and gold threads unraveled and wove themselves into the fragile wings of the frozen mariposas, converting the tiny creatures into magical designs stitched meticulously into the bodice of La Llorona's gown.

To crown her beauty, a floral wreath appeared on her head, transforming her into an Aztec princess. The metamorphosis was bedazzling, and I was mesmerized by her exquisite face, her dark luminous eyes, her appreciative smile. It was so breathtaking, the change in Llorona, that it rendered me speechless. Then out of the corner of my eye, a light swirled and unfurled beside us. I took a step back as *la Virgen de Guadalupe*, Tonantzin, materialized. Shocked by her appearance, both La Llorona and I dropped to our knees and bowed our heads.

"Great Mother," La Llorona said, as she knelt before Tonantzin. "We are grateful for your divine presence."

"It is I who am grateful," the *Virgen* said in her serene, heavenly voice. "Rise, my most cherished children, *mis Mariposas*."

"The Virgin Mother is kind and generous." La Llorona remained kneeling, clutching the roses to her chest. "She honors me with this transformation."

"You have done well, my daughter. Your migration through the voyage of pain and sorrow has been hard, but you are at the end of your journey. The Ancients have waited a long time for you to emerge, to spread your wings, to take flight. And now, they are ready for you to come home."

The *Virgen* lifted her right arm and opened her hand. Millions of tiny specks of gold flew out from the center of her palm. The iridescent particles soared above La Llorona and fell over her in a divine shower that bathed her in what I can only describe as sunlight. Lighter and lighter La Llorona grew until she was more than translucent; she was a silhouette of radiance.

"Rise, Malitzin. Rise, faithful daughter," Tonantzin commanded. "It is time for you to be reunited with your loved ones, time for you and your children to claim your place among the stars."

Beside me, La Llorona's silhouette began to disappear until she was completely gone. Then, to my amazement, I heard distant but distinct sounds, a whisper of music and something else, the laughter of children coming from high up in the sky. In the heavens, five bright blue stars climbed out of the horizon and up into the studded sky. They circled each other playfully before settling to the right among a cluster of smaller stars, forming a new constellation just below Ursa Major—woman and her two children, forever reunited in the sky.

"So this is what it was all about, a new constellation—*new life in the universe*," I whispered, overwhelmed by the magic my sisters and I had helped the goddess create.

"Yes, restoring that which was once lost. You have done your part, my tiniest of butterflies," Tonantzin said, turning to me. "Odilia, you are a true princess, and you've made your ancestors very proud. The courage and wisdom you have acquired through this ordeal, this odyssey, will serve you well as you grow into womanhood. You will have a very prosperous life."

"Thank you, I really appreciate that," I said meekly, and then because I couldn't help it, I had to ask. "But what about Mamá? At first, I gave her the flowers. Then when nothing happened, I realized they were intended for La Llorona, so I delivered them to the right person. But I'm still worried about Mamá. Will she be all right without Papá?"

"Your Mamá is *Mariposa* too, tenacious and fierce, but generous with her love," the *Virgen* assured me. "She will be transformed soon enough. From this pain, she too will gain the strength to fly. But now, it is time for me to take my leave. Thank you once again, for letting your heart be your guide."

With that, the *Virgen de Guadalupe*, Tonantzin, our Great Mother in the sky, disappeared. Her splendid image dissolved into the brush, and I was left standing by myself in the shadow of a thin, waning moonlight.

"Will we ever see you again?" I whispered, trembling all alone in the darkness. "Will you ever come back to help us if we need you, or must we face things alone from now on?"

"Only the sun is alone in the sky," the *Virgen*'s voice answered me from beyond the shadows of the night. I couldn't see anything, but I could feel her presence all around me. "I am with you every day. I am the moon, the stars, the sky. I am the river. I am the morning sigh. Remember, *mi Mariposa pequeña*. You are one of many. You are one of us."

At her words, a swarm of butterflies fluttered out of the

hackberry shrubs and flitted around me, dusting me with delight. With her voice still echoing in my ears, I got on my bicycle and pedaled home. A brood of cheerful, incandescent snout-nosed butterflies trailed behind me, glistening in the moonlight—like fireflies, like hope.

22

***La Luna:** "La luna todo lo ve,*

pero nada dice."

The Moon: "The moon sees everything,

but says nothing."

It surprised me quite a bit that we should miss Papá. After all, he'd been out of our lives for almost a year before his return. Nevertheless, for weeks after the incident, the girls sat around discussing it, wishing things could have been different. That he had loved us more. That we had been enough of a family to keep him home.

Not me. I kept my feelings for Papá tucked away, like a tiny rosebud hidden within the pages of an old forgotten book. Back in the darkest corner of my heart it lay, so well pressed that its fragile edges might chip, break off, even disintegrate if I tried to touch it.

Some days, however, for no apparent reason and without my awareness, sorrow would crack my resolve. I'd be tending my herb garden, clipping sprigs of fragrant leaves or replanting tender roots, then all of a sudden, a single tear would fall down my face without my awareness, surprising me. Perplexed, I would touch it and wonder what had happened to bring it forth. The answer was always there, tucked away within the brittle pages of that closed book—*Papá*.

After a while, however, my wounds began to heal, and I found that I didn't cry unexpectedly anymore. My heart had accepted the loss, and like my sisters, I too began to move on. School started up again, and we all went willingly, even gratefully, back to a normal life. I tended my herb garden every day and when Mamá cut her hand peeling *nopales*, I put *milenrama* on it. When she saw that it had healed quickly, Mamá suggested I might become a doctor someday. I think I like that.

The weekend after Easter, we celebrated my birthday with a Sweet Sixteen party. The event was strange and unusual to us. Our friends and loved ones were used to attending debutant balls, but since I didn't have one the year before, this party was like my make-up *quinceañera*.

It was a beautiful reception. Mamá had taken extra care to decorate the backyard with white ribbons. There were calla lilies at every table, and the deck was shining with the twinkling of white icicle lights that trailed over trees and shrubs to create the illusion of a fairyland, a garden for *mariposas*.

Juanita and the twins were my official *damas*, my female attendants, and each of us had been assigned a nice, handsome dancing partner, a *chambelán*. We'd fretted about finding boys to be our official escorts, but Mamá had a lot of *comadres* and they had a lot of sons from which to choose. She did a nice job, because I was assigned the handsomest boy in the neighborhood. His name was Mario Cortés, and he had big green eyes. I liked him very much.

The night of the party was soft and dreamy, with a warm breeze drifting in and out of our backyard. The girls and I danced with our escorts until the balls of our feet hurt, and we were forced to slip off our heels and dance in our bare feet. Mario kept stepping on my toes, so I had to jump back every time he got *creative*. It was silly, but we laughed about it most of the night.

By midnight, I was still keeping an eye on his shiny shoes when I saw something moving behind the trees to the left of our house. At the rustle of leaves, I froze and Mario bumped into me head-on, almost knocking me to the ground. He grabbed at my corsage to try to keep me from falling.

"Ouch," he said, releasing me suddenly.

"Are you all right?" I asked, keeping an eye to the left of me, trying to figure out who was hiding in the foliage. For a second I thought it might be Pita looking for fireflies, but she was standing at the cake table, digging into her second helping.

"I cut myself on your corsage," Mario said, sucking on the side of his index finger.

"Let me see," I said, examining his hand. "It's just a pinprick. You'll live."

"Oh yeah, tell that to Sleeping Beauty," Mario protested teasingly.

A man stepped out of the shadows into the well-lit yard. "Oh my God!" I whispered.

"What? What's going on?" Mario asked, following my gaze.

Papá stood in front of our two lime trees, looking across the dance floor with his hands in his pockets. However, it wasn't me he was looking at, but Mamá, who was dancing at the other end of the yard with a man in a pinstriped shirt and navy blue slacks, a man we had all come to know and love.

"I'll be right back," I said, leaving Mario to wonder what was going on.

As I walked toward him, Papá turned to look at me, and his face broke into a rueful smile that didn't quite match the sadness in his hazel eyes.

"It gladdens my heart to see you like this, Odilia. All grown up," Papá whispered as I leaned in and allowed him to give me a small, reserved hug. I had not expected to see him that night, but the mildness in his voice told me he had not come to make trouble. *"Feliz cumpleaños, m'ija."*

"Thank you. You look handsome tonight," I said, returning his rueful smile.

"Thanks," he said, fiddling with the boot slider on his bolo tie and looking at the ground nervously. "I didn't want to embarrass you on your special night."

"Right," I said, not sure of what else to say to him.

"I know you probably weren't expecting me, but I just needed to come. I wanted to talk with your Mamá. I had hoped . . . well, that she and I . . ." He looked sideways toward Mamá, who was still dancing, oblivious to us.

"Oh," I said, suddenly understanding.

“She looks happy,” he said.

I turned around just in time to see Special Agent Aaron Gonzales spin and twirl Mamá to the beat of a fast paced *cumbia*. Aaron had been right about CPS. After a brief investigation, they decided there was nothing wrong with our little family, but the experience deeply affected Mamá. It had taken a long time, months and months, but Mamá changed. She had inched herself into the process, like a caterpillar. First, she had changed her work schedule so she could go to night school. Within months she'd taken her GED test and received her certificate. After that, she started to attend community college and got a new job as a clerk in a private school, where her boss didn't mind if she kept a close eye on her daughters. She had grown in many ways, but especially in love.

In Aaron, Mamá had found a strong heart, and she'd attached herself to the offered hand slowly, cautiously, making sure he was the right man with whom to start a new life. But when she'd emerged from the safety of her cocoon, Mamá was happier and more radiant than we'd ever seen her. In our eyes, she was reborn into beauty—celestial, divine. And we couldn't be happier for her.

“She's like a butterfly—radiant,” I said, letting out a long held breath. “Everything's all right now.”

“Listen, about what happened . . .” Papá began, his voice suddenly full of emotion, and I felt kind of sorry for him because I knew what he was about to divulge.

Stories about him and what had transpired after he left our house that last time were everywhere in our neighborhood. My sisters and I couldn't go anywhere without someone giving us the latest gossip, filling in the holes where someone else had left off. The rumor mill had it that six weeks into his marriage, his new wife ran off with a rancher who had a big house on a hundred-acre spread in Nuevo Laredo. But that wasn't the bad part. She'd cleaned out his bank account before she left him, taking with her every penny he'd ever saved from his years as a quasi-famous Tejano singer. I heard he was singing again, but tonight I didn't feel up to asking him where or when. It seemed irrelevant, nothing more than idle chitchat.

"It's okay," I interrupted. "We don't have to talk about it."

"No. It's not okay," Papá continued. His voice was suddenly clipped, terse, as if what he was about to say made him angry. "What I did was wrong. I made a terrible mistake."

"Well, it's over now," I said, hugging him quickly, woodenly, trying to pull myself away from the situation. "I should get back to the party."

"Odilia." Papá took my hand and tugged on it gently, pulling me in closer to kiss me on the cheek and caress my hair. "You look beautiful. Have a good time."

"Thanks for coming," I said, taking my hand out of his and turning away from him.

"Okay," he whispered. Then, taking one last look around the yard, he turned around and walked away. As he disappeared behind the lime trees lining the side of our house, I stood trembling in my bare feet, wondering if we'd ever be close again, the way we were before he'd abandoned us.

Juanita came up behind me. She stood silently beside me, looking past the trees and shrubs at the lone figure of a man moving away from our house, crossing the street, and finally driving away in his car.

"And he didn't even bring a present," Juanita lamented. She put her arms around me protectively and leaned in to kiss my cheek.

"He did," I said, swallowing my tears. Her warmth engulfed me. "You just can't see it."

I turned around and looked for Mamá. She wasn't dancing anymore. She was standing across the yard pulling the twins and Pita into her arms and laughing at something. It was at that very moment that I knew with certainty we would always be one, together forever, protecting our loved ones, braving the wind and illuminating the sky.

Author's Note

I have always been fascinated by the knowledge and wisdom of our ancestors, the *Aztecas*. Their culture, their scientific observations, their religion, their architecture, their language, their myths and legends—everything about them is extraordinary. I wanted to write a story that brought all the magic and wonder of my ancestors to my readers. I wrote *Summer of the Mariposas* with the intention of showcasing both our modern and ancient *mitos y leyendas* by juxtaposing them against one of the greatest stories ever told, *The Odyssey*.

People ask me why I chose the horrible, much-feared La Llorona to be the mystical mentor or spiritual guide for my beloved girls. I think it's because I've always believed La Llorona to be much maligned, and in a sense I wanted to show her in a positive light.

I think of La Llorona in all her various mythological and legendary forms, and I feel sorry for her. As Malitzin, the Aztec slave girl given to Hernán Cortés, I find her to be one of our culture's most controversial and misunderstood historical figures. Legend says that when she became Cortés's interpreter and mistress she caused the fall of Tenochtitlan, and so the people refused to call her by her given name and began to refer to her as Malinche, the traitor.

However, while some defame Malitzin, she is celebrated by others. They see her as a savior, the founder of Mexico, for without her assistance Hernán Cortés would never have defeated the indigenous tribes of Mexico and given birth to a new nation. Malitzin's son by Cortés, Don Martín, was one of the first Mestizos born in Mexico.

Over the years, history and legend blended and the truth became blurred and smudged, but somewhere along the way Malitzin became associated with the mythological figure La Llorona. According to the stories, Cortés left Mexico to go back to court. There he became enamored of and engaged to a Spanish noblewoman, so he returned to Mexico to retrieve his children. It was that treacherous act that supposedly sent Malinche into such a rage as to take her two children and drown them in the river to spite Cortés.

Somehow, I find that too abhorrent an act for any mother to carry through. I'd like to believe that something else happened, something horrible and unexpected and completely out of her hands. Why else would she refuse to rest, to wail an eternal penance, to look for her children for centuries? Why would she lose herself in her pain if she was anything but innocent? I think it was just easy for people to villainize Malitzin and believe her capable of killing her own children because she was so detested.

However, by presenting Malitzin in a modern setting, I am giving her the occasion to tell "her side" of the story, to make us look into her heart and know that a mother's love is pure, not selfish or malignant. Using La Llorona as a mystical guide afforded me the opportunity to redeem her. After all, as parents, we all make mistakes and we all deserve a chance to make things right, much like Mamá does at the end of this book when she transforms herself.

Above all else, I wrote this story because I wanted to celebrate the extraordinary bond between children and their mamás. Mothers are very important. They have a special place *en mi corazón*.

Mothers are for love.

Glossary

abuelita (ah-bweh-LEE-tah): affectionate form of *abuela* ("grandmother"), similar to "grandma"

aduana (ah-DWAH-nah): customs station at the United States entrance of a Mexican border town

agua (AH-gwah): water

agua bendita (ah-gwah behn-DEE-tah): holy water

agua de tamarindo (AH-gwah de tah-mah-REEN-doh): cold drink made from the tamarind plant

aguas frescas (AH-gwahs FREHS-kahs): cool drinks made from fresh fruit juices

águila (AH-gee-lah): eagle

ahora (ah-O-rah): now or today

aire (AY-reh): air

al (ahl): to the

alacrán (ah-lah-KRAHN): scorpion

amigo (ah-ME-go): friend

Aramés, aramás, todavía nada más, ven aquí, ven acá, aire frío, aire mío, hazlas mías, cinco hermanitas, cinco estrellitas, serán mías, aramés, aramás: nonsensical phrases created to sound like a convoluted, mysterious spell, translated as: "Arames, aramas, already nothing, come here, come there, cold air, air of mine, make them mine, five little sisters, five little stars, will be mine, arames, aramas."

araña (ah-RAH-nyah): spider

árbol (AHR-bol): tree

argolla (ahr-GO-yah): earring

arrepiéntanse (ah-rreh-pee-EHN-tahn-seh): repent

atarántala (ah-tah-RAHN-tah-lah): stun [her]

Ave María (AH-veh mah-REE-ah): Holy Mary

Ay (ay): Oh

Ay María Purísima (Ay mah-REE-ah poo-REE-see-mah): Oh, purest Holy Mary

"¡Ay mis hijos!" (aye mees EE-hos): a saying credited to the mythological La Llorona, "Woe to my children!"

Aztecas (ahs-THE-kah): the Aztecs

babas (BAH-bahs): slobbering fool

bebito (beh-BEE-toh): baby

bendita (behn-DEE-tah): holy

bien (bee-ehn): good, well, or very

bien águila (bee-ehn AH-gee-lah): very smart, clever

bobo (bo-bo): dummy

borracho [as in borracho beans] (bo-RRAH-cho): drunk [here: pinto beans cooked with beer]

bruja/brujo (BROO-hah/ BROO-ho): witch/warlock
buen/buena/bueno (boo-EHN) (boo-EH-nah) (boo-EH-noh): good
buenas noches (boo-EHN-ahs NO-chehs): good night
buenos días (boo-EHN-ohs DEE-ahs): good morning, good day
bulto (BOOL-to): [here] a bundle, bulk, shape, shadow, a piece of luggage
cabeza (cah-BEH-sah): head
cabrito (cah-BREE-to): a young goat cooked in a ground pit
caca (CAH-kah): feces, excrement
cada (CAH-dah): every
caiga (CAY-gah): fall
calabacita (cah-lah-bah-SEE-tah): squash [here: zucchini]
calabaza (cah-lah-BAH-sah): squash [here slang: pumpkin-heads, dummies]
calavera (cah-lah-VEH-rah): skull
cállate (CAH-yah-teh): be quiet
cálmate (CAHL-mah-the): settle down
campechana (kahm-peh-CHAH-nah): flaky, buttery, honey-glazed sweet bread
canícula (cah-NEE-koo-lah): dog days of summer
cantor (cahn-TOR): singer, also one who calls out the *Lotería* cards as they are drawn in the game
canto (CAHN-to): song, melody
caso (CAH-so): consideration, concern
cazo (CAH-so): cooking pot
cerro (SEH-rro): hill

chambelán (chahm-beh-LAHN): male escorting a female attendant at a *quinceañera*

chanclas (CHAHN-klahs): sandals

chaparrón (chah-pah-RRON): rain

chalupa (chah-LOO-pah): a canoe or small rowing boat

chalupita (chah-loo-PEE-tah): a small canoe, small rowing boat

chiflada (chee-FLAH-dah): spoiled brat

chilaquiles (chee-lah-KEE-lehs): breakfast food made with pieces of corn tortilla, eggs, and other savory ingredients: usually tomatoes, onions, and hot peppers (chiles)

chiles (CHEE-lehs): hot peppers

chinampa (chee-NAHM-pah) man-made island, commonly used during Aztec times on Lake Texcoco to grow crops

chinchontle (cheen-CHON-tleh): fictitious plant used to sedate Odilia and her sisters

chiquito (chee-KEE-to): little one, child

chismosa (cheez-MOH-sah): person fond of gossiping

chupacabras (choo-pah-KAH-brahs): mythological creature from Mexican folklore said to kill goats and other farm animals by sucking their blood

cielo (see-EH-loh): sky

Cihuacóatl (see-wah-CO-ahtl) *[Nahuatl]*: Aztec Mother Goddess, goddess of motherhood and fertility as well as midwives.

cinco hermanitas (SEEN-koh ehr-mah-NEE-tahs): five little sisters

claro que sí (CLAH-ro keh SEE): of course, yes

clínica (CLEE-nee-kah): clinic, medical center

cluecas (cloo-EH-cahs): brooding, slang for agitated or nervous

cola (CO-lah): tail

comadre (co-MAH-dreh): girlfriend, godparent

comercio (co-MEHR-see-oh): store

como (CO-mo): like

compadre (com-PAH-dreh): close male friend, sometimes also godfather

con (con): with

cóndor (CON-dor): condor, large vulture

corazón (co-rah-SOHN): heart

Corazón Salvaje (co-rah-SOHN sahl-VAH-heh): the title of a popular Mexican soap opera which has been remade several times, most recently in 2009

coyote (co-YO-teh): coyote

cuando (coo-AHN-doh): when

cuatita (kwah-TEE-tah): twin girl

cueva (coo-EH-vah): cave

cumbia (COOM-bee-ah): a type of dance with Colombian roots, often played at quiceañeras and other events where dancing is part of the celebration

cumpleaños (coom-pleh-AH-nyos): birthday

curandera (coo-rahn-DEH-rah): healer, especially one who uses medicinal herbs (feminine form)

dama (DAH-mah): lady, title given to a girl who is part of the royal court in a *quinceañera*'s celebration.

dan (dahn): give

de (deh): of

del (dehl): of the

dejes (DEH-hehs): allow (past tense)

demonias (deh-MO-nee-ahs): female demons, slang for "brats"

desaparecida (deh-sah-pah-reh-SEE-dah): those who have disappeared (feminine)

descuidada (dehs-coo-ee-DAH-dah): neglectful

desprendió (dehs-prehn-dee-OH): detached

diablito (dee-ah-BLEE-to): little devil

diablo (dee-AH-blo): devil

días (DEE-ahs): days

diles (DEE-lehs): tell them

Dios (dee-ohs): God

Dios Santísimo (dee-ohs sahn-TEE-see-mo): Holy Father

dorada (doh-RAH-dah): golden

egoísta (eh-go-EES-tah): selfish, egotistical

ejido (eh-HEE-doh): a system of communal or cooperative farming

El Sacrificio (ehl sah-kree-FEE-see-oh): a small town in Coahuila, Mexico, off Hwy 57

El Santuario de Nuestra Señora de Guadalupe (ehl sahn-too-AH-ree-oh deh NWEHS-trah seh-NYO-rah deh gwah-dah-LOO-peh): Our Lady of Guadalupe, a Catholic church in Piedras Negras, Coahuila, Mexico

enchilada (en-chee-LAH-dah): rolled tortilla filled with cheese and sometimes beef or chicken and baked covered in red chili sauce

en su gloria (ehn soo GLO-ree-ah): in all her splendor/glory

es (ehs): is

escalera (ehs-cah-LEH-rah): ladder

escuincles (ehs-QUEEN-klehs): from Nahuatl *itzcuintli* ("dog"), meaning little kid

está (ehs-TAH): is (refers to the speaker's observation or perception of how something looks, feels, tastes, etc.)

Estados Unidos (ehs-TAH-dos oo-NEE-dohs): the United States (of America)

estás (ehs-TAHS): you are

estrella (ehs-TREH-yah): star

estrellita (ehs-treh-YEE-tah): little star

fajita (fah-HEE-tah): skirt steak, usually grilled

fantasma (fahn-TAHS-mah): phantom

farmacia (fahr-MAH-see-ah): pharmacy

Federales (feh-deh-RAH-lehs): Federal officers

feliz cumpleaños (feh-LEES coom-pleh-AH-nyos): happy birthday

fideo (fee-DEH-oh): vermicelli noodles cooked with chicken broth and salsa, Mexican style

fiesta (fee-EHS-tah): party, celebration

frontera (fron-TEH-rah): border

gallina (gah-YEE-nah): hen

gracias (GRAH-see-ahs): thank you

greñas (GREH-nyahs): hair

guacamole (gwah-kah-MO-leh): avocado dip made with salsa and lime

guapo (GWAH-poh): handsome

guato (GWAH-toh): outburst, fit, making a show

Hacienda Dorada (ah-see-EHN-dah do-RAH-dah): Abuelita Remedios's fictitious ranch in the woods beyond El Sacrificio, Coahuila, Mexico

hago (AH-go): (I) make

hija (EE-hah): daughter

hijo (EE-ho): son

horchata (orr-CHAH-tah): cold drink made with rice, barley, sesame seeds, and almonds

hormiguita (orr-mee-GEE-tah): little ant

huisache (wee-SAH-cheh): short, thorny tree with fernlike fronds, similar to mesquites

Huitzilopochtli (weet-see-lo-POCHT-lee) *[Nahuatl]*: solar Aztec god, the wizard god

jabalina (hah-bah-LEE-nah): peccary, javelina, skunk hog

jaras (HAH-rahs): arrows

jícama (HE-kah-mah): the spherical, elongated taproot of a yam bean

jojotle (ho-HO-tleh): fictitious medicinal remedy for grogginess or drug overdose

la aurora (lah ah-oo-RO-rah): the dawn

La Laguna de Texcoco (lah lah-GOO-nah deh tehx-CO-co): Texcoco Lake, Mexico City, Mexico

La Llorona (lah yo-RO-nah): the "Weeping Woman," a legendary character whose eternal penance for having drowned her children is to try to find them, said to carry off children who misbehave

La Sirena (lah see-REH-nah): the siren or mermaid

lechuzas (leh-CHOO-sahs): barn owls, or in Mexican folklore, mythological creatures said to have the body of a bird and the face of a witch, believed to punish evildoers

levantan (leh-VAHN-tan): awaken

limosnas (lee-MOS-nahs): money attained from begging

limosnera (lee-mos-NEH-rah): beggar, street urchin

llores (YO-rehs): cry

llueva (yoo-EH-vah): to rain

Lotería (lo-teh-REE-ah): a popular board game in Mexico, played with individual game boards called *tablas* and calling cards with images like *La Sirena*, the Siren.

Lupita (loo-PEE-tah): nickname for Guadalupe

¡Madre de Dios! (MAH-dreh deh dee-os): exclamation, *Mother of God!*

mal aire (mahl AY-reh): bad air

malas (MAH-lahs): bad

malcriadas (mahl-cree-AH-dahs): spoiled

Malitzin [also known as **Malinche**] (mah-LEEN-tzeen): Aztec Princess who betrayed her people and handed over the Aztec kingdom to the Spanish Conquistador, Hernán Cortés

Mamá (mah-MAH): Mom

mamita (mah-MEE-tah): slang, little sister

mariposa (mah-ree-POH-sah): butterfly

marranito (mah-rrah-NEE-toh): dense pastry shaped like a piglet made with sweet molasses and spices

mecate (meh-CAH-teh): rope

mía/mío (MEE-ah/MEE-oh): mine

migra (MEE-grah): slang, border patrol

m'ija/m'ijita (MEE-hah/mee-HEE-tah): term of endearment meaning "beloved daughter"

milenrama (meel-ehn-RRAH-mah): yarrow (or *acquilea*, after Achilles), an herb used to heal wounds and hemorrhaging

mira (MEE-rah): see

mis (MEES): my

mojarra (mo-HAH-rrah): perch

molcajete (mol-kah-HEH-teh): mortar

mole (MOH-leh): rich brown sauce made of chili peppers, spices, chocolate, and peanut butter, usually served with chicken or turkey

molino (mo-LEE-no): windmill

Monclova (mon-CLO-vah): city in Coahuila, Mexico, off Hwy 57

moño (MO-nyo): a bow

mordida (mor-DEE-dah): bite

muchachita (moo-chah-CHEE-tah): little or young girl

mujer (moo-HEHR): woman

mundo (MOON-do): world

muñeca (moo-NYEH-kah): doll

músico (MOO-see-co): musician

muy (MOO-ee): a lot, much

nagual (NAH-goo-ahl): warlock

nietecita (nee-eh-teh-SEE-tah): little granddaughter

niña (NEE-nyah): little girl

Niño Fidencio (NEE-nyo fee-DEHN-see-oh): a famous Mexican healer, a folk saint, unrecognized by the Catholic Church

nopal (no-PAHL): cactus

nuestro (noo-EHS-tro): our

Nueva Rosita (noo-EH-vah rro-SEE-tah): A village in Coahuila, Mexico, along Hwy 57

ojito (o-HEE-to): slang for a stream or creek

Padre Nuestro (PAH-dreh noo-EHS-tro): Our Father, prayer

pajarillo (pah-hah-REE-yo): little bird

pájaro (PAH-hah-ro): bird

paliza (pah-LEE-sah): beating

paloma (pah-LO-mah): dove

Pancho Villa (PAHN-cho VEE-yah): famous Mexican revolutionary who led the Northern division in Chihuahua during the Mexican Revolution

Papá (pah-PAH): father

para (PAH-rah): for

pasar (pah-SAHR): to pass

pequeña (peh-KEH-nyah): little

Pérdido (PEHR-dee-do): a play on the pronunciation of the word *perdido*, meaning "lost"

piojos (pee-OH-hos): lice, bugs

pobrecita (po-breh-SEE-tah): poor little one

poco (PO-co): little, not much

pollo (PO-yo): chicken

por favor (por fah-VOR): please

preciosa (preh-see-OH-sah): precious

pues (poo-ehs): well then

puesticito (pos-teh-SEE-toh): little corner store

purísima (poo-REE-see-mah): purest

puro (POO-ro): pure, whole

puros (POO-ros): only

qué (keh): what

¡qué diablos! (keh dee-AH-blos): slang, "What in the world!"

¿qué pasa? (keh PAH-sah): What is going on?

¿qué pasó? (keh pah-SO): What happened?

quiere (kee-EH-reh): wants

quiero (kee-EH-ro): (I) want

quinceañera (keen-seh-NYEHR-ah): celebration of a girl's fifteenth birthday, usually a large party, that is her formal social debut; a *quinceañera* is also a fifteen-year-old girl

ranchito (rrahn-CHEE-to): little ranch

raspa (RRAHS-pah): snowcone

ratoncita (rah-ton-SEE-tah): little female mouse; slang term for "petty thief"

remedios (rreh-MEH-dee-os): remedies

revolución (rreh-vo-loo-see-ON): revolution

rosada (rro-SAH-dah): pink

rosas de castilla (RRO-sahs deh kahs-TEE-yah): roses of Castile, originally brought to the Americas from Castile, Spain, by missionaries and land grant owners during the Spanish conquest of Mexico; is now an iconic symbol of beauty and Mexican heritage

rumor (roo-MOR): rumor

Sabinas (sah-BEE-nahs): a city in Coahuila, Mexico, along Hwy 57

sacrificio (sah-kree-FEE-see-oh): sacrifice

sala (SAH-lah): living room, family room, or receiving room
santísimo (sahn-TEE-see-mo): holy
semillita (seh-mee-YEE-tah): little seed
señora (seh-NYOH-rah): lady, married woman
señorita (seh-nyoh-REE-tah): young lady; also a title given to an unmarried woman of any age
serpiente (sehr-pee-EHN-teh): snake
sí (see): yes
sol (sol): sun
sopapilla (so-pah-PEE-yah): puffy pastry treat made from flour tortilla pieces, fried and dusted with sweetened cinnamon or powdered sugar. It puffs up with hot air and is often served with honey on the side.
sospechoso (sos-peh-CHO-so): suspicious-looking man
su (soo): your
tablas de Lotería (TAH-blahs deh lo-teh-REE-ah): individual game boards for Lotería, much like bingo cards
taco (TAH-koh): often crisply fried tortilla folded over a variety of fillings such as seasoned meat, lettuce, tomatoes, and cheese
tamal (tah-MAHL): a specialty dish made from a corn based dough, filled with spicy pork, meat, chicken, or other protein, wrapped in corn husks and broiled. Served as a main dish. Dessert tamales are filled with a combination of fruit and cheeses.
taquito (tah-KEE-toh): smaller version of tacos, tortillas filled with meat, chicken, or any other breakfast or lunch protein and served as a main dish.

tarada (tah-RAH-dah): brainless, dim-witted

Tejano (teh-HAH-no): Texan, of or originating from Texas

telaraña (teh-lah-RAH-nyah): spider web

Tenochtitlan (teh-nosh-TEE-tlahn) *[Nahuatl]*: capital of the Aztec civilization, now the capital of Mexico, modern-day Mexico City

tiene (tee-EH-neh): has

tlacuache (tlah-coo-AH-cheh): possum

tocar (to-CAHR): to play (instrument) or touch

Tonantzin (to-NAHN-tzin): Aztec mother goddess

torta (TOR-tah): pie

tortilla (tor-TEE-yah): thin, round bread made with flour or cornmeal, rolled flat, and usually served hot with a filling or topping

traidor (trah-ee-DOR): traitor

tu (too): your

tuna (TOO-nah): prickly pear, cactus fruit

un (oon)/**una** (OO-nah): one

vago (VAH-go): vagabond or wanderer, lazy person

vámonos (VAH-mo-nos): let's go

velorio (veh-LO-ree-oh): viewing of a body before burial, accompanied by rosary prayers

venadas (veh-NAH-dahs): deer

verde (VEHR-deh): green

virgen (VEER-hen): Virgin

virgencita (veer-hen-SEE-tah): little virgin

viuda (veh-OO-dah): widow

y (ee): and

ya (yah): all right

yerbabuena [sometimes *hierba*] (yehr-bah-boo-EH-nah): a species of mint [spearmint], used in teas to sooth body aches or stomach cramps

zopilote (so-pee-LO-teh): vulture

Acknowledgments

First, I'd like to acknowledge my husband, Jim, who gets me as a writer, but always manages to keep it light. Once, when I apologized for having to write madly, passionately, and for long, exhausting periods of time, he said, "Baby, you are beyond obsessed—you are possessed, but I love you anyway!"

On crazy writing nights, he puts up with the punching of the keys while he's trying to sleep. On crazy writing days, he forgives me for not listening to everything he had to say and brings Diet Coke and tacos to my computer desk to keep the creative muse from starving or dehydrating me. On crazy weeks-long writing binges (like Christmas break), he stays out of the writing cave and fields all calls and lets me play in there all by myself without being bothered.

Thank you for being my first reader, and looking at everything

I write with a critical eye and a kind heart, and for believing in me and my work. *Gracias, mi amor,* for being a great father and soulmate, and for taking care of so much while I chase this dream.

I'd also like to thank my editor at Tu Books, the talented Stacy Whitman, who fell in love with my girls and helped me tell their story honestly and with integrity while letting me be my poetic self. Thank you, Stacy, for being a fantastic editor, a great teacher not afraid to use a red pen, all the while asking a million valid questions and guiding me in absolutely the right path. You taught me so much in such a short amount of time—I am a better writer for it, and tremendously indebted to you.

I'd like to also thank Isaac Stewart for creating a magical, gorgeous cover for *Summer of the Mariposas*. You are a genius!

I can't forget to thank my sisters, Alicia, Virginia, Diamantina, Angelica, *y* Roxana, for being themselves: sharing, arguing, caring, fighting, hugging—but always in the most sisterly way. Your love, courage, and sense of adventure inspired these characters—I am blessed to have you as *mis cinco hermanitas.*

Once again, I'd also like to thank my McAuliffe family, my brothers and sisters in education, most especially my writing cheerleaders, and dearest friends: Veronica Huerta, Ceilia Bowles, Maria Ramirez, Rosalinda Casillas, Nina Huerta, Gabriela Sandoval, Gayle King, and Mayo and Amalia Caceres. Your encouraging words give me wings—thank you.

About the Author

Guadalupe Garcia McCall received the Pura Belpré Award for her debut YA novel, *Under the Mesquite.* She was born in Mexico and moved to Texas as a young girl, keeping close ties with family on both sides of the border. Trained in Theater Arts and English, she now teaches English/Language Arts at a junior high school. Her poems for adults have appeared in more than twenty literary journals. McCall lives with her husband and their three sons in the San Antonio, Texas, area. You can find her online at guadalupegarciamccall.com.

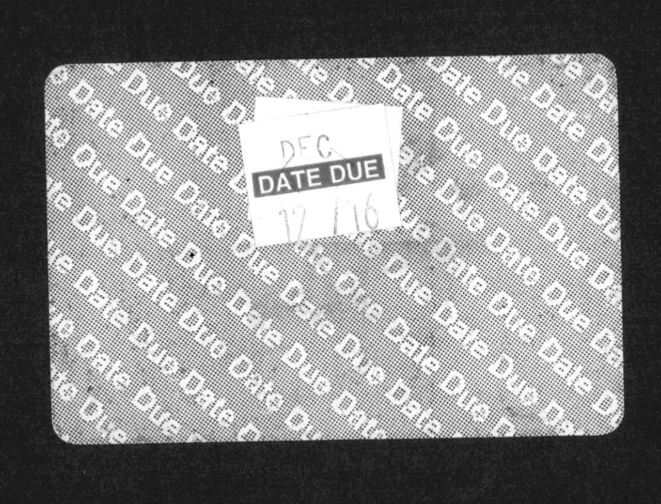
DATE DUE